Acclaim for Robert Silverberg's Majipoor Cycle

"There are two things that abide: absolute awe at Silverberg's capacity for creating images . . . he makes you see, believe, be there witnessing . . . and [the] overarching compassion that colors every word and all souls in his enormous planet."
Los Angeles Times

"I was happy to visit Majipoor again, and to know there's room on that great and grand world for even more events to be chronicled."
Asimov's Science Fiction Magazine

"A grand picaresque tale by one of the great storytellers of the century."
Roger Zelazny

"A brilliant concept of the imagination."
Chicago Sun-Times

"Silverberg has created a big planet, chockablock with life and potential stories."
Washington Post

By Robert Silverberg

THE MAJIPOOR CYCLE
Lord Valentine's Castle
Valentine Pontifex
Majipoor Chronicles
The Mountains of Majipoor
Sorcerers of Majipoor

OTHER TITLES
Starborne
Hot Sky at Midnight
Kingdoms of the Wall
The Face of the Waters
Thebes of the Hundred Gates
The Alien Years

ROBERT SILVERBERG

LORD PRESTIMION

An Imprint of HarperCollinsPublishers

This is a work of fiction. Names, characters, places, and incidents are products of the author's imagination or are used fictitiously and are not to be construed as real. Any resemblance to actual events, locales, organizations, or persons, living or dead, is entirely coincidental.

EOS
An Imprint of HarperCollins*Publishers*
10 East 53rd Street
New York, New York 10022-5299

First Eos paperback printing: June 2000
First HarperPrism hardcover printing: August 1998

Eos Trademark Reg. U.S. Pat. Off. and in Other Countries, Marca Registrada, Hecho en U.S.A. HarperCollins® is a trademark of HarperCollins Publishers Inc.

Printed in the U.S.A.

WCD 10 9 8 7 6 5 4 3 2 1

For Jim Burns
who has shown me how Majipoor really looks

The smallest act of a king, his merest cough,
has consequences somewhere in the world.
As for his greater deeds, they reverberate
through all the cosmos forever.

—AITHIN FURVAIN
The Book of Changes

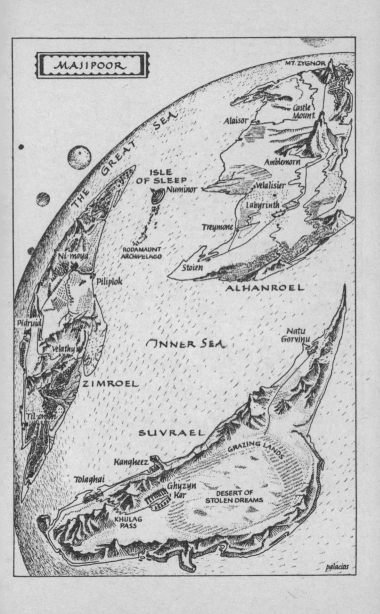

CASTLE MOUNT AND GLAYGE VALLEY

Castle Mount
HOME OF THE CORONAL

MT. ZYGNOR

Morpin

Halanx

Stee

KAZKAS PROMONTORY

Dumdilmir

Stipool

TOLINGAR GARDENS

Chilmoge

MT. HAIMON

Bombifale

Ertsud Grand

Tentag

NORMORK CREST

Normork

Amblemorn

PIGMY FOREST

RIVER

Pendiwane

Bishak East

Gayles

RIVER

Yerrick

Mitripond

Velalisier

N

TO THE LABYRINTH

TO THE WINE REGION

RIVER STEE

LAKE ROGHOIZ

palacios

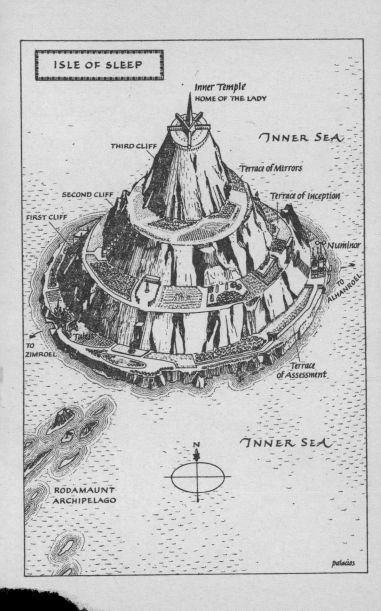

ISLE OF SLEEP

Inner Temple
HOME OF THE LADY

INNER SEA

THIRD CLIFF

Terrace of Mirrors

SECOND CLIFF

Terrace of Inception

FIRST CLIFF

Numinor

TO
ALHANROEL

TO
ZIMROEL

Talea

Terrace
of Assessment

N

INNER SEA

RODAMAUNT
ARCHIPELAGO

palacios

I

The Book of Becoming

1

THE CORONATION CEREMONY, WITH its ancient ritual incantations and investitures and ringing trumpet-calls, and the climactic donning of the crown and the royal robes, had ended fifty minutes ago. Now came a space of several hours in the festivities before the celebratory coronation feast. There was a furious, noisy bustling and hustling throughout the vastness of the great building that from this day onward would be known to the world as Lord Prestimion's Castle, as the thousands of guests and the thousands of servitors made ready for that evening's grand banquet. Only the new Coronal himself stood apart and alone, in a sphere of echoing silence.

After all the strife and turmoil of civil war, the usurpation and the battles and the defeats and the heartbreak, the hour of victory had come. Prestimion was the anointed Coronal of Majipoor at last, and eager to take up his new tasks.

But—to his great surprise—something troublesome, something profoundly unsettling, had surfaced within him in this glorious hour. The sense of relief and achievement that he had felt at the knowledge that his reign was finally beginning was, he realized, being unexpectedly tempered by a strange core of uneasiness. Why, though? Uneasiness over what? This was his moment of triumph, and he should be rejoicing. And yet—even so—

A powerful hunger for privacy amid all the frenzy of the day had come over him toward the end of the coronation ceremony, and, when it was over, he had abruptly gone off to sequester himself in the immensity of the Great Hall of Lord Hendighail, where he could be alone. That huge room was where the celebratory gifts that had been arriving steadily all month, a river of wonderful things flowing toward the Castle without cease from every province of Majipoor, lay piled in glittering array.

Prestimion had only the haziest notion of when Lord Hendighail had lived—seven, eight, nine hundred years be-

fore, something like that—and none at all of the man's life
and deeds. But it was obvious that Hendighail had believed
in doing things on a colossal scale. The Hendighail Hall was
one of the biggest rooms in the entire enormous Castle, a
mighty chamber ten times as long as it was wide, and lofty
in proportion, with a planked ceiling of red ghakka-timber
supported by groined vaults of black stone whose intricately
interwoven traceries were lost in the dimness far overhead.

The Castle, though, was a city in itself, with busy central
districts and old, half-forgotten peripheral ones, and Lord
Hendighail had caused his great hall to be built on the northern side of Castle Mount, which was the wrong side, the
obscure side. Prestimion, although he had lived at the Mount
most of his life, could not remember ever having set foot in
the Hendighail Hall before this day. In modern times it had
been used mainly as a storage depot, where objects that had
not yet found their proper places were kept. Which was how
it was being employed today: a warehouse for the tribute
coming in from all over the world for the new Coronal.

It was packed now with the most astounding assortment
of things, a fantastic display of the color and wonder of
Majipoor. The custom was, when a new ruler came to the
throne, for all the myriad cities and towns and villages of
Majipoor to vie with one another in bestowing gifts of great
splendor upon him. But this time—so said the old ones, the
ones whose memories went back more than forty years to
the last coronation—they had outdone themselves in gen-
erosity. What had arrived thus far was three, five, ten times
as much as might have been expected. Prestimion felt
stunned and dazed by the profusion of it all.

He had hoped that inspecting this great flow of gifts from
all the farflung districts of the world might lift his spirits in
this unexpectedly cheerless moment. Coronation gifts, after
all, were meant to tell a new Coronal that the world welcomed him to the throne.

But to his distress he discovered immediately that they
were having the opposite effect. There was something disturbing and unhealthy about so much excess. What he
wanted the world to be saying to him was that it was happy

to have a bold and vigorous young Coronal taking the place of the old and weary Lord Confalume atop Castle Mount. This extraordinary torrent of costly presents was altogether too great a display of gratitude, though. It was extreme; it was disproportionate; it indicated that the world was undergoing a kind of wild frenzy of delight over his accession, altogether out of keeping with the actual fact of the event.

That worldwide overreaction mystified him. Surely they had not been that eager for Lord Confalume to go. They had loved Lord Confalume, who had been a great Coronal in his day, although everyone knew that Confalume's day now was over and it was time for someone new and more dynamic to occupy the seat of kingly power, and that Prestimion was the right man. Even so, this outpouring of gifts upon the transfer of authority seemed almost as much an expression of relief as one of joy.

Relief over what? Prestimion wondered. What had triggered such a superfluity of jubilation, verging on worldwide hysteria?

A fierce civil war had lately come to a happy outcome. Were they rejoicing over that, perhaps?

No. No.

The citizens of Majipoor could not possibly know anything about the sequence of strange events—the conspiracy and the usurpation and the terrible war that followed it—that had brought Lord Prestimion by such a roundabout route to his throne. All of that had been obliterated from the world's memory by Prestimion's own command. So far as Majipoor's billions of people were aware, the civil war had never happened. The brief illegitimate reign of the self-styled Coronal Lord Korsibar had vanished from memory as though it had never been. As the world understood things, Lord Confalume, upon the death of the old Pontifex Prankipin, had succeeded to Prankipin's title, whereupon Prestimion had serenely and uneventfully been elevated to the Coronal's throne, which Confalume had held for so long. So, then, why this furore? Why?

Along all four sides of the huge room the bewildering overabundance of gifts rose high, most of them still in their packing-cases, mountains of stacked treasure climbing toward the distant roof-timbers. Room after room of this rarely used northern wing of the Castle was fiilled with crates from far-off districts whose names meant little or nothing to Prestimion. Some of them were familiar to him only as notations on the map, others not known to him at all. New loads of cargo were arriving even now. The chamberlains of the Castle were at their wits' end to deal with it all.

And what lay before him here was only a fraction of what had come in. There were the live gifts, too. The people of the provinces had sent an extraordinary assortment of animals, a whole zoo's worth of them and then some, the most bizarre and fantastic beasts to be found on Majipoor. The Divine be thanked, they were being kept somewhere else. And strange plants as well, for the Coronal's garden. Prestimion had seen some of those yesterday: some huge trees with foliage like swords of gleaming silver, and grotesque succulent things with twisted spiky leaves, and a couple of sinister carnivorous mouthplants from Zimroel, clanking their central jaws to show how horrendously eager they were to be fed, and a tub of dark porphyry filled with translucent gambeliavos from Stoienzar's northern coast, that looked as if they were made of spun glass and gave off soft tinkling sighs when you passed your hand over them—and much more besides, botanical splendors beyond enumeration. All those too were elsewhere.

The sheer volume of all this, the great size of the offering, was overwhelming. His mind could not take it all in.

To Prestimion it seemed as if this great piled-up mass of objects was Majipoor itself in all its size and complexity: as if the entire massive world, largest planet in the galaxy, had somehow forced its way into this one room today. Standing in the midst of his mounds of gifts, he felt dwarfed by the lavishness of the display, the dazzling extravagant prodigality of it. He knew that he should be pleased; but the only emotion he could manage, surrounded by so much tangible evidence of his new grandeur, was a kind of numbed dismay. That unexpected and baffling sense of hollowness that had been mounting in him throughout the lengthy formalities of the rite that had made him Coronal Lord of Majipoor, leaving him mysteriously saddened and somber in what should have been his hour of triumph, now threatened to engulf his entire soul.

As though in a dream Prestimion wandered around the hall, randomly examining some of the packages that his staff had already opened.

Here was a shimmering crystal pillow, within which could be seen a richly detailed rural landscape, green carpets of moss, trees with bright yellow foliage, the purple roof-tiles of some pretty town unknown to him, everything as vivid and real as though the place portrayed were actually contained within the stone. A scroll attached to it declared it to be the gift of the village of Glau, in the province of Thelk Samminon, in western Zimroel. With it came a scarlet coverlet of richly woven silken brocade, fashioned, so the scroll said, of the fine fleece of the local water-worms.

Here was a casket brimming with rare gems of many colors, which gave off a pulsating glow in gold and bronze and purple and crimson like the finest of sunsets. Here was a glossy cloak of cobalt blue feathers—the feathers of the famous fire-beetles of Gamarkaim, said the accompanying note, giant insects that looked like birds and were invulnerable to the touch of flame. The wearer of the cloak would be as well. And here, fifty sticks of the precious red charcoal of Hyanng, which when kindled had the ability to drive any disease from the body of the Coronal.

Here, an exquisite set of small figurines lovingly carved from some shining translucent green stone. They depicted, so their label informed him, the typical wildlife of the district of Karpash: a dozen or more images of unfamiliar and extraordinary beasts, portrayed down to the tiniest details of fur and horns and claws. They began to move about, snorting and scampering and chasing one another around the box that held them, as soon as Prestimion's breath had warmed them to life. And here—

Prestimion heard the great door of the hall creaking open

behind him. Someone entering. He would not be allowed to be alone even here.

A discreet cough; the sound of approaching footsteps. He peered into the shadows at the far end of the room.

A slender, lanky figure, drawing near.

"Ah. There you are, Prestimion. Akbalik told me you were in here. Hiding from all the fuss, are you?"

The elegant, long-legged Septach Melayn, second cousin to the Duke of Tidias, it was: a peerless swordsman and fastidious dandy, and Prestimion's lifelong friend. He still wore his finery of the coronation ceremony—a saffron-hued tunic embroidered in golden chasings of flowers and leaves, and gold-laced buskins tightly wound. Septach Melayn's hair, golden as well and tumbling to his shoulders in elaborately arranged ringlets, was bedecked with three gleaming emerald clasps. His short, sharply pointed yellow-red beard was newly trimmed.

He came to a halt some ten feet from Prestimion and stood with arms akimbo, looking around in wonder at the multitude of gifts.

"Well," he said, finally, in obvious awe. "So you're Coronal at last, Prestimion, after all the fuss and fury. And here's a great pile of treasure to prove it, eh?"

"Coronal at last, yes," said Prestimion in a sepulchral tone.

Septach Melayn's brow furrowed in puzzlement. "How dour you sound! You are king of the world, and yet you don't sound particularly pleased about it, do you, my lord? After what we've been through to put you here!"

"Pleased? Pleased?" Prestimion managed a half-chuckle. "Where's the pleasure in it, Septach Melayn? Tell me that, will you?" He felt a sudden strange throbbing behind his forehead. Something was stirring with him, he knew, something dark and furious and inimical that he had never known was in him at all. And then, pouring out of him uncontrollably, came a most surprising cascade of singularly intense bitterness. "King of the world, you say? What does that mean? I'll tell you, Septach Melayn. Years and years of hard work face me now, until I'm as dried out as an old piece of leather, and then, whenever old Confalume finally dies, I go to live in the dark dismal Labyrinth, never to see the light of day again. I ask you: What pleasure? Where?"

Septach Melayn gaped at him in amazement. For an instant he seemed unable to speak. This was a Prestimion he had never seen before.

At length he managed to say, "Ah, what a dark mood is this for your coronation day, my lord!"

Prestimion was astounded himself by that eruption of fury and pain. This is very wrong, he thought, abashed. I am speaking madness. I must do something to change the tone of this conversation to something lighter. He wrenched himself into some semblance of his usual self and said, in an altogether different manner, consciously irreverent, "Don't call me 'my lord,' Septach Melayn. Not in private, anyway. It sounds so stiff and formal. And obsequious."

"But you are my lord. I fought hard to make you so, and have the scars to prove it."

"I'm still Prestimion to you, all the same."

"Yes. Prestimion. Very well. Prestimion. Prestimion. As you wish, my lord."

"In the name of the Divine, Septach Melayn—!" cried Prestimion, with an exasperated grin at that last playful jab. But what else could he expect from Septach Melayn, if not frivolity and teasing?

Septach Melayn grinned as well. Both of them now were working hard to pretend that Prestimion's startling outburst had never happened. Extending a pointing hand toward the Coronal, a lazy, casual gesture, he said, "What is that thing you're holding, Prestimion?"

"This? Why, it's—it's—" Prestimion consulted the scroll of tawny leather that had come with it. "A wand made of gameliparn horn, they say. It will change color from this golden hue to a purplish-black whenever waved over food containing poison."

"You believe that, do you?"

"The citizens of Bailemoona do, at any rate. And here— here, Septach Melayn, this is said to be a mantle woven from the belly-fur of the ice-kuprei, that lives in the snowy Gonghar peaks."

"The ice-kuprei is extinct, I think, my lord."

"A pity, if it is," said Prestimion, idly fondling the thick smooth fabric. "The fur is very soft to the touch. —In here," he went on, tapping a square bale bound in ornate seals, "here we have an offering from someplace in the south, strips of the highly fragrant bark of the very rare quinoncha tree. And this handsome cup is carved from the jade of Vyrongimond, which is so hard that it takes half a lifetime to polish a piece the size of your fist. And this—" Prestimion struggled with a half-opened crate out of which some shimmering marvel of silver and carnelian was protruding. It was as though by rummaging so frantically amongst these crates he might somehow pull himself out of the edgy, half-despondent mood that had driven him to this room in the first place.

But he could not deceive Septach Melayn. Nor could Septach Melayn maintain his studied indifference to Prestimion's earlier show of anguish any longer.

"Prestimion?"

"Yes?"

The swordsman came a step or two nearer. He towered over Prestimion, for the Coronal was a compact man, strong-shouldered but short in the leg, and Septach Melayn was so slim and lengthy of limb that he seemed almost frail, though in fact he was not.

Quietly he said, "You need not show me every one, my lord."

"I thought you were interested."

"I am, up to a point. But only up to a point." In a tone that was quieter still, Septach Melayn said, "Prestimion, just why have you gone slinking away by yourself to this room just now? Surely not to gloat over your gifts. That's never been your nature, to covet and fondle mere objects."

"They are very fine and curious objects," said Prestimion staunchly.

"No doubt they are. But you should be dressing for tonight's feast now, not prowling around by yourself in this

storehouse of strangenesses. And your peculiar words of a
few minutes past—that cry of pain, that bitter lament. I tried
to ignore it as some odd aberration of the moment, but it
keeps echoing in my mind. What did all that mean? Were
you sincere, crying out against the burden of the crown? I
never thought to hear such things from your lips. You're
Coronal now, Prestimion! The summit of any man's ambition. You will rule this world in glory This should be the
most splendid day of your life."

"It should be, yes."

"And yet you withdraw to this dismal hall, you brood in
solitude, you distract yourself with these silly pretty trinkets
in your own great moment of attainment, you cry out against
your own kingship as though it's a curse someone has laid
upon you—"

"A passing mood."

"Then let it pass, Prestimion. Let it pass! This is a day
of celebration! It's not two hours since you stood before the
Confalume Throne and put the starburst crown on your forehead, and now—now—if you could see your own face,
now, my lord—that look of gloom, that bleak and tragic
stare—"

Prestimion offered Septach Melayn an exaggerated comic
smile, all flashing teeth and bulging eyes.

"Well? Is this better?"

"Hardly. I am not in any way fooled, Prestimion. What
can possibly distress you this way, on this day of days?"
And, when Prestimion made no response: "Perhaps I know."

"How could you not?" And then, without giving Septach
Melayn a chance to answer: "I've been thinking of the war,
Septach Melayn. The war."

Septach Melayn seemed caught by surprise for an instant.
But he made a quick recovery.

"Ah. The war, yes. The war, of course, Prestimion. It
marks us all. But the war's over. And forgotten. No one in
the world remembers the war but you and Gialaurys and I.
All those who are gathered here at the Castle today for your
coronation rites: they have no memory whatever of that

other coronation that took place in these halls not so long ago."

"We remember, though. We three. The war will stay with us forever. The waste, the needlessness. The destruction. The deaths. So many of them. Svor. Kanteverel. My brother Taradath. Earl Kamba of Mazadone, my master in the art of the bow. Iram, Mandrykarn, Sibellor. And hundreds more, thousands, even." He closed his eyes a moment, and turned his head away. "I regret them all, those deaths. Even the death of Korsibar, that poor deluded fool."

"You have left one name unspoken, and not a trivial one," said Septach Mélayn; and delicately he provided it, as if to lance an inflamed and swollen wound. "I mean that of his sister the Lady Thismet."

"Thismet, yes."

The name that could not be avoided, hard as Prestimion had tried. He could hardly bear to speak of her; but she was never absent long from his mind.

"I know your pain," said Septach Melayn softly. "I understand. Time will heal you, Prestimion."

"Will it? Can it?"

They were both silent for a time. Prestimion let it be known by his eyes alone that he wished not to speak further of Thismet now, and so for the moment they spoke of nothing at all.

"You know that I do rejoice in being Coronal," said Prestimion finally, when the strain of not speaking out had grown too great. "Of course I do. It was my destiny to have the throne. It was what I was shaped by the Divine to be. But did there have to be so much bloodshed involved in my coming to power? Was any of it necessary? All that blood pollutes my very accession."

"Who knows what's necessary and what is not, Prestimion? It happened, that's all. The Divine intended it to happen, and it did, and we dealt with it, you and I and Gialaurys and Svor, and now the world is whole again. The war's a buried thing. We saw to that ourselves. No one alive but us has any idea it ever took place. Why dredge it all up today, of all days?"

"Out of guilt, perhaps, at coming to the throne over the bodies of so many fine men."

"Guilt? Guilt, Prestimion? What guilt can you mean? The war was all that idiot Korsibar's fault! He rebelled against law and custom! He usurped the throne! How can you speak of guilt, when he alone—"

"No. We must all have been at fault, somehow, to bring down a curse like that upon the world."

Septach Melayn's pale-blue eyes went wide with surprise once again. "Such mystic nonsense you speak, Prestimion! Talking so seriously of curses, and allowing yourself to take even a scintilla of blame for the war on yourself? The Prestimion I knew in other days was a rational man. He'd never utter such blather even in jest. It would never enter his mind. —Listen to me. The war was Korsibar's doing, my lord. Korsibar's. Korsibar's. His sin alone, his and no one else's. And what's done is done, and you are Majipoor's new king, and all is well on Majipoor at last."

"Yes. So it is." Prestimion smiled. "Forgive me this fit of sudden melancholy, old friend. You'll see me in a happier frame of mind at the coronation feast tonight, I promise you that." He walked up and down the room, lightly slapping at the sealed crates. "But for the moment, Septach Melayn—these gifts, this warehouse full of stuff—how it all oppresses me! These gifts weigh upon me like the weight of the world." He said, with a grimace, "I ought to have it all taken out and burned!"

"Prestimion—" said Septach Melayn warningly.

"Yes. Forgive me again. I fall too easily into these lamentations today."

"Indeed you do, my lord."

"I should be grateful for these presents, I suppose, instead of being troubled by them. Well, let me see if I can find some amusement in them. I'm much in need of amusement right now, Septach Melayn." Prestimion moved away and went rambling once more through the aisles of stacked-up boxes, pausing to peer into those that lay open. A fire orb, here. A sash of many colors, constantly shifting its hues. A flower fashioned from precious bronze, from whose petaled depths came a low humming song of great beauty. A bird carved from a vermilion stone, that moved its head from side to side and squawked at him indignantly. A scallop-edged cauldron of red jade, satin-smooth and warm to the touch. "Look," said Prestimion, uncovering a scepter of sea-dragon bone, carved with infinite cunning. "From Piliplok, this is. See, here, how well they've encircled it with—"

"You should come away from here now," said Septach Melayn sharply. "These things will wait, Prestimion. You need to dress for the banquet."

Yes. That was so. It was wrong to sequester himself in here like this. Prestimion knew he must throw off the alto-gether uncharacteristic access of sadness and desolation that had overtaken him in these past few hours, rid himself of it like a cast-off cloak. He would have to show the banqueters this evening the radiant look of contentment and fulfillment that was proper and befitting to a newly crowned Coronal.

Yes. Yes. And that he would do.

2

PRESTIMION AND SEPTACH MELAYN went from the Hendi-ghail Hall together. The two great burly Skandar guards on duty outside the storeroom offered Prestimion an excited flurry of starburst salutes, which he acknowledged with a nod and a wave. At a word from Prestimion Septach Melayn tossed a silver coin to each of them.

But as they made their way through the innumerable drafty winding passages and corridors of the Castle's north-ern wing, Prestimion found himself sliding back into bleak-ness. The task of regaining his poise was proving harder than he had expected. That dark shroud clung to him re-lentlessly.

He should have risen to the Coronal's throne without difficulties. He had been the unquestioned choice of his pre-decessor, Lord Confalume. It was understood by all that the crown would be his when the old Pontifex, Prankipin, died, and Lord Confalume moved on to the Labyrinth to take up

Prankipin's post of senior monarch. But when Prankipin did eventually die, it was Korsibar, Lord Confalume's impressive-looking but slow-witted son, who had seized the royal power, at the urging of his pack of sinister companions and with the aid of an equally sinister magus. It was unlawful for a Coronal's son to succeed his father on the throne, and so there had been civil war, from which Prestimion emerged in time in possession of his rightful crown.

But such unnecessary destruction—so many lives lost—such a scar slashed across Majipoor's long and peaceful history—

Prestimion had healed that scar, so he hoped, by decreeing the radical act of obliteration by which a phalanx of sorcerers had wiped all recollection of the war from the minds of everyone in the world. Everyone, that was, other than he and his two surviving companions-at-arms, Gialaurys and Septach Melayn.

But one scar would not heal, nor could he ever obliterate it. That was from the wound he had suffered at the climactic moment of the final battle. A wound to the heart, it was: the murder of the rebel Korsibar's twin sister, the Lady Thismet, the great love of Prestimion's life, at the hands of the sorcerer Sanibak-Thastimoon. No magic would bring Thismet back, and none would replace her in Prestimion's affections. There was only a void where their love had been. What had it profited him to be made Coronal, if in the attaining of the throne he had lost the person who mattered most to him?

Prestimion and Septach Melayn were at the entrance now to the courtyard that led to Lord Thraym's Tower, where most Coronals of modern times had had their private apartments. Septach Melayn paused there and said, "Shall I leave you here, Prestimion? Or do you want me to remain with you while you prepare yourself for the banquet?"

"You'll need to change your outfit also, Septach Melayn. Go. I'll be all right."

"Will you, now?"

"I will. My word on that, Septach Melayn."

*   *   *

Prestimion went inside. The grand apartments that were
his official residence now were mostly still bare. Lord Confalume, he who was Confalume Pontifex now, had shipped
his incomparable collection of rarities and wonders off to
his new residence in the depths of the Labyrinth. During the
time of his usurpation Korsibar had furnished these rooms
to his own taste—a host of highly ordinary things, some
flashy and vulgar, some drab and common, all of them un-
interesting—but the same act of sorcery that had wiped Korsibar's illicit reign from the world's memory had cleared
away all of Korsibar's possessions. Korsibar had never existed, now. He had been deleted retroactively from existence. In due time Prestimion would have some of his own
things transferred to the Castle from his family estate at
Muldemar, but he scarcely had had the opportunity yet for
thinking about that, and he had little about him now except
some furnishings brought over from the lesser apartment
that he had occupied in former times in the Castle's eastern
wing, where high princes of the realm were allotted residential quarters.

Nilgir Sumanand, the gray-bearded man who had long
been Prestimion's aide-de-camp, was waiting for him, fretting in obvious impatience. "The coronation banquet, lordship—"

"Yes. Yes, I know. I'll bathe quickly. As for what I'll
wear tonight, you probably already have it waiting, right?
The green velvet banqueting robe, the golden stole, the starburst brooch that I wore this afternoon, and the lighter
crown, not the big formal one."

"All is ready for you, my lord."

A ceremonial guard of high lords of the realm escorted
him to the banquet hall. The two senior peers led the way—
Duke Oljebbin of Stoienzar, the outgoing High Counsellor,
and the immensely wealthy prince Serithorn of Samivole—
and the pompous Prince Gonivaul of Bombifale, the Grand
Admiral of Majipoor, marched just behind them. These three
had thrown their considerable influence to Korsibar at the
time of the civil war; but they no longer were aware of that,
and Prestimion felt that it would be useful for him to forgive

them for their disloyalty, now that it had been rendered null anyway, and treat them with the respect that was owing to men of their positions and power.

Septach Melayn flanked Prestimion on his right and the hulking mountainous warrior Gialaurys was on his left. To the new Coronal's rear walked his two surviving younger brothers, the hotheaded young Teotas and the tall, vehement Abrigant. The cunning and thoughtful third brother, Taradath, had perished in the war at the disastrous battle of the Iyann Valley, when Korsibar's men had breached Mavestoi Dam and buried thousands of Prestimion's troops under a wall of water.

The coronation banquet, as ever, was being held in the Grand Festival Hall in the Tharamond wing of the Castle. That was a room bigger even than the Hendighail Hall, and much more centrally located; but even so huge a space as that was incapable of holding all the invited guests, the princes and dukes and counts of so many hundreds of cities, and the mayors of those cities as well, and the miscellaneous nobility of Castle Mount, descendants of scores of Coronals and Pontifexes of years gone by. But Lord Tharamond, one of the most cunning builders among the many Coronals who had left their imprint on the Castle, had so designed things that his great hall led to a chain of others, five, eight, ten lesser feasting-halls in a row, whose connecting doors could be opened to make a single linked chamber of truly Majipoorian size; and in these, room after room after room, the attendees of the coronation banquet were distributed according to carefully measured weightings of rank and protocol.

Prestimion had little liking for such inflated events as these. He was a straightforward and unpretentious man, practical and efficient, with no special desire for self-aggrandizement. But he understood the proprieties very clearly. The world expected a great coronation festival from him; and so there would be one, the formal ceremony of crowning this afternoon, and now the great banquet, and tomorrow the speech to the assembled provincial governors, and the day after that the traditional coronation games, the jousting and the wrestling and the archery and all the rest of that. After which Prestimion's coronation festival would end, and the heavy task of governing the giant world of Majipoor would begin.

The banquet seemed to last ten thousand years.

Prestimion greeted and embraced old Confalume and led him to his seat of honor at the dais. Confalume was still a sturdy and stalwart man even here in the eighth decade of his life, but much diminished in vigor and alertness from the heroic Confalume of old. He had lost both his son and his daughter in the civil war. Of course he had no notion of that, or even that Korsibar and Thismet had ever existed at all; but some sense of a vacancy in his spirit, an absence of something that should have been there, seemed evident in the often muddled expression of his eyes in these latter days.

Did he ever suspect the truth? Prestimion wondered. Did any of them? Was there ever a moment when someone, be he a high lord of the realm or a humble farmer, stumbled by happenstance across some outcropping of the hidden reality that underlay the false memories implanted in his mind, and came up frowning in bewilderment? If so, no one gave any indication of it. And probably never would. But even if the sorcery that had altered the history of Majipoor might not hold true in every last case, it was the sort of thing that one would think wisest to keep concealed, Prestimion supposed, for fear of being thought a madman. He profoundly hoped so, at any rate.

Another place of honor at the long dais went to Prestimion's mother, the vivacious and sparkling Princess Therissa, who by virtue of her son's ascent to the throne would soon herself assume the title of Lady of the Isle of Sleep, and take charge of the machinery by which guidance and solace were dispensed to the citizenry of Majipoor while they slept. Beside her on the dais sat the formidable Lady Kunigarda, Confalume's sister, who had held the rank of Lady of the Isle during Confalume's reign as Coronal, and now was about to retire from her duties. Then the various high lords of the Council, with Septach Melayn and Gialaurys among them. And at the end of the row were the high magus Gominik Halvor of Triggoin and his wizardly son Heszmon Gorse, smiling at him thoughtfully. Those smiles, he knew, indicated the claim they had on him: for, little as he cared for sorcery and the other esoteric phenomena, he could never deny that the skill at magicking that these two possessed had played no small part in his gaining of the throne.

Prestimion went to each of these people in turn, formally welcoming them to this banquet that honored him.

And then, after he had taken his own seat but before the food was served, it was the turn of the lesser but still major lords to make their obeisance to him—this great one and that, humbly coming up to offer their felicitations to Prestimion, their hopes for the era just dawning—

Now came the start of the ceremony itself. The ringing of bells. The prayers and incantations. The endless toasts. Prestimion merely sipping at his wine, careful not to seem ungracious, but wary of drinking too much during this taxing event.

Then, at long last, the meal. A procession of delicacies from every region of the world, prepared by the most skillful of chefs. Prestimion barely picked at his food. Afterward, a round of poetic recitations: the resounding verses of Furvain's great epic, The Book of Changes, on and on with the account of the semi-mythical Lord Stiamot's conquest of the aboriginal Shapeshifter race, and then the chanting of The Book of Powers and The Heights of Castle Mount and any number of other historical sagas of Pontifexes and Coronals of centuries gone by.

The after-dinner singing, then. Thousands of voices raised in ancient hymns. Prestimion chuckled at the sound of Gialaurys's uncouth heavy basso groaning along beneath the others nearby.

There was much more, ancient rituals prescribed by musty lore. The ceremonial display of the Coronal's shield, with the starburst rendered in shining silver embellished with rays of gold, and Prestimion's ceremonial placing of his hands on it. Confalume rising to deliver a longwinded blessing on the new Coronal, and ceremonially embracing him before all the gathering. The Lady Kunigarda doing the same. The Princess Therissa accepting the circlet of the Lady of the Isle from Kunigarda. And so on and so on, interminably. Prestimion patiently endured it all, though it was far from easy.

But to his great surprise he discovered that somewhere along the way, during the course of this long and arduous event, he had shed the strange leadenness of heart that had come over him earlier. All that dejection and bitter cheerlessness had dropped away, somehow. Tired as he was, here at the very end of the banquet, he had found his way back to joyfulness at last. And more than joyfulness: for, somewhere in the course of the evening, he had felt a sense of being truly kingly coming over him for the first time.

One supreme fact had been established today. His name had at last been enrolled in the long roster of Coronals of Majipoor now, after many a travail in the course of his path to the throne.

Coronal of Majipoor! King of the most wondrous world in all the universe!

And he knew that he would be a good Coronal, an enlightened Coronal, whom the people would love and praise. He would do great things, and he would leave Majipoor a better place for his having lived and reigned. And this was what he had been born to accomplish.

Yes. Yes. So all was for the best this glorious day, despite the momentary cloud of gloom that had dimmed its glory for him for a time a few hours before.

Septach Melayn saw the change come over him. During a lull in the festivity he came to Prestimion's side and said, looking at him warmly, "The despair you spoke of a little while ago in the Hendighail Hall has gone from you, has it not, Prestimion?"

Unhesitatingly Prestimion replied, "We had no conversation in Hendighail Hall this day, Septach Melayn."

There was something new in his tone, a strength, even a harshness, that had never been there before. Prestimion himself was taken unawares when he heard it ringing in his ears. Septach Melayn heard it too; for his eyes widened an instant, and the corners of his mouth quirked in surprise, and he caught his breath in sharply. Then he inclined his head in a formal way and said, "Indeed, my lord. We did not speak in the Hendighail Hall." And made the starburst sign, and returned to his seat.

Prestimion signaled for his wine-bowl to be refilled.

This is what it means to be a king, he thought. To speak coldly even to your best beloved friends, when the occasion demands. Does a king even have friends? he wondered. Well, he would find that out in the weeks ahead.

The banquet was at its climactic moment. Everyone was standing now, hands aloft in the starburst salute. "Prestimion! Lord Prestimion!" they were crying. "Hail, Lord Prestimion! Long life to Lord Prestimion!"

And then it was over. The hour had come for the breaking-up of the banquet into smaller gatherings, groups filtering themselves apart by rank and affinity of friendship. At long last, with dawn approaching, the time arrived when the newly consecrated Coronal Lord of Majipoor was permitted to seek his rest, and could tactfully declare the revels ended, and withdraw, finally, to the privacy and peace of his own apartments, his own bedroom.

His empty apartments. His lonely bed.

Thismet, he thought, as he tumbled down in utter exhaustion toward the pillow. In the midst of his great joy he could not find a way to hide from the unending pain of losing her. I am king of the world tonight, and where are you, Thismet? Where are you?

3

IN THE GREAT CITY of Stee, well down the slopes of Castle Mount, there was trouble in the household of the immensely wealthy merchant banker Simbilon Khayf.

A fourth-floor chambermaid of the house of Simbilon Khayf had fallen victim suddenly to a fit of madness and flung herself from an attic window of the banker's grand mansion, killing not only herself but two passers-by in the street below. Simbilon Khayf himself was nowhere near the scene when this occurred: he was away at the Castle, attending Lord Prestimion's coronation ceremonies as the guest of Count Fisiolo of Stee. And so it had become the task of his only daughter, Varaile, to deal with the grisly tragedy and its consequences.

Varaile, a tall, slender, dark-eyed woman with jet-black hair that fell to her shoulders in a shining cascade, was only in her nineteenth year. But her mother's early death had made her the mistress of the great house when she was still a girl, and those responsibilities had given her a maturity beyond her years. When the first strange sounds from the street reached her ears—a horrible cracking thud, and then another, less distinct, a moment later, followed by shouts and piercing shrieks—she moved calmly and purposefully toward the window of her own third-floor study. Quickly she took in the grim scene: the bodies, the blood, the gathering crowd of agitated witnesses. She headed at once for the stairs. Servants of the house came rushing up toward her, all crying out at once, gesticulating, sobbing.

"Lady—lady—it was Klaristen! She jumped, lady! From the top-story window, it was!"

Varaile nodded coolly. Within herself she felt shock and horror and something close to nausea, but she dared not allow any of that to show. To Vorthid, the chamberlain of the house, she said, "Summon the imperial proctors immediately." To the wine-steward, Kresshin, she said, "Run and get Dr. Thark as fast as you can." And to Bettaril, the strong and sturdy master of the stables, she said, "I have to go out there to see after the injured people. Find yourself a cudgel and stand beside me, in case matters become unruly. Which very possibly they will."

Of the Fifty Cities of Castle Mount, Stee was by far the grandest and most prosperous; and Simbilon Khayf was one of the grandest and most prosperous men of Stee. Which made it all the more startling that such a misfortune could strike his house. And a great many envious folks both within and without Stee, resentful of Simbilon Khayf's phenomenal rise to wealth and power out of the back streets of the city, secretly rejoiced at the difficulties that his fourth-story chambermaid's lunatic plunge had entangled him in. For Stee, ancient as it was, was looked upon by its neighbors on the Mount as something of an upstart city, and Simbilon Khayf, the wealthiest commoner in Stee, was himself, beyond any doubt, an upstart among upstarts.

The fifty magnificent cities that occupied the jagged sides of immense Castle Mount, the astounding mountain that swept upward to a height of thirty miles above the lowlands of the continent of Alhanroel, were arranged in five distinct bands situated at varying altitudes—the Slope Cities near the bottom, then the Free Cities, the Guardian Cities, the Inner Cities, and, just below the summit itself, the nine that were known as the High Cities. Of the Fifty Cities, the ones whose citizens had the highest opinions of themselves were those nine, the High Cities that formed a ring that encircled the Mount's uppermost reaches, almost on the threshold of the Castle itself.

Because they were closest to the Castle, these were the cities most often visited by the glittering members of the Castle aristocracy, lords and ladies who were descended from Coronals and Pontifexes of the past, or who might someday attain to those great titles themselves. Not only did the Castle folk often journey down to such High Cities as High Morpin or Sipermit or Frangior to partake of the sophisticated pleasures that those cities offered, but also there was a steady upward flow from the High Cities to the Castle: Septach Melayn was a man of Tidias, Prestimion had come from Muldemar. Therefore many folk of the High Cities tended to put on airs, regarding themselves as special persons because they happened to live in places that stood far up in the sky above the rest of Majipoor and rubbed elbows on a daily basis with the great ones of the Castle.

Stee, though, was a city belonging to the second band from the bottom—the Free Cities, they were called. There were nine of them, all quite old, dating back at least seven thousand years to the time when Lord Stiamot was Coronal of Majipoor, and probably they were much older than that.

No one was quite certain what it was that the Free Cities were free from. The best scholarly explanation of the name was that Stiamot had awarded those cities an exemption from some tax of his day, in return for special favors received. Lord Stiamot himself had been a man of Stee. In Stiamot's time Stee had been the capital city of Majipoor, until his decision to build a gigantic castle at the summit of the Mount and move the chief administrative center to it.

Unlike most of the cities of Castle Mount, which were tucked into various craggy pockets of the colossal mountain, Stee had the advantage of being located on a broad, gently sloping plain on the Mount's northern face, where there was enormous room for urban expansion. Thus it had spread out uninhibitedly in all directions from its original site along the swift river from which it had taken its name, and by Prestimion's time had attained a population of nearly twenty-five million people. On Majipoor it was rivaled in size only by the great city of Ni-moya on the continent of Zimroel; and for overall wealth and grandeur, even mighty Ni-moya had to take second place to Stee.

Stee's magnitude and location had afforded it great commercial prosperity, a prosperity so great that citizens of other cities tended to regard Stee and its barons of industry as more than a little vulgar. Its chief mercantile center was the splendid row of towering buildings faced with facades of reflective gray-pink marble that were known as the Riverwall Buildings, which ran for miles along both banks of the River Stee. Behind these twin walls of offices and warehouses lay the thriving factories of industrial Stee on the left bank, and the palatial homes of the rich merchants on the right. Further back on the right bank were the great country estates of the Stee nobility and the parks and game preserves for which Stee was famous throughout the world, and on the left, for mile after mile, the modest homes of the millions of workers whose efforts had kept the city flourishing ever since the remote era of Lord Stiamot.

Simbilon Khayf had been one of those workers, once. But earlier he had been even less than that: a street beggar, in fact. All that, though, was forty and fifty years in his past.

Luck, shrewdness, and ambition had propelled him on a swift climb to his extraordinary position in the city. Now he consorted with counts and dukes and other such great men, who pretended to regard him as a social equal because they knew they might someday have need of his banking facilities; he entertained at his grand mansion the high and mighty of many other cities when business dealings brought them to Stee; and now, even as the hapless housemaid Klaristen was hurling herself to her death, he was mingling cheerfully with the most exalted members of the Majipoor aristocracy at Lord Prestimion's great festival.

Varaile, meanwhile, found herself kneeling in blood in the street just outside her house, staring down at grotesquely broken bodies while a hostile and ever-growing crowd exchanged sullen muttered comments all around her.

She gave her attention to the two fallen strangers, first. A man and a woman, they were; both handsomely dressed, obviously well-to-do. Varaile had no idea who they were. She noticed an empty floater parked by the grassy strip across the street, where sightseers who had come for a look at Simbilon Khayf's mansion often left their vehicles. Perhaps these people were strangers to Stee, who had been standing in the cobblestoned plaza outside the west portal, admiring the finely carved limestone sculptures of the house's facade, when the body of the housemaid Klaristen had come smashing down out of the sky upon them.

They were dead, both of them. Varaile was certain of that. She had never seen a dead body before, but she knew, crouching down and peering into the glazed eyes of the two victims, that no impulse of life lurked behind them. Their heads were at grotesque angles. Klaristen must have dropped directly down on them, snapping their necks. Death would have been instantaneous: a blessing of sorts, she thought. But death all the same. She fought back instinctive terror. Her hands moved in a little gesture of prayer.

"Klaristen is still breathing, lady," the stablemaster Bettaril called to her. "But not for long, I think."

The housemaid had evidently ricocheted from her two victims with great force, landing a dozen or so feet away.

When Varaile was convinced that there was nothing she could do for the other two, she went to Klaristen's side, ignoring the onlookers' sullen stares. They seemed to hold her personally responsible for the calamity, as though Varaile, in a moment of pique, had thrown Klaristen out the window herself.

Klaristen's eyes were open, and there was life in them, but no sign of consciousness. They were set in a fixed stare like those of a statue; and only when Varaile passed her hand before them, which produced a blink, did they give any indication that her brain was still functioning. Klaristen looked even more broken and twisted than the other two. A two-stage impact, Varaile supposed, shuddering: Klaristen hitting the two strangers first, rebounding from them, coming down again and landing hard, perhaps head first, against the cobblestoned street.

"Klaristen?" Varaile murmured. "Can you hear me, Klaristen?"

"She's leaving us, lady," said Bettaril quietly.

Yes. Yes. As she watched, Varaile could see the expression of Klaristen's eyes changing, the last bit of awareness departing, a new rigidity overtaking them. And then the texture of the eyes themselves altered, becoming weirdly flat and strangely flecked, as if the forces of decay, though only just unleashed, were already taking command of the girl's body. It was a remarkable sight, that transition from life to death, Varaile thought, greatly astonished at her own analytical coolness in this terrible moment.

Poor Klaristen. She had been no more than sixteen, Varaile supposed. A good, simple girl from one of the outlying districts of the city, out by the Field of Great Bones, where the fossil monsters had been discovered. What could have possessed her to take her own life this way?

"The doctor's here," someone said. "Make way for the doctor! Make way!"

But the doctor very quickly ratified Varaile's own diagnosis: there was nothing to be done. They were dead, all three. He produced drugs and needles and attempted to jolt them back to life, but they were beyond rescue.

A big rough-voiced man called out for a magus to be
fetched, one who could witch the dead ones alive again with
some potent spell. Varaile glared at him. These simple people, with their simple faith in wizards and spells! How embarrassing, how annoying! She and her father employed
mages and diviners themselves, of course—it was only sensible, if you wanted to steer clear of unpleasant surprises in
life—but she hated the modern credulous popular faith in
occult powers that so many people had embraced without
reservation or limit. A good soothsayer could be very useful,
yes. But not in bringing the dead back to life. The best of
them did seem to be able to glimpse the future, but the
working of miracles was more than their skills could encompass.

And why, come to think of it, Varaile asked herself, had
their household magus, Vyethorn Kamman, given them no
warning of the dreadful deed that the housemaid Klaristen
was planning to enact?

"Are you the Lady Varaile?" a new voice asked.
"Imperial proctors, ma'am." She saw men in uniforms, gray
with black stripes. Badges bearing the pontifical emblem
were flashed. They were very respectful. Took in the situation at a glance, the bodies, the blood on the cobblestones;
cleared the crowd back; asked her if her father was home.
She told them that he was attending the coronation as Count
Fisiolo's guest, which produced an even deeper air of deference. Did she know any of the victims? Only one, she
said, this one here. A maid of the house. Jumped out of a
window up there, did she? Yes. Apparently so, said Varaile.
And had this girl been suffering from any emotional disturbance, ma'am? No, said Varaile. Not that I know of.

But how much could she really ever know, after all, of
the emotional problems of a fourth-floor chambermaid? Her
contact with Klaristen had been infrequent and superficial,
limited mostly to smiles and nods. Good morning, Klaristen.
Lovely day, isn't it, Klaristen? Yes, I'll send someone up
to the top floor to fix that sink, Klaristen. They had never
actually spoken with each other, as Varaile understood the
term. Why should they have?

It quickly became clear, though, that things had been seriously amiss with Klaristen for some time. The team of proctors, having finished inspecting the scene in the street and gone into the house to interview members of the household staff, brought that fact out into the open almost at once.

"She started waking up crying about three weeks ago," said plump jolly old Thanna, the third-floor maid, who had been Klaristen's roommate in the servants' quarters. "Sobbing, wailing, really going at it. But when I asked what the matter was, she didn't know. Didn't even know she'd been crying, she said."

"And then," said Vardinna, the kitchen-maid, Klaristen's closest friend on the staff, "she couldn't remember my name one day, and I laughed at her and told it to her, and then she went absolutely white and said she couldn't remember her own name, either. I thought she was joking. But no, no, she really seemed not to know. She looked terrified. Even when I said, 'Klaristen, that's your name, silly,' she kept saying, 'Are you sure, are you sure?' "

"And then the nightmares began," Thanna said. "She'd sit up screaming, and I'd put the light on and her face would be like the face of someone who had just seen a ghost. Once she jumped up and tore all her nightclothes off, and I could see she was sweating all over her body, so wet it was like she'd gone for a bath. And her teeth chattering loud enough to hear in the next street. All this week she had the nightmares real bad. Most of the time she couldn't tell me what the dreams had been, just that they were awful. The only one she could remember, it was that a monstrous bug had sat down over her face and started to suck her brain out of her skull, until it was altogether hollow inside. I said it was a sending of some kind, that she ought to go and see a dream-speaker, but of course people like us have no money for dream-speakers, and in any case she didn't believe she was important enough to be receiving sendings. I never saw anyone so frightened of her dreams."

"She told me about them too," Vardinna said. "Then, the other day, she said she was starting to have the nightmares while she was awake, also. That something would start

throbbing inside her head and then she'd see the most horrid
visions, right in front of her eyes, even while she was working."

To Varaile the head proctor said, "You received no report
of any of this, lady?"

"Nothing."

"The fact that one of your housemaids was apparently
having a mental breakdown on your premises was something that you never in any way noticed?"

"Ordinarily I saw very little of Klaristen," said Varaile
coolly. "An upstairs maid in a large household—"

"Yes. Yes, of course, lady," said the proctor, looking
flustered and even alarmed, as though it was only belatedly
dawning on him that he might be seeming to lay some share
of responsibility for this thing upon the daughter of Simbilon Khayf.

Another of the proctors entered now. "We have identities
of the dead people," he announced. "They were visitors
from Canzilaine, a man and a wife, Hebbidanto Throle and
his wife Garelle. Staying at the Riverwall Inn, they were.
An expensive hotel, the Riverwall: only people of some substance would stay there. I'm afraid there will be heavy in-
demnities to pay, ma'am," he said, glancing apologetically
toward Varaile. "Not that that would be any problem for
your father, ma'am, but even so—"

"Yes," she said absently. "Of course."

Canzilaine! Her father had important factories there. And
Hebbidanto Throle: had she ever heard that name before? It
seemed to her that she had. The thought came to her that
he might have been some executive in her father's employ,
even the manager of one of the Canzilaine operations. Who
had come to Stee with his wife on a holiday, perhaps, and
had wanted to show her the stupendous mansion of his fab-
ulously wealthy employer—

It was a chilling possibility. What a sad ending for their
journey!

Eventually the proctors were finished asking questions,
at least, and were huddling off in one corner of the library
conferring among themselves before leaving. The bodies

had been removed from the street outside and two of the gardeners were hosing away the bloodstains. Bleakly Varaile contemplated the tasks immediately ahead of her.

First, to get a magus in here to purify the house, cleanse it of the stain that was on it now. Suicide was a serious business; it brought down all sorts of darknesses upon a house. Then to track down Klaristen's family, wherever they might live, and convey condolences and the information that all burial expenses would be paid, along with a substantial gift as an expression of gratitude for the dead girl's services. Next, to get in touch with someone on her father's staff in Canzilaine, and have him find out just who Hebbidanto Throle and his wife had been, and where their survivors could be reached, and what sort of consolatory gesture would be appropriate. Some large sum of money at the very least, but perhaps other expressions of sympathy would be required.

What a mess! What an awful mess!

She had been very bitter about being left at home while her father went off to the coronation with Count Fisiolo. "The Castle will be too wild and drunken a place this week for the likes of you, young lady," Simbilon Khayf had said, and that was that. The truth of it, Varaile knew, was that her father wanted to be wild and drunken himself this week, he and his lordly aristocratic friend the foul-mouthed and blasphemous Count Fisiolo, and didn't care to have her around. So be it: no one, not even his only daughter, ever defied the will of Simbilon Khayf. She had obediently remained behind; and how lucky it was, she thought, that she had been here to cope with this thing today, rather than having left the house and its responsibilities to the servants.

As the proctors were leaving, the head man said in a low voice to her, "You know, lady, we've had several cases like this lately, though nothing quite as bad as this one. There's some kind of epidemic of craziness going around. You'd do well to keep a close eye on your people here, in case any of the others happens to start going over the edge."

"I'll bear that in mind, officer," said Varaile, though the

thought of monitoring the sanity of her staff was unappealing to her.

The proctors departed. Varaile felt a headache now beginning to come on, but went up to the study to set about what needed to be done. Everything had to be under control before Simbilon Khayf returned from the coronation.

An epidemic of craziness?

How odd. But these were unusual times. Even she had felt uncharacteristic moments of depression and even confusion in recent days. Some hormonal thing, she supposed. But moods of that sort had never been a problem for her before.

She sent for Gawon Barl, the head steward of the house, and asked him to set about arranging for the purification rites immediately. "Also I need to have the address of Klaristen's father and mother, or some kin of hers, at least," she said. "And then—these poor people from Canzilaine—"

4

ONCE AGAIN THE CASTLE was the scene of coronation games, the second time in the past three years. Once again grandstands had been constructed along three sides of the great sunny greensward that was Vildivar Close, just downhill from the Ninety-Nine Steps. Once again the greatest ones of the realm, the other two Powers and the members of the Council and the earls and dukes and princes of a hundred provinces, were gathered to celebrate the accession of the new king.

But no one but Prestimion and Gialaurys and Septach Melayn was able to remember those earlier games, the ones that had been held in honor of the Coronal Lord Korsibar, any more than anyone remembered Korsibar himself. The foot races, the jousting, the wrestling, the contests at archery and all the rest—forgotten by winners and losers alike. Removed from memory. Obliterated by Prestimion's team of sorcerers, acting together in one mighty effort of the magical art. All that had happened in that other round of games had

been unhappened. Today's games were the games of Lord
Prestimion, lawful successor to Lord Confalume. Lord Korsibar had never been. Even the sorcerers who had worked
the unhappening had had to forget their own deed, by Prestimion's command.

"Let the archers come forth!" cried the Master of the
Games. Duke Oljebbin of Stoienzar held that honorary title
this day.

As the contestants filed onto the field, a little murmur of
wonderment went up from the crowd. Lord Prestimion himself was among them.

No one had expected the new Coronal to be on the field
this day. But it should not have been a huge surprise, really.
Archery had ever been Prestimion's great sport: he was a
master of the art. And also a man within whose breast the
fires of competition burned fiercely at all times. Those who
knew him well knew that it would not have been at all like
him to pass up a chance to demonstrate his skill. But even
so—for the Coronal to compete in his own coronation
games—how strange! How unusual!

Prestimion had gone out of his way today to seem like
nothing more than an eager seeker for the prize at archery.
He was clad in the royal colors, a close-fitting golden doublet and green breeches, but he wore no circlet about his
forehead, nor any other badge of office. Some stranger who
had no idea which of these dozen men who carried bows
was Coronal might perhaps have identified him by the look
of great presence and authority that had always been the
mark of his demeanor; but more likely the short statured
man with the close-cropped dull-yellow hair would have
gone unnoticed in that group of robust, heartily athletic men.

Glaydin, the long-limbed youngest son of Serithorn of
Samivole, was the first to shoot. He was a skillful archer,
and Prestimion watched approvingly as he let his arrows fly.

Then came Kaitinimon, the new Duke of Bailemoona,
who still wore a yellow mourning band about his arm in
honor of his father, the late Duke Kanteverel. Kanteverel
had died with Korsibar at the bloody battle of Thegomar
Edge; but not even Kaitinimon knew that. That his father

was dead, yes, that much he understood. But the true circumstances of Kanteverel's death were clouded, as were the deaths of all who had fallen in the battles of the civil war, by the pattern of sorcery that Prestimion's mages had woven around the world.

That spell of oblivion had been cunningly designed to allow the survivors of the war's numberless victims to weave explanatory fantasies of their own that would fill the inner void created by the bare knowledge, unadorned by any factual detail, that their kinsmen no longer were among the living. Perhaps Kaitinimon believed that Kanteverel had died of a sudden seizure while visiting his western estates, or that a swamp-fever had taken him off during a tour of the humid south. Whatever it was, it was anything but the truth.

Kaitinimon handled his bow well. So did the third competitor, the tall hawk-faced forester Rizlail of Megenthorp, who, like Prestimion, had learned the art of bowmanship from the famed Earl Kamba of Mazadone. Then a stir went through the crowd when the next archer stepped forward, for he was one of the two members of the contending group that came from non-human stock, and a Su-Suheris at that, a member of that strange double-headed race that had lately begun to settle in some numbers on Majipoor. His name was announced as Gabin-Badinion.

How would someone with two heads take proper aim? Might the heads not disagree about the best placement of the bow? But it was no problem, evidently, for Gabin-Badinion. With icy precision he ably filled the inner rings of the target with his shafts, and gave the crowd a brusque two-headed nod by way of acknowledging its applause.

It was Prestimion's turn now.

He carried with him the great bow that Earl Kamba had given him when he was still a boy, a bow so powerful that few grown men could draw it, though Prestimion handled it with ease. In the battles of the civil war he had worked much destruction with this bow; but how much better, he thought, to be employing it in a contest of skill, instead of taking the lives of honorable men!

Upon reaching the base-line Prestimion paid homage, as all the earlier archers had done, to the high Powers of the Realm who were looking on. He bowed first to the Pontifex Confalume, who was seated in a great gamandrus-wood throne at the center of the grandstand along the right-hand side of Vildivar Close. The ceremony by which a Pontifex chose a new Coronal was essentially one of adoption, and so, by the custom of Majipoor, it was proper for Prestimion now to regard Confalume as his father—his true father was long dead, anyway—and behave with appropriate reverence.

Prestimion's next bow of obeisance went to his mother, the Princess Therissa. She sat on a similar throne in the left-hand grandstand, with her predecessor as Lady of the Isle of Sleep, the Lady Kunigarda, beside her. Prestimion swung about then and saluted his own vacant seat in the third grandstand, by way of making an impersonal acknowledgement of the majesty of the Coronal, a gesture to the office itself, not to the man.

Then he took the great bow firmly in hand, Kamba's bow, the bow that he had cherished so long. It was a source of distress to Prestimion that the good-hearted, ever-cheerful Kamba, that supreme master of archery, was not here to take part in this contest today. But Kamba was one of those who had thrown in his lot with the usurping Korsibar, and he had died for it, with so many other brave warriors, at The-gomar Edge. The spells of the mages had been able to cause the war itself to be forgotten, but they could not bring fallen soldiers back to life.

Standing quietly at the base-line, Prestimion held himself altogether still for a time. He was often impulsive, but never when he stood before a target. With narrowed eyes he scrutinized his goal until at last he felt his soul at perfect center. He raised his bow then, and sighted along the waiting shaft.

"Prestimion! Prestimion! Lord Prestimion!" came the cry from a thousand throats.

Prestimion was aware of that great roar, but it was of no consequence to him just now. The thing that mattered was staying attuned to the task at hand. What pleasure there was in this art! Not that sending a shaft through the air was of any great importance in itself; but to do a thing with supreme excellence, to do it perfectly, whatever that thing might be—ah, there was joy in that!

He smiled and released his arrow, and watched it travel straight and true to the heart of the target, and heard the satisfying thump as it embedded itself deep.

"There's no one to equal him at this, is there?" asked Navigorn of Hoikmar, who was sitting with a group of men of high rank in one of the boxes on the Coronal's side of the field. "It isn't fair. He really ought to sit back and let someone else win an archery title, just for once. Quite aside from the fact that it's of somewhat questionable taste for a Coronal to be competing in his own coronation games."

"What, Prestimion sit back and allow another to win?" said the Grand Admiral of the Realm, Gonivaul of Bombifale. Gonivaul, a dour man whose dark beard was so dense and his thick black hair so low across his forehead that the features of his face could scarcely be seen, offered Navigorn a look that was in fact the Grand Admiral's version of a smile, though a stranger might have taken it to be a scowl. "It's just not in his nature, Navigorn. He seems a decent well-bred sort, and so he is, but he does insist on winning, does he not? Confalume saw that in him right away, when he was only a boy. Which is why Prestimion rose through the Castle hierarchy as quickly as he did. And why he's Coronal of Majipoor today."

"Look at that, now! He has no shame," said Navigorn, more in admiration than criticism, as Prestimion split his first arrow with his second. "I knew he'd try that trick again. He does it every time."

"I understand from my son," said Prince Serithorn, "that Prestimion isn't actually competing for the prize today, but is performing only for the pure pleasure of the art. He's asked the judges not to calculate his score."

"And that means," Gonivaul said sourly, "that the winner, whoever he turns out to be, must understand that he's simply

the best archer on the field who happens not to be Prestimion."

"Which taints the glory of winning a bit, wouldn't you
say?" asked Navigorn.

"My son Glaydin made a similar comment," said Serithorn. "But you show the man no mercy. Either he competes
and, most likely, wins, or he disqualifies himself and thereby
casts a shadow on the winner. So what is he to do? —Pass
the wine, will you, Navigorn? Or do you mean to drink it
all yourself?"

"Sorry." Navigorn handed the flask across.

On the field, Prestimion was still running through his
flamboyant repertoire of fancy shooting, to the accompani-
ment of uproarious approval from the crowd.

Navigorn, a powerfully built dark-haired man of impressive stature and confident nature, watched Prestimion's performance with ungrudging approval. He appreciated
excellence wherever he encountered it. And he admired
Prestimion immensely. For all his lordly bearing, Navigorn
himself had never had royal ambition; but it did please him
to be near to the fount of power, and Prestimion had told
him just yesterday that he had chosen him to be a member
of the incoming Council. That had been unexpected. "You
and I have never been particularly close friends," Prestimion
had said. "But I value you for your qualities. We need to
come to know each other better, Navigorn."

Prestimion at last yielded up his place on the field, to
thunderous applause. He went running off, grinning, in a
bouncy, boyishly jubilant stride. A slim young man wearing
tight blue leggings and a brilliant scarlet-and-gold tunic typical of the distant west coast of Zimroel came forth next.

"He looked so happy just now," Prince Serithorn observed. "Far more so than he was at the banquet the other
night. Did you see how preoccupied he seemed then?"

"There was a black look about him that night," said Admiral Gonivaul. "Well, he's never happier than when he's
at his archery. But perhaps his long face at the banquet was
meant to tell us that he's already begun to take a sober view
of what being Coronal actually involves. Not just grand pro-

cessionals and the cheers of the admiring multitudes. Oh, no, no, no! A lifetime of grueling toil is what's in store for him now, and the truth of it must be starting to sink in. —You know what 'toil' means, don't you, Serithorn? No, why would you? The word isn't in your vocabulary"

"Why should it be?" replied Serithorn, who despite his considerable age was smooth-skinned and trim, an elegant, light-hearted man, one who rejoiced unabashedly in the enormous wealth that had descended to him from a whole host of famous ancestors going back to Lord Stiamot's time. "What work could I possibly have done? I never thought I had much to offer the world in the way of useful skills. Better to do nothing all one's life, and do it really well, than to set out to do something and do it badly, eh, my friend? Eh? Let those who are truly capable do the work. Such as Prestimion. He'll be a marvelous Coronal. Has real aptitude for the job. Or like Navigorn here: a natural-born administrator, a man of genuine ability. —I hear he's named you to the Council, Navigorn."

"Yes. An honor I never sought, but am proud to have received."

"Plenty of responsibility, being on the Council, let me tell you. I've put in more than my share of time on it. Prestimion's asked me to stay on, matter of fact. What about you, Gonivaul?"

"I long for retirement," the Grand Admiral said. "I am no longer young. I will return to Bombifale and enjoy the comforts and pleasures of my estate, I think."

Serithorn smiled lightly. "Ah? You mean Prestimion hasn't reappointed you as Admiral, is that it? Well, we'll miss you, Gonivaul. But of course it's a lot of ghastly drudgery, being Grand Admiral. I can hardly blame you for being willing to lay the job down. —Tell me, Gonivaul, did you ever set foot on board a seagoing vessel so much as once, during your entire term of office? No, surely not. A risky thing it is, going to sea. Man can drown, doing that."

It was an old business, the duels of sarcastic byplay between these two great lords.

The part of Gonivaul's face that was visible turned bright red with wrath.

"Serithorn—" he began ominously.

"If I may, gentlemen," said Navigorn, cutting smoothly across the banter just as matters were threatening to become unruly.

Gonivaul backed off, grumbling. Serithorn chuckled in satisfaction.

Navigorn said, "I've not yet officially come into my new post, and already I've been handed a most peculiar problem to deal with. Perhaps you two, who know all the ins and outs of Castle politics as few others do, can advise me."

"And what problem may that be?" said Serithorn, making no great show of interest. He was looking not at Navigorn but at the field below.

The second of the day's two non-human contestants was at the baseline now, a great shaggy Skandar wearing a soft woolen jerkin boldly striped in black and orange and yellow. His bow, broader and more powerful even than Prestimion's, dangled casually from one of his four huge hands like a plaything. The herald's announcement gave his name as Hent Sekkiturn.

"Do you recognize the colors this archer wears, by any chance?" asked Navigorn.

"They are those of the Procurator Dantirya Sambail, I believe," said Serithorn, after a moment's inner deliberation.

"Exactly. And where is the Procurator himself, do you think?"

"Why—why—" Serithorn looked around. "You know, I don't actually see him. He should be sitting right up here near us, I'd say. Do you have any idea of where he is, Gonivaul?"

"I haven't laid eyes on him all week," said the Grand Admiral. "Come to think of it, I can't remember the last time I did see him. He's not what you'd call an inconspicuous man, either. Could it be that he's skipped the coronation altogether and stayed home, back there in Ni-moya?"

"Impossible," Serithorn said. "A new Coronal is being crowned for the first time in decades, and the most powerful prince in Zimroel doesn't bother to show up? That would be absurd. For one thing, Dantirya Sambail would want to be on the scene when the new appointments and preferences are handed out. And so he was, I'm quite certain, during the months when old Prankipin was dying. He'd have stayed for the coronation, certainly. Besides, Prestimion would surely take mortal offense if the Procurator were to snub him like this."

"Oh, Dantirya Sambail's at the Castle, all right," said Navigorn. "That's precisely the problem I want to discuss. You haven't noticed him at any of the festivities because he happens to be a prisoner in the Sangamor tunnels. And now Prestimion's set me in charge of him. I'm to be his jailer, it seems. My first official duty as a member of the Council."

A look of incredulity appeared on Serithorn's face. "What are you saying, Navigorn? Dantirya Sambail, a prisoner?"

"Apparently so."

Gonivaul seemed equally amazed. "I find this altogether unbelievable. Why would Prestimion put Dantirya Sambail in the tunnels? The Procurator's his own cousin—well, some sort of relative, anyway, right? You'd know more about that than I do, Serithorn. What is this, a family quarrel?"

"Perhaps it is. More to the point," Serithorn said, "how could anybody, even Prestimion, succeed in locking up someone as blustering and obstreperous and generally vile as Dantirya Sambail? I'd think it would be harder than locking up a whole pack of maddened haiguses. And if it's actually been done, why haven't we heard about it? I'd think it would be the talk of the Castle."

Navigorn turned his hands outward in a shrug. "I have no answers for any of this, gentlemen. I don't understand the least thing about it. All I know is that the Procurator's in the lockup, or so Prestimion assures me, and the Coronal has assigned me the job of making sure he stays there until he can be brought to judgment."

"Judgment for what?" Gonivaul cried.

"I don't have the slightest idea. I asked him what crime

the Procurator was accused of, and he said he'd discuss that with me some other time."

"Well, what's your difficulty, then?" asked Serithorn crisply. "The Coronal has given you an assignment. You do as he says, that's all. He wants you to be the Procurator's jailer? Then be his jailer, Navigorn."

"I hold no great love in my heart for Dantirya Sambail. He's little more than a wild beast, the Procurator. But even so—if he's being held without justification, purely at Prestimion's whim, am I not an accomplice to injustice if I help to keep him in prison?"

Gonivaul said, amazed, "Are you raising an issue of conscience, Navigorn?"

"You might call it that."

"You've taken an oath to serve the Coronal. The Coronal sees fit to place Dantirya Sambail under arrest, and asks you to enforce it. Do as he says, or else resign your office. Those are your choices, Navigorn. Do you believe Prestimion's an evil man?"

"Of course not. And I have no desire to resign."

"Well, then, assume that Prestimion believes there's just cause for locking the Procurator away. Put twenty picked men on duty in the tunnels round the clock, or thirty, or however many you think are necessary, and have them keep watch, and make sure they understand that if Dantirya Sambail manages to charm his way out of his cell, or to bully and bluster his way out, or to get out in any other way at all, they'll spend the rest of their lives regretting it."

"And if men of Ni-moya, the Procurator's men, that unsavory crew of murderers and thieves that Dantirya Sambail likes to keep about him, should come to me this afternoon," said Navigorn, "and demand to know where their master is and on what charges he's being held, and threaten to start an uproar from one end of the Castle to the other unless he's released immediately—?"

"Refer them to the Coronal," Gonivaul said. "He's the one who put Dantirya Sambail in jail, not you. If they want explanations, they can get them from Lord Prestimion."

"Dantirya Sambail a prisoner," said Serithorn in a wondering tone, as though speaking to the air around him. "What a strange business! What an odd way to begin the new reign! —Are we supposed to keep this news a secret, Navigorn?"

"The Coronal told me nothing about that. The less said the better, I'd imagine."

"Yes. Yes. The less said the better."

"Indeed," said Gonivaul. "Best to say no more." And they all nodded vigorously.

"Serithorn! Gonivaul!" a hearty, raucous voice cried just then, from a couple of rows above. "Hello, Navigorn." It was Fisiolo, the Count of Stee. With him was a short, stocky, ruddy-faced man with dark, chilly eyes and a high forehead. A formidable mass of stiff silvery hair swept upward from that forehead to a prodigious and somewhat alarming height. "You know Simbilon Khayf, do you?" Fisiolo asked, with a glance toward his companion. "Richest man in Stee. Prestimion himself will be coming to him for loans before long, mark my words."

Simbilon Khayf favored Serithorn and Gonivaul and Navigorn with a quick, bland, beaming inclination of his head, studiedly modest. He seemed very much flattered to find himself in the presence of peers of such lofty position. Count Fisiolo, a square-faced, blunt-featured man who was never one to stand on ceremony, immediately beckoned Simbilon Khayf to follow him down into the box that the other three occupied, and he lost no time in doing so. But he gave the distinct impression of being someone who knew that he was far out of his depth.

"Have you heard?" Fisiolo said. "Prestimion's got Dantirya Sambail penned up in the tunnels! Has him hanging on the wall in heavy irons, so I'm told. Can you imagine such a thing? It's the talk of the Castle."

"We've only just learned of it," said Serithorn. "Well, if the story's true, no doubt the Coronal had good reason for putting him there."

"And what could that have been? Did nasty Dantirya

Sambail say something dreadfully rude? Dantirya Sambail make the starburst sign the wrong way, maybe? Dantirya Sambail break wind at the coronation ceremony? —Come to think of it, was Dantirya Sambail even at the coronation ceremony?"

"I don't remember seeing him arrive at the Castle at all," Gonivaul said. "When we all came back here after Prankipin's funeral."

"Nor I," said Navigorn. "And I was here when the main caravan from the Labyrinth arrived. Dantirya Sambail wasn't with it."

"Yet we are reliably informed that he is here," said Serithorn. "Has been for some time, it seems. Long enough to offend Prestimion and be imprisoned, and yet nobody remembers seeing him arrive. This is very strange. Dantirya Sambail creates whirlwinds of noise about himself wherever he goes. How could he have come to the Castle, and none of us know it?"

"Strange, yes," said Gonivaul.

"Strange indeed," added Count Fisiolo. "But I confess that I like the idea that Prestimion has managed somehow to put that repulsive loathsome monster in irons. Don't you?"

5

THE PROCURATOR OF NI-MOYA was much on Prestimion's mind, too, in the days that followed the coronation festival. But he was in no hurry to deal with his treacherous kinsman, who had betrayed him again and again in the twistings and turnings of the late civil war. Let him languish some while longer in the dungeon into which he had been cast, Prestimion thought. It was necessary first to figure out some way of handling his case.

Beyond any question Dantirya Sambail was guilty of high treason. More than anyone, except, perhaps, the Lady Thismet herself, he had spurred Korsibar on to his insane rebellion. The breaking of the dam on the Iyann had been his doing, too, a savage act that had caused unthinkable destruction. And in the battle of Thegomar Edge he had lifted his hand against Prestimion in single combat, jeeringly offering to let the contest decide which of them would be the next Coronal and attacking Prestimion with axe and sa- ber. Prestimion had prevailed in that encounter, though it was a close thing. But he had been unable to slay his de- feated kinsman then and there on the battlefield, which was what he deserved. Instead Prestimion had had Dantirya Sambail and his malevolent henchman Mandralisca hauled away as prisoners, to be brought to judgment at a later time.

But how, Prestimion wondered, could the Procurator be put on trial for crimes that nobody, not even the accused man himself, was able to remember? Who would stand forth as his accuser? What evidence could be adduced against him? "This man was the chief fomenter of the civil war," yes. But what civil war? "It was his treasonous intention to seize the royal throne for himself once he had arranged the death of his puppet Korsibar." Korsibar? Who was Korsi- bar? "He is guilty of menacing the life of the legitimate Coronal on the field of battle with deadly weapons." What battle, where, when?

Prestimion had no answers to these questions. And there were, anyway, more pressing problems to deal with first, here in the early weeks of his reign.

The coronation guests, most of them, had scattered far and wide to their homes. The princes and dukes and earls and mayors had gone back to their own domains; the former Cor- onal who now was Confalume Pontifex had taken himself down the River Glayge on the long somber voyage that would deliver him to his new subterranean home in the Labyrinth; the archers and jousters and wrestlers and swords- men who had come to show their skills at the coronation games were dispersed as well. The Princess Therissa had gone back to Muldemar House to prepare for her journey to the Isle of Sleep and the tasks that awaited her there. The Cas- tle was suddenly a much quieter place as Prestimion entered into the tasks of the new regime.

And there was so much to do. He had desired the throne and its duties with all his heart; but now that he had had his wish, he was awed by the boundless tasks he faced.

"I hardly know where to begin," he confessed, looking up wearily at Septach Melayn and Gialaurys.

The three of them were in the spacious room, inlaid everywhere with rare woods and strips of shining metal, that was the core of the Coronal's official suite. The throne-room was for the pomp and grandeur of state; these chambers were where the actual business of being Coronal took place.

Prestimion was seated at his splendid starburst grained desk of red palisander, and long-legged Septach Melayn lounged elegantly beside the broad curving window over-looking the sweeping, airy depths of the abyss of space that bordered the Castle on this side of the Mount. The thick-bodied, heavy-sinewed Gialaurys sat hunched on a backless bench to Prestimion's left.

"It's very simple, lordship," said Gialaurys. "Begin at the beginning, and then continue to the next thing, and the next, and the one after that."

Coming from Septach Melayn, such advice would have been mockery; but big steadfast Gialaurys had no capacity for irony, and when he spoke, in that deep, slow, gritty rumble of a voice of his, the words flattened by the blunt accents of his native city of Piliplok, it was always with the greatest seriousness. Prestimion's mercurial little compan-ion, the late and much lamented Duke Svor, had often mis-taken Gialaurys's stolidity for stupidity. But Gialaurys was not stupid at all, just ponderously sincere.

Prestimion laughed amiably. "Well said, Gialaurys! But which thing is the first one, and which the next? If only it were that easy to know."

"Well, Prestimion, let us make a list," said Septach Me-layn. He ticked things off on his fingers. "One: appointing new court officials. On which we've made a fairly good start, I'd say. You've got yourself a new High Counsellor, thank you very much. And Gialaurys here will be a superb Grand Admiral, I'm sure. Et cetera et cetera. Two: repairing the prosperity of the districts that suffered damage during the war. Your brother Abrigant has some thoughts on that subject, incidentally, and wants to see you later in the day. Three—"

Septach Melayn hesitated. Gialaurys said at once, "Three: doing something about bringing Dantirya Sambail to trial."

"Let that one go for a while," Prestimion said. "It's a complicated matter."

"Four," went on Gialaurys, undaunted: "Interviewing everyone who fought on Korsibar's side in the late war, and making certain that no lingering disloyalties remain that could threaten the security of—"

"No," said Prestimion. "Strike that from the list. There never was any war, remember? How could anyone still be loyal to Korsibar, Gialaurys, when Korsibar never existed?"

Gialaurys offered a scowl and a grunt of displeasure. "Even so, Prestimion—"

"I tell you, there's nothing to worry about here. Most of Korsibar's lieutenants died at Thegomar Edge—Farholt, Mandrykarn, Venta, Farquanor, all that crowd—and I have no fear of the ones who survived. Navigorn, for instance. Korsibar's best general, he was. But he begged forgiveness right on the battlefield, do you recall, when he came up to surrender just after Korsibar was killed? And sincerely so. He'll serve me well on the Council. Oljebbin and Serithorn and Gonivaul—they sold out to Korsibar, yes, but they don't remember doing it, and they can't do any harm now in any case. Duke Oljebbin will go to the Labyrinth and become High Spokesman for the Pontifex, and good riddance. Gonivaul gets sent into retirement in Bombifale. Serithorn's useful and amusing; I'll keep him around. Well, who else? Name me the names of people whom you suspect of being disloyal."

"Well—" Gialaurys began, but no names came to his lips.

"I'll tell you one thing, Prestimion," said Septach Melayn. "There may not be any Korsibar loyalists left around, but there isn't anybody at the Castle, other than the three of us, who's not seriously confused in some way by the witchery that you invoked at the end of the war. The war itself is wiped from everyone's mind, yes. But they all know that something big happened. They just don't know what it was. A lot of important men are dead, whole huge regions of Alhanroel are devastated, the Mavestoi Dam has mysteriously given way and flooded half a province, and yet everybody has been given to understand that there's been a smooth and uneventful transition from Confalume's reign to yours. It doesn't add up right, and they know it. They keep running up against that big throbbing blank place in their memories. It bothers them. I see mystified looks coming over people's faces right in the middle of a sentence, and they stop speaking and frown and press their hands against the sides of their heads as if they're groping in their minds for something that isn't there. I've begun to wonder if it was such a good idea to remove the war from history like that, Prestimion."

This was a subject Prestimion would have preferred not to discuss. But there was no avoiding it now that Septach Melayn had wrestled it out into the open.

"The war was a terrible wound to the soul of the world," said Prestimion tautly. "If I had left it unexpunged, grievances and countergrievances would have been popping up forever between Korsibar's faction and mine. By having all memories of the war wiped clean, I gave everyone a chance to make a fresh start. To borrow one of your own favorite phrases, Septach Melayn, what's done is done. We have to live now with the consequences, and we will, and that's all there is to it."

Inwardly, though, he was not so sure. He had heard disquieting reports—everyone had—of strange outbreaks of mental imbalance here and there on the Mount, people attacking strangers without motive in the streets, or bursting into uncontrollable sobbing that went on for days and days, or throwing themselves into rivers or off cliffs. Such tales had come in lately from Halanx and Minimool, and Haplior also, as though some whirling eddy of madness could be spiralling outward and downward from the Castle to the adjacent cities of the Mount. Even as far down the Mount as Stee, it seemed, there had been a serious incident, a housemaid in some rich man's mansion who had leaped from a window and killed two people standing in the street below.

What reason was there, though, to link any of this to the general amnesia that he had had his sorcerers induce at the end of the war? Perhaps such things inevitably happened at the time of the changing of kings, especially after so long and happy a reign as that of Lord Confalume. People thought of Confalume as being a loving father to the entire world; they were unhappy, perhaps, to see him disappearing into the Labyrinth; and hence these disturbances. Perhaps.

Septach Melayn and Gialaurys were going on and on, extending into a host of new areas the already sufficient list of problems that were awaiting solutions:

He needed, they told him, to integrate the various magical arts, which had come to take on such importance on Majipoor in Confalume's time, more fully into the fabric of society. This would require conversations with such folk as Gominik Halvor and Heszmon Gorse, who had remained at the Castle for just that purpose, said Gialaurys, rather than return to the wizards' capital at Triggoin.

He needed also to do something about a horde of synthetically-created monsters that Korsibar had planned to use against him on the battlefield if the war had lasted just a little longer: according to Gialaurys, a number of them had escaped from their pens and were rampaging through some district north of Castle Mount.

Then, too, he ought to deal with some complaint that the Metamorphs of Zimroel had raised, having to do with the boundaries of the forest reservation on which they were required to live. The Shapeshifters were complaining of illegal encroachments on their domain by unscrupulous land-developers out of Ni-moya.

And also there was this to do, and this, and that—

Prestimion was barely listening, now.

They were so insufferably sincere, these two, Septach Melayn in his elegant knightly way, Gialaurys in his own blunter style. Septach Melayn had always posed as one who never took anything seriously, but it was, Prestimion knew,

only a pose; and as for Gialaurys, he was nothing else but
stolid seriousness, a great massive sturdy lump of it. Prestimion felt, more keenly than ever, the loss of the slippery
little Duke Svor, who had had many faults but never the
one of excessive sincerity. He had been the perfect mediator
between the other two.

How idiotic it had been of Svor to step out onto the
battlefield of Thegomar Edge, when his proper place had
been behind the scenes, scheming and plotting! Svor had
not been any sort of warrior. What lunacy had driven him
to take part in that murderous battle? And now he was gone.
Where, Prestimion wondered, will I find a replacement for
him?

And for Thismet, also. Especially, especially, Thismet.
The biting pain of that loss would not leave him, would not
so much as diminish with the passing weeks. Was it Thismet's death, he wondered, that had cast him into this miserable despondency?

Much work awaited him, yes. Too much, it sometimes
seemed. Well, he would manage it somehow. Every Coronal
in the long list of his predecessors had faced the same sense
of immense responsibilities that had to be mastered, and
each had shouldered those responsibilities and played his
part, for good or ill, as history related—as history would
one day relate also of him. And most of them had done the
job reasonably well, all things considered.

But he could not shake off that mysterious, damnable
sense of weariness, of hollowness, of letdown and dissatis-
faction, that had poisoned his spirit since the first day of his
reign. He had hoped that the taking up of his royal duties
would cure him of that. It did not seem to be working out
that way.

Very likely the tasks before him would seem far less
immense, Prestimion thought, if only Thismet had lived.
What a wonderful partner of his labors she would have
been! A Coronal's daughter herself, aware of the challenges
of the kingship, and doubtless more than capable of handling
many of them—Thismet would have been ever so much
more capable of governing, he was sure, than her foolish

brother: she would gladly have shared a great deal of his burden. But Thismet, too, was lost to him forever.

Still talking, Septach Melayn? And you, Gialaurys?

Prestimion toyed with the slim circlet of bright metal that lay before him on the desk. His "everyday" crown, as he liked to call it, to distinguish it from the exceedingly magnificent formal crown that Lord Confalume had had fashioned for himself, with those three immense many-faceted purple diniabas gleaming in its browband, and its finials of emeralds and rubies, and its inlaid chasings of seven different precious metals.

Confalume had loved to wear that crown; but Prestimion had worn it only once, in the first hours of his reign. He meant to reserve it henceforth for the very highest occasions of state. He found it mildly absurd even to have this little silver band around his head, hard though he had fought for the right to wear it. But he kept it constantly by him, all the same. He was Coronal of Majipoor, after all.

Coronal of Majipoor.

He had set his goal high, and after terrible struggle he had attained it.

As his two dearest friends droned on and on with their seemingly unending recitation of the tasks that awaited him and their interminable discussion of priorities and strategies, Prestimion was no longer even pretending to be paying attention. He knew what his tasks were: all of these, yes, and one that Septach Melayn and Gialaurys had not mentioned. For above all else he must make himself, here at the outset, the master of the officials and courtiers who were the real heart of the government: he must demonstrate his kingliness to them, he must show them that Lord Confalume, with the guidance of the Divine, had chosen the right man for the post.

Which meant that he must think like a Coronal, live like a Coronal, walk like a Coronal, breathe like a Coronal. That was the prime task; and all else would follow inevitably from the doing of it.

Very well, Prestimion: you are Coronal. Be Coronal.

The husk of him remained where it was, behind his desk,

pretending to listen as Septach Melayn and Gialaurys earnestly laid out an agenda for the early months of his reign. But his soul flew upward and outward, into the cool open sky above the tip of Castle Mount, and journeyed toward the world, traveling in miraculous simultaneity to all directions of the compass.

He opened himself now to Majipoor and let himself feel its immensity flowing through him. Sent his mind roving outward across the vastness of the world that in these days just past had been entrusted to his care.

He must embrace that vastness fully, he knew, take it into himself, encompass it with his soul.

—The three great continents, sprawling, vast, many-citied Alhanroel and gigantic lush-forested Zimroel and the smaller continent of Suvrael, that sun-blasted land down in the torrid south. The giant surging rivers. The countless species of trees and plants and beasts and birds that filled the world with such beauty and wonder. The blue-green expanse of the Inner Sea with its roving herds of great sea-dragons moving unhurriedly about their mysterious migrations, and the holy Isle of Sleep that lay in its center. The other ocean, the enormous unexplored Great Sea that stretched across the unknown farther hemisphere of the world.

—The marvelous cities, the fifty great ones of the Mount and the uncountable multitude beyond, Sippulgar and Sefarad and Alaisor and wizardly Triggoin, Kikil and Mai and Kimoise, Pivrarch and Lontano, Da and Demigon Glade, and on and on, across to the far shore of the Inner Sea and the distant continent of Zimroel with its multiplicity of ever-burgeoning megalopolises, Ni-moya, Narabal, Til-omon, Pidruid, Dulorn, Sempernond, and all the rest.

—The billions and billions of people, not only the humans but those of the other races, Vroons and Skandars, Su-Suheris and Hjorts and the humble slow-witted Liimen, and also the mysterious shape-shifting Metamorphs, whose world this had been in its entirety until it was taken from them so many thousands of years ago.

All of it now placed in his hands.

His.

His.

The hands of Prestimion of Muldemar, yes: who now was Coronal of Majipoor.

Suddenly Prestimion found himself feverishly yearning to go forth not merely in a vision but in the flesh, and explore this world that had been given into his charge. To see it all; to be everywhere at once, drinking in the infinite wonders of Majipoor. Out of the pain and loneliness of his strange new life as Coronal came, in one great turbulent rush, the passionate desire to visit the lands from which those coronation gifts had come. To repay the givers, in a sense, with the gift of himself.

A king must know his kingdom at first hand. Until the time of the civil war, when he had trekked back and forth across Alhanroel from one battlefield to another, his life had been centered almost entirely on Castle Mount, and at the Castle itself. He had been to some of the Fifty Cities, of course; and there had been the one journey to the eastern coast of Zimroel when he was hardly out of boyhood, that time when he had met and fallen into friendship with Gialaurys at Piliplok, but otherwise he had seen little of the world.

The war, though, had given Prestimion an appetite for traveling. It had taken him up and down the heartland of Alhanroel, to cities and places he had never expected to see: he had beheld the astonishing might of the Gulikap Fountain, that uncheckable spume of pure energy, and had crossed the forbidding spine of the Trikkala Mountains into the lovely agricultural zones on the other side, and had impelled himself across the grim dread desert of the Valmambra to reach the remote city of the wizards, Triggoin, far in the north. And yet he had seen only a tiny sliver of the magnificence that was Majipoor.

He longed, abruptly, to experience more. He had not realized, until this moment, how powerful that longing was. The desire seized him and took full possession of him. How much longer could he remain holed up in isolated majesty in the luxurious confines of the Castle, drearily passing one day after another in such matters as interviewing potential members of the Council and reviewing the legislative program that he had been handed by Lord Confalume's administration, when the whole glorious world beyond these walls beckoned to him, urging him to go forth into it? If he could not have Thismet, well, he would have Majipoor itself to console him for the loss. To see all that it held, to touch, to taste, to smell. To drink deep; to devour. To present himself to his subjects, saying, Look, see, here I am before you, Prestimion your king!

"Enough," he said suddenly, glancing up and interrupting Septach Melayn in full spate. "If you will, my friends, spare me the rest of it for now."

Septach Melayn peered down at him from his great height. "Are you all right, Prestimion? You look very strange, suddenly."

"Strange?"

"Tense. Strained."

Indifferently Prestimion said, "I've slept badly these few nights past."

"That comes of sleeping alone, my lord," said Septach Melayn, with a wink and a little sniggering leer.

"No doubt that's so," said Prestimion icily. "Another problem to be solved, at another time." He allowed Septach Melayn to see plainly that he was not amused. Then he said, after a long chilly moment of silence, "The true problem, Septach Melayn, is that I feel a great restlessness churning within me. I've felt it since the hour this crown first touched my forehead. The Castle has begun to seem like a prison to me."

Septach Melayn and Gialaurys exchanged troubled glances.

"Is that so, my lord?" said Septach Melayn cautiously.

"Very much so."

"You should talk to Dantirya Sambail about what being a prisoner is really like," Septach Melayn said, giving Prestimion an exaggerated roll of his eyes.

The man is irrepressible, Prestimion thought.

"In due time I will certainly do just that," he replied unsmilingly. "But I remind you that Dantirya Sambail's a criminal. I'm a king."

"Who dwells in the greatest of all castles," said Gialaurys. "Would you rather be back on the battlefield then, my lord? Sleeping in the rain beneath a bower of vakumba-trees in Moorwath forest? Struggling in the mud by the banks of the Jhclum? Making your way through the swamps of Beldak marsh? Or wandering about deliriously in the desert of Valmambra once more, perhaps?"

"Don't talk nonsense, Gialaurys. You don't understand what I'm saying. Neither of you do. Is this the Labyrinth, and I the Pontifex, that I'm required to stay in one place forever and ever? The Castle's not the boundary of my life. These few years past all my efforts have been spent on making myself Coronal; and now I am; and it seems to me now that all I've achieved for myself is to make myself the king of documents and meetings. The coronation festivities have come and gone. I sit in this office, grand as it is, day after day, yearning with all my heart to be anywhere else. —My friends, I need to get out into the world for a time."

In some alarm Septach Melayn said, "Surely you're not thinking of a grand processional, Prestimion! Not yet! Not in the first month of your reign—nor even the first year, for that matter."

Prestimion shook his head. "No. It's much too soon for that, I agree." What did he want, though? It was far from clear even to himself. Improvising hastily, he said, "Short visits somewhere, perhaps—not a grand processional but a little one, through half a dozen of the Fifty Cities, let's say—two or three weeks going here and there on the Mount. To bring myself closer to the people, to get to know what's on their minds. I've been too busy in these years of war to pay any attention to anything except raising armies and making battle plans."

"Yes, certainly, travel to some of the nearby cities. Yes, by all means, do," said Septach Melayn. "But it'll take time—weeks, even months—to arrange even the simplest of official journeys. Surely you know that. The arrangements for proper royal accommodations, the programs of events to be drawn up, the receptions, the banquets that must be organized—"

"More banquets," said Prestimion glumly.

"They are unavoidable, my lord. But I have a better suggestion, if you merely want to escape from the Castle for quick visits to the neighboring cities."

"And what is that?"

"Korsibar, I'm told, also wanted to travel about on the Mount while he was Coronal. And did so secretly, in disguise, making use of some shapechanging device that the sneaky Vroon wizard Thalnap Zelifor invented for him. You could do the same, taking on this guise or that one, as it pleased you, and no one the wiser."

Prestimion looked at him dubiously. "I remind you, Septach Melayn, that at this very moment Thalnap Zelifor is on his way to exile in Suvrael, and all of his magical devices have gone with him."

Frowning, Septach Melayn said, "Ah. In truth I had forgotten that." But then his eyes brightened. "Yet there's really no need of such magic, is there? I understand it failed one day for Korsibar anyway, while he was in Sipermit, I think, and he was seen changing to his true semblance. Which gave rise to the silly fable that Korsibar was a Metamorph. If you were to wear a false beard, though, and a kerchief around your head, and dressed yourself in commoner's clothing—"

"A false beard!" said Prestimion, with a guffaw.

"Yes, and I would go with you, or Gialaurys, or the two of us both, also in disguise, and we'd sneak off to Bibiroon, or Upper Sunbreak, or Banglecode or Greel or wherever it is you want to go, and spend a night or two sniffing around having high sport far from the Castle, and no one would ever know? What do you say to that, Prestimion? Would that ease this restlessness of yours at least a little?"

"I do like the idea," Prestimion said, feeling a spark of joy rising within his breast for the first time in more weeks than he cared to count. "I like it very much!"

*   *   *

And would gladly have set forth from the Castle that very evening. But no, no, there were more meetings to attend, and proposals to consider, and decrees that must be signed. He had never fully comprehended until now the meaning of the old saying that it was folly to yearn to be the master of the realm, for you would discover in short order that you were in fact its servant.

"Lordship, it is Prince Abrigant of Muldemar to see you," came the voice of Nilgir Sumanand, who held the post of major-domo to the Coronal now.

"Admit him," Prestimion said.

Tall slender Abrigant, seven years Prestimion's junior and the elder of his two living brothers, came striding into the royal office. The Prince of Muldemar, he was, now, having succeeded to Prestimion's old title upon Prestimion's becoming Coronal. Prestimion was seriously thinking of giving him a seat on the Council as well, not at once, perhaps, but after young Abrigant had had a chance to ripen into his maturity a little further.

Abrigant might more readily have been Septach Melayn's brother than Prestimion's, so different in physical type was he. He was slim where Prestimion was stocky, and lanky where Prestimion was short statured, and his hair, though golden like his brother's, had a sheen and a radiance that Prestimion's had never had. He cut a fine figure, did Abrigant: dressed this evening as though for a formal public occasion of court, with a tight-fitting, high-waisted pinkish-purple doublet of rich Alaisor make, and soft long-legged breeches of the same color, tucked into high boots of the distinctive yellow leather of Estotilaup that were topped with fine lace ruffles.

He offered his brother not only the starburst gesture but a grand sweeping bow, greatly overdone. Irritatedly Prestimion made a quick brushing motion with his hand, as if to sweep the effusive obeisance away.

"This is a little too much, Abrigant. Much too much!"

"You are Coronal now, Prestimion!"

"Yes. So I am. But you are still my brother. A simple starburst will be sufficient. More than sufficient, indeed." He began once more to toy with the slender crown lying on his desk. "Septach Melayn tells me you have ideas to put before me. Dealing with, so I understand it, the matter of bringing some relief to the regions currently suffering from crop failures and other such disruptions."

Abrigant looked puzzled. "He said that, did he? Well, not exactly. I know that certain places here and there around Alhanroel are in bad shape, all of a sudden. But I don't know the whys and wherefores of any of that, except for a few obvious things like the collapse of the Mavestoi Dam and the flooding of the Iyann Valley. The rest's a mystery to me, what might be causing these sudden local outbreaks of food shortages, or whatever. The will of the Divine, I suppose."

Statements of that kind troubled Prestimion, and he was hearing them more and more often. But what could he expect, when he had kept everyone around him in ignorance of the major event of the era? Here was his own brother, one of his most intimate friends, whom he hoped would also become, eventually, one of his most useful advisers, a member of the Royal Council. And he knew nothing of the war and its effects. Nothing!

A great civil war had devastated great sectors of Alhanroel for two whole years, and Abrigant had no inkling that it had ever occurred. Living in such darkness, how could he be expected to make rational decisions about public affairs? For a moment Prestimion was tempted to confess the truth. But he checked himself. He and Septach Melayn and Gialaurys had agreed most vehemently that they should be the only ones to know. There could be no revelations after the fact, not now, not even for Abrigant.

"You're not here to talk about remedies for the afflicted provinces, then?"

"No. What I have are ideas concerning ways to increase the general economic well-being of the entire world. If all the world grows wealthier, then the distressed districts will be helped along with everyone else. Which must be what led Septach Melayn to misunderstand my purpose."

"Go on," said Prestimion uncomfortably.

This new earnestness of Abrigant's was very strange in his ears. The Abrigant he knew was energetic, impetuous, even somewhat hotheaded. In the struggle against the usurping Korsibar he had been a valiant, ferocious warrior. But a man of ideas, no. Prestimion had never known his brother to show much aptitude for abstract thought. An athlete, was what he was. Hunting, racing, sport of all kinds: that was where Abrigant's interests always had lain. Perhaps maturity was coming upon him faster than Prestimion had expected, though.

Abrigant hesitated. He seemed uncomfortable too. After a moment he said, as if reading his brother's mind, "I'm well aware, Prestimion, that you think I'm a pretty shallow sort. But I do a lot of reading and studying now, I've hired experts to tutor me on matters of public affairs. I—"

"Please, Abrigant. I realize that you're not a boy any longer."

"Thank you. I just want you to know that I've given a lot of thought to these things." Abrigant moistened his lips and drew his breath in deeply. "What I have to say is simply this. We've enjoyed, of course, a great economic upturn on Majipoor all through Lord Confalume's years as Coronal, and through Lord Prankipin's reign before that. A case could be made that we've been living through a golden age. But even so, we're not nearly as prosperous as we ought to be, considering the wealth of natural resources we have here, and the overall tranquility of our political system."

Overall tranquility?

With a terrible war only a few weeks in the past? Prestimion wondered whether there was some irony there—whether Abrigant might remember more of the recent events than he was letting on. No, he thought. There was not the slightest trace of ambiguity in Abrigant's steady, earnest gaze. His eyes, sea-green like Prestimion's own, were focused on him with solemn uncomplicated intensity.

"The big stumbling-block," Abrigant was saying, "is the scarcity of metals here, of course. We've never had enough iron on Majipoor, for example, or nickel, or lead, or tin. We've got some copper, yes, and gold and silver, but not much else in the way of metal. We've been greatly short-changed in that regard. Do you know why that's so, Prestimion?"

"The will of the Divine, I suppose?"

"You could say that, yes. It was the will of the Divine to provide most worlds of the universe with good heavy cores of iron or nickel, and those worlds have plentiful supplies of such metals in their crusts, too. But Majipoor's much lighter within and without. We've got light rock, or great airy caverns, where other worlds have those masses of solid metal. And there's not much metal in our world's crust, either. This is why gravity doesn't have a really powerful pull here, even though Majipoor is so big. If this planet was composed of as much metal as other worlds are, people like us would probably be crushed flat by the tremendous force of gravity. Even if we weren't, we wouldn't be sufficiently strong to lift a single finger. Not a single finger, Prestimion! Do you follow me so far?"

"I understand something of the laws of gravity," said Prestimion, amazed at being lectured in such matters by Abrigant, of all people.

"Good. You'll agree with me, then, that this lack of metals has been something of an economic handicap for us? That we've never been able to build spacegoing vessels, or even an adequate system of air and rail transport, because of it? That we're dependent on other worlds for a lot of the metal we do use, and that this has been costly to us in all sorts of ways?"

"Agreed. But you know, Abrigant, we haven't really done too badly. No one goes hungry here, big as our population is. There's ample work for all. We have splendid cities of enormous size. Our society's been remarkably stable under a worldwide government for thousands of years."

"Because we have a wonderful climate almost everywhere, and fertile soil, and any number of useful plants and animals both on land and sea. But plenty of people are going hungry right now, so I hear, in places like the Iyann Valley.

I hear about bad harvests elsewhere in Alhanroel, empty granaries, factories having to shut down because something has been strange lately about the shipment of raw materials from place to place, and so forth."

"These are temporary problems," said Prestimion.

"Maybe so. But such things will put a great strain on the economy, won't they, brother? I've been doing a lot of reading, I told you. I've come to understand how one disruption over here can lead to another over there, which causes troubles in a third place entirely that's very far away, and before you know it the problem has spread all across the world. Which is something you may find yourself facing before you've spent many months on the throne, I'm afraid."

Prestimion nodded. This conversation was getting tiresome.

"And what do you suggest, then, Abrigant?"

Eagerly Abrigant said, "That we bring about an increase in our supply of useful metal, particularly iron. If we had more iron, we could manufacture more steel for use in industry and transportation, which would permit a great expansion of trade both on Majipoor itself and with our neighboring worlds."

"How is this to be achieved, exactly? By sorcery, perhaps?"

Abrigant looked wounded. "I beg you, brother, don't be condescending. I've been doing a great deal of reading lately."

"So you keep telling me."

"I know, for example, that there's said to be a district somewhere deep in the south, and off to the east of Aruachosia Province, where the soil is so curiously rich in metal that the plants themselves contain iron and copper in their stems and leaves. Which need only to be heated to yield a rich harvest of useful metal."

"Skakkenoir, yes," Prestimion said. "It's a myth, Abrigant. No one's ever been able to find this wonderful place."

"How hard has anyone ever tried? All I can turn up in the archives is an expedition in Lord Guadeloom's time, and that was thousands of years ago. We should go looking for it again, Prestimion. I'm quite serious. But I have other suggestions to make, too. Do you know, brother, that there are ways of manufacturing iron, zinc, and lead out of baser substances such as charcoal and earth? I don't mean through wizardry, although science of this sort certainly seems to verge on wizardry; but it is science all the same. Research has already been done. I can bring you people who have achieved such transformations. On a small scale, yes, a very small scale—but with proper backing, generous funds appropriated from the royal treasury—"

Prestimion gave him a close look. This was a new Abrigant, all right.

"You actually know of such people?"

"Well, at second hand, I have to admit. But reliable second hand. I urge you most strongly, brother—"

"No need for further urging, Abrigant. You pique my interest with this. Bring me your metal-making wizards and let me speak with them."

"Scientists, Prestimion. Scientists."

"Scientists, to be sure. Though anyone able to conjure iron out of charcoal sounds very much like a magus to me. Well, mages or scientists, whatever they may be, it's worth an hour of my time to learn more about their art. I do agree with your basic argument. A greater store of metal will make for great economic benefits for Majipoor. But can we really obtain the metal?"

"I'm confident of it, brother."

"We'll see about that," said Prestimion.

He rose and led Abrigant across the richly inlaid floor, artfully decorated with stripes of ghazyn and bannikop and other precious woods, to the door of the office. Abrigant paused there and said, "One more thing, Prestimion. Is it true that our kinsman Dantirya Sambail is a prisoner here in the Castle?"

"You've heard about that, have you?"

"Is he?"

"He is, yes. Hidden away snugly in the Sangamor tunnels."

Abrigant made a holy sign. "You can't be serious,

brother! What insanity is this? The Procurator's too dangerous a man to treat this way."

"It's specifically because he is dangerous that I've put
him where he is."

"But to offend a man who wields so much power, and
who is so free with his wrath—"

"The offense," said Prestimion, "was from him to me,
not the other way around, and merits what I've done to him.
As for the circumstances of the offense, those are of no
concern to anyone but me. And however much power Dantirya Sambail may wield, I wield more. In the fullness of
time I'll deal with his case as it deserves, I assure you, and
justice will be served. —I thank you most warmly for this
visit, brother. May it lead to good things for us all."

6

"AND THE NEW CORONAL," Dekkeret said. "What do you
think of him, now?"

"What is there to think?" his cousin Sithelle replied.
"He's young, is all I know. And quite intelligent, I hear.
We'll find out the rest as time goes along. —They do say
that he's very short, I understand."

"As if that matters," said Dekkeret scornfully. "But I suppose it does, at least to you. He'd never marry you, would
he? You'd be much too tall for him, and that wouldn't do."

They were walking along the broad rim of the immense
impregnable wall of black stone monoliths that surrounded
their home city of Normork, which was one of the twelve
Slope Cities of the Mount, a long way down the giant mountain from Lord Prestimion and his Castle. Dekkeret was not
quite eighteen, tall and strapping, with a powerful broad-
shouldered frame and an air of strength and confidence
about him. Sithelle, two years younger, was nearly of a
height with him, though of a lithe and willowy build that
made her seem almost fragile beside her sturdy cousin.

She laughed, a silvery, tinkling sound. "Me, marry the

Coronal? Do you suppose any such thing has ever entered my mind?"

"Of course I do. Every girl on Majipoor is thinking the same thing these days. 'Lord Prestimion is young and handsome and single, and he'll be taking a consort sooner or later, and why not a girl like me?' Am I right, Sithelle? No. No, of course not. I'm always wrong. And you'd never admit that you were interested in him if it was so, would you?"

"What are you saying? Coronals don't marry commoners!" She slipped her arm through his. "You're being silly," she said. "As usual, Dekkeret."

He and Sithelle were the best of friends. That was the problem. Their families had always hoped that they would marry some day; but they had grown up together, and looked upon each other almost as brother and sister. She was a handsome girl, too, with long springy hair the color of fire and bright, mischievous gray-violet eyes. But Dekkeret knew that he was no more likely ever to marry Sithelle than—well, than Sithelle was to marry Lord Prestimion. Less likely, indeed, because it was at least conceivable that she would somehow meet and marry the Coronal, but Dekkeret knew that Sithelle could never be his own choice as a wife.

They strolled along in silence for a time. The wall's rim was so wide that ten people could walk abreast on the road that ran along it, but there were few others up there now. The hour was getting late, the hour of long shadows. The green-gold orb of the sun was low in the sky and in just a short while it would move around behind the tremendous upjutting mass of Castle Mount and be lost to their view.

"Look there," Dekkeret said. He pointed downward into the city. They were at the place where the wall, as it followed the craggy contours of the Mount, made a great curve outward to carry past an out-thrusting rocky spur. The ancient palace of the Counts of Normork was tucked into that sweeping bulge.

A low, squat, almost windowless square building of gray basalt, it was, topped by six menacing-looking minarets. It seemed more like a fortress than a palace. Everything in

Normork had that look—secure, inward-looking, well guarded—as though the city's builders had looked upon the likelihood of invasion from some neighboring city as a perpetual threat. The outer wall, Normork's most famous landmark, enclosed the city like a tortoise's shell. It was so great a wall that it might almost be fair to call Normork itself an appendage to the wall, rather than speaking of the wall as an aspect of the city.

There was just one gate in the wall that so supremely enfolded Normork, and that was a mingy little thing that since time immemorial had been sealed tight every evening, so that if you didn't enter the city before dark, you waited until morning. Normork's wall, so it was said, was patterned after the great one of huge stone blocks, now mostly in ruins, that once had protected the prehistoric Metamorph capital of Velalisier. But thousands of years had gone by since there last had been war on Majipoor. Who were the enemies, Dekkeret often wondered, against whom this colossal rampart had been erected?

"The palace, you mean?" Sithelle said. "What about it?"

Long yellow streamers were draped across the palace's featureless face. "They've still got the mourning badges hanging from the facade," said Dekkeret.

"Well, why shouldn't they? It isn't all that long since the Count and his brother died."

"It seems like a long time to me. Months."

"No. Just a few weeks, in fact. I know, it does seem much longer. But it's not."

"How strange," Dekkeret said. "That the two of them should be dead so young." A boating accident on Lake Roghoiz, so it had been announced, where the princes had been sport-fishing. "Can it be true that the thing really happened the way we were told it did?"

Sithelle gave him a mystified look. "Is there any reason to doubt it? The nobility get killed in fishing and hunting accidents all the time."

"We are asked to accept that Count Iram hooked a scamminaup so big that it pulled him right into the lake and drowned him. That scamminaup must have been as big as a sea-dragon, Sithelle! I can't help wondering why he didn't simply let go of the line. And then Lamiran going in after him to rescue him, and drowning also? It's all very hard to believe."

Sithelle said, shrugging, "What purpose would anyone have in lying about it? And what difference would it make? They're dead, aren't they, and Meglis is Count of Normork, and that's that."

"Yes," he said. "I suppose so. Odd, though."

"What is?"

"So many deaths all about the same time. Significant deaths, dukes and earls and counts. But plenty of ordinary people too. My father travels pretty widely up and down the Mount on business, you know. Bibiroon, Stee, Banglecode, Minimool, all sorts of places. And he tells me that wherever you go, you see the mourning badges hanging from important public buildings and private residences. A lot of people have died recently. A lot. That's hard to explain."

"I suppose," Sithelle said. She didn't seem very interested.

Dekkeret persisted. "It bothers me. A lot of things do, lately. It's all been something of a blur, these last weeks, wouldn't you say? Not just the death of the Count and his brother. The old Pontifex dying too, Lord Confalume taking his place, Prestimion becoming Coronal. Everything seemed to happen so fast."

"Things weren't happening fast while his majesty was dying. That seemed to take forever."

"But once he did die—whiz, bang, all manner of things going on at once, Prankipin's funeral one week and Lord Prestimion's coronation practically the next—"

"I don't think they were actually so close together," said Sithelle.

"Maybe not. But it seemed that way to me."

They were beyond the palace, now, coming around to the side of the city that faced outward from the flank of the Mount, affording a glimpse of nearby Morvole on its thrusting promontory. A watchtower set into the wall provided a viewing-point here from which one could see, to the left, the highway winding down through the serrated rocky spine of Normork Crest into the foothills of the Mount, and in the other direction, looking upward, the cities of the next ring. There was even the merest shadowy hint, impossibly high above, of the lofty circlet of perpetual mist that cloaked the upper zones of the great mountain, hiding the summit and its Castle from the eyes of those below.

Sithelle scrambled swiftly up the narrow stone steps of the tower, leaving him well behind. She was a slim, leggy girl, enormously quick and agile. Dekkeret, following her, climbed in a more plodding way. His limbs were relatively short in proportion to his solid, massive torso, and he usually found it wisest to move carefully and unhurriedly.

When he joined her, she was holding the rail and peering out at nothing in particular. Dekkeret stood close beside her. The air was clear and cool and sweet, with just a taste of the light rain that would be coming, as it did every day, later in the evening. He let his eyes rove upward, up to where he imagined the Castle lay, clinging to the highest crags of the Mount, miles overhead and invisible from here.

"I hear the new Coronal's going to pay us a visit soon," he said, after a bit.

"What? A grand processional already? I thought Coronals didn't do that until they'd been on the throne at least two or three years."

"Not a full processional, no. Just a brief visit to some of the Mount cities. My father said so. He hears a lot of news as he travels around."

Sithelle turned toward him. Her eyes were glowing. "Oh, if only he would! To see an actual Coronal—!"

Her breathless eagerness bothered him. "I saw Lord Confalume once, you know."

"You did?"

"In Bombifale, when I was nine. I was there with my father, and the Coronal was a guest at Admiral Gonivaul's estate. I watched them come riding out together in a big floater. You can't mistake Gonivaul—he's got a great shaggy beard all over his face and nothing shows through it but his eyes and his nose. And there was Lord Confalume sitting next to him—oh, he was splendid! Radiant. He was in his prime, then. You could practically see light streaming from him. As they went past I waved to him, and he waved back, and smiled, such an easy calm smile, as if to tell me how much he loved being Coronal. Later that day my father brought me to Bombifale Palace, where Lord Confalume was holding court, and he smiled at me again, by way of saying to me that he recognized me from seeing me before. It was an extraordinary sensation just to be in his presence, to feel the strength of him, the goodness. It was one of the great moments of my life."

"Was Prestimion there?" Sithelle asked.

"Prestimion? With the Coronal, you mean? Oh, no, no, Sithelle. This was nine years ago. Prestimion wasn't anybody important then, just one of the young princes of Castle Mount, and there are plenty of those. His rise to the top came much later. But Confalume—ah, Confalume! What a wonderful man. Prestimion will have a lot to live up to, now that he's Coronal."

"And do you think he will?"

"Who can say? At least everyone agrees that he's bright and energetic. But time will tell." The sun was gone now. A few sprinkles of rain were beginning to fall, hours before the customary time. Dekkeret offered her his jacket, but she shook her head. They began to descend from the watch-tower. —"If Prestimion's really coming to Normork, Sithelle, I'm going to make every effort to meet him. Personally, I mean. I want to speak with him."

"Well, then, just walk right up to him and tell him who you are. He'll invite you to sit right down and have a flask of wine with him."

Her sarcasm bothered him. "I mean it," he said. The rain already seemed to be giving out, after having pattered for just a moment or two. It had left a pleasant touch of fragrance in the air. They continued on their westward route along the black spine of the wall. "You can't suppose that I want to spend the rest of my life in Normork, working at my father's trade."

"Would that be so awful? I can think of worse things."

"No doubt you can. But it's my plan to become a Castle knight and rise to a high government position."

"Of course. And become Coronal some day, I suppose?"

"Why not?" Dekkeret said. She was being very annoying. "Anyone can be."

"Anyone?"

"If he's good enough."

"And has the right family connections," said Sithelle. "Commoners don't usually get chosen for the throne."

"But they can be," Dekkeret said. "You know, Sithelle, it's possible for anybody at all to get to the top. You just have to be chosen by the outgoing Coronal, and nothing says he absolutely has to choose someone from among the Castle nobility if he doesn't want to. And what's a nobleman, anyway, if not the descendant of some commoner of long ago? It isn't as though the aristocracy is a separate species. —Listen, Sithelle, I'm not saying that I expect to be Coronal, or even that I want to be Coronal! The Coronal thing was your idea. I simply want to be something more than a small-scale merchant who's required to spend his entire life wearily traveling up and down the Mount from one city to the next peddling his wares to indifferent customers, most of whom treat him like dirt. Not that there's anything disgraceful about being a traveling merchant, I mean, but I can't help thinking that a life of public service would be ever so much—"

"All right, Dekkeret. I'm sorry I teased you. But please stop making speeches at me." She touched the tips of her fingers to her temples. "You're giving me a headache, now."

His irritability vanished instantly. "Am I? —You complained of a headache yesterday, too. And I wasn't making speeches then."

"Actually," said Sithelle, "I've been having headaches a lot of the time, the last couple of weeks. Terrible pounding ones, some of them are. I've never had that problem before."

"Have you seen anyone for it? A doctor? A dream-speaker?"

"Not yet. But it worries me. Some of my friends have

been having them, too. —What about you, Dekkeret?"

"Headaches? Not that I've noticed."

"If you haven't noticed, you aren't having them."

They came to the broad stone staircase that led downward from the top of the wall into Melikand Plaza, the gateway to Old Town. The city here was a warren of ancient narrow streets paved with oily-looking gray-green cobblestones. Dekkeret much preferred the broad curving boulevards of the New City, but he had always thought of Old Town as quaint and picturesque. Tonight, though, it seemed oddly sinister to him, even repellent.

He said, "No headaches, no. But I have had some odd moments now and then, of late." He groped for words. "How can I express this, Sithelle? It's like I feel that there's something very important hovering right at the edge of my memory, something that I need to think about and deal with, but I can't get a handle on what it is. My head starts to spin a little whenever that happens. Sometimes it spins a lot. I wouldn't call it a headache, though. More like dizziness."

"Strange," she said. "I get that same feeling, sometimes. Of something that's missing, something that I want to find, but I don't know where to look for it. It gets to be very bothersome. You know what I mean?"

"Yes. I think I do."

They paused at the parting of their roads. Sithelle gave him a warm smile. She took his hand in hers. "I hope you get to see Lord Prestimion when he comes here, Dekkeret, and that he makes you a knight of the Castle."

"Do you mean that?"

She blinked. "Why wouldn't I mean it?"

"In that case, thank you. If I do get to meet him, do you want me to tell him about my beautiful cousin who's somewhat too tall for him? Or shouldn't I bother?"

"I was trying to be nice," Sithelle said ruefully, letting go of his hand. "But you don't know how to do that, do you?" She stuck her tongue out at him and went sprinting away into the tangle of little streets that lay before them.

"THE MIDNIGHT MARKET OF Bombifale!" said Septach Melayn grandly, and beckoned Prestimion forward with a sweeping gesture of his broad-brimmed hat.

Prestimion had visited Bombifale many times before. It was one of the closest of the Inner Cities, just a day's journey below the Castle, and no one would dispute its rank as first in beauty among the cities of the Mount. Once, many hundreds of years earlier, it had given Majipoor a Coronal—Lord Pinitor—and Pinitor, a hyperactive and visionary builder, had spared no expense in transforming his native city into a place of wonder. The burnt orange sandstone of its scalloped walls had been brought from the forbidding desert country back of the Labyrinth by countless caravans of pack-animals; the spectacular four-sided slabs of blue seaspar inlaid in those walls came from an uninhabited district along Alhanroel's eastern coast that had rarely been explored before or since; and all along the perimeter of the city the walls were crowned with an uncountable series of slim, graceful towers of the most delicate design, giving Bombifale the magical look of a city that has been built by supernatural creatures.

But not all of Bombifale was magical and delicate and fantastical. Where Prestimion and Septach Melayn stood just now—on a patch of cracked and furrowed pavement sloping sharply downward into a dimly lit district of slant-roofed warehouses at the city's outer rim, no great distance within Lord Pinitor's fabled walls—was as squalid and dank-smelling a place as one might expect to find in some fifth-rate port town.

Something about this neighborhood seemed familiar. Perhaps the bundles of loosely wrapped trash piled against the building walls, Prestimion thought. Or the stench of stagnant sewage too close nearby. And the ramshackle look of the nearby brick-walled buildings, ancient ones leaning crookedly up against one another, rang chimes in his memory.

"I've been in this part of town before, haven't I?"

"Indeed you have, my lord." Septach Melayn indicated a small, shabby inn on the far side of the street. "We stayed here one night not long before the war, when we were coming back from the Labyrinth after the Pontifex's funeral as outcasts, returning to the Castle to see whether Korsibar could make good on his seizure of the throne."

"Ah. I do remember. We had churlish unwilling hospitality at yonder hostelry that night, as I recall." And added, speaking very softly, "You shouldn't call me 'my lord' in this place, Septach Melayn."

"Who'd believe it, in such a place, looking as you do?"

"Even so," said Prestimion. "If we come in secrecy, let's be secretive about all things, is that agreed? Good. Come, now: show me this midnight market of yours."

It was not that Prestimion feared for his safety. No one would dare raise a hand against the Coronal in this place, he was certain, if his true identity should be discovered. In any event he could look after himself in any brawl, and the swordsman had not yet been born who could deal with Septach Melayn. But it would be deeply embarrassing to be found out—Lord Prestimion himself, skulking around this seamy, disreputable place in a grease-stained cloak and patched leggings, with half his face muffled up in a beard as black as Gonivaul's and a wig of rank, mushroom-colored hair falling to his shoulders? What possible reason could he offer for such an excursion? He'd be the butt of Castle jokes for months, if the story ever got around. And it would be a long time before Kimbar Hapitaz, the commander of the Coronal's guard, permitted him to slip away from the Castle so easily again.

Septach Melayn—he was in disguise too, a hideous mop of red hair stiff as straw hiding his immaculate golden ringlets, and a shaggy, ragged black neckerchief concealing his elegantly tapered little beard—led him down the weed-speckled road toward a huddle of dilapidated buildings at the end of the street. There were only the two of them. Gialaurys had been unable to accompany them on this adventure; he was off in the north, chasing after the artificially-created war-monsters that Korsibar had never had a chance to use in the war. Some of them had broken loose and were devastating the unfortunate Kharax district.

"In here, if you will," Septach Melayn said, pulling a heavy, creaking door aside.

Prestimion's first impressions were of dimness, noxious fumes, noise, chaos. What had appeared from the outside to be a group of buildings was actually one long, low structure divided into narrow aisles that stretched on and on until their farthest reaches were lost to sight. A string of glowfloats bobbing near its rafters provided the primary lighting, which was far from adequate. An abundance of smoldering torches mounted in front of the various booths provided little additional illumination and a great deal of foul black smoke.

"Whatever sort of thing you may care to buy," Septach Melayn murmured in his ear, "it will be available for purchase somewhere in here."

Prestimion had no doubt of that. It seemed that an infinite array of merchandise lay before him.

Much of what he saw at the booths closest to the entrance was the sort of stuff one might find in any marketplace anywhere. Huge burlap bags of spices and aromatics—bdella and malibathron and kankamon, storax and mabaric, gray coriander and fennel, and many more besides; various kinds of salt, dyed indigo and red and yellow and black to distinguish them from one another; fiery glabbam powder for the hot stews beloved of Skandars and sweet sarjorelle to give flavoring to the sticky cakes of the Hjorts, and much more. Beyond the spice-peddlers were the meat-vendors, with their offerings dangling in great slabs from huge wooden hooks, and then the sellers of eggs of a hundred different kinds of birds, eggs of all hues and some startling shapes, and after them the tanks where one might purchase live fishes and reptiles, and even young sea-dragons. Deeper yet and they were peddling baskets and panniers, fly-whisks and brooms, palm mats, bottles of colored glass, cheap beads and badly made bangles, pipes and perfumes, carpets and brocaded cloaks, writing-paper, dried fruits, cheese and butter and honey, and on and on and on, aisle after aisle, room beyond room.

Prestimion and Septach Melayn passed through a place of wickerwork cages, where live animals were being sold for uses which Prestimion did not care even to guess. He saw sad little bilantoons huddled together, and snaggle-toothed jakkaboles, and mintuns and droles and manculains and a horde of others. At one point he turned a corner and found himself staring into a cage of sturdy bamboo that contained a single smallish red-furred beast of a kind he had never beheld before, wolf-like, but low and wide, with enormous paws, a broad head that was huge in proportion to its body, and thick curving yellow teeth that looked as though they could not only rip flesh but easily crush bone. Its yellow-green eyes glared with unparalleled ferocity. A stale smell came from it, as of meat that had been left too long to dry in the sun. As Prestimion looked at it in wonder, it made a deep ugly sound, midway between a growl and a whine, throbbing with menace.

"What is that thing?" he asked. "It's the most hideous beast I've ever seen!"

"A krokkotas, it is," said Septach Melayn. "It roves the northern desert-lands, from Valmambra eastward. They say it has the power of imitating human speech, and will call a man's name by night in the wastelands, and when he approaches, it pounces and kills. And devours its victim down to the last scrap, bones and hair and toenails and all."

Prestimion made a sour face. "And why would such an abomination be put up for sale in a city marketplace, then?"

"Inquire of that from the one who offers it," Septach Melayn said. "I myself have no idea."

"Perhaps it's best not to know," said Prestimion. He stared at the krokkotas once more; and it seemed to him that its whining growl had intelligible meaning, and that the beast was saying, "Coronal, Coronal, Coronal, come to me."

"Strange," Prestimion murmured. And they moved along.

But then the merchandise grew even stranger.

"We are entering the market of the sorcerers," said Septach Melayn quietly. "Shall we stop here first, do you think, for something small to eat?"

Prestimion had no idea what was being sold from the little group of food-stalls that now confronted them; nor, so it appeared, did Septach Melayn. But the aromas were enticing. Some questioning revealed that this stall offered minced bilantoon meat mixed with chopped onions and palm tips, that this one had peppered vyeille wrapped in vine leaves, that the one next to it specialized in the flesh of a red gourd called khiyaar, stewed with beans and tiny morsels of fish. The vendors all were Liimen, the impassive flatfaced three-eyed folk to whom the humblest tasks of Majipoor invariably fell, and they answered Septach Melayn's queries about their offerings in husky, thickly accented monosyllables, or sometimes not at all. In the end Septach Melayn bought a little array of items more or less at random—Prestimion, as was his custom, carried no money—and they paused at the entrance to the sorcerers' market to eat. Everything was remarkably tasty; and at Prestimion's urging, Septach Melayn bought them a flask of some rough, vigorous wine, still bubbling with youth, to wash it down.

Then they went forward.

Prestimion had seen sorcerers' markets in the city of Triggoin during his time of exile: places where strange potions and ointments could be bought, and amulets of all sorts, and spells deemed to be efficacious in a host of situations. In dark and mysterious Triggoin such places had seemed altogether appropriate and expectable, a natural sort of merchandise for a city where sorcery was the center of economic life. But it was eerie to find such things being sold here in pretty Bombifale, hardly a stone's throw beneath the walls of his Castle. This place showed him once again what great inroads the occult arts had made in recent years into the everyday existence of Majipoor. There had not been all this sorcery and magicking going on when he was a boy; but the mages called the tune now, and all Majipoor danced to it.

The outer zone of the midnight market had been only sparsely occupied compared with this part. Out there, a scattering of people whose daily lives were lived at unusual hours, or those who had neglected to do their everyday marketing at everyday times, could be seen shopping in a desultory way for the next day's meat and vegetables. But back here, where goods of a more esoteric kind were sold, the aisles were choked with buyers to the point where it was difficult for Prestimion and Septach Melayn to make their way through them.

"Is it like this every night, I wonder?" Prestimion asked.

"The sorcerers' market is open only on the first and third Seadays of the month," the swordsman replied. "Those who need to buy do their buying then."

Prestimion stared. Here, too, were booths bounded by rows of burlap sacks, too, but not sacks of spices and aromatics. In this place, so the vendors tirelessly chanted, one could obtain all the raw materials of the necromantic arts, powders and oils galore—olustro and elecamp and golden rue, mastic pepper, goblin-sugar and myrrh, aloes and vermilion and maltabar, quicksilver, brimstone, thekka ammoniaca, scamion, pestash, yarkand, dvort. Here were the black candles used in haruspication; here were specifics against curses and demonic possession; here were the wines of the resuscitator and the poultices that warded off the devil-ague. And here were engraved talismans designed to invoke the irgalisteroi, those subterranean prehistoric spirits of the ancient world whom the Shapeshifters had locked up under dire spells twenty thousand years before, and who could sometimes, with the right incantation, be induced to do the bidding of those who called upon them. Prestimion had learned of these beings and others akin to them during his stay in Triggoin, when he was a fugitive taking refuge from Korsibar's armies.

It was dizzying to behold this infinity of bizarre amulets and mantic instruments and simples and specifics laid out all about him for sale; it was disturbing to see the citizens of Bombifale moving through this marketplace of strangenesses by the hundreds, jostling against each other in their eagerness to put down their hard-earned crowns and royals for such things. They were ordinary folk, modestly dressed; but they were throwing their money about like a throng of earls.

"Is there more?" Prestimion asked in astonishment.

"Oh, yes, yes, much more."

The floor of the building that housed the market now seemed to take on a downward slant. Evidently they were entering a part of the structure that lay beneath the surface of the street.

It was even smokier here, and more musty. In this sector was a mixture of vendors and entertainers; Prestimion saw some jugglers at work, a group of four-armed Skandars with grayish-red fur energetically flinging knives and balls and lighted torches to each other with high abandon, and musicians with coin jars in front of them grinding away grimly at their viols and tamboors and rikkitawms amidst all the other noise of the place, and ordinary sleight-of-hand magicians who made no pretense at sorcery doing age-old magical tricks with snakes and bright-colored kerchiefs and padlocked chests and knives seemingly passed through throats. Scribes called out, offering to write letters for those who lacked that art; water-carriers with gleaming copper panniers begged to ease the thirst of those around them; bright-eyed little boys invited passersby to gamble at a game that involved the impossibly quick manipulation of small bundles of twigs.

In the midst of all this hubbub Prestimion became aware of a zone of sudden silence, a perceptible avenue of hushed-ness cutting down the center of the crowd. He had no idea at first what could be causing this extraordinary effect. Then Septach Melayn pointed; and Prestimion saw two figures in the uniforms of officers of the Pontificate advancing through the marketplace, creating apprehension and unease as they went.

The first was a Hjort, rough-skinned and puffy-faced and bulging of eye like all his kind, and carrying himself in the exaggeratedly upright stance that always made Hjorts seem pompous and self-important to their fellow inhabitants of

Majipoor, though their posture was simply a matter of the way their thick, middle-heavy bodies were constructed. From the Hjort's shoulders dangled a large pair of scales, which struck Prestimion as being more a badge of office than anything that might have practical use.

It was the second figure, though, that seemed to be the cause of the consternation. A man of the Su-Suheris race, this one was: tremendously tall, nearly as tall, in fact, as a Skandar, and bearing his pair of cold-eyed, hairless, immensely elongated heads atop a narrow, forking neck more than a foot in length. He was a disconcerting sight. His kind always was. Just as a Hjort could not help seeming squat-looking and coarse-featured and comically ugly to people of other races because of his protuberant eyes and ashen-hued pebbly skin, so too did the two gleaming pallid heads of the Su-Suheris unfailingly give them a sinister and utterly alien air.

"The inspector of weights and measures," said Septach Melayn, in response to an unspoken question from Prestimion.

"In here? I thought you said that no governmental agency regulates this market."

"None does. Yet the inspector comes, all the same. It is his own private enterprise, which he carries out after the normal hours of his work. He orders each shopkeeper to prove that he gives fair measure and honest price; and whoever fails to pass muster is taken outside and flogged by the other vendors. For this he gets a fee. The dealers here want no improper business activities."

"But it's all improper here!" Prestimion cried.

"Ah, but not to them," said Septach Melayn.

Indeed. This was a world in and of itself, this midnight market of Bombifale, thought Prestimion. It existed outside the normal bounds of Majipoor, and neither Pontifex nor Coronal had any authority here.

The inspector of weights and measures and his Hjort herald moved solemnly onward, deeper into the marketplace. Prestimion and Septach Melayn followed in their wake.

Dealers in divination devices had their stalls here. Prestimion recognized some of their wares from the training he had undertaken while in Triggoin. This sparkling stuff in small cloth packets was zemzem-dust, to sprinkle on those who were gravely ill in order to know the course that their malady would take. Its source was Velalisier, the haunted ruined capital of the ancient Metamorphs. These charred-looking little loaves were rukka-cakes, which had the capacity to influence the course of love-affairs; and this slimy stuff was mud of the Floating Island of Masulind, that had the power of guiding one in commercial transactions. This was the powdered delem-aloe, that told when it was a woman's fertile time of the month by bringing out thin red circles around her breasts. And this curious device—

"That is of no value whatever, my lord," said someone suddenly to his left, someone with a deep, resonant voice that reached Prestimion from a point high above. "You would do well not to squander your attention on it."

Prestimion was holding, just then, a little machine in the form of a magic square, which, when manipulated by an adept, was reputed to give answers to any question in numerical form that required decoding. He had picked it up idly from a table. At the unexpected comment from the stranger at his side he tossed it down again as though it were as hot as a burning coal, and glanced up at the speaker.

It was, he saw, another of the Su-Suheris kind: a towering ivory-skinned figure clad in a simple black robe belted with a red sash, whose high-vaulted leftward head was staring down at him with a cool dispassionate gaze, while the other one was looking off in a different direction entirely.

Prestimion felt an instant sense of innate discomfort and distaste.

It was hard to feel at ease with these tall two-headed beings, so strange was their appearance, so frosty their mien. One could far more easily adapt to the presence of great furry four-armed Skandars, or tiny many-tentacled Vroons, or even the reptilian Ghayrogs that had settled in such numbers on the other continent. Outworlders like Skandars and

Vroons and Ghayrogs were no more human than Su-Suheris folk, but at least they had just one head apiece.

Prestimion had his own reasons for antipathy toward the Su-Suheris race, besides. Sanibak-Thastimoon, Korsibar's private magus, had been a Su-Suheris. It was the icy-souled Sanibak-Thastimoon, perhaps more than anyone else, who had prodded the malleable, foolish Korsibar onward to his catastrophic usurpation with false predictions of a glorious success. It was by virtue of spells cast by Sanibak-Thastimoon that Korsibar's forces had managed to keep the upper hand in the civil war for so long. And it was in the final moments of that war, when all was lost for Korsibar, that Sanibak-Thastimoon, finding himself under attack by his defeated and now desperate puppet-Coronal, had slain Korsibar and had taken the life of his sister Thismet as well, when in fury she had rushed at him brandishing the fallen Korsibar's sword.

But Sanibak-Thastimoon had perished moments later at the hand of Septach Melayn, and the very fact of his existence had been swept away, along with so much else, by the sorcerers who had blotted the civil war from the world's memory. This Su-Suheris here, whoever he might be, was a different one entirely, who could hardly be held accountable for the sins of his kinsman. And the Su-Suheris people, Prestimion reminded himself, were citizens of Majipoor with full civil rights. It was not for him to treat them with disdain.

Therefore he answered calmly enough, "You have reason, I suppose, to mistrust these little machines?"

"What I feel for them, my lord, is contempt, rather than mistrust. They are useless things. As are most of the devices offered for sale in this place." The two-headed being swept his long gaunt arm about the room in a wide-ranging gesture. "There is true divination and there is the other kind, and these are, by and large, contemptible useless products manufactured for the sake of deceiving foolish people."

Prestimion nodded. Very softly he said, gazing up far above him into the alien creature's chilly emerald-hued eyes, "You called me 'my lord.' Twice. Why?"

Those eyes narrowed in surprise. "Why, because it is fitting and proper, my lord!" And the Su-Suheris flicked his bony fingers outward in the starburst gesture. "Is that not so?"

Septach Melayn moved closer in, hand to the pommel of his sword, face dark with displeasure. "I tell you, fellow, you are much mistaken. This is a line of chatter you'd be wisest not to pursue any further."

Now both heads were trained on Prestimion from that great height, and all four eyes were focused keenly on the Coronal's sturdy, compact figure. In a voice that could not have been heard by anyone but Prestimion and his companion the left-hand head said, "Good my lord, forgive me if I have done anything wrong. Your identity is obvious. I had no idea you meant to go undetected."

"Obvious?" Prestimion tapped his false beard, tugged at his black wig. "You see my face, do you, beneath all this stuff?"

"I perceive your nature and standing quite easily, my lord. And that of the High Counsellor Septach Melayn beside you. These things cannot be hidden by wigs and beards. At least, not from me."

"And who may you be, then?" Septach Melayn demanded.

The two heads inclined themselves in a courteous bow. "My name is Maundigand-Klimd," the Su-Suheris said suavely. It was the right head that spoke, this time. "A magus by profession. When my calculations showed that you would be in this place tonight, it behooved me, I felt, to place myself in your presence."

"Your calculations, eh?"

"Rather different ones, I must tell you, from the ones performed with such devices as these." Maundigand-Klimd laughed frostily and pointed to the magic-square machines on the table before them. "They make a pretense at magic, and a worthless pretense at that. What I practice has the true mathematics at the heart of its divining."

"It is a science, then, your prognosticating?"

"Most distinctly a science, lordship."

Prestimion glanced across, at that, at Septach Melayn. But his countenance studiously revealed nothing at all.

To Maundigand-Klimd he said, "So there was nothing accidental, then, about your being here next to me in this place just now?"

"Oh, my lord," said Maundigand-Klimd, with the closest thing to a smile that Prestimion had ever seen on the face of a Su-Suheris. "There is no such thing as an accident, my lord."

8

"FOLLOW THIS WAY IF you please, Lord Prestimion," said Navigorn of Hoikmar. He and Prestimion were at the entrance to Lord Sangamor's tunnels, that tangled maze of underground chambers with brilliantly glowing walls that a Coronal of thousands of years before had caused to be constructed on the western face of Castle Mount. "I don't suppose you've ever had occasion to be in this place before, your lordship," Navigorn said. "It's quite extraordinary, really"

"My father brought me here once, when I was a small boy," said Prestimion. "Just to let me see the show of colors in the walls. The tunnels hadn't been used as a prison, of course, for hundreds and hundreds of years."

"Not since the time of Lord Amyntilir, in truth." The sentry on duty stepped aside as they approached. Navigorn touched his hand to the shining metal plate in the door and it swung obediently open, revealing the narrow passageway that led to the tunnels proper. "What a perfect site for dungeons, though! As you can see, the only access is through this easily guarded corridor. And then we continue underground right out to Sangamor Peak, which juts up from the Mount in such a way that it's impossible to scale, impossible to reach in any way except from beneath."

"Yes," Prestimion said. "Very ingenious."

He did not trouble to tell Navigorn that this was his third visit to the tunnels, not his second; that only two years before, in fact, he had been a prisoner in these chambers, the first such captive in centuries, sent here by order of the Coronal Lord Korsibar, as Korsibar then was pleased to style himself. And had hung by his wrists and ankles from the wall of a stone chamber whose every square inch emitted great sweeping blasts of brilliant red color, visible even when he closed his eyes. That inexorable outpouring of light had pounded and throbbed against his brain in a way that had come close to driving him mad.

Prestimion had no idea how long Korsibar had kept him imprisoned. Three or four weeks, at least, though it had felt like months to him. Years, even. He had emerged from the tunnels feeble and shaken, and had been a long while recovering.

Navigorn, though, lacked any awareness of that. Prestimion's stay in the Sangamor tunnels was another thing that had been expunged from everyone's remembrance. Everyone's, that is, but his own. If only he could forget it, too! But the memory of that terrible time would stay with him forever.

But he was here now as Coronal, not as a prisoner. Navigorn led him inward through the tunnel vestibule, chattering like a tour guide. Prestimion was amused to see how well Navigorn had taken to the jailer's role.

"The walls, you see, are faced with a substance much like stone, though it's actually of an artificial nature. It is the special quality of that substance, my lord, that it unceasingly gives off great quantities of colored light. A scientific secret of the ancients which, alas, we have lost in modern times."

"One of many," said Prestimion. "Though I confess I don't see much utility to this one."

"There's great beauty in these colors, my lord."

"Up to a point. I imagine they could become infuriating after a while, those tremendous pulsing jolts of light that can't be turned off."

"Perhaps so. But over a short period of time—"

Well, when he had been imprisoned here by Korsibar it had not been for any short period of time, not short at all, and the cumulative impact of his cell's interminable pulsing jolts of ruby light had seemed well-nigh lethal as the long days dragged on. Prestimion had not found it within himself to do to Dantirya Sambail what Korsibar had done to him; and so, although the tunnels were the most secure prison that the Castle had, and there had been no choice but to put the Procurator away in them, Prestimion had seen to it that Dantirya Sambail was placed in one of the more comfortable chambers.

The rumor was loose in the Castle, Prestimion knew, that Dantirya Sambail lay chained day and night in some dismal desolate hole where he suffered the worst torments that the tunnel walls could hurl at him. That was not so. Instead of being manacled to the walls as Prestimion had been, the Procurator had a good-sized room with plenty of space in it for him to roam freely about, and a bed, and a couch, and his own table and desk. Nor was the emanation from this cell's wall of the kind that battered your mind and stunned your very soul; it was a gentle lime-green, where Prestimion had had to endure those constant unrelenting pounding waves of brilliant red.

Prestimion had not bothered to contradict the rumors, though. Let them believe what they liked. He would discuss the status of Dantirya Sambail with no one. It was not a bad thing for a new Coronal to arouse a little uneasiness in those around him in the Castle.

He and Navigorn passed through a zone where a dull, throbbing jade-colored light, heavy as the waters at the bottom of the sea, came pulsating forth, and beyond it a place of a sizzling pink as keen as knifeblades, and then one of somber, overwhelming ochre with the force of steady muffled drumbeats. Upward now they went, spiraling around the flank of the upthrust stone dagger that was Sangamor Peak, and Prestimion had a glimpse, quick but sickening, of the crushing rubyred light of the cell that once had been his own. Adjacent to it was one with the stinging brightness of newly smelted copper. Then the colors became more mellow: cinnamon, hyacinth blue, aquamarine, mauve.

And at last a soft chartreuse, and Prestimion found himself at the threshold of the place where the Procurator of Ni-moya was being detained.

Prestimion had put this visit off as long as possible, but it could be avoided no longer, he knew. At some point it was necessary to confront the fact that Dantirya Sambail was held prisoner for high crimes and misdemeanors of which the Procurator had no knowledge at all. Prestimion was still unsure of the way to deal with the paradoxes inherent in that situation. But he understood that they must now at last be addressed.

"Well, cousin!" cried Dantirya Sambail with implausible heartiness, when Navigorn had gone through the lengthy series of intricate procedures that opened the door of the Procurator's chamber. "They told me you'd be coming to pay me a visit today; but I thought it was only out of playfulness or mischief that they said it. What a delight it is to behold your handsome young face again, Prestimion! —But I should call you 'Lord Prestimion,' should I not? For I understand that your coronation day has come and gone already, although through some misunderstanding I was not invited to the ceremony."

And the Procurator, smiling, held out both his hands, which were girded together at the wrists by a metal band, and waggled his fingers comically in a jovial semblance of the starburst gesture.

Prestimion had been aware that he might expect almost anything from Dantirya Sambail when they first came face to face, but a show of joviality was not high on the list. Which was why he had ordered the Procurator's wrists to be manacled before his arrival; for Dantirya Sambail was a man of bull-like strength, who might well be so furious over his incarceration that he would launch himself at Prestimion in a murderous frenzy the moment that the Coronal entered his cell.

But no. Dantirya Sambail was all smiles and twinkles, as if this were some charming inn where he had taken up lodging, and Lord Prestimion were his guest this day.

To Navigorn Prestimion said, "Unlock his shackles."

After a moment's hesitation Navigorn obeyed. Prestimion held himself poised and ready in case Dantirya Sambail's joviality should turn instantly to wrath once his bonds were taken from him. But the Procurator remained where he was on the other side of the room, standing between the long, low couch and a desk of curving contours on which half a dozen books were casually stacked. He seemed utterly at ease. Prestimion knew only too well, though, what roiling fires roared through his kinsman's soul.

The calm, unflickering pale-green glow flowed steadily from the walls. It swathed and enfolded everything in a cool benign presence. "I'm pleased to see that your chamber is a pleasant one, cousin. There are worse accommodations to be had in these tunnels, I think."

"Are there, Prestimion? I wouldn't know about that. — But yes, yes, quite pleasant. The delicate viridescence that comes from the walls. This fine furniture; these charming flagstone floors across which I stroll during my daily walks from that side of the room to this. You could have been far less kind."

The voice was a purr; but there was no mistaking the rage that lay just beneath.

Prestimion studied Dantirya Sambail with care. He had not looked upon the Procurator's face since that horrific day at Thegomar Edge, when, with Korsibar already beaten and very likely dead, Dantirya Sambail had presented himself before him with a sword in one hand and a farmer's hatchet in the other, and challenged him to single combat with the throne as the prize. And had come close to striking him down before Prestimion, although bruised by a flat-sided blow in the ribs, prevailed with a sudden quick thrust of his rapier that cut the tendon of the arm holding the axe, and another that sliced a bloody line across the Procurator's sword-arm. There were signs that Dantirya Sambail was wearing poultices on those wounds beneath his loose, billowing blouse of golden silk even now, though they must be nearly healed.

The Procurator was splendid in his ugliness: a heavy-bodied man of middle years, with a massive head set atop a thick neck and heavy shoulders. His face was pale, but spotted everywhere with a horde of brilliant red freckles. His hair was orange in hue, rank and coarse, forming a dense fringe around the high curving dome of his forehead. His chin was a powerful jutting one, his nose broad and fleshy, his mouth wide and savage, drawn far out to its corners. It was the face of some dire beast. But out of it stared strangely gentle violet-gray eyes, eyes improbably warm with tenderness and compassion and love. The contrast between the sensitivity of those eyes and the ferocity of his features was the most frightful thing about him: it marked him as a man who encompassed the whole range of human emotion and was willing to take any position at all in the service of his implacable desires.

He stood now in his customary posture, his great head thrust forward, his chest inflated defiantly, his short thick legs splayed apart to provide him with a base of maximum stability. Dantirya Sambail was ever in a mode of attack, even when at rest. In his native continent of Zimroel he had ruled virtually as an independent monarch from the vast city of Ni-moya over a domain of enormous size; but he had not been content with that, it seemed, and hungered for the throne of Majipoor also, or at least the right to name the man who held it. He and Prestimion were distant relatives, third cousins twice removed. They had always pretended to a cordiality between them that neither of them felt.

Some moments went by, and Prestimion did not speak.

Then Dantirya Sambail said, still in that quiet sardonic tone of formidable self-control, "Would you do me the honor, my lord, of telling me how much longer you plan to offer me your hospitality in this place?"

"That has not yet been determined, Dantirya Sambail."

"There are duties of state awaiting me in Zimroel."

"Undoubtedly so. But the question of your guilt and punishment must be answered first, before I can allow you to resume them. If ever I do."

"Ah," said Dantirya Sambail gravely, as though they were discussing the making of fine wines, or the breeding of bidlak bulls. "The question of my guilt, you say. And my punishment. What is it, then, that I'm guilty of? And what punishment, precisely, do you have in mind for me? Eh, my lord? It would be kind of you to explain these little things to me, I think."

Prestimion gave Navigorn a quick sidelong glance. "I'd like to speak with the Procurator privately a moment, Navigorn."

Navigorn frowned. He was armed; Prestimion was not. He shot a glance toward Dantirya Sambail's discarded fetters. But Prestimion shook his head. Navigorn went out.

If Dantirya Sambail meant to attack him, Prestimion thought, this was the moment. The Procurator was bulkier by far than the relatively slight Prestimion and stood half a head taller. He seemed, though, to have no such madness in mind. He held himself as aggressively as before, but remained where he was, far across the room, his deceptively beautiful amethyst eyes regarding Prestimion with what looked like nothing more than amiable curiosity.

"I'm perfectly willing to believe that I've committed dreadful deeds, if you say I have," said Dantirya Sambail equably, when the cell door had closed. "And if I have, why, then I suppose I should suffer some penalty for them. But why is it that I know nothing about them?"

Prestimion remained silent. He realized that his silence was beginning to extend too far. But this was all even more difficult than he had anticipated.

"Well?" Dantirya Sambail said, after a time. There was an edge on his tone, now. "Will you tell me, cousin, why it is that you've put me away down here? For what cause, by what law? I've committed no crime that merits any of this. Can it be just on the general suspicion that I'll make some sort of trouble for you, now that you're Coronal, that you've jailed me?"

Further procrastination was impossible. "It's well known from one end of the world to the other, cousin," said Prestimion, "that you're a perpetual danger to the security of the realm and to the man who sits on the throne, whoever he may be. But that's not the reason why you're here."

"And what is, then?"

"You are imprisoned not for anything you might do, but for things you have done. Namely, acts of treason against the crown and violence against my person."

A look of total bewilderment crossed Dantirya Sambail's face at that. He gaped and blinked and lowered his head as though the weight of it was suddenly too much for him to carry. Prestimion had never seen him look so utterly dumfounded. For a moment he felt something very close to sympathy for the man.

Hoarsely the Procurator said, "Are you insane, cousin?"

"Far from it. The peace was breached. Unlawful deeds were done. You happen to be without awareness of the sins of which you're guilty, that's all. But that doesn't mean that they weren't committed."

"Ah," said Dantirya Sambail again, without even the most minimal show of comprehension.

"There are wounds on your body, are there not? One here, and one here?" Prestimion touched his left armpit, and then ran his hand along the inside of his other arm from elbow to wrist.

"Yes," said the Procurator grudgingly. "I meant to ask you about—"

"You received those wounds at my hands, when you and I fought on the field of battle."

Dantirya Sambail slowly shook his head. "I don't have any recollection of that. No. No. Such a thing never happened. You are insane, Prestimion. By the Divine! I'm the prisoner of a madman."

"On the contrary, cousin. Everything that I tell you here is true. There were acts of treason; there was strife between us; I barely escaped with my life. Any other Coronal would have sentenced you to death for what you did without hesitating as long as a moment. For some unfathomable reason, perhaps growing out of our kinship, such as it is, I find myself unwilling to do that. But neither can I set you free— at least not without some understanding between us of your unquestioning loyalty henceforth. And would I trust that, even if you gave it?"

Color was coming to Dantirya Sambail's face now, so that his myriad freckles stood out like the fiery marks of some irascible pox. His fingers were curling fretfully in a gesture of frustration and rising anger. An odd growling sound, distant and indistinct, seemed to be coming from the depths of his huge chest. It reminded Prestimion of nothing so much than the growl of the caged krokkotas in the midnight market of Bombifale. But Dantirya Sambail did not speak. Could not, perhaps, just then.

Prestimion went on: "The situation's a very strange one, Dantirya Sambail. You have no knowledge of your crimes, that I know. But you should believe me when I tell you that you are guilty of them nevertheless."

"My memory has been tampered with, is that the story?"

"I'll not respond to that."

"Then it has been. Why was that? How could you dare? Prestimion, Prestimion, Prestimion, do you think you're a god of some sort, and I nothing more than an ant, that you can feel free to hurl me into prison under trumped-up charges, and to meddle with my mind in the bargain? — But enough of this farce. You want my loyalty? You can have as much of it as you deserve. I've been incredibly patient, Prestimion, all these days or weeks or months, or however long it is that you've had me in this place. Let me out of here, cousin, or there'll be war between us. I have my supporters, you know, and they're not few in number."

"There has already been war between us, cousin. I keep you here to make certain that there never will be again."

"Without trial? Without so much as lodging a charge against me, except this vague mumbling about treason, and crimes against your person?" Dantirya Sambail had recovered his poise, Prestimion saw. The baffled look was gone from him, and so, too, was the outward show of fury. He had his old terrible calmness back, the calmness that Prestimion knew to hide volcanic forces kept under control by ferocious inner strength. "Ah, Prestimion, you vex me greatly. I would lose my temper, I think, if not for my certain feeling that you've taken leave of your senses, and that it's folly to be angry with a madman."

A predicament. Prestimion pondered it. Should he tell the Procurator the full truth of the great obliteration? No, no: he would simply be handing Dantirya Sambail an unsheathed blade and telling him to strike. The tale of what had been done to the world's memory was a secret that must never be revealed.

Nor could he lock Dantirya Sambail up in here indefinitely without bringing him to trial. The Procurator had not been speaking idly when he said he had his supporters. Dantirya Sambail's power spread far and wide over the other continent. Quite conceivably Prestimion might find himself embroiled before long in a second civil war, this one between Zimroel and Alhanroel, if he went on holding the Procurator without explanation in this seemingly arbitrary and even tyrannical way.

But a man lacking all awareness of his crimes could not be brought fairly to justice for committing them. That was a puzzle of Prestimion's own making. And he was, he realized, as far from a resolution of it as ever.

The time had come to withdraw, to regroup, to seek the counsel of his friends.

"I had a man who stood by my side to serve me," Dantirya Sambail was saying. "Mandralisca was his name. Good and true and loyal, he was. Where is he, Prestimion? I'd like him sent to me, if I am to be kept here longer. He tasted my food for me, you know, to be sure there was no poison in it. I miss his wondrous jollity. Send him to me, Prestimion."

"Yes, and the two of you can sing merry songs together all the night long, is that it?"

It was almost comical to hear Dantirya Sambail calling the poison-taster Mandralisca jolly. Him, that thin-lipped hard-eyed villain, that spawn of demons, that stark skull-and-crossbones of a man?

But Prestimion had no intention of bringing those two scorpions together. Mandralisca too had played an evil role at Thegomar Edge, and had been hauled in, wounded and a prisoner, spewing venom with every breath, after engaging Abrigant in a duel. He was in another cell, much less pleasant than Dantirya Sambail's, in another part of the tunnels. And there he would stay.

This conversation was leading nowhere. Moving toward the door, Prestimion said, "I bid you farewell, cousin. We'll speak again another time."

The Procurator gaped at him. "What? What? Did you come here simply to mock me, Prestimion?"

There was that rumbling krokkotas growl again. There was untrammeled rage on Dantirya Sambail's face, though the strange eyes were as soft and gentle as ever within the contorted mask of fury. Coolly Prestimion opened the cell door, stepped through, closed it just as Dantirya Sambail began to lurch toward him with upraised arms.

"Prestimion!" the Procurator cried, hammering clangorously against the door as it slammed in his face. "Prestimion! Damn you, Prestimion!"

9

IT WAS RARE FOR any travelers to approach the Castle by the northwestern road, which came up the back side of the Mount by way of the High City of Huine, and thence to the road known as the Stiamot Highway, a wide but poorly maintained thoroughfare, old and rutted, that reached the Castle at the infrequently used Vaisha Gate. The usual way to go was through the gently rising plateau of Bombifale Plain to High Morpin, and up the ten flower-bordered miles of the Grand Calintane Highway to the Castle's main entrance at the Dizimaule Plaza.

But someone was definitely coming up the northwestern road today—a little group of vehicles, four of them, moving slowly, with a particularly bizarre one at the head of the procession. That one was a sight of such surpassing strangeness that the young guard captain who had been stuck with the dreary assignment of patrolling the Vaisha Gate station gasped in wonder as it came into view, seven or eight turns below him along the winding road. He stood agog a moment, not believing the evidence of his eyes. A huge flat-

bed wagon of strange antique design, it was, so broad it
filled the width of Stiamot Highway from one shoulder to
the other—and that fluid, rippling wall of light surrounding
it on all sides with a cold white pulsing glow—that cargo
of dimly glimpsed monsters, half hidden behind that shield
of dizzying brightness—

The captain of guards at Vaisha Gate was twenty years
old, a man of Amblemorn at the foot of Castle Mount. His
training had not fitted him for dealing with anything remotely like this. He turned to his subaltern, a boy from
Pendiwane in the flatlands of the Glayge Valley. "Who's the
officer of the day today?"

"Akbalik."

"Find him, fast. Tell him his presence is required out
here."

The boy went sprinting inside. But finding anyone in the
virtually infinite maze of the Castle was far from an easy
task, even the officer of the day, who was supposed to make
himself readily accessible. Some thirty minutes went by before the boy returned, Akbalik in tow. By then the flat-bed
wagon had pulled up in the spacious gravel-strewn tract in
front of the gate; the three floaters that had accompanied it
in its journey up the Mount were parked beside it; and the
captain of guards from Amblemorn found himself in the
extraordinary situation of standing with drawn sword against
no less a figure than the formidable warrior Gialaurys,
Grand Admiral of the Realm. Half a dozen grim-faced men,
Gialaurys's companions, were arrayed just behind him, frozen into positions of imminent attack.

Akbalik, the nephew of Prince Serithorn and a man much
respected for his common sense and steady nature, took the
scene in quickly. With no more than a single startled blink
at the cargo of the wagon he said in a crisp voice to the
guard captain, "You can put your weapon down, Mibikihur.
Don't you recognize the Admiral Gialaurys?"

"Everyone knows the lord Gialaurys, sir. But look at
what he's got with him! He has no permit to bring wild
animals into the Castle. Even the lord Gialaurys needs a

permit before he can drive a wagonload of things like this inside!"

Akbalik's cool gray eyes surveyed the wagon. He had never seen a vehicle so big. Nor had he seen, ever before, such creatures as were being transported in it.

It was difficult to make them out, for they were constrained from leaving the wagon by some kind of bright curtain of energy that completely encircled it—a curtain that was like a sheet of lightning rising from the ground, but lightning that stayed and stayed and stayed. It seemed to Akbalik that lesser energy-walls within the wagon divided the creatures one from another. And those creatures—those revolting, hideous monsters!—

Gialaurys seemed in high fury. He stood with clenched fists, his great-muscled arms rippling with barely contained strength, and the look of rage on his face could have melted rock. "Where is Septach Melayn, Akbalik? I sent word ahead for him to meet me at the gate! Why are you here, and not him?"

Imperturbably Akbalik said, "I came because I was summoned by a guardsman, Gialaurys. A truckload of weird monsters was coming up the highway to the Castle, I was told, and these men here hadn't been given any instructions to expect such a thing, and they wanted to know what to do. —By the Lady, Gialaurys, what are these beasts?"

"Pets to amuse his lordship," Gialaurys said. "I captured them for him out Kharax way. More than that is of no immediate to concern to you or anyone else. —Septach Melayn was supposed to receive me here! This cargo of mine needs to be properly stowed, and I charged him with the task of arranging it. I ask you again, Akbalik, where is Septach Melayn?"

"Septach Melayn is here," came the light, easy voice of the swordsman, appearing just then at the Castle's gate. "Your message was a little slow getting to me, Gialaurys, and by error I came by way of Spurifon Parapet, which took me somewhat out of the way." Languidly he strolled through the gate and gave Gialaurys a quick, affectionate tap on the shoulder by way of welcome. Then he stared into the wagon.

"These are what were running loose in Kharax?" he said, in a voice congested with astonishment. "These, Gialaurys?"

"These, yes. Hundreds of them. Running free all over Kharax Plain. It was a bloody terrible task, my friend, tracking those creatures down and slaughtering them. Our Coronal owes me something for it. —But do you have a place ready for these fellows, Septach Melayn? A very secure place? They are some samples of what I encountered there."

"I have one, yes. In the royal stables, it is. Will this wagon of yours pass through the gate, though?"

"Through this one, yes. Not through the Dizimaule, which is why I arrived at this side of the Castle." Gialaurys turned to his men. "Here, now! Get that wagon moving! Into the Castle with it, now! Into the Castle!"

It took an hour to convey the creatures to the hold that Septach Melayn had prepared for them and to settle them in, each in its own cage, safely locked away behind sturdy bars that would not be easily sundered. Septach Melayn had found a disused wing of the Castle stables: a great stone barn deep down beneath the ancient Tower of Trumpets that must have been employed for housing royal mounts a thousand or two years ago, in Lord Spurifon's time, or Lord Scaul's, when this part of the Castle was more frequently used than it had been of late. Craftsmen working with great speed had transformed it under Septach Melayn's direction into a receiving chamber for Gialaurys's pleasant specimens.

When the job was done, Gialaurys and Septach Melayn dismissed Akbalik and the others who had helped them with the work. Just the two of them remained behind. Septach Melayn said, staring in wonder and horror at the baleful things pacing and snorting within their cages, "How would we have fared in the war, I'd like to know, if Korsibar had succeeded in turning such atrocities as these loose against us?"

"You can thank the Divine that he never did. Perhaps even Korsibar had wisdom enough to know that once they were set free to attack us, they'd continue on through the world, a menace to everyone ever after."

"Korsibar? Wisdom?"

"Well, there is that point," Septach Melayn conceded. "But what held him back from using them, then? I suppose it was that the war came to an end before he could." He peered into the cages and shuddered. "Foh! How they stink, these beasts of yours! What a pack of monstrosities!"

"You should have seen them when they were wandering about all over Kharax Plain. Wherever your eye came to rest there was something hideous to behold, snarling at something even more hideous. Like a scene out of your worst nightmare, it was. A lucky thing for us that the plain is closed on three sides by granite hills, so that we were able to drive them into a trap, and even get them to set upon one another, while we were picking them off at the edges."

"You killed them all, I hope?"

"All the loose ones, one by one, until none remained," said Gialaurys. "Except these, which I brought back as souvenirs for Prestimion. But there are hundreds more still in their pens that never broke free. The keepers have no idea what they are, you know. Having no memory of Korsibar, or of the war, how could they? All they understood was that out there in Kharax—and a gray ugly place Kharax is, too, my friend, not a tree for miles—there was this huge pen of horrors, which are supposed to be kept under guard, only something went wrong and some of them got out. Do you want to hear their names?"

"The names of the keepers?" Septach Melayn asked.

"Of the animals," said Gialaurys. "They do have names, you know. I suppose Prestimion will want to know them." He drew from his tunic a dirty, folded scrap of paper, which he pondered in a laborious way, reading not being one of Gialaurys's great skills. "Yes. This one here"—he indicated a long white bony thing like a serpent made of a string of razor-sharp sickles welded together, that lay writhing and fiercely hissing in the cage on the far left—"this one's a zytoon. And this, with the pink baggy body and all those legs and red eyes and that disgusting hairy tail with the black stingers in it, that's the malorn. Behind it we have the vour-hain"—that was a green, pustulent-looking bear-like creature with curving tusks as long as swords—"and then the zeil, the min-mollitor, the kassai—no, that's the kassai, with the crab-legs, and that one's the zeil—and can you make out the weyhant back there, the one with the mouth so big it could swallow three Skandars at once—" Gialaurys spat. "Oh, Korsibar! You should be killed all over again for having even dreamed of letting these things loose against us. And we should find the wizards who made them and eradicate them also."

Turning away with a grimace from the caged monsters, Gialaurys said, "Tell me, Septach Melayn, what new and interesting things have happened at the Castle while I was off among the zeils and the vourhains?"

"Well," said the swordsman, grinning wickedly, "the Su-Suheris is new and interesting, I suppose."

Gialaurys gave him a perplexed look. "What Su-Suheris do you mean?"

"Maundigand-Klimd is his name. We met him, Prestimion and I, in the midnight market of Bombifale. Or, rather, he met us: saw through our disguises, walked right up to us, greeted us for who we really were." Once more the wicked grin. "It will amuse you to learn that he's Prestimion's new court magus."

"He's what? A Su-Suheris, you say? I thought Heszmon Gorse was to be head magus here."

"Heszmon Gorse goes back shortly to Triggoin, where he'll rule over the wizards there as adjutant to his father, and eventually succeed him. No, Gialaurys, this Su-Suheris has been awarded the job at court. He impressed himself upon the Coronal at once, that night in Bombifale market. Was summoned to the Castle, a day or two later, at Prestimion's express order. And now they are fast friends. It's not just that he's a master of his arts, although evidently he is. Prestimion is captivated by him; loves him as he loved Duke Svor, I think. It's plain, Gialaurys, he needs someone about him that has a darker soul than yours or mine. And has found one now."

"But a Su-Suheris—" Gialaurys threw up his hands in bewilderment. "To have those two repellent snaky heads looking down at you all the time—those cold eyes—! And the treacherous nature of the race, there's a consideration too, Septach Melayn! How can Prestimion have forgotten Sanibak-Thastimoon so quickly?"

"I must tell you," the swordsman said, "that this one is a different pot of ghessl from Sanibak-Thastimoon. There was the reek of evil about that other one. It came boiling up from his pallid skin like a noxious fume. This man is steady and straightforward. Dark he is within, yes, I suppose, and very sinister to behold; but that's the nature of his kind. Still, one is tempted to put one's trust in him. Why, he even shows Prestimion the secret of his geomantic spells."

"Does he? Can that be so?"

"Yes, and makes it seem so mathematical and pure that even Prestimion is impressed, skeptical of mind though the Coronal is, beneath all his pretended acceptance of sorcery. I, too, as a matter of fact, must admit that I—"

"A Su-Suheris in the inner circle," Gialaurys said, grumbling. "I like this very little, Septach Melayn."

"Meet the man, first, and judge him afterward. You'll sing a different tune." But then Septach Melayn frowned and said, taking his sword from its sheath and drawing its tip in a thoughtful way across the earthen floor of the old stable, making idle patterns that were something like the mystic symbols of the geomancers of his native city of Tidias, "There is, I must say, one bit of advice he's given Prestimion already that makes me a trifle uneasy. They were speaking yesterday, Prestimion and Maundigand-Klimd, of the problem of Dantirya Sambail; and the magus came forth with the idea of restoring the Procurator's memories of the war."

Gialaurys started at that.

"To which," continued Septach Melayn, sweeping serenely onward, "the Coronal responded quite favorably, saying, yes, yes, that might very likely be the right thing to do."

"By the Lady!" Gialaurys howled, throwing up his hands and making half a dozen holy signs in one feverish blur of incantation. "I leave the Castle for just a few weeks, and madness instantly takes root in it! —Restore the Procurator's memories? Prestimion's gone unhinged! This wizard must have sprung him entirely free of his wits!"

"Do you think so, now?" came the Coronal's voice just then, echoing across the huge stables toward them from the rear of the room. Prestimion stood by the entrance, beckoning. "Well, Gialaurys, come close, and look me in the eye! Do you see any vestige of lunacy lurking in my gaze? Come, Gialaurys! Come, let me embrace you and welcome you back to the Castle, and tell me whether you still think I've gone mad."

Gialaurys went toward him. He saw now the Su-Suheris, looming behind the Coronal: a towering formidable figure in the richly brocaded purple robes, shot through with bright golden threads, of a magus of the court. His long, forking white neck and the two hairless elongated heads that it bore rose above his heavy, jewel-encrusted collar like an eerily carved column of ice. Gialaurys, with a quick hostile glance at the alien, opened his arms to Prestimion, and held the smaller man tightly for a long moment.

"Well?" Prestimion said, stepping back. "What do you say? Am I a madman, do you think, or is this the Prestimion you knew before you went off to Kharax?"

"You speak of restoring Dantirya Sambail's memories of the war, I hear," Gialaurys said. "That seems very like madness to me, Prestimion." And glanced sullenly, again, at the Su-Suheris.

"Seems like madness, perhaps, but whether it is is yet to be determined, I think," said Prestimion. The Coronal paused and sniffed and made a face. —"What a fetid offensive stench this place has! It's these pretty animals of yours, I suppose. You must show them to me in a moment or two." Then his face took on an easier look. "But introductions are in order, first." The Coronal indicated his companion. "This is our newly appointed magus of the court, Gialaurys. Maundigand-Klimd's his name. I assure you he's made himself more than useful already." And to the Su-Suheris he said, "And this is our famous Grand Admiral, Gialaurys of Piliplok. Though surely you must know that already, Maundigand-Klimd."

The Su-Suheris smiled with the left head, nodded with the right one. "In truth I did, lordship."

Prestimion said, "We'll talk of Dantirya Sambail later, Gialaurys. But the simple essence of the thing, I tell you now, is the issue we've discussed before amongst us—our inability to put a man on trial for crimes that he can't remember, that indeed no one in the world knows anything about save us. Who is to stand up in court as his accuser? And how, once accused, can he plead his cause? Even a murderer's entitled to defend himself. Then, how can he repent, once we find him guilty? There's no repentance when there's no cognizance of guilt."

"We already know of these problems, Prestimion," said Gialaurys.

"So we do. But we've found no solution to them. Now Maundigand-Klimd proposes that we put a counterspell on him that undoes the obliteration, so that we can try him while he's in full consciousness of his deeds. And then, afterward, wipe his memory clean again. —But, as I say, we'll talk of all that later. Show me your precious lovely creatures, now."

"Yes," Gialaurys said. "Yes, I will," but made no move toward the cages. Something else had belatedly occurred to him. After a little pause he said, in the bleak, ponderous way by which he communicated high displeasure, "It seems evident from what you tell me, my lord, that your new magus has been made privy to knowledge of the obliteration. Which, as I understood our compact, was not to be made known to anyone, not to anyone at all."

Now it was Prestimion's turn to be silent for a time.

Plainly he was abashed. A touch of ruddiness came to his face, and uneasiness to his eyes. He replied, finally, "Maundigand-Klimd had already worked out the secret for himself, Gialaurys. I merely confirmed that which he suspected. Technically it was, I agree, a violation of our oath. But in fact—"

"Are we to have no secrets from this man, then?" Gialaurys demanded, with some heat in his tone.

Prestimion held up one hand in a soothing gesture. "Peace, Gialaurys, peace! He is a great magus, is Maundigand-Klimd. You understand much more of the arts of the magus than I do, friend. Surely you know that keeping secrets from a true adept is no simple matter. Which is why I thought it wisest to bring him into my service, eh? —I tell you, Gialaurys, we'll speak of all this afterward. Let me see what you've brought back for me from Kharax."

Gruffly Gialaurys led Prestimion to the front of the cages and showed the Coronal his prizes, drawing forth his tattered slip of paper and reading off the monsters' names, explaining to Prestimion which the malorn was, and which the minmollitor, and which the zytoon. Prestimion said very little. But it was obvious from his demeanor that he was appalled by the surpassing ugliness of the things, and the pungent, acrid smells that came from them, and the aura of menace conveyed by their various fangs and claws and stingers. "The zeil," Prestimion said, half to himself. "Ah, there's a nasty one! And the vourhain—is that what that pestilent bloated one is called? What sort of mind would devise such things? How loathsome they are. And how strange!"

"These were not the only strange things I discovered in the north, your lordship. I must tell you: I saw people laughing aloud in the streets."

Prestimion looked amused. "They must have been happy, then. Is happiness such a strange thing, Gialaurys?"

"They were alone, my lord. And laughing very loud. I saw two or three who were laughing in this fashion, and not a happy laugh, either. And one other that was dancing. All by himself, very wildly, in the public square of Kharax."

"I've been hearing more such tales myself," said Septach Melayn. "Odd behavior everywhere. There's more madness abroad in the land these days than ever there used to be, I think."

"You may well be right," Prestimion said. His voice held a note of concern. But there was a certain remoteness in his tone, too, as though his mind was focused on three or four things at once and none held his full attention. He moved away from the others and walked up and down before the cages, shaking his head, solemnly murmuring the names of the synthetic killer-beasts to himself in the manner of an incantation. "Zytoon . . . malorn . . . min-mollitor . . . zeil." There could be no doubt he was strangely affected by the disagreeable shapes and unquestionable ferocity of the odious beasts that Korsibar's mages had devised for use in the war. By the overwhelming hideousness of their appearance, by the very needlessness of their mere existence, they seemed to conjure back to life the spirit of the terrible war itself.

He stepped back from the cages after a time, and gestured with his head and shoulders in away that indicated he wanted to clear his mind of what he had just seen.

"What do you say, Prestimion, should we destroy the lot of them, now that you've had a look?" Gialaurys asked.

At first the Coronal seemed not to have heard the question. Then he said, speaking as though from a great distance, "No. No, I think not. We'll keep them, I think, as reminders of what might have been, if only Korsibar had lasted a little while longer." And, after another pause: "Do you know, Gialaurys, I believe we can use these things to test the valor of our young knights."

"How so, my lord?"

"By setting them up against your malorns and zytoons in straightforward combat, and seeing how well they cope. That should show us who the really resourceful and courageous ones are. What do you think? Is that not a splendid idea?"

Gialaurys could not find the words for a response. The idea seemed grotesque to him. He glanced toward Septach Melayn, who offered only a tiny, almost imperceptible shake of his head.

But the thought seemed to amuse Prestimion. He looked off toward the monsters' lairs for a moment, smiling strangely, as though in the eye of his mind he already saw the lordlings of the Castle facing these hissing horrors in the arena.

Then the Coronal returned from whatever strange place he had entered and said, in a far more businesslike tone of voice, "Let's address this so-called epidemic of madness, now, shall we? Perhaps we have a problem here that bears closer investigation. I need a first hand look at the situation, I suspect. —Septach Melayn, what progress has been made on arranging that processional for me through the cities of Castle Mount?"

"The plans are nearly complete, my lord. Another two months and everything should be in order."

"Two months is a very long while, if people are laughing by themselves and dancing crazily in the streets of Kharax. And hurling themselves from upper-story windows, too— has there been any more of that sort of thing, I wonder? I want to go out and have a look at things right now. Tomorrow, or at worst the day after tomorrow. Get new disguises made for us, Septach Melayn. Better ones than last time, too. That wig was atrocious, and that preposterous beard. I want to go to Stee, I think, and then Minimool, say, and maybe Tidias—no, not Tidias, someone will recognize you there—Hoikmar, it'll be. Hoikmar, yes. That lovely place of the quiet canals."

A great howling and bellowing came from the cages. Prestimion looked around.

"The weyhant, I suspect, would like to eat the zeil. Do I have the names right, Gialaurys?" Once again he shook his head. Revulsion was plain on his face. "Kassai . . . malorn . . . zytoon! Foh! What monsters! May the man who devised them sleep uneasily in his grave!"

10

COMING INTO THE FREE City of Stee by the landward route around the face of Castle Mount would have been an impracticably protracted journey for Prestimion and his companions; for so great was Stee that its outskirts alone took three days to traverse in that fashion. Instead they went overland only as far as golden-walled Halanx, not far downslope from the Castle, where they boarded the snub-nosed thick-walled high-speed ferry that carried travelers down the swift River Stee to the city of the same name. No one paid the slightest heed to them. They were dressed in coarse linen robes, dull and flat in hue, the sort favored by traveling merchants; and Septach Melayn's hairdresser had ingeniously transformed their appearances with wigs and mustaches and, for Prestimion, a sleek little beard that ran tightly along the line of his jaw.

Gialaurys, who, like his predecessor as Grand Admiral of Majipoor had never felt much fondness for travel by water, had a foul time of it almost from the moment the ferry was under way. After the first few plunging moments he shifted about so that he was sitting with his broad back to the porthole, and muttered a series of prayers under his breath, all the while devoutly rubbing with his thumbs two small amulets that he held folded into the palms of his hands.

Septach Melayn showed him little mercy. "Yes, dear man, pray with all your might! For it's well known that this ferry sinks almost every time it attempts the voyage, and hundreds of lives a week are lost."

Anger flashed in Gialaurys's eyes. "Spare me your wit for once, will you?"

"The river does certainly move quickly, though," said Prestimion, to put an end to the banter. "There can't be many swifter ones in all the world."

He felt none of Gialaurys's queasiness. But their vessel's velocity here in the upper reaches of the Mount was indisputably startling. It seemed at times as if the ferry were taking a completely vertical path down the mountain. After a while there was a leveling-off, though, and the ferry's pace grew less alarming. It made stops to discharge passengers and collect new ones at Banglecode of the Inner Cities and Rennosk in the Guardian ring, and then proceeded by a wide westward swing to the next level down. By the time it was among the Free Cities and drawing close to Stee, late that afternoon, the river's course had flattened so much that its flow seemed almost tranquil.

The towers of Stee now rose up tall before them on both sides of the river. With twilight coming on, the pinkish-gray marble walls of the right bank towers had acquired the bronze hue of the setting sun, and the equally lofty buildings that lined the opposite bank were already shrouded in darkness.

Septach Melayn consulted a glistening map of blue and white tiles inset into the curving side of the ferryboat's hull. "I see here that there are eleven quays in Stee. Which one shall we take, Prestimion?"

"Does it matter? One's as good as another, for us."

"Vildivar, then," said Septach Melayn. "That's just this side of the center of town, or so it would seem. The fourth quay from here, it is."

The ferry, moving now at an unhurried pace, cruised smoothly from slip to slip, discharging a cluster of passengers at each; and in a little while a glowing sign on shore told them that they had arrived at Vildivar Quay. "None too soon," muttered Gialaurys darkly. His face was three shades more pale than usual, so that the brown bristles of his long dense sideburns stood out like angry bars against his cheeks.

"Come, now!" Septach Melayn cried cheerfully. "Great Stee awaits us!"

It was everyone's fantasy to visit Stee at least once in his life. When Prestimion was a small boy his father had taken him there, as he had to so many other famous places, and Prestimion, overwhelmed by the sight of those miles of mighty towers, had vowed to return for a longer look when he was older. But then his father's unexpected death had delivered the duties of Prince of Muldemar to him while he was still quite young, and soon after that his rise to importance among the knights of the Castle had begun, and Prestimion had had little time for pleasure-travel after that. Now, staring at the splendor of Stee through the eyes of a grown man, he was astounded to see that the city looked every bit as awesome to him today as it had when he was a child.

But Vildivar Quay turned out to be not quite as central as Septach Melayn had calculated. The towers flanking the river in this section of the city were industrial factories, and they had begun to close for the day. Workers bound for their homes in the residential districts on the opposite side of the water were streaming aboard the commuter ferries and small passenger-boats that served in lieu of bridges across the immensity of the river. Soon the neighborhood in which they had come ashore would be deserted. "We'll hire a boatman to take us along to the next quay," Prestimion decided, and they made their way back down to the water's edge.

Indeed there was a riverboat waiting in the section of the quay where private craft were allowed to tie up. It was a small, sturdy-looking vessel of the kind known as a trappagasis, made of grease-caulked planks fastened together not with nails but thick black cords of guellum fiber. At bow and stern it bore weatherbeaten figureheads that might once have been representations of sea-dragons. Its captain—most likely its builder, too—was a sleepy-looking old Skandar whose gray-blue fur had faded almost to white. He sat slouchingly in the stern, looking patiently upward at the darkening sky, with his four arms wrapped about his barrel of a chest as though he were thinking of settling in for a nap.

Gialaurys, who was fluent in the Skandar dialect, went to him to speak about booking passage. And returned, after a brief discussion that did not appear to have gone well for him, wearing a very strange expression on his face.

"What is it, Gialaurys?" asked Prestimion. "Is it that he's not for hire?"

"He tells me, lordship, that it's unwise to travel downriver at this time of day, because this is the hour when the

Coronal Lord Prestimion usually sails upstream in his great yacht toward his palace."

"The Coronal Lord Prestimion, you say?"

"Indeed. The newly crowned master of the world: none other than the Coronal Lord Prestimion. The Skandar advises me that he has taken up residence of late in Stee, and makes the river journey every night from his friend Count Fisiolo's palace to his own. There are some evenings, he says, when the Coronal Lord is in exuberant spirits and pleased to hurl purses full of ten-crown pieces to the boatmen that he passes on the way; but on other evenings, when his mood is more somber, the Coronal Lord has been known to order his pilot to ram into any boats that take his fancy the wrong way, and sink them. No one interferes with this, because he is the Coronal, after all. Our Skandar here prefers to wait until Lord Prestimion has gone past before taking on any passengers. For safety's sake, he says."

"Ah. The Coronal Lord Prestimion has a palace in Stee?" Prestimion said, bemused. This was all very curious. "Why, I had no idea! And diverts himself at sundown by sinking riverboats at random? —We need to know more about this, I think."

"In truth we do," said Septach Melayn.

This time all three of them went down to the quay. Gialaurys once again told the Skandar they wished to engage his services; and when the Skandar threw both his upper arms upward in a gesture of refusal, Septach Melayn drew forth his velvet purse and allowed the glint of silver-hued five-crown pieces to be seen. The boatman stared.

"What's your usual fare for the journey up to the next quay, fellow?"

"Three crowns fifty weights. But—"

Septach Melayn held up two bright shining coins. "Here we have ten crowns. That is a tripling of your fare, eh? Will that entice you, perhaps?"

Morosely the Skandar said, "And if the Coronal Lord takes it into his head to sink my boat? Just last Twoday he sank Friedrag's, he did, and three weeks past it was Rhezmegas's that went down. If he sinks mine, what becomes of my livelihood, then? I'm not young, good sire, and the task of building boats is far too much for me now. Your ten crowns will do me precious little good if I lose my boat."

Prestimion made a quick sign, just the littlest flick of his fingertips. Septach Melayn jingled his purse again and a heavy silver coin of impressive size, one that made the five-crown pieces look like trifles, dropped into his palm. He held it up. "Do you know what this thing is, friend?"

The Skandar's eyes grew wide. "A ten-royal piece, is it?"

"Ten royals, yes. One hundred crowns, that is to say. And look: here's a second one, and a third. No need to build a new trappagasis, eh? You should be able to buy yourself another one, don't you think, with thirty royals? That'll be your indemnity, if the Coronal Lord's in a ship-sinking mood tonight. Well? What do you say, fellow?"

Hoarsely the Skandar replied, "May I see one of those things, lordship?"

"I'm no lord, fellow, simply a well-to-do merchant come over from Gimkandale town with my friends, here to see the wonders of Stee. —You think the money's false, do you?"

"Oh, no, lordship, no, no!" A busy fluttering of depre-catory gestures, all four hands touching forehead, came from the Skandar. "It's only that I've never as much as seen a ten-royaler, never once ever in my life! Let alone possessing one. May I have a look? And then I'll take you where you want to go, sure enough!"

Septach Melayn handed one of the big coins across. The Skandar studied it with awe, as though it were some gem of rare hue: turning it over and over, rubbing his hairy fingers across the faces it bore, the Coronal Lord Confalume on the obverse and the late Pontifex Prankipin on the other side. Then, with a trembling hand, he returned it. "Ten royals! What a sight that is to me, I can hardly tell you! Get in, lordships! Get in, get in!"

When the three of them were aboard, the huge old man rose and pushed out into the stream. But he could not seem to get over having handled a coin of such great value. Again and again he shook his head and stared at the fingers that had handled the shining piece.

As the trappagasis moved out into the river, Prestimion, who like most of the lords of Castle Mount had never had much occasion to handle money, leaned across toward Septach Melayn and murmured, "Tell me, what will one of those coins buy?"

"A tenner? A fine thoroughbred mount, I'd say. Or a few months' lodging at a decent hostelry, or enough of the good wine of Muldemar to satisfy a year's thirst, at least. It's probably as much as our boatman's able to earn in six or seven months. And probably near as much as this boat of his is worth."

"Ah," said Prestimion, struggling to grasp the dimensions of the gulf that separated this Skandar's existence from his. There were, he was aware, coins of higher denomination even than the tens, a fifty-royal piece and a hundred-royal one also, actually: he had just the other day approved the designs for the whole series of new coins that would soon bear his own visage along with that of the Pontifex Confalume.

One hundred royals, though—represented by a single thick coin that Septach Melayn might be carrying in his purse even now—why, that was an inconceivable fortune for the common folk of the world, who dealt in humble bronze weight pieces and shiny one-crown coins that contained just a bit of silver much alloyed with copper. The royal-denominated coinage might just as well be the money of some other world, for all the bearing it had on the everyday lives of these people.

It was sobering and instructive for him to contemplate that, in view of all the times he had seen the likes of Dantirya Sambail or Korsibar casually wagering fifty and a hundred royals at a time at the Castle games. There is much I still need to learn, he thought, about this world that has made me its king.

*   *   *

The creaking old trappagasis made its leisurely way downstream, the Skandar, in the stern, now and then putting a hand on the tiller to keep it in mid-channel. The river was inordinately wide and almost sluggish here, though Prestimion knew that matters changed beyond the city, where the great stream shattered against the row of low jagged hills known as the Hand of Lord Spadagas and broke up into a multitude of unimportant riverlets that lost themselves in the lower reaches of the Mount.

"Where shall we go, then, lordships?" the boatman called out to them. "Havilbove Quay's the next, and then Kanaba, and the one after that's the Guadeloom Quay."

"Take us to the center of things, wherever that may be," replied Prestimion.

And to Septach Melayn he said, "What do you suppose he could have been talking about, this business of Lord Prestimion going out in his yacht and sinking boats? It made no sense to me. These people must surely be aware that Lord Prestimion hasn't had time yet even to pay an official visit to Stee, and that there's no likelihood at all that he'd be living here and riding up and down the river by night making trouble for people."

"Do you think they give much thought to the realities of the Coronal's life, lordship?" Gialaurys said. "He's a myth to them, a legendary figure. For all they know, he has the power to be in six places at once."

Prestimion laughed. "But still—to imagine that the Coronal, even if he were here, would run down ships in the channel just for sport—"

"Trust me in this, my lord. I know more of the common folks' minds than you ever will. They'll believe anything and everything about their kings. You have no idea how remote from their lives you are in every way, living far above them atop the Mount as you do. Nor can you imagine what wild fables and fantasies they spin about you."

"This is something other than a fable, Gialaurys," said Septach Melayn impatiently. "This is simply a delusion. Don't you see that the old man's as mad as all those people you saw laughing to themselves in Kharax? Solemnly telling us that the new Coronal goes about sinking riverboats! Why, what can that be, if not one more example of this new insanity that's spreading through the populace like a plague?"

"Yes," Gialaurys said. "I think you're right. Madness. Delusion. The man doesn't seem stupid. So he must be crazy, then, and no question about it."

"A most peculiar delusion, though," said Prestimion. "Comic, in its way, of course. And yet I would have hoped they'd have had more love for me than to suppose me capable of—"

Just then came a sharp cry from the boatman. "Look, my lords, look!" He was pointing frantically forward with all four arms. "There! Just upstream from us!"

A disturbance of some kind, not at all imaginary, was quite definitely going on up ahead.

The river was churning with activity. Ferries and riverboats of all sizes were scurrying busily about, cutting toward one shore or the other at sharp angles as if making hasty alterations to their routes. And it was possible to see, a little farther on, a large and luxurious vessel—a ship of virtually regal grandeur—making passage toward them down the center of the channel with all its lights ablaze.

"It is the Coronal Lord Prestimion, come to sink my boat!" the Skandar moaned in a strangled-sounding voice.

This no longer seemed as amusing as it had been. It needed to be investigated. "Steer us toward him," Prestimion commanded.

"Lordships! No—I beg you—"

'Toward him, yes," said Gialaurys firmly, and added a couple of rough Skandar expletives.

Still the terrified boatman hesitated, imploring their mercy. Septach Melayn, grinning a broad shameless grin, turned and lifted his hand, showing it agleam with great round ten-royal coins. "For you, fellow, if there's any trouble! Full indemnity for your losses! Thirty royals here, do you see? Thirty!"

The poor Skandar looked miserable; but he acceded gloomily and put a couple of his hands to the tiller, and kept the trappagasis on its course.

It was all alone, now, solitary and exposed: the only vessel, other than the yacht of the supposed Lord Prestimion, that still remained in midchannel. And it was bringing them nearer, moment by moment, to the majestic and overbearing ship that held dominion over this section of the river.

They were very close to it, now. Unsettlingly close; for it would be a very easy business, Prestimion was beginning to realize, for this great ship to pass right over their little boat and grind it to matchsticks, and sail away from the encounter without having felt the slightest tremor.

He was no expert on maritime matters; but it was obvious enough to him that this craft looming up loftily before them in the channel was built on a grand princely scale, the sort of yacht that a Serithorn or an Oljebbin might own. Its hull was fashioned of some black glistening wood bright as burnished steel, and abovedecks it bristled everywhere with a host of fanciful spars and booms and stays and banner-bedecked masts and glowlamps in a dozen colors, and from its bow rose the fanged and gaping head of some imaginary monster of the deep, elaborately carved and vividly painted in scarlet and yellow and purple and green. The whole effect was dazzling, awe-inspiring, just a little frightening.

As for the flag that it flew, Prestimion saw to his amazement that it was the Coronal's own sea-going flag, a green starburst on a field of gold.

"Do you see it?" he cried, tugging furiously at Gialaurys's arm. "That flag—that starburst flag—"

"And there is the Coronal himself, I think," said Septach Melayn coolly. "Although I had heard that Lord Prestimion was a better-looking man than that; but perhaps it was only rumor."

Prestimion gazed wonderstruck across the way at the man that claimed to be his very self. He stood proudly on the foredeck of this grand ship clad in robes of the Coronal's colors, staring out in regal manner into the night.

He looked, indeed, nothing at all like the man whom he pretended to be. He seemed taller than Prestimion, as many men were, and much less sturdy through the shoulders and chest. His hair was a golden brown, not the flat yellow of

Prestimion's, and he wore it in curving waves, not simply and straight, as Prestimion did. His face was fleshy and full and not at all pleasing, the eyebrows too heavy, the nose too sharply hooked. But he bore himself with a prideful kingly stance, his head thrown back and one hand stiffly thrust into the slit of his green velvet surcoat.

Behind him stood a tall slender man in a buff jerkin and flaring red breeches, who perhaps was meant to be this Coronal's version of Septach Melayn, and on his other side was a heavyset slab-jawed fellow in breeches of Piliplok style, surely intended to represent Gialaurys. Their presence made this bizarre masquerade all the more troublesome; it extended it into new levels of duplicity that destroyed the last trace of Prestimion's earlier bemuscment, and awoke in him something now approaching anger.

He had already lived through one usurpation; he had no tolerance in his soul for another, if that was in fact what this strange affair was intended to be.

The Skandar boatman's teeth were chattering with fear. "We will die, lordships, we will die, we will die—please, I beg you, let me turn the boat—!"

Turning was beside the point now, though. The two vessels were so close that the false Lord Prestimion could easily run them down in the channel, if that were his wish. But his mood appeared to be a kindly one tonight. As the riverboat went past the great yacht on its starboard side the supposed Lord Prestimion cast his glance downward, and his eyes met those of Prestimion far below, and for a long moment the two men stared at each other in deep, intense contemplation. Then the grandly dressed Prestimion on the deck smiled to the simply garbed Prestimion in the humble riverboat far below, as a king may sometimes smile to a common man, and nodded in a grand courtly way, and the hand came forth from the surcoat clutching a small round bag of green velvet, which he flung casually outward in Prestimion's general direction.

Prestimion was too flabbergasted even to reach for it. But Septach Melayn of the lightning-swift reflexes leaned forward and snapped the fat bulging bag from the air just as it was about to hurtle past into the water. Then the yacht continued splendidly onward, leaving the Skandar's little boat by itself in mid-river, wallowing in the great ship's wake.

For a moment there was a stunned silence aboard the riverboat, broken finally by the low droning of the Skandar's prayer of thanks for having escaped destruction, and then by an angry shout from Prestimion. "Bythois and Sigei!" he cried, in fury and shock. "He threw money to me! He threw me a purse of money! Me! Who does he think I am?"

"He plainly must not have any idea, my lord," said Septach Melayn. "And as for who he thinks he is, well—"

"Remmer take his soul!" Prestimion cried.

"Ah, my lord, you should not invoke those great demons," said Gialaurys worriedly. "Not even in jest, my lord."

Prestimion nodded indulgently. "Yes, Gialaurys, yes, I know." Those awesome names were just noises to him, mere empty imprecations. But not so to Gialaurys.

His sudden burst of anger began to ease. This was too baroque to be seriously threatening; but he had to know what it all signified.

Looking toward Septach Melayn, he said, "Is it real money, at least?"

Septach Melayn extended a hand brimming with coins. "Looks adequately real to me," he said. "Ten-crown pieces, they are. Two or three royals' worth, I'd say. Would you like to see?"

"Give them to the boatman," Prestimion said. "And tell him to take us to shore. The right bank. That's where Simbilon Khayf would live, isn't it? Have him put us down at whichever quay is closest to the home of Simbilon Khayf."

"Simbilon Khayf? You intend to visit Sim—"

"He's the most important man of commerce in Stee, or so I've been told. Anyone who possesses money on a scale that allows him to hurl bags of ten-crown pieces at strangers in riverboats would be known to Simbilon Khayf. He'd certainly be able to tell us who this proud yachtsman is."

"But—Presthnion, the Coronal can't possibly impose himself on a private citizen without warning! Not even one as wealthy as Simbilon Khayf. Any sort of official visit needs great preparation. You don't really think that you can drop in just like that, do you? 'Hello, Simbilon Khayf, I happened to be in town, and I wanted to ask you a few questions about—' "

"Oh, no, no," Prestimion said. 'We won't tell him who we are. What if there's a conspiracy of some kind, and he's part of it? This false Prestimion here may be his cousin, for all we know, and it'll be the last the world sees of us if we present ourselves in our true guises. No, Septach Melayn, we are so beautifully disguised today: we'll come as modest merchants asking a loan. And tell him what has just befallen us, and see what he says."

"My father will be down shortly," said the lovely young dark-haired woman who greeted them in the downstairs parlor of Simbilon Khayf's great mansion. "Will you have some wine, gentlemen? We favor the wine of Muldemar, here. From Lord Prestimion's own family's cellars, so my father says."

Her name was Varaile. Prestimion, studying her covertly from his seat at the side of the imposing room, could not fathom how someone as coarse-featured and disagreeable-looking as Simbilon Khayf, a man who was scarcely more handsome than a Hjort, could ever have spawned a daughter so beautiful.

And beautiful she was. Not in the mysterious, delicate way of Thismet; for Thismet had been small, almost tiny, with slender limbs and a startlingly narrow waist above the dramatic flare of her hips. Her superb features were perfectly chiseled, with dark and fiery eyes that sparkled with a lustrous mischievous gleam out of a face as pale as that of the Great Moon, and her skin was of a surpassing whiteness. This woman was much taller, as tall as Prestimion himself, and did not have that look of seeming fragility masking sinewy strength that had made Thismet's beauty so extraordinary. There had been a radiance about Thismet that Simbilon Khayf's daughter could not equal, nor did she move with Thismet's coolly confident majesty.

But these comparisons, he knew, were unfair. Thismet, after all, had been a Coronal's daughter, reared amidst the trappings of great power. Her life at court had enfolded her in a glow of royal dignity that could only have enhanced the innate shapeliness of her striking form. And beyond all dispute this Varaile was a woman of extraordinary beauty in her own way, sleek and elegant and finely made. She seemed calm and poised within, too, a woman—a girl, really—of unusual self-assurance and grace.

Prestimion found it surprising that he was so fascinated by her.

He was still in mourning for his lost love. He had been granted only those few weeks of surpassing passion with Thismet on the eve of the deciding battle of the civil war—Thismet who had been his most potent enemy, until her abandonment of her foolish feckless brother and her journey to Prestimion's side—and then she had been taken from him just as their life together was beginning to unfold. One did not recover quickly from such a loss. Prestimion thought, at times, that he never would. Since Thismet's death he had scarcely looked at another woman, had put completely out of his mind any thought of involving himself with one, even in the most superficial way.

Yet here he was taking wine from this Varaile's hand—the good rich wine of his own family's vineyards, yes, though she had no way of knowing that—and looking upward at her, and meeting her eyes with his; and what was that if not a little shiver of response traveling down his back, and a minute tremor of speculation, even of desire—?

"Do you plan to be in Stee for very long?" she asked. Her voice was deep for a woman's, rich, resonant, musical.

"A day or two, no more. We have business in Hoikmar also to pursue, and after that, I think, in Minimool, or perhaps it's Minimool first and Hoikmar afterward. And then we return to our homes in Gimkandale."

"Ah, you three are men of Gimkandale, then?"

"I am, yes. And Simrok Morlin here. Our partner Ghev-

eldin"—Prestimion looked toward Gialaurys—"is from Piliplok, originally." There was no concealing Gialaurys's
broad accent, which marked him at once as a man of eastern
Zimroel; best not to pretend otherwise where pretense was
needless, Prestimion thought.

"Piliplok!" Varaile cried. A glint of yearning came into
her eyes. "I've heard so much of that place, where all the
streets run so straight! Piliplok, and of course Ni-moya, and
Pidruid and Narabal—like names out of some legend, they
are to me. Will I ever visit them, I wonder? Zimroel's so
very far away."

"Yes, the world is large, lady," said Septach Melayn pi-
ously, giving her the solemn stare of one who utters pro-
fundities. "But travel is a wonderful thing. I myself have
been as far as Alaisor in the west, and Bandar Delem in the
north; and one day I too will set sail for Zimroel." And
then, with a salacious little smirk: "Have you been to Gimkandale, Lady? It would be my great pleasure to show you
my city, should you ever care to visit it."

"How splendid that would be, Simrok Morlin!" she said.

Before he could halt himself Prestimion shot Septach
Melayn an astounded glance. What did the man think he
was up to? Offering her a tour of Gimkandale, was he? And
with such a flirtatious leer? It was a risky tactic. They were
in this house as supplicants, not as suitors. Since when was
Septach Melayn so flirtatious with women, besides, even
one as handsome as this? —And, Prestimion wondered in
some astonishment, could that be a trace of jealousy that I
feel?

Simbilon Khayf's daughter poured more wine for them.
She dispensed the costly stuff with a very free hand, Prestimion observed. But of course this was a house of great
wealth. From the moment of their entrance into it they had
seen trappings and furnishings that were worthy of the Castle itself: doors of dark thuzna-wood inlaid with filigree of
gold, and a hall of royal opulence where a jetting plume of
perfumed water spumed ceiling-high from a twelve-sided
fountain of crimson tiles edged with turquoise, and this parlor here, furnished with costly carpets of tight-knit Makro-

posopos weave and thickly brocaded cushions. And this was
only the first floor of four or five. It looked as though it had
all been put together in the last three years; but whoever
had done the job for Simbilon Khayf, he had done it very,
very well.

"Ah, here's my father now," Varaile said.

She clapped her hands and instantly a liveried servant
entered by a door to the left, carrying a chair so elaborately
inlaid with jewels and rare metals that it seemed very much
like a throne; and at the same moment, through a door at
the opposite side of the parlor, Simbilon Khayf entered
briskly, offered curt nods to his unexpected guests, and took
the noble seat that had been provided for him. He was uglier
even than Prestimion remembered from the one quick
glimpse of him he had had during Coronation week: a hard-
faced little man with a big nose and thin cruel lips, whose
most conspicuous feature was a great excessive mound of
silvery hair that he wore absurdly piled up atop his head.
He was dressed with pretentious formality, a maroon waist-
coat shot through with glittering metallic strands over close-
fitting blue breeches trimmed with red satin braid.

"Well," he said, rubbing his hands together in what was
perhaps the involuntary gesture of a hungry tradesman
scenting a deal, "so there's been some confusion about an
appointment, is there? Because, I tell you plainly, I can recall nothing whatsoever about having agreed to see three
merchants of Gimkandale this evening at my home. But I
didn't get where I was by turning away honest business out
of false pride, eh? I am at your service, gentlemen. —My
daughter has been treating you well, I hope?"

"Magnificently, sir," said Prestimion. He raised his glass.
"This wine—the best I've ever tasted!"

"Of the Coronal's own cellars," replied Simbilon Khayf.
"The finest Muldemar, it is. We drink nothing else."

"How enviable," said Prestimion gravely. "I am named
Polivand, sir; my partner to the left is Simrok Morlin, and
over here, sir, is Gheveldin, who comes originally from Piliplok."

He paused. This was a tense moment. Simbilon Khayf

had attended the coronation banquet; since he had been in the company of Count Fisiolo that day, he must have been seated reasonably close to the high dais. Could the thought be dawning in him that the three merchants before him in his parlor were in fact the Coronal Lord Prestimion, the High Counsellor Septach Melayn, and the Grand Admiral Gialaurys, all of them tricked out in ridiculous disguise? And, if he had seen through their false whiskers, was he even now on the verge of blurting out some stupid question about their reasons for this remarkable attempt at deception? Or would he hold back to see what hand the Coronal might be playing?

He gave no clue. He looked complacent and even a bit bored, as a man of his stature in the world of business might well be when finding himself in the uninvited and unanticipated presence of such a trio of nobodies. Either he was a superb actor—which was altogether conceivable, considering his astounding ascent to immense wealth in just a few years—or he did in fact believe that his visitors were what they claimed to be and nothing more, earnest businessmen of Gimkandale with a proposition to set before him, and that they did indeed have an appointment with him that he somehow had forgotten.

Prestimion proceeded smoothly onward. "Shall I tell you why we're here, good Simbilon Khayf? It is that we have developed a machine for keeping business accounts and other financial records, a machine far more efficient and swift than any now available."

"Indeed," said Simbilon Khayf, without much display of interest. He rested his hands on his belly and steepled his fingers. His eyes, which were icy and unpleasant, showed the beginnings of a glare. Evidently he had come to an instant appraisal of the prospects that these visitors offered, and found not much here to interest him.

"There'll be immense demand for it once it's on the market," Prestimion continued fervently, with a show of eager need. "Such immense demand that great quantities of borrowed capital will be required to finance the expansion of our factory. And therefore—"

"Yes. I see the rest. You have brought with you, of course, a working model of your device?"

"We had one, yes," said Prestimion, sounding stricken. "But there was an unfortunate accident on the river—"

Septach Melayn took up the tale. "The boat which we hired to take us from Vildivar Quay to a landing nearer to your house came perilous close to overturning, sir, in a collision that we almost had with a great ship of the river that charged right down upon us, giving us no room, no room whatever," he said, with such hayseed earnestness that it was all Prestimion could do to keep from bursting into laughter. "We might have drowned, sir! We clung hard to our seats, sir, and managed to stay inside the boat and save ourselves; but two pieces of our luggage went over the side. Including, sir, I am most regretful to tell you, the one—"

"That contained the model of your device. I see," said Simbilon Khayf drily. "What an unfortunate loss." There was little sympathy in his tone. But then he chuckled. "You must have had an encounter with our mad Coronal, is what it sounds like to me. A great garish ludicrous-looking yacht, with lights all over it, was it, that tried to run you down in the middle of the river?"

"Yes!" cried Prestimion and Gialaurys, both at once. "Yes, that's it exactly, sir!"

"True enough," added Septach Melayn. "It come a foot or two closer to us and we'd have been smashed to smithereens. To utter absolute smithereens, sir!"

"The Coronal is mad, is that what you said?" Prestimion asked, evincing an expression of the keenest curiosity. "I fail to take your meaning, I think. The Coronal Lord, surely, is atop Castle Mount at this moment, and we have no reason to believe his mind's in any way impaired, do we? For that would be a terrible thing, if the new Coronal should be—"

"You must realize that my father's not speaking of Lord Prestimion, now," Varaile put in smoothly. "As you say, there's every reason to believe that Lord Prestimion's as sane as you or I. No, this is a local madman he means, a young kinsman of our Count Fisiolo, whose reason has entirely fled from him in recent weeks. There's much insanity loose in Stee these days. We had a dreadful event ourselves a month or two ago, a housemaid losing her mind and leaping from a window, killing two people who happened to be passing by below—"

"How awful," said Septach Melayn, with an exaggerated gesture of shock.

"This kinsman of the Count," Prestimion said. "He's deluded, then? And it's his particular delusion that he's our new Coronal?"

"That it is," Varaile replied. "And therefore can do as he pleases, just as though he owns the world."

"He should be locked in some deep dungeon, no matter whose kinsman he might be," Gialaurys said emphatically. "Such a man should not be loose on the river to the endangerment of innocent travelers!"

"Ah, I quite agree," said Simbilon Khayf. "There's been a great disruption of commerce lately, as he rampages up and down with that gaudy ship of his. But Count Fisiolo—who is, I should tell you, a dear friend of mine—is a merciful man. Our lunatic is his wife's brother's son, Garstin Karsp by name, whose father Thiwid died suddenly not long ago in the full flower of health. His father's unexpected death quite knocked young Garstin from his moorings; and when the word came forth that the old Pontifex had also died and that Prestimion would be Coronal after Lord Confalume went to the Labyrinth, Garstin Karsp let it be known that Prestimion was not in fact a man of Muldemar, as was commonly given out, but actually one of Stee. And that indeed he himself was Prestimion, who as Coronal would make his capital here in Stee, as Lord Stiamot did in the ancient days."

"And is that claim generally accepted here?" Septach Melayn asked.

Simbilon Khayf shrugged. "Perhaps by some very simple folk, I suppose. Most of the citizenry understand that this is only Thiwid Karsp's son, who has gone insane with grief."

"The poor man," said Septach Melayn, and made a holy sign.

"Ah, not so poor, not so poor! I am banker to the family,

and it is no great breach of confidence when I tell you that the vaults of the Karsps overflow with hundred-royal coins the way the skies overflow with stars. He spent a small fortune on that ship of his, did Garstin Karsp. And hired a huge crew to sail it nightly up and down our river for him while he terrifies the riverboat men. Some nights he tosses rich purses full of coins to the boats he passes, and other nights he ploughs right through them as though they aren't visible. No one knows what his mood will be from one night to the next, so everyone flees when his craft approaches."

"And yet the Count spares him," Prestimion said.

"Out of pity, for the young man has suffered so from the loss of his father."

"And the boatmen whose livelihood he wrecks? What about their sufferings?"

"They are compensated by the Count, so I understand."

"We lost our own merchandise. Who will compensate us? Shall we apply to the Count?"

"Perhaps you should," said Simbilon Khayf, frowning a little, as though Prestimion's sudden forcefulness of speech had indicated to him that he was not quite so humble a person as he had previously shown himself to be. —"Oh, I agree, my man, this can't be allowed to go on much longer. So far no one has actually been drowned; but before long someone will, and then Fisiolo will tell the boy that it's time to end this masquerade, and he'll quietly be sent away for treatment somewhere, and things will get back to normal on the river."

"I pray they do," said Septach Melayn.

"For the time being," Simbilon Khayf went on, "it would appear that we have a Coronal of our very own amongst us in Stee, and so be it, such as he is. As my daughter mentioned, many things are not right nowadays. The sad incident in our household here is evidence of that." He rose from his little throne. The interview, quite clearly, was ending. "I regret the inconvenience you suffered on the river," he said, though there was not a shred of regret in his tone. "If you will be so good as to return with a new model of your device, and make another appointment with my people, we'll see about making an investment in your company. Good day, gentlemen."

"Shall I show them out, father?" Varaile asked.

"Gawon Barl will do it," said Simbilon Khayf, clapping for the servant who had brought him his chair.

"Well, at least we have no conspiracy in this city to unseat me," Prestimion said, when they were outside. "Only a wealthy lunatic whom Count Fisiolo unwisely indulges in his insanity. There's some relief in knowing that, eh? We'll send word to Fisiolo when we get back that these crazy voyages of young Karsp must come to an end. And all his talk of his being Lord Prestimion, as well."

"So much madness everywhere," Septach Melayn murmured. "What can be going on?"

"Did you notice," said Gialaurys, "that we were here simply to ask for a loan, and very quickly he was talking of 'making an investment'? If we actually had a company that produced anything worthwhile, I see, he'd have controlling ownership of it in short order. I think I understand more clearly now how he came by such great wealth so swiftly."

"Men of his sort are not famous for gentle business dealings," said Prestimion.

"Ah, but the daughter, the daughter!" said Septach Melayn. "Now, there's gentility for you, my lord!"

"You're quite taken by her, are you?" Prestimion asked.

"I? Yes, in an abstract way, for I respond to beauty and grace wherever I find it. But you know I feel little need for the company of women. It was you, I thought—you, Prestimion—who'd come away from there singing her praises the loudest."

"She is a very beautiful woman," Prestimion agreed. "And marvelously well bred, for the child of such a boorish rogue. But I have other matters on my mind than the beauty of women just now, my friend. The Procurator's trial, for one. The famines in the war-smitten districts. And also these strange incidents of madness cropping up again and again. This kinsman of Count Fisiolo's, this other Lord Prestimion, who's allowed to go free to terrorize the river! Who's the bigger madman, I wonder, the boy who says he's me, or

Fisiolo who tolerates his lunacy? —Come. Let's find a hostelry; and in the morning it's on to Hoikmar, eh? We may discover three Prestimions holding court there!"

"And a couple of Confalumes as well," said Septach Melayn.

From the window of her third-floor bedroom the daughter of Simbilon Khayf followed the three visitors with her eyes as they made their way across the cobbled plaza and into the public park beyond.

There was something unusual about each of them, Varaile thought, that set them apart from most of the men who came here to get money from her father. The one who was so very tall and slender, whose movements were as graceful as a dancer's: he spoke like a bumpkin, but it was plainly only a pretense. In reality he was sharp and quick, that one—you could see it in that piercing blue stare of his, which took in everything at a glance and filed it away for future use. And sly and cunning too; there was a note of mockery underlying everything he said, however straightforward it was meant to seem on the surface—a shrewd and playful and perhaps very dangerous man. And the second one, the big man who had said very little, but spoke with that thick Zimroel accent when he did: how strong he seemed, what a sense of tremendous power under tight restraint he showed! He was like a great rock.

And then, that third man, the short broad-shouldered one. How compelling his eyes were! How magnificent his face, though the oddly inappropriate beard and mustache did him no credit. I suspect he would be quite beautiful without them, though, Varaile thought. He is a splendid man. There is a lordly presence about him. It is hard for me to believe that such a man is merely a dreary merchant, a grubby manufacturer of accounting devices. He seems so much more than that. So very much more.

11

THEY WENT UP THE Mount to the ring of Guardian Cities, with Hoikmar as their first stop. There, in a public garden abloom with tanigales and crimson eldirons, alongside a quiet canal bordered by short red-tinged grass soft as thanga fur, they encountered a beggar, a ragged and tattered old gray-haired man, who gripped Prestimion's wrist with one hand and that of Septach Melayn with the other and said with a strange urgency in his voice, "My lords, my lords, give me a moment's heed. I have a box of money for sale at a good price. A very good price indeed."

His eyes were bright with a look of great intensity and even, perhaps, keen intelligence. And yet he wore a beggar's foul rags, torn and stinking. An old pale-red scar crossed the entirety of his left cheek and vanished near the corner of his mouth. Septach Melayn glanced across the top of the man's head to Prestimion and smiled crookedly as though to say, Here we have another sorry madman, I think, and Prestimion, distressed by the thought, nodded solemnly.

"A box of money for sale?" he said. "What can you mean by that?"

The old man meant just that, apparently. He brought forth from a shabby cloth bag at his waist a rusted strongbox, much encrusted with soil and bound with sturdy straps of faded crumbling leather. Which he opened to reveal that the box was packed to its brim with coins of high denomination, dozens of them, royals and five-royal pieces and a few tens. He dug his gnarled fingers into the horde and stirred the coins about, making a silvery chinking sound. "How pretty they are! And they are yours, my lords, at whatever price you care to pay."

"Look," Septach Melayn said, scooping up one silver piece and tapping it with his fingernail. "Do you see this lettering of antique style at the edge? This is Lord Arioc here, whose Pontifex was Dizimaule."

"But they lived three thousand years ago!" Prestimion exclaimed.

"Somewhat more than that, I think. And who is this? Lord Vildivar, I believe it says. With Thraym's face on the other side."

"And here," said Gialaurys, reaching past Prestimion to pull a coin out of the box, and puzzling over the inscription on it. "This is Lord Siminave. Do you know of a Siminave?"

"He was Calintane's Coronal, I think," said Prestimion. He looked sternly at the old man. "There's a fortune in this box! Five hundred royals, at the least! Why would you sell this money to us for a quick price? You could simply spend the coins one by one and live like a prince for the rest of your life!"

"Ah, my lord, who would believe that a man like me could have amassed a treasure like this? They'd call me a thief, and lock me away forever. And this is very ancient money, too. Even I can see that, though I can't read; for these are strange faces, these Coronals and Pontifexes here. People would be suspicious of money this old. They'd refuse it, not knowing the faces of these kings. No. No. I found the box by a canal, where the rain had washed away the soil. Someone buried it long ago for safe keeping, I suppose, and never returned for it. But it does me no good, my lords, to have such money as this." The old man grinned slyly, showing a few snaggled teeth. "Give me—ah, let us say two hundred crowns, in money I can spend—give it me in ten-crown pieces, or even smaller coins—and the box is yours to deal with as you wish. For I see that you three are men of consequence, my lords, and will know how to dispose of money of this sort."

"Is a babbling old moon-calf," said Gialaurys, tossing his coin back in the box and tapping his forefinger to his forehead. "No one would refuse good silver royals, however old they be." And Septach Melayn nodded and smiled and twirled his forefinger in a little circle.

With which opinion Prestimion found himself in agreement. He felt pity for the dirty, bedraggled old man. That burning brightness in his gaze was insanity, not intelligence.

Surely this was one more dismaying instance of the strange madness that seemed to be polluting the world. He might indeed be a thief, yes, who had taken these coins from some collector of antiquities. Or, what was more likely from the looks of the box that held them, he really had found them beside the canal. But either way it was a madman's act to be offering them so cheaply, the merest fraction of their true value, to strangers met by happenstance.

Nor did Prestimion want any entanglement in these dealings. How could he, of all people in the world, be party to a transaction by which he bought hundreds of royals' worth of silver from a beggar for a double handful of crowns? He felt a touch of horror at standing this close to madness. Longing profoundly to be gone from this place, he told Septach Melayn to give the man fifty crowns and let him keep the treasure for some other buyer.

The beggar looked astonished as Septach Melayn counted out five ten-crown pieces and passed them across. But he took the money and tucked it in a belt beneath his robe. Then his crafty eyes widened and an expression that might have been fear flashed across his face. "Ah, but one must ever give value for money." He snatched three coins from his own horde. Seizing Prestimion once more by the wrist, the old man pressed them into the palm of his hand, and went scurrying rapidly away, clutching his box of coins to his bony bosom.

"What a strange business," Prestimion said. The sour aroma of the old lunatic's tattered garments lingered after him. He poked gingerly at the ancient coins with his fingertip, turning them from side to side. "They're odd-looking old things, aren't they? Kanaba and Lord Sirruth, I think we have here, and Guadeloom and Lord Calintane, and this one—no, I can't make these names out at all. Well, no matter. Here, take care of these for me," he said, giving them to Septach Melayn. They moved along. —"Two hundred crowns for the whole box?" Prestimion said, after a time. "He could have asked twenty times as much. A fool, do you think, or a thief, or a madman?"

"Why not all three?" said Septach Melayn.

Putting the episode from their minds, they spent two days more in languid Hoikmar, drifting about the taverns and markets of that serene lakeside city. Two other troublesome incidents disturbed the tranquility of the visit. A lanky raddled-looking woman with utterly vacant eyes drifted up to Septach Melayn in the main avenue and draped a costly stole of scarlet gebrax hide around his shoulders, murmuring that the Pontifex had instructed her to give it to him. Upon saying which, she turned instantly and lost herself in the busy traffic of the street. And a little later that day, while they were buying a meal of grilled sausages from a Liiman in the city plaza, a well-dressed man of middle years quietly waiting on line behind them, a man who might have been a university professor or the proprietor of a prosperous jewelry boutique, suddenly cried out in a wild voice that the Liiman was selling poisoned meat. Shouldering his way forward, he up-ended the cart onto the pavement, sending hot coals and skewers of half-cooked sausages spraying everywhere about, and went marching furiously away growling to himself.

These were disquieting things. Prestimion's purpose of going out with his companions in disguise had been to see at first hand the other side of Majipoor life, something other than that of the Castle and its gilded lords. But he had not anticipated so much darkness and strangeness, such a welter of irrational behavior.

Had it always been this way out in the cities? he wondered—open displays of madness, public manifestations of the bizarre? Or, as Septach Melayn had sometime ago suggested, was all this some sort of aftereffect of the obliteration of the memory of the war upon the minds of the most sensitive and vulnerable citizens? Either way the thought was distasteful. But Prestimion felt particular alarm at the possibility that he himself, by his desire to cleanse in an instant way the wound that the Korsibar insurrection had inflicted on the world, was responsible for this entire epidemic of madness, this strange plague of mental derangement, that appeared to be increasing in virulence from one week to the next.

In Minimool, Hoikmar's neighbor in the Guardian Cities, further signs of such things made themselves manifest. Prestimion found two days there more than sufficient for him.

He had heard that Minimool was a place of distinctive and arresting appearance, but in his present mood he found it oppressively strange: a huddled-together city made up of clumps of tall narrow buildings with white walls and black roofs and tiny windows, crowded one up against another like so many bundles of spears. Steep vertiginous streets that were little more than alleyways separated one clump from the next. And here, too, he heard weird shrill laughter out of open windows high overhead, and saw more than a few people walking in the streets with fixed expressions and glassy eyes, and collided in a doorway with someone in a frantic hurry who burst into gulping breathless sobs as she went sprinting frenetically away.

His sleep was punctuated by troubled dreams as well. In one the beggar with the coin-box from Hoikmar came to him, grinning his evil snaggle-toothed grin, and opened the box and showered him with coins, hundreds of them, thousands, until he was half buried beneath their weight. Prestimion woke, trembling and sweating; but later he slept again, and another dream came, and this time he stood at the edge of a lovely pearly-hued lake at sunrise with Thismet, quietly admiring a sky suffused with pink and emerald streaks, and Simbilon Khayf's dark-haired daughter came up to them out of nowhere and swiftly thrust the silent unresisting Thismet into the water, where she vanished without a trace. This time Prestimion cried out harshly as he awakened, and Septach Melayn, lying on a nearby cot in the hostelry where they were spending the night, reached across and gripped him by the forearm until he was calm.

There was no more sleep for him that night in Minimool. From time to time strange tremors of distress came over him, and for a moment, just before dawn, it seemed to him almost as though the general madness were reaching up and engulfing him with its dread contagion. Then he brushed the feeling aside. It would not touch him, whatever it might be. But O! The people! The world!

"I have had enough of this tour, I think," Prestimion said in the morning. "Today we return to the Castle."

Plainly much was amiss out there in the world of everyday life; and Prestimion, once he was back, gave orders for the planning for his official visit to the cities of the Mount to be accelerated. No more skulking around in false whiskers and shabby costumes, not now. In the full panoply of the Coronal Lord he would go forth to six or seven of the most important cities among the Fifty, and confer with dukes and counts and mayors, and take the measure of the crisis that seemed to be enveloping the world with such rapidity here in the opening months of his reign.

First, though, the problem of Dantirya Sambail's continued captivity needed a resolution of some sort.

He paid a call on the magus Maundigand-Klimd, who by now had established his headquarters in a group of vacant rooms on the far side of the Pinitor Court that had been the apartment of Korsibar before his seizure of the throne. Prestimion had expected to find the place filled by this time with all the arcane gear of the sorcerer's trade, astrological charts on the walls, and heaps of mysterious leather-bound folios full of magical lore, and enigmatic mechanical instruments of the sort he had seen in the chambers of Gominik Halvor, the master of wizardry with whom he had studied the dark arts during his time in Triggoin: phalangaria and ambivials, hexaphores and ammatepilas, armillary spheres and astrolabes and alembics, and all of that.

But there were none of those things here. Prestimion saw just a few small unimportant looking devices laid out in indifferent order on the upper shelves of a simple unpainted bookcase that was otherwise empty. Their nature was unknown to him; they might easily have been calculating machines or other items of prosaic arithmetical function, not very different from those that Prestimion had pretended to deal in when he was in Stee. Or the cheap little geomantic devices that he had seen for sale in the midnight market of Bombifale, that night when he first had met Maundigand-

Klimd, and which the Su-Suheris had scornfully dismissed as fraudulent and worthless. Maundigand-Klimd was not likely to have such things here, Prestimion decided. He was surprised by such sparseness, though.

Maundigand-Klimd had furnished the apartment only in the most stark and minimal way. In the main room Prestimion saw a sleeping-harness of the sort used by the Su-Suheris folk, and a couple of chairs for the benefit of human visitors, and a small table on which a handful of books and leaflets of little apparent significance lay casually strewn. There seemed to be little, if anything, in the rooms beyond, and throughout the place the ancient stone walls were altogether bare of ornament. The effect was sterile and chilling.

"This was a troubled trip for you, I think," the magus said at once.

"You can see that, can you?"

"One scarcely needs to be a master of the mantic arts to see that, your lordship."

Prestimion smiled grimly. "It's that apparent? Yes. I suppose it is. I saw things I'd rather not have seen, and dreamed things I'd have been better off not dreaming. It's exactly as I was told: there's madness out there, Maundigand-Klimd. Much more of it than I had supposed there to be."

Maundigand-Klimd replied with his disconcerting double nod, but made no other response.

"There were some who walked as though asleep in the streets, or laughed to themselves, or cried or screamed," Prestimion said. "A kinsman of Count Fisiolo in Stee calls himself Lord Prestimion, and randomly sinks boats that he meets along the river for his own pleasure. In Hoikmar—" He had with him the three coins that the beggar had pressed into his hand, and, remembering them now, he brought them out and laid them before Maundigand-Klimd. "I had these of a poor sad crazy old man there, who came upon us all eager to sell us a rusty box heavy with good silver royals for a handful of crowns. Look you, Maundigand-Klimd: these coins are thousands of years old. Lord Sirruth, this is, and Lord Guadeloom, and here—"

The Su-Suheris set the three coins out in a precise row in the palm of his own gaunt white hand. The left head gave Prestimion a quizzical look. "You bought the whole box of them, did you, my lord?"

"How could I? But we gave him a little money for charity's sake, and he forced these three on us in return, and turned and fled."

"He was not so mad as you suppose, I think. And you did well not to make him an offer. These coins are false."

"False?"

Maundigand-Klimd placed one hand over the other, closing the coins between, and held them that way for a time. "I can feel the vibration of their atoms," he said. "These coins have cores of bronze, and just a thin wash of silver over them. I could easily scrape through to the base metal with my fingernail. How likely is it that Lord Sirruth's ten-royal pieces had bronze cores?" The Su-Suheris handed back the coins. "There are madmen galore roaming the world, my lord, but your poor old man of Hoikmar is not one of them. A simple swindler is all he is."

"There's some comfort in that," Prestimion said, in as light a tone as he could manage just then. "At least there's one out there who still has his wits! —But where's all this madness coming from, do you suppose? Septach Melayn says it may be connected with the obliteration. That there's a vacuum in people's minds where the memories of the war once were, and strange things go rushing in when vacuums are created."

"I find a degree of wisdom in that notion, my lord. On a certain day some months past I felt what I thought of as an emptiness entering me, though I had no idea of its cause. As it happened I was strong enough to withstand its effects. Others evidently are not so fortunate."

A pang of guilt and shame seared through Prestimion at the Su-Suheris sorcerer's words. Could it be? Was the whole world to be infected with madness because of his spur-of-the-moment decision on the battlefield at Thegomar Edge?

No, he thought. No. No. No. Septach Melayn's theory is wrong. These are isolated, random instances. A world of

many billions of people will always have a great many madmen among those billions. It is only coincidence that so
much of this is coming to our attention just now.

"Be that as it may," Prestimion said, pushing back his
discomfort, "we'll look into the truth of it at some other
time. Meanwhile: I'll shortly be leaving the Castle again for
some weeks, or even months, to make formal visits to several of the cities of the Mount. The unfinished matter of
Dantirya Sambail has to be dealt with before I go."

"And what is your pleasure, my lord?"

"You spoke not long ago of giving him back his memory
of the civil war," Prestimion said. "Can such a thing actually
be done?"

"Any spell can be reversed by the one who cast it."

"It was Heszmon Gorse of Triggoin, and his father Gominik Halvor. But they have gone off to their home in the
north, and would be many weeks in returning if I summoned
them back now. And in any case they themselves no longer
have any inkling of what it was I asked them to do."

A flicker of surprise crossed Maundigand-Klimd's faces.
"Is that so, my lord?"

"The obliteration was complete, Maundigand-Klimd.
Septach Melayn and Gialaurys and I were the only ones
excepted from it. And since the day it was done you are the
only one who's been told that it happened."

"Ah."

"I'm not eager to allow knowledge of it into the possession of anyone else, not even Gominik Halvor and his son.
But Dantirya Sambail was the prime agent of the usurpation,
and for that he has to be punished, and it's evil to punish a
man for something he doesn't know he's done. I want to
see some shred of remorse from him before I pronounce
sentence. Or some awareness, at the very least, that he deserves what I intend to impose on him. Tell me this,
Maundigand-Klimd: could you undo the obliteration in
him?"

The Su-Suheris took a moment to reply.

"Quite probably I could, my lord."

"You hesitated. Why?"

"I was contemplating the consequences of doing such a thing, and I saw—well, certain ambiguities."

Prestimion gave him a puzzled frown. "Make yourself perfectly clear, Maundigand-Klimd."

Another brief pause. "Do you know how I see into the future, my lord?"

"How could I possibly know that?"

"Let me explain it, then." The Su-Suheris touched his right hand to his right forehead, and then to the other one. "Alone among all intelligent species of the known universe, my lord, my race is constructed with a double mind. Not a double identity, despite our custom of carrying a pair of names apiece; merely a double mind. One self divided between two brain-cases. I may speak with this mouth or that, as I please; I may turn this head, or that one, to observe something; but I am a single self none the less. Each brain has the capacity to carry on an independent train of thought. But they are also capable of joining in a united effort."

"Indeed," said Prestimion, scarcely understanding at all, and mystified by where this might be heading.

"Do you think, lordship, that our insight into things to come is brought about by lighting incense and muttering incantations, invoking demons and dark forces, and such? No, my lord. That is not how it is done by us. Such folk as the geomancers of Tidias may rely on such methods, yes, their bronze tripods and colored powders, their chanting, their spells. But not us." He passed one hand, long fingers outspread, before both his faces. "We establish a linkage between one mind and the other. A vortex, if you will: a whirlpool of tension as the neural forces meet and swirl round each other. And in that vortex we are thrust forward along the river of time. We are given glimpses of what lies ahead."

"Reliable glimpses?"

"Usually, my lord."

Prestimion tried to imagine what it was like. "You see actual scenes of the future? The faces of people? You hear the words they speak?"

"No, nothing like that," said Maundigand-Klimd. "It's far

less concrete and specific, my lord. It is a subjective thing, a matter of impressions, inferences, subtle sensations, intuitions. Insight into probabilities. There's no way I could make you really understand. One must experience it. And that—"

"Is impossible for someone who has only one head. All right, Maundigand-Klimd. At least it sounds rational to me. You know I have a bias in favor of rationality, don't you? I'm not truly comfortable with the sorcery of incantations and aromatic powders, and I don't expect I ever will be. But there's an aspect of science, or something like science, in what you say. A telepathic communion of your two minds—a temporal vortex, a whirlpool that carries your perceptions forward in time—that' s easier for me to swallow than the whole superstitious rigmarole of ammatepilas and pentagrams and magical amulets. —So tell me, Maundigand-Klimd: What do you see, when you cast the auguries for restoring the Procurator's lost memories?"

Again that little moment of hesitation. "A multitude of forking paths."

"I can see that much myself," Prestimion said. "What I need to know is where those paths lead."

"Some, to complete success in all your endeavors. Some to trouble. Some to great trouble. And then there are some whose destinations are utterly unclear."

"This is not helpful, Maundigand-Klimd."

"There are sorcerers who will tell a prince whatever he wishes to hear. I am not one of those, my lord."

"I understand that, and I'm grateful for it." Prestimion let out his breath in a soft whistling sound. —"Give me a reasonable assessment of risk, at least. I feel the moral necessity of making Dantirya Sambail's mind intact again as a prerequisite to passing sentence on him. Do you see anything inherently dangerous in that?"

"Not if he remains your prisoner until the sentence is carried out, my lord," said Maundigand-Klimd.

"You're certain of that?"

"I have no doubt."

"Well, then. That sounds good enough for me. Let's go to the tunnels and pay him a little visit."

The Procurator was in a far less amiable mood than on the occasion of his last interview with Prestimion. Obviously the additional weeks of confinement had told on his patience and temper: there was nothing in the least affable or jovial about the basilisk glance that he gave Prestimion now. And when the Su-Suheris entered his cell a moment after the Coronal, stooping low to negotiate the arching entrance, Dantirya Sambail looked altogether vitriolic.

Along with rage, though, there seemed to be a certain expression of fear in his amethyst-hued eyes. Prestimion had never before seen the slightest flicker of dismay on the Procurator's features: he was a man of utter self-confidence, ever in command of his soul. But the sight of Maundigand-Klimd appeared to have shaken that command now.

"What is this, Prestimion?" Dantirya Sambail asked acidly. "Why do you bring this alien monstrosity into my lair?"

"You do him an injustice with such harsh words," said Prestimion. "This is Maundigand-Klimd, high magus to the court, a man of science and learning. He's here to repair your injured mind, cousin, and bring you back to full consciousness of certain deeds that have been stripped from your recollections."

The Procurator's eyes went bright as flame. "Aha! You admit it then, that you tampered with my mind! Which you denied, Prestimion, on your last visit."

"I never denied it. I simply made no reply when you accused me of it. Well, cousin, you were indeed tampered with, and I regret that now. I come here today to see that it's undone. And we will now proceed. —How will you go about this, Maundigand-Klimd?"

Fury and terror in equal proportion made Dantirya Sambail's fleshy face redden and swell. His great spreading nostrils widened like yawning chasms and his eyes shrank down to slits, so that their strange beauty was concealed and only his malevolence could be seen. He shrank back against the green-glowing wall of the cavernous cell, making angry throttling gestures with his hands as though defying the Su-Suheris to approach him. Something like a snarl came from his throat.

But that ugly sound died away suddenly into a placid murmur, and his puffed-up features relaxed, and his meaty shoulders slumped and went slack. He stood as though bewildered before the looming form of the towering sorcerer and made no further attempt at resistance.

Prestimion had no idea what kind of transaction was passing between the two of them. But it seemed clear that one was in progress. Maundigand-Klimd's heads stood forward in eerie rigidity at the summit of the long massive column that was his neck. The two tapering skulls appeared to be touching, or almost so, along their crests. Something invisible but undeniably real hovered in the air between the Su-Suheris and Dantirya Sambail. There was a terrible crackling silence in the room. There was a sense of almost unbearable tension.

Then the tension broke; and Maundigand-Klimd stepped back, nodding that weird double nod of his in what looked very much like satisfaction.

Dantirya Sambail seemed stunned.

He took a couple of staggering steps backward and slipped limply into a chaise along the wall, where he sat slumped for a moment with his head in his hands. But quickly the formidable strength of the man appeared to be reasserting itself. He looked up; gradually the old demonic power returned to his expression; he smiled ferociously at Prestimion, the clearest sign that he was his full self again, and said, "It was a close thing, I see, that day by Thegomar Edge. A little better aim with that axe and I'd be Coronal right now instead of a prisoner in these tunnels of yours."

"The Divine guided me that day, cousin. You were never meant to be Coronal."

"And were you, Prestimion?"

"Lord Confalume, at least, thought so. Thousands of

good men died to back his choice. All of whom would be alive today, but for your villainies."

"Am I such a villain? If that's the case, then so were Korsibar and his magus Sanibak-Thastimoon. Not to mention your friend the Lady Thismet, cousin."

"The Lady Thismet lived long enough to see the error of her ways, and amply demonstrated her repentance," said Prestimion coolly. "Sanibak-Thastimoon had his punishment on the battlefield at the hands of Septach Melayn. Korsibar was a mere dupe; and in any event he's dead also. Of the shapers of the insurrection, cousin, you're the only one who lives on to contemplate the foolishness and wickedness and shameful wastefulness of the entire infamous thing. Contemplate it now. The opportunity to do so is yours."

"Foolishness, Prestimion? Wickedness? Wastefulness?" Dantirya Sambail laughed a great boisterous laugh. "The foolishness was yours, and bloody foolishness it was, at that. The wickedness and the wastefulness: they were yours as well, not any of my doing. You talk of insurrection, do you? That was your insurrection, not Korsibar's. Korsibar was Coronal, not you! He had been crowned in this very Castle; he was on the throne! And you and your two henchmen willingly chose to launch a rebellion against him, to the cost of how many lives, I could not begin to tell you!"

"You believe that, do you?"

"It was nothing but the truth."

"I won't argue the legalities with you, Dantirya Sambail. You know as well as I that a Coronal's son does not succeed his father. Korsibar simply grabbed the throne, with your encouragement, and Sanibak-Thastimoon bamboozled old Confalume with some wizardly hypnosis to make him accept it."

"And it would have been better off for everyone, Prestimion, if you'd let things stand that way. Korsibar was an idiot, but he was a good uncomplicated man who would have run things in the proper way, or at least would have let those who know how to run things in the proper way do so without interference. Whereas you, determined to put your mark on every little thing, determined in your pathetic boyish fashion to be a Great Coronal Who Will Be Remembered in History, will manage to bring the whole world down into calamity and ruin by insistently getting in the way of—"

"Enough," Prestimion said. "I understand completely how you would have liked the world to be run. And have devoted several difficult years of my life to making certain that it isn't going to happen that way." He shook his head. "You feel no remorse at all, do you, Dantirya Sambail?"

"Remorse? For what?"

"Well done. You've condemned yourself out of your own mouth. And therefore I find you guilty of acts of high treason, cousin, and hereby sentence you—"

"Guilty? What about a trial? Where's my accuser? Who speaks in my defense? Do we have a jury?"

"I am your accuser. You choose not to speak in your own defense, and no one else will. Nor is there need of a jury, though I can call in Septach Melayn and Gialaurys, if you prefer."

"Very amusing. What will you do, Prestimion, have my head cut off before a mob in the Dizimaule Plaza? That'll put you into the history books, all right! A public execution, the first one in—what? Ten thousand years? Followed, of course, by a civil war, as all of irate Zimroel rises against the tyrannical Coronal who dared to put the legitimate and anointed Procurator of Ni-moya to death for reasons that he was entirely unable to explain."

"I should put you to death, yes, and damn the consequences, Dantirya Sambail. But that's not what I plan to do. I lack the necessary barbarity." Prestimion gave Dantirya Sambail a piercing look. "I pardon you of the capital crimes of which you are guilty. You are, however, stripped forever of the title of Procurator, and deprived for the rest of your life of all authority beyond the confines of your own estate, though I leave you your lands and wealth."

Dantirya Sambail gazed at him through half-closed eyelids. "That is very kind of you, Prestimion."

"There's something more, cousin. Your soul's a cesspool of poisonous thoughts. That must be altered, and will be, before I can allow you to leave the Castle and return to your home across the sea. —Maundigand-Klimd, would it be possible, do you think, to adjust this man's mind in such a way as to make him a more benign citizen? To strip him of wrath and envy and hatred as I've just stripped him of rank and power, and send him out into the world a more decent person?"

"For the love of the Divine, Prestimion! I'd rather you cut off my head," bellowed Dantirya Sambail.

"Yes, I believe you would. You'll be a total stranger to yourself, won't you, once all that foul venom has been pumped out of you? —What do you say, Maundigand-Klimd? Can it be done?"

"I think it can, yes, my lord."

"Good. Get about it, then, as quickly as you can. Wipe away these memories of the civil war that you've just restored, now that he has seen what he did to merit the sentence I pronounced—wipe those away now, immediately—and then do what you must to transform him into a being fit for life in civilized society. I'll be leaving very soon, you know, on a journey to Peritole and Strave and several other cities of the Mount. I want this man rendered harmless, and I want it done quickly. —And after I've come back, Dantirya Sambail, we'll have one more little chat, and if I decide then that I can take the risk of setting you free, why, free you'll surely be! Is that not kind of me, cousin? And merciful, and loving?"

12

IT WAS NOT A grand processional, not in the strict sense of the term, for that would have required him to let himself be seen in the farthest-flung regions of the realm, not merely the cities of Alhanroel but also those of the other continents, places he knew of only in the sketchiest way, Pidruid and Narabal and Til-omon on Zimroel's far coast, and Tolaghai and Natu Gorvinu, at least, in burning Suvrael. The full journey would take years. It was too soon in his reign for such a prolonged absence from Castle Mount.

No, not a grand processional, only a state visit to some neighboring cities. But it was certainly a processional, and very grand in its own way. Out through the Dizimaule Gate and down the Grand Calintane Highway the Coronal went, aboard the first of a long succession of ornate royal floaters, and with him went his brothers Abrigant and Teotas and half the high officials of his young administration, the Grand Admiral Gialaurys and the Counsellors Navigorn of Hoikmar and Belditan the younger of Gimkandale and Yegan of Low Morpin, and Septach Melayn's kinsman Dembitave, Duke of Tidias, and many more. Septach Melayn himself had remained behind as regent at the Castle: it seemed best not to leave the place entirely bereft of its major figures, even for the few weeks of this tour.

Prestimion meant to stop in one city of each of the five rings of the Mount. The various host city mayors had, of course, been notified weeks before, and were ready to meet the high and crushingly costly responsibility of providing lodgings and proper festivities for a Coronal and his entourage.

Muldemar was the chosen stop among the High Cities: Prestimion's own native place, where he could sleep once more at his family's great estate of Muldemar House, and hunt sigimoins and bilantoons in his own game preserve, and embrace the loyal retainers who had served his parents and his grandparents before them, and accept the homage of the good people of Muldemar City, to whom he was not only their Coronal but their prince and their friend. Here he quietly asked the stewards and chamberlains whether there had been any problems among the workers of late; and was told, yes, yes, a few strange things had occurred, people complaining of a kind of forgetfulness of trivial and nontrivial things, and even some serious instances of deep confusion and inner distress verging on—well, on madness. But it was only a passing thing, Prestimion was told, and no reason for great concern.

Then it was on to Peritole of the Inner Cities, where seven million people lived in splendid isolation amid some of the most spectacular scenery of the upper Mount: subordinate mountain ranges of wild beauty, and strange purple conical peaks rising to great heights out of gray-green graveled plains, and above all the magnificent natural stone staircase of Peritole Pass, that gave access from above to the long sloping sprawl of the tremendous mountain's midsection. In Peritole, too, Prestimion heard tales of breakdown and mental confusion, though those who told these stories to him brushed them quickly aside as insignificant, and urged the Coronal to sample another tray of the pungent smoked meats that were the specialty of the city.

Downward. Strave of the Guardian Cities, a place of the grandest architectural exuberance, no two structures remotely alike, great palaces chock-a-block defying one another in their glorious excess, profusions of towers and pavilions and belvederes and steeples and belfries and cupolas and rotundas and porticos sprouting madly everywhere like giant mushrooms. The city had only recently emerged from a period of official mourning, for Earl Alexid of Strave had died not long before—of a sudden seizure, it was said. The new earl, Alexid's son Verligar, was hardly more than a boy, and plainly overawed by the presence of the Coronal at his side. But he pledged his loyalty most graciously. That was a taxing moment for Prestimion, who was privately aware that his one-time friend and hunting companion Earl Alexid had died not of any inward failing of his flesh but in fact under the sword of Septach Melayn, in the battle of Arkilon plain, during the early days of the Korsibar insurrection.

There had been some outbreaks of mental disturbances in Strave as well, it seemed, though neither Earl Verligar nor anyone else was greatly eager to speak of them. The subject seemed an embarrassment to them, as it had been in Muldemar.

When the feasting was done in Strave the Coronal and his companions moved on to their next destination. That was white-walled Minimool, of the Guardian Cities; and from there, after a few days, a journey of seventy miles down the long sloping flank of the lower Mount brought Prestimion to Gimkandale of the Free Cities, and then another hundred miles of zigzagging highways at the mountain's widespreading base took him to the final city of his tour, ancient Normork, second oldest of the Slope Cities.

"This is a dark heavy place," Gialaurys murmured to Prestimion, as their floater passed through the curiously inconspicuous gate that was the single opening in Normork's gigantic wall of black stone. "I feel its weight on me already, and we're scarcely inside the town!"

Prestimion, who was leaning from his floater's window, waving and smiling to the crowd that lined the road, felt it also. Normork clung to the dark fangs of the range known as Normork Crest the way some hunted animal clings to a precarious perch that it knows to be beyond its enemies' reach. The great black wall that protected the city—against whom? Prestimion wondered—was entirely out of proportion to the towers of gray stone behind it, a fantastically overbearing fortification impossible to justify by any rational means. And that lone tiny gate—what a strange statement that made! Was this not Majipoor, where all peoples lived in peace and harmony? Why hide yourselves like frightened mice in such a miserable inward-turning fashion as this?

But he was Coronal of all Majipoor, the strange cities as well as the beautiful ones, and it was not for him to disapprove of the way any place cared to display itself to the world. And so he favored the Normork folk with dazzling smiles and enthusiastic salutes, and made starbursts to them as they made them to him, and let them see by every aspect of his demeanor how pleased he was to be entering their splendid city. And to Gialaurys he said, hissing under his breath, "Smile! Look happy! This place is much beloved by those who dwell here, and we are not here as its judges, Gialaurys."

"Beloved, is it? I'd sooner embrace a sea-dragon!"

"Pretend you are in Piliplok," said Prestimion. A sly remark, that was; for Gialaurys's own native city, somber Piliplok where no street deviated so much as an inch from the rigid plan that had been laid out thousands of years before, was itself widely considered a grim and depressing place by those who did not happen to have been born there. But Prestimion's light-hearted gibe slipped easily past the Grand Admiral, as such gibes often did, and in his diligent way Gialaurys summoned up the closest thing he could manage to a sunny smile and thrust his head out the window on his side of the floater to show the Normork folk what delight he felt at beholding their pretty town.

It was a bright golden day, at least, and the gray stone blocks out of which the buildings of Normork were constructed took on a pleasantly radiant shimmer. Once one is inside the wall, Prestimion thought, the city has a certain kind of ponderous charm.

There was nothing charming, though, about the fortress-like palace of the Counts of Normork. It was a solid mass of stone, crouching in a curving bay of the wall like a great predatory beast about to spring upon the city it dominated. The plaza in front of it was packed with people, thousands of them, with untold thousands more jammed into the narrow streets beyond. "Prestimion!" they were shouting. "Prestimion! Lord Prestimion!" Or so he supposed the words to be; but the outcry blurred into chaotic incoherence as it rebounded from the rough stone walls all around, and became merely a dull booming rhythmic sound.

Count Meglis—a new man; Prestimion did not know him well; he was some distant relative of Iram, the former count who had been slain in the civil war—came out to greet him. This Meglis was a swarthy man, wide and blocky and built low to the ground like the palace of which he was now the possessor, with unpleasant little bloodshot eyes and a great startling space between his front teeth both above and below. There was something about his square-sided frame and solidly anchored stance that reminded Prestimion uncomfortably of Dantirya Sambail. It would have been much more pleasing to be received here today by the good-hearted red-haired Count Iram, that superb chariot-racer and more than able archer.

But Iram had fallen fighting in the service of Korsibar, and so had his lithe young brother Lamiran; and the welcome that this Count Meglis offered seemed genuine and warm enough. He stood firmly planted on the lowest steps of his palace, arms outspread, grinning a great snaggle-toothed grin that conveyed complete and absolute delight at the idea that the Coronal of Majipoor was to be his guest at dinner tonight.

Prestimion stepped from his floater. Gialaurys was just to his left; capable gray-eyed Akbalik, Prince Serithorn's nephew, was the officer of the guard at his right. To Prestimion's surprise, Count Meglis did not stir from his spot. Protocol called for the Count to come forward to the Coronal, not for the Coronal to go to the Count; but Meglis, still grinning, still holding his arms out wide, stood where he was, twenty or thirty paces away, as though he expected Prestimion to ascend the palace steps to him in order to receive his embrace.

Well, why not stand there, fool that he obviously was? What would this man, catapulted upward with so little preparation into his title by the premature deaths both of Iram and his brother, know of court protocol? But someone should have coached him. Prestimion, though rarely a stickler for proper procedure, nevertheless could hardly make the first move himself, and Meglis did not seem to understand what was required of him.

So each maintained his position, and the moment of stasis stretched on and on. Then, just as it began to seem to Prestimion that the deadlock would never end, something unexpected happened. A high female voice from the crowd called out, "Lordship! Lordship!" Prestimion saw a pretty young woman—no, a girl; she was fifteen, sixteen at most detach herself from the front row of the crowd and set out in his direction, carrying an elaborate floral bouquet, crimson-and-gold halatingas and bright yellow morigoins and deep-green treymonions and many more blooms that he could not have named, all woven together in the most beautiful way.

Prestimion's guards moved immediately to cut off her approach. But her boldness amused him. He shook his head and beckoned for her to advance. Since the squat, ugly Count Meglis was still stupidly waiting up there with grinning face and widespread arms, and seemed to intend to wait like that there forever, it would be a pleasant and diverting interruption of the present awkwardness, Prestimion thought, to accept these splendid flowers from this lovely girl.

She was very attractive: tall and slender—a bit taller than he was himself, he saw—with a great mass of reddish-gold curls cascading about her face and shining gray-violet eyes. Her expression was a charming mixture of fear and awe and eagerness and—yes—love. That was the only word for it. He had never seen such unqualified adoration in a person's eyes, never.

She was trembling as she extended the bouquet.

"How marvelous they are," Prestimion said, taking them from her. "I'll keep them beside my bed tonight." She flushed a bright scarlet and made a fluttering starburst at him and began to back away, but Prestimion, captivated by the shy and innocent loveliness of her, was not ready to have her go. He took a step or two in her direction. "What's your name, girl?"

"Sithelle, your lordship." Her voice was husky with terror. She could barely get the sounds out.

"Sithelle. A lovely name. You live here in Normork, do you? Are you still at school?"

She began to make some sort of reply. But Prestimion was unable to hear whatever she might have said, because in that moment chaos descended on the scene. Out of the multitudes packed close in the plaza a second person abruptly emerged, a thin wild-eyed bearded man who came prancing forward, screaming wildly, bellowing clotted unintelligible words, the gibberish of a lunatic. He was brandishing in his upraised right hand a farmer's sickle, honed to glittering sharpness. The girl was all that separated Prestimion from him. As the madman came bearing down upon them she turned automatically in the direction of the disturbance and virtually collided with him as she stepped forward.

"Look out!" Prestimion cried.

She had no chance. Unhesitatingly, almost without giving

it a thought, the man slashed at her with the sickle, a quick impatient chopping swipe as though he wanted merely to clear her from his path. The girl fell away to one side and slumped to the pavement, kicking convulsively and clutching desperately at her throat. With the peculiar intense clarity that comes over one at such moments Prestimion saw unceasing streams of blood flowing between her clamped fingers.

An instant later the madman rose up before him, the bloody sickle lifted high. Gialaurys and Akbalik, aware by now of what was taking place, rushed toward him. But someone else reached Prestimion first. A burly young man of impressive size had burst out of the crowd only seconds behind the man with the sickle, and now, acting with startling speed, he caught up with the assassin, seized his right arm by the wrist, and bent it sharply backward. The sickle dropped from his hand, hit the ground with a tinny clatter, and skittered harmlessly away. The young man, crooking his other arm, wrapped it around the madman's throat and closed it on him with remorseless twisting force.

There was a sharp snapping sound. The madman went limp, his head lolling loosely. The big young man hurled him contemptuously away from him like a discarded doll.

He knelt then beside the wounded girl, whose entire upper body was covered in bright blood. She was no longer moving. A great moan came from the boy as he inspected her frightful wound. For a moment he seemed overwhelmed by shock and grief. Then, tenderly scooping her into his arms, he rose and walked off into the crowd with his burden.

The whole extraordinary event had taken no more than a few seconds. Prestimion felt dazed by it all. He struggled to regain his poise.

Akbalik was standing grim-faced above the fallen and motionless assassin, now, pinning him to the ground with the tip of his sword as if expecting him to rise and begin swinging the sickle again. The other guardsmen arrayed themselves in a close formation in front of the astounded townspeople, cutting the Coronal off from their view. Gialaurys loomed up like a wall in front of Prestimion.

"Lordship?" he cried, wide-eyed with alarm. "Are you safe?"

Prestimion nodded. He was badly shaken, but the sickle had come nowhere near him. Quickly he turned and trotted up the palace steps toward Meglis, who was still standing there, gaping like a drowned habbagog. The royal party hurried inside. Someone brought a bowl of chilled wine, and Prestimion gulped it greedily. The vision of that bloodied girl—struck down before his eyes, dying, perhaps already dead—blazed in his mind. And the lunatic assassin: his wild howls, those crazed eyes, that flashing blade! But for the accident that the girl had happened to be standing right in front of him, Prestimion knew, he would probably be lying dead in the plaza this very moment. Her presence there had saved him, yes, and that of the sturdy young man who had grabbed the assailant's arm.

How strange, he thought, to be the target of an assassination attempt! Had a Coronal ever died in such a way? Cut down in front of the cheering populace by a man swinging a blade? He doubted it. It went against all reason. The Coronal was the embodiment of the world; to kill him was to shatter a continent, to send all of Alhanroel, say, to the bottom of the sea. Korsibar's seizing of the throne was something he could almost understand: it was one prince asserting a claim, however invalid it might be, against the rights of another. Not this: this was new. This was madness: an emptiness in someone's soul driving him to create an emptiness in the world. Prestimion gave thanks to the Divine that it had failed. Not merely for his own sake; that was too obvious to be worth thinking about. But for the world's. The world could not afford to have the Coronal struck down in the street like some beast in a slaughterhouse.

Prestimion turned to Akbalik. "Find that boy, and bring him here right away. I want to know how the girl is, too." And, to Gialaurys: "What's become of the assassin?"

"Dead, lordship."

"Damnation! I didn't want him killed, Gialaurys. He should have been held for questioning."

Akbalik, who had reached the palace door, paused and

turned. "Nothing could be done, my lord. His neck had been broken. I was standing over a corpse."

"Let's get some information about who he was, at any rate. Just a solitary lunatic? Or do we have a conspiracy here, I wonder?"

Meglis now came bumbling up, muttering imbecilic apologies, inarticulately craving the Coronal's pardon for this unfortunate incident. He was an altogether contemptible person, Prestimion decided. Another hard consequence of Korsibar's terrible folly: the flower of Majipoor's aristocracy had perished in the war, and all too many of the great titles were in the hands of fools or boys.

In late afternoon Akbalik returned to the palace. The young man who had saved Prestimion's life was with him.

"This is Dekkeret," Akbalik said. "The girl was his cousin."

"Was?"

"She died within moments, my lord," said the boy. His voice quavered just a little. He was very pale, and could barely meet Prestimion's gaze. The overpowering grief he felt was obvious; but he appeared to have it under tight control. "It is the most terrible loss. She was my best friend. And talked for weeks of nothing else but your visit, and how badly she wanted to have a glimpse of you at close range when you were here. And for you to have a glimpse of her, my lord. I think she was in love with you."

"I think so too," Prestimion said. He gave the boy a long, careful look. He seemed very impressive. Prestimion had learned long ago that there are some people whose qualities are instantly apparent, and that was the way with this Dekkeret: no doubt but that he was intelligent, sensitive, strong within and without. And, perhaps, ambitious. The boy was behaving very well, too, under the impact of his lovely cousin's awful death.

An idea began suddenly to form in him. "How old are you, Dekkeret?"

"Eighteen last Fourday, sir."

"Are you in school?"

"Two more months, my lord."

"And then?"

"I haven't decided, sir. Governmental service, possibly. At the Castle, if I can manage it, or else some post with the Pontificate. My father's a salesman, who goes from city to city, but that has no appeal to me." And then, as if speaking of himself were of no interest to him: —"The man who killed my cousin? What is going to happen to him, my lord?"

"He's dead, Dekkeret. You pulled his neck back a little too far, I'm afraid."

"Ah. I don't always know my own strength, sir. Is it a bad thing that I killed him, lordship?"

"In fact I would have preferred to have had the opportunity of asking him a question or two about why he felt the way he apparently did about me. But in the heat of the moment you could hardly have been expected to handle him with any special delicacy. And it was good that you moved as quickly as you did. —Are you serious about a career at the Castle, boy?"

Color rose to Dekkeret's cheeks. "Oh, my lord! Yes, my lord! Yes. Yes. There's nothing I would want more in life than that!"

"If only everything could be arranged so easily as this can," Prestimion said, with a genial smile. He glanced toward Akbalik. "When we head back to the Castle, he comes with us. Enroll him as a knight-initiate and see that he's given accelerated training. Take him under your wing. I put you in charge of him, Akbalik. Set him on his way."

"I'll look after him well, my lord."

"Do that. Who knows? We may have found the next Coronal here today, eh? Stranger things have happened."

Dekkeret's face was a fiery red and he was blinking rapidly, as though this astonishing fulfillment of his wildest fantasies had brought him to the edge of tears and he was struggling to fight them back. But then he regained his poise. With great dignity he dropped to his knees before Prestimion and made a solemn starburst, and offered his thanks in a low, unsteady voice.

Prestimion gently told him to stand. "You'll do well

among us, I know. —And I'm deeply sorry about your cousin. I could tell, just in those few moments of speaking with her, what a wonderful girl she must have been. Her death will haunt me for a long time to come." Those were no empty words. The ghastly purposeless murder of that beautiful child had stirred grim memories in him. Rising, he said to Gialaurys, "Send word to Meglis that the banquet for tonight is canceled, if he hasn't managed to figure that out himself. Have a light dinner brought to me in my quarters. I don't want to see anyone or talk to anyone, is that clear? In the morning we'll set out for the Castle."

The Coronal spent a dark, brooding evening alone. The sight of that flashing sickle, those spurting gouts of blood, would not leave him. The girl's gentle face, wide-eyed with adoration and fear, kept blurring into a swirling mist before him and transforming itself into Thismet's very different features. Again and again his tormented mind conjured up for him the grim scene that had come bursting into his mind so many times before, the bloody field of Beldak marsh in the final moments of the battle of Thegomar Edge, the sorcerer Sanibak-Thastimoon rearing up before Thismet with the dagger in his hand—

He dared not sleep, knowing what dreams were likely to come. A few books were in his baggage. He chose one at random and sat up reading far into the night. *The Heights of Castle Mount,* it was, that creaky old epic of the long-ago past, rich with tales of valiant Coronals riding forth into remote and perilous corners of the planet. Gladly he lost himself in its pages. Had any of them really existed, those ancient glorious heroes, or were they only names out of fantasy? And would someone, someday, write a poem about him, the tragic and heroic Lord Prestimion, who had loved and lost his enemy's sister, and then—

A knock at the door. This late?

"Who's there? What is it?" Prestimion said, not troubling to conceal his annoyance.

"Gialaurys, my lord."

"I wanted no company tonight."

"I know that, Prestimion. But there's an urgent message from Septach Melayn at the Castle. For your eyes alone, immediate response required. I couldn't let it wait until morning."

Prestimion sighed. "Very well." He flung his book aside and went to the door.

The letter bore Prestimion's own seal. Septach Melayn had sent it in his capacity as regent, then. Urgent indeed: connected, perhaps, to this afternoon's attempt on his life? Hastily he cracked the blob of red wax and unfolded the letter.

"No," he said, after scanning it a moment. A drumbeat pounding started at his temples. He closed his eyes. "By all the demons of Triggoin, no!"

"My lord?"

"Here. Read it yourself."

The message was a brief one. Even Gialaurys, carefully tracing out the words with his fingertip, speaking them silently aloud as he moved along the line, needed only an instant or two to absorb its import.

He looked up. His stolid face was gray with shock.

"Dantirya Sambail has escaped from the Castle? And Mandralisca too? Heading for Zimroel, so it says here, to set up a government in opposition to yours. But this is impossible, my lord! How can it be? —Do you think this is Septach Melayn's idea of a joke, Prestimion?"

Prestimion managed a somber smile. "Not even his notion of wit could stretch as far as this, Gialaurys."

"Dantirya Sambail!" Gialaurys cried, prowling restlessly now about the room. "Always Dantirya Simbail! —There's been some treason here, my lord. If only we'd put him to death without hesitation, right there on the battlefield, this would never have—"

"If only, yes. If only. That is not a useful thought, Gialaurys." Prestimion took back the letter and stared numbly at it, reading it again and again as though he expected to find its message changing after a time into something less horrific.

But it was ever the same. And he could hear Maundigand-Klimd's words now echoing in his ears, from that day when they had spoken of what the magus had seen as he pondered the possible consequences of giving Dantirya Sambail back his lost memories: *I saw—well—certain ambiguities. A multitude of forking paths.*

Yes, Prestimion thought. A multitude of forking paths. And now I must traverse them all.

II

*The Book
of Seeking*

1

"HOW CAN I REMAIN at the Castle after this?" Navigorn demanded. His strong-featured face was a study in the most intense anguish. "I am in disgrace, my lord. I can't bear to look anyone in the eye. You gave me a task, and see how hideously I have bungled it! What else can I do now but withdraw from this place and go into retirement? I beseech you, my lord, permit me to—"

Prestimion held up his hand. "Peace, Navigorn. I don't doubt that all this has been upsetting for you, but I still need you here beside me. Your request to retire is refused. Calm down and tell me how the escape came about."

"If only I could be sure, my lord—"

"Well, what do you think happened, then."

"Yes. As best I can, lordship."

Navigorn rose from his seat on the bench to Prestimion's left and began to pace about like some caged beast that has but little space in which to roam.

The meeting was being held not in Prestimion's official quarters but in the modest and austere throne-room of Lord Stiamot, a curious survival from ancient times situated just at the edge of the zone of majestic and splendid chambers that was the modern Castle's core. It was a small, stark room, furnished with a simple marble seat in antique style for the Coronal, low benches for his ministers, and a Makroposopos carpet in subdued colors that supposedly was a reproduction of the one from Lord Stiamot's time.

But Lord Stiamot's time was seven thousand years in the past. The throne-chamber he had used had long since been supplanted by a grand throne-room built by Lord Makhario, and that in turn had given way after many centuries to the even more magnificent royal chamber of Lord Confalume, which Prestimion's predecessor had furnished with a throne of such supreme grandeur that it might seem better befitted for a god than a mere worldly king. Prestimion, though, since his return to the Castle from his travels on the Mount, had taken to using the unostentatious little Stiamot throne-room as his working headquarters, preferring its simplicity to the splendor of his formal office or the impossibly opulent surroundings of Lord Confalume's throne-chamber. He had been amused to learn that Korsibar had shown the same preference after the first few weeks of his short reign.

Only the innermost members of Prestimion's circle were at the meeting: Septach Melayn, Gialaurys, Maundigand-Klimd, and Prestimion's brothers Abrigant and Teotas. Prestimion was aware that it might have been appropriate to invite Vologaz Sar, whom the Pontifex Confalume had lately designated to be the official representative of the Pontificate at the Castle, and also the hierarch Marcatain, as representative for that arm of the government which was headed by the Lady of the Isle. But he was not yet certain how to go about admitting the great deception that he had practiced on the world to his mother the Lady, or to the Pontifex. Especially to the Pontifex. And so, thus far, he had been governing as though he were the sole Power of the Realm, sharing nothing with the two high officials who were in fact senior to him by constitutional rank.

That could not continue much longer. Already, this new crisis over Dantirya Sambail had compelled him to reveal to his astonished brothers the fact of the memory-obliteration. He could trust them to remain silent as long as that was his wish. But he knew that he had no authority to compel silence from his mother, or from Confalume.

Navigorn, without ceasing his pacing, said, "There was bribery involved. Of that I'm certain. Mandralisca, it was—"

"That demon!" Gialaurys exclaimed.

"That demon, yes. The Procurator's poison-taster, and poisonous is he himself. We had him locked safely away, so we thought, but somehow he began to suborn his guards, promising them—it isn't clear—vast estates in Zimroel, or something of the kind. Four of them have disappeared, at any rate. Set him free, they did, and slipped away to points unknown."

"You have their names?" Septach Melayn asked.

"Of course."

"They'll be found, no matter where they've fled. Duly punished to the limits of the law." Septach Melayn made quick whicking gestures with his wrist as though flourishing an invisible sword in the air. "Has there ever been such a fountain of iniquity in our world as this vile Mandralisca, I wonder? The very first time I set eyes on him I knew—"

"Yes, I remember," Prestimion said, with a bleak smile. "It was at the funeral games for the old Pontifex, when you and I had the wager on the baton-dueling, and you bet against Mandralisca just out of sheer loathing for him, though he was the better baton-man. And lost five crowns to me." The Coronal looked toward Navigorn again. "All right. We return to your story. Mandralisca has succeeded in getting free. How does he manage to make his way to Dantirya Sambail in a different part of the tunnels entirely?"

"Unclear, lordship. More bribery, no doubt."

"How badly do you pay your men, Navigorn, that they so readily sell their honor to prisoners?" asked Teotas fiercely.

Navigorn whirled on Prestimion's younger brother as though he had been slapped. Hot fury crackled in his eyes. But Teotas, a slender golden-haired youth who bore a startling resemblance to his royal brother but had a far more fiery temper, met Navigorn's glare with anger of his own. For a moment it seemed as though they might fight. Then, just as Prestimion was on the verge of signaling Gialaurys to intervene, Navigorn turned away with a look of weariness and defeat on his face and said in a low voice, "Your question does not deserve an answer, boy. But I tell you all the same, I could have given them a hundred royals a week, and it would have made no difference. He took possession of their souls."

"This is so," said Septach Melayn, lightly touching his fingertips to Teotas's chest before the young prince could reply. "Mandralisca deals in demons' coinage. On the right day he could suborn anyone he chooses. Anyone."

"Me? You? Prestimion?" snapped Teotas, angrily pushing the hand aside. "Demon or no, he can't buy everyone. You speak only for yourself here, Septach Melayn!"

"Enough of this," Prestimion said impatiently. "We're losing our way. —What do you say, Navigorn? How could Mandralisca have been able to get to his master's cell?"

"I can't tell you that. One of the four bribed ones must have helped him, I suppose. I can say to you only that he did get to him, got him loose, led him from the tunnels without anyone trying to stop them. Quite likely he cast some spell that allowed him to cloud the minds of those on duty at the gates, and walked by them as though they were asleep."

"I never knew this Mandralisca to be versed in sorcery!" said Prestimion, startled.

"Anyone can master a simple spell or two," Maundigand-Klimd said. "And that one would be simple."

"For you, perhaps. But he'd have used it the day he first was imprisoned, if he'd known the art of it from the beginning," Prestimion said. "It must have been brought to him covertly just the other day."

"By whom?" Gialaurys asked.

"By some other member of the Procurator's retinue, smuggling it into the tunnels," cried Septach Melayn. "Getting it in, perhaps, the same way Mandralisca got himself and his master out. A conspiracy! The Ni-moya folk found out where Dantirya Sambail was, and contrived by magical arts to get him free!"

"This is shameful," Teotas said, glowering again at Navigorn. "If prisoners can be freed so casually from the tunnels by wizardry, why was no sort of counterspell put on the place to protect against that very thing?"

"Spells—counterspells—there would be no end of that," Prestimion said irritably. "We couldn't have guarded against every eventuality, Teotas." He looked toward the Su-Suheris. "I asked you to strip the Procurator's mind of certain special memories, Maundigand-Klimd. And I instructed you, also, to remove from it every possibility of acting on evil impulses. Were those things done?"

"Only the initial and very preliminary phase, the removal of those certain memories. The greater work, the suppression of the evil that's so deeply rooted in his character, must

be executed with care, my lord, if the man's not to be reduced to a babbling idiot."

"Small loss that would have been," said Gialaurys.
—"Well, then: a pretty mess, Dantirya Sambail loose with
most or all of his foulness still intact within him, and on his
way to Zimroel to raise an army. But we'll handle it. We'll
get messengers out, top speed, west and south. I'll slap a
surveillance order on all ports along both those coasts.
Stoien, Treymone, Alaisor—we'll cut him off from home,
and track him down, and bring him back here in chains. It's
not as though the Procurator's a difficult man to recognize."

"That he is not," said Abrigant, speaking for the first
time. "But he may not have gone west or south, though."

"What?" said Gialaurys and Septach Melayn in the same
instant.

Abrigant unfolded a despatch. "Akbalik brought this to
me five minutes before I entered this meeting," he said. "According to what I see here, someone looking very much like
the Procurator of Ni-moya was sighted these two days past
in Vrambikat province. I point out that Vrambikat lies due
east of Castle Mount."

"East," said Gialaurys in a baffled tone. "What good's
his going east? This must be wrong. You can't get to Zimroel from here by traveling east!"

"You can if you get yourself to the shore of the Great
Sea and sail clear across to the other side," said Septach
Melayn with a sly smile.

Gialaurys grunted in annoyance. "Nobody in all of history has ever sailed across the Great Sea. What makes you
think Dantirya Sambail would attempt such an impossible
project now?"

"Let's hope he has," said Abrigant, grinning. "He'll never
be seen again!"

A bright cascade of laughter came from Septach Melayn.
"Or if by some miracle he does get all the way over to
Zimroel after a year or two at sea," he said, "it'll take him
half a year more just to make the trip from Pidruid or Nar-
abal, or wherever he comes ashore, to his home in Ni-moya.
Where we'll have troops waiting to arrest him."

Prestimion alone failed to register amusement. "The thought of the Procurator's making such a voyage at all is completely imbecilic," he said. "It can't be done."

"There is an old tale," said Maundigand-Klimd, "that the thing was attempted in the time of Lord Arioc, a vessel setting out from the port of Til-omon and sailing westward in the Great Sea, but it became tangled in floating dragon-grass, and then miscarried its direction altogether, and wandered at sea for five years, or, some say, eleven, before finally finding its way back to the port from which it had—"

"All well and good," said Prestimion sharply, "but I refuse to believe that Dantirya Sambail has any such enterprise in mind. If he really has set out eastward, it's no doubt some sort of trick. Eastern Alhanroel's a remote, isolated place. He can disappear into it and easily avoid capture, and eventually he could change course entirely and head up north to Bandar Delem or Vythiskiorn and find a Zimroel-bound ship there. Or swing around abruptly to the south, and go out by way of the tropics. The one idea I don't give any credit to at all is that he's actually planning to make his way home by way of a sea that nobody has ever been able to navigate."

"What are you going to do, then?" asked Septach Melayn.

"Send a military force toward Vrambikat and try to track him down before he vanishes altogether." Prestimion pointed toward Gialaurys. "Under your command, Gialaurys," he said. "Yours and Abrigant's, jointly. I want you on the road to Vrambikat within fifty hours." He hesitated a moment and added, gesturing to the Su-Suheris, "You'll go with them, Maundigand-Klimd. And I want a Vroon, also. Vroons are wondrous good at magicking up the right direction for travel. Have you a Vroon among your wizardly acquaintances, Maundigand-Klimd, who could accompany you?"

"There is one I know, named Galielber Dorn. He has the skills we would need."

"And where's he to be found?"

"High Morpin, my lord. He has a mind-reading concession there, at the park of the mirror-slides."

"That's not far. Get word to him right away that he's to present himself at the Castle by tomorrow afternoon. Offer him whatever fee he thinks he needs for serving as our guide."

The thought came to Prestimion then of what it would be like to go into the east-country, where he had never been, where hardly anyone ever went. The excitement of venturing into territory so little known as this region of Alhanroel throbbed suddenly within him; and he felt himself overcome once more by that powerful wanderlust, that irresistible desire to leave the Castle's multitude of echoing rooms behind him and set forth into the infinite wonder that was Majipoor, that had come to be for him the one consolation for the absence of his true consort.

He would not let them go into those strange lands yonder without him.

Could not.

And if he needed to provide a plausible pretext for allowing himself once more to be drawn from the Castle, why, this search for Dantirya Sambail would serve the purpose well enough, he told himself.

And so he said, flashing a sudden smile at them after another pause: "Do you know, Septach Melayn, I think I'll want you to serve as regent again. Because I mean to be part of this expedition also."

2

HE KNEW ALMOST AT once that he had made the right choice. This was uncommonly beautiful country, out here east of the Mount. Prestimion was not the only member of the party to whom this was a new land. None of them had ever gone into the east-country, except perhaps the little Vroon, Galielber Dorn, who was their guide. It was not clear whether the Vroon had actually traveled in these parts before, but certainly he behaved as if he had, calling out the landmarks to them one after another with the confident air of one who has been here many times. But that was a special

skill of Vroons, Prestimion knew: their near-infallible sense
of direction, their all-knowing awareness of the relationship
of places. It was as though they came into the world with
detailed maps of every region of the universe already in
place behind their great golden eyes. Yet in fact Galielber
Dorn might be just as much a stranger to the east-country
as they were themselves.

The mighty pedestal of Castle Mount filled the sky behind them. Just ahead lay the misty valley of Vrambikat;
and beyond that was the unknown. Already they were able
to spy strangenesses and wonders in the distance, for the
land was still sloping away from the Mount, and their view
extended for many miles to north and south and east.

"That patch of red, Galielber Dorn," said Abrigant, pointing off to the southeast, where there was a startling dot of
bright color against the horizon. "What's that? A place that's
rich in iron ore, is it? For iron has that reddish hue."

Prestimion chuckled. "He looks for metals everywhere,"
he said quietly to Gialaurys. "It is his obsession now."

"Only sand, that is," the Vroon replied. "Those are the
blood-red dunes of Minnegara that you see, which border
on the scarlet sea of Barbirike. The sand is made up of the
myriad shells of the tiny creatures that give the sea its ruddy
tint."

"A scarlet sea," Prestimion murmured, shaking his head.
"Blood-red dunes."

Which came into clearer view three days later: parallel
rows of crescent dunes as sharp along their crests as scimitars, and so vivid in color that the air shimmered red above
them; and, farther on, stretching beyond sight, a long narrow
body of water that seemed like nothing so much as a great
pool of blood. It was a handsome and startling sight, but
ominous as well. Abrigant, ever eager for sources of metals,
was all for a side journey to explore it; but the Vroon maintained that no iron would be found there, and Prestimion
peremptorily told his brother to put the project from his
mind. They were on a different quest just now.

In Vrambikat city they interviewed the three citizens who
had reported seeing Dantirya Sambail. Commoners, they

were, two women and a man, all of them so tongue-tied at finding themselves summoned before people of such obvious high rank that it was almost impossible for them to get their story out. Had they known that they were facing the Coronal and his brother, and the Grand Admiral of the Realm, they very likely would have fallen down fainting. As it was, the best they could do was fumble and stammer.

But again Galielber Dorn proved himself useful. "Allow me," the Vroon said, and stepped forward, extending his ropy, twining tentacles toward the jabbering trio.

He was a tiny creature, no more than knee-high to the shorter of the women, yet they backed away uncertainly as the Vroon approached them. Three clipped clicking sounds came from his curving golden beak and they halted, shifting their weight uncertainly from leg to leg. Galielber Dorn went from one to the next, reaching out with two delicate, intricately branched tentacles and wrapping them about their wrists, and with each one he maintained his grip for some moments while staring upward into their eyes.

By the time he was done with the last of them, all three were as calm as though they had been given some soothing potion. And when, under further prompting from Prestimion, they began finally to speak, the story came from them in a copious flow.

They had indeed encountered a pair of brusque, disagreeable men who answered well to the descriptions of Dantirya Sambail and his minion Mandralisca. The one man was long-limbed and slim, with an athlete's wiry grace about him and a dour, hard face, cheekbones like knifeblades, eyes like polished stones. The other, a shorter and sturdier-looking man, had worn a kerchief over his face as though to protect himself from wind and sun, but they had seen his eyes, and they were even more remarkable in their way than those of the other man: lovely violet-hued eyes, as gentle and tender and warm as the taller man's dark ones had been cold and hostile.

"There can be no doubt, can there?" said Gialaurys. "There are no other eyes in the world like the Procurator's."

The fugitives had come riding into Vrambikat city on two

plump mounts that looked as if they had been driven to the last extremes of exhaustion. They needed to sell these creatures, they explained, and to purchase new ones with which to continue their journey, and they had no time to waste. "I laughed," said the man, "and told them that no stableman would pay fifty weights for two half-dead beasts like that, The tall one struck me and knocked me to the ground, and I think would have put an end to me right then, if the other hadn't stopped him. Then Astakapra here"—he indicated the older of the women—"told him where he could find a stable nearby, and off they went, and good riddance, say I."

"Where is this stable?" Prestimion asked, "Is it easy to reach from here?"

"Nothing easier, sir," the man said. "This wide street here, that's Eremoil Way. Two blocks, corner of Amyntilir, turn right, second building in from the corner on your left, with the bales of hay out front. Can't miss it."

"Pay them something," said Prestimion to Abrigant, and they moved along.

The ostlers at the stable remembered their visitors only too well. It had not been difficult for them to identify the mounts on which Mandralisca and Dantirya Sambail had been traveling as stolen ones, for they bore the markings of a well-known mount-breeder of the foothill city of Megenthorp on their haunches, and the Megenthorp man had sent word out into the hinterlands not long before that two strangers had broken into his compound and taken a pair of valuable mares. Which were these two beasts before them now, sadly reduced by days of harsh usage; and the two men who had come to the stable, the fierce-looking gaunt one and the other, shorter one with the strange purple eyes, had proceeded at once to draw weapons on the ostlers and relieve them of two fresh animals, leaving the winded ones from Megenthorp in their place.

"So they have swords now too," said Abrigant. "Supplied by the accomplices in their escape, I wonder, or acquired along the way?"

"Along the way, it would seem," Prestimion said. "As with the mounts." To the ostlers he said, "Do you have any idea which direction they were heading in as they went out of town?"

"Oh, yes, my lord, yes. East. They asked us where the main eastward highway could be found; and we told them, oh, yes, we told them truly, as who would not, with a sword's tip at his throat?"

East.

How far east? As far as the Great Sea? That was untold thousands of miles away. Surely, surely, they weren't insane enough to be thinking of getting back to Zimroel that way. Where, Prestimion wondered, were they really heading?

"Come," he said. "Time's wasting."

"We're riding in floaters and they on mounts," said Gialaurys. "We're bound to overtake them sooner or later."

"They can find floaters for themselves the same way they found mounts," Prestimion said. "Let's get moving."

Beyond Vrambikat the countryside grew emptier, only widely scattered little towns now and the occasional camp of imperial troops on maneuvers, and lonely watchtowers along the rim of hills flanking the road. No one had seen two strangers on mounts come riding this way lately, although it would have been easy enough for Dantirya Sambail and Mandralisca to slip by these places unnoticed under cover of darkness. And in dreams the next two nights both Prestimion and Gialaurys had a sense of their quarry moving swiftly and steadily through the territory ahead of them. "Dreams must be trusted," said Gialaurys, and Prestimion did not dispute him.

Eastward, then. What else could be done?

Scenes of extraordinary beauty unfolded before their eyes as they journeyed on. The long scarlet sea became a mere slit in the landscape that lay off to their right, and then it vanished altogether; but now, in the same direction, they saw pale green mountains soft as velvet that ran through the rising spine of the land, and, when they looked down over the other way, into the low country of the north, the travelers beheld a chain of small, perfectly round lakes, black as the darkest onyx and just as glistening, that stretched on and on in a triple row to the limits of their vision. It was as if the hand of a master artist had distributed them in the landscape with the greatest of care.

A lovely sight, but an inhospitable place. "The Thousand Eyes, they are called," Galielber Dorn told them. "Where those lakes are, that is entirely a barren zone. There are no settlements in the district before us down there. Nor wild animals either, for no living thing can abide that black water. It burns one's skin like fire, and to drink of it means death."

Four days later they came to the mouth of a great serpentine chasm that angled off to the northeast, toward the place where earth and sky met. Its steep walls, forbiddingly vertical, were shining like gold in the midday sun. "The Viper Rift," said the Vroon. "It runs three thousand miles, or somewhat more, and its depth is immeasurable. There's a river of green water at its bottom, but I think no explorer has ever been able to climb down those mountain walls to reach it."

And then a place of trees with long, many-angled red needles that sang like harps in the breeze, and one where boiling-hot streams came pouring down out of a cliff a thousand feet high, and a district of vermilion hills and purple gullies bridged by glistening spider-threads strong as powerful cables, and one where the scarlet energy of a tireless volcano rushed with a great roaring whoosh far up into the sky from a triangular rupture in the ground.

All very fascinating, yes. But this territory was vast and empty. In much of it a terrifying silence ruled. Dantirya Sambail could be anywhere in it, or nowhere. Did it make sense to continue his seemingly hopeless pursuit? Prestimion began to give some consideration to turning back. It was irresponsible of him to go on and on for mere curiosity's sake, when vital tasks awaited him at the Castle and this quest seemed ever more unlikely to meet with success.

But then, at last, unexpectedly, came some word of the fugitives:

"Two men on mounts?" a phlegmatic flat-faced villager said, in a shoddy little town that sat square in a crossroads

between two highways that bore no traffic at all.
Maundigand-Klimd had found him. He seemed to take the
fact that a Su-Suheris had suddenly manifested himself in
his remote town utterly for granted; but evidently he took
everything utterly for granted. "Oh, yes, yes. They came this
way. A tall lean man and one who was older and heavier.
Ten, twelve, fourteen days ago." He pointed toward the horizon. "Heading east, they were."

East. East. Always east.

But the east seemed to go on forever.

They rode on. It was, at any rate, a lovely district to be
traveling in. The air was clear and pure, the weather mild,
the winds gentle. The soil looked fertile. Every day's sunrise
was a golden-green delight. But there were only the tiniest,
most forlorn towns out here, each one dozens of miles from
its neighbor; and the inhabitants stared in amazement at the
sight of well-born travelers venturing among them in a procession of glossy floaters bearing the starburst crest.

It was almost unthinkable, Prestimion told himself, that
after all the thousands of years of human existence on Majipoor there should be such near-emptiness out here, not
very many weeks' journey east of Castle Mount. He knew
that great tracts of central Zimroel were still unoccupied;
but to see this silent realm of immense open spaces virtually
in the shadow of the Mount—that was unexpected, and
strange. And humbling, too. It taught one, once again, the
meaning of size. Even after all these thousands of years of
human settlement, the vastness of Majipoor was such that
ample room for expansion still remained.

Surely this region was one that could be usefully developed. A project for the future, Prestimion thought. As
though he did not have enough before him already.

The road they were following, a broad, straight highway,
veered slightly to the south now, though it still ran predom-
inantly eastward. The few villages were even farther apart,
here, tiny collections of strawroofed huts with scruffy
kitchen-gardens around them. Green meadows and forest
gave way to the dark blur of wilderness to the north and a
line of rocky blue hills in the south. Straight ahead, still, lay

a grassy land of streams and small lakes, quiet, peaceful, inviting.

But there was evidence that this place was not altogether a bucolic paradise. Flights of big dusky-winged raptorial birds often passed by high overhead—khestrabons, they were, or perhaps the even larger and fiercer surastrenas—with their long yellow necks at full extension and their beady eyes hungrily taking in all that lay below them. Now and again, far in the distance, they could be seen swooping down by twos and threes as though to snatch up some hapless migratory creatures of the ground. There were some fearsome insects here, too, beetles twice the size of thuvna eggs, with six horns an inch long on their heads and black armor spotted with sinister blotches of red covering their wings. An army of them, half a mile in length, came marching five abreast along the edge of the road one morning, making a terrifying clacking sound with their huge beaks as they advanced.

"What are these things called?" Gialaurys wanted to know, and the Vroon replied: "Calderoules, they are. Which in the dialect of eastern Alhanroel means 'poison-spitters'—for they'll throw fiery acid at you out of spouts under their wings from ten feet away, and woe betide you if any of it touches your lips or nostrils."

"I think this pretty place is less charming than it looks," observed Abrigant, with a hiss of displeasure, and Prestimion had word sent to the floaters behind theirs in the convoy that no one was to set foot outside of his vehicle until they had left these insects well behind them.

As for the plants in this region, they were like no plants Prestimion and his companions had ever seen. Confalume, when he was Coronal, had been deeply interested in botany as in so many other things, and Prestimion had often strolled with him through one or another of the glass-roofed garden-houses that the older man had caused to be built at the Castle, admiring the strange and wonderful plants that had been collected for him in every part of the world; and in time something of Lord Confalume's passion for horticultural curiosities had passed to him. At Prestimion's request, Galielber Dorn put names to as many of the plants they were seeing now as he could: these are moonvines, this is gray carrionfurze, that low stubby weed is mikkusfleur, that is barugaza, this with the white trunk and fruit like globes of green jade is the kammoni tree. Perhaps the Vroon was inventing the names as he went, perhaps they were the true ones; but after a time even he could name them no more, and replied with a shrug of his many tentacles whenever he was asked to identify some curious specimen spied by the roadside.

Yet he still knew the names of the natural features they were passing. There was a surprising place that he called the Fountain of Wine, where, he said, creatures too small to see carried out natural fermentation in a subterranean basin, and a geyser sprayed the product of their labors into the air five times a day. "You would not want to taste it, though," the Vroon warned, when Gialaurys expressed an interest.

And then, the Dancing Hills—the Wall of Flame—the Great Sickle—the Web of Jewels—

The miles fled behind them. Days went by. Weeks. Ever eastward ran their course, the Mount now beginning to drop from sight to the rear of them, no villages at all along the way any more, nothing at all to be seen except broad flat fields of grass, each of a different color: a great swath of topaz grass, then one where the jutting blades were deep cobalt, and then claret, indigo, creamy primrose, saffron, chartreuse. "We must be coming to the Great Sea," Abrigant said. "Look how low the land lies here. And only grass will grow, as though the ground is a sandy swamp. The sea can't be very far off."

"I doubt this very much," Gialaurys said gruffly. He had long since lost all appetite for continuing this expedition, which had come by now to strike him as a foolhardy if not downright impossible endeavor. Gialaurys looked questioningly toward the Vroon. "The sea's a year's journey from us yet, if it's a day. What do you say, little one?"

"Ah, the sea, the sea." Galielber Dorn made a small percussive sound with his beak, the Vroonish equivalent of a smile, and gestured vaguely toward the east. "Far, yet," he

said. "Very, very far." And soon the last of the grassy sa-
vannahs was behind them and they were in a district of
purplish granite hills, not in any way resembling a coastal
landscape, which gave way to a dense forest of rich black
soil where big bright globular fruits of some unknown kind
clung to every bough of the thick-leaved trees like golden
lamps in a green night.

Prestimion, for all Gialaurys's grumbling, was not yet
ready to abandon the quest for the Procurator. They began,
now, all of them, to search purposefully for Dantirya Sambail in dreams. That was often a useful way to gain access
to information that could not be had by other means.

And indeed the method produced an immediate rich harvest of results. Too rich, in fact: for Abrigant, after com-
mending himself to sleep and the mercy of his mother the
Lady of the Isle, had a clear vision of the Procurator and
his henchman encamped at a village of low, round, blue-
tiled dwellings beside a swift stream, and awakened convinced that that place was no more than sixty miles north
of their present position. But dreaming Gialaurys had seen
the fugitives too, camped in that sweet meadowland to their
rear where those flights of yellow-necked raptorial birds had
passed overhead. The voice that spoke to Gialaurys in his
dream told him quite explicitly that the expedition had gone
unknowingly past its quarry in the night, weeks ago, and
was already a thousand miles too far to the east. One of
Prestimion's captains, though, a man from the northwestern
part of Alhanroel named Yeben Kattikawn, was just as pos-
itive that he had had a true vision of the Procurator moving
rapidly ahead of them, traveling in a stolen floater; according to the dream of Yeben Kattikawn, Dantirya Sambail was
almost to the shore of Lake Embolain of the silken-smooth
water, which was the one place in eastern Alhanroel that
everyone had heard of, though hardly anyone could tell you
precisely where it was. And Prestimion himself, wrestling
with the problem throughout an entire night of uneasy sleep,
emerged with the conviction that Dantirya Sambail had bypassed them in the Dancing Hills, which Prestimion saw in
the most vivid detail, quivering and swaying as the ground

beneath them trembled, and the Procurator and his sinister companion riding steadily over their unstable crest, heading northward with the intent of turning at some point and making a great westerly loop back beyond Castle Mount to the other coast of the continent.

This welter of contradictions gave no guidance at all. At midday, while they were camped beside a grove of tall gray-leaved tree-ferns whose trunks were hairy with scarlet fur, Prestimion drew Maundigand-Klimd aside and asked him for a clarifying opinion, telling him that their night's dreaming had produced only confusion; and the Su-Suheris, who had not taken part in the dream-quest, for his people did not seek information in that way, replied that he suspected sorcery at work. "These are false trails that your enemy has planted in all your minds, I think. There are certain spells of dispersion that a fleeing man can cast, to deflect those who seek him from his proper route. And these dreams give every evidence that the Procurator has cast just such spells, or had them cast for him."

"And you? Where do you think he is?"

Maundigand-Klimd disappeared at once into a trance, one head communing with the other, and for a long while stood swaying before Prestimion without speaking. Seemingly he was in some other realm. A soft sweet wind blew from the south, but it barely stirred the fronds of the gray ferns. The world was still and silent for an endless long time. Then the four eyes of the magus opened all in the same instant and he said, looking more somber even than he ordinarily did, "He is everywhere and nowhere at the same time."

"And the meaning of that," Prestimion prompted patiently, when no better explanation was forthcoming, "is—?"

"That we have let ourselves be badly deceived by him, my lord. That—just as I suspected—he, or some sorcerer in his pay, has spread confusion all over these empty provinces, so that the people we meet imagine him traveling this way or that, in a floater or upon mounts. The information they've given us is worthless. The same is true of what

Abrigant has discovered in his dream, and Kattikawn also, I fear."

"Did your trance show you where he is, then?"

"Alas, only where he is not," said Maundigand-Klimd. "But I suspect the truth will prove to be closer to your dream and that of Gialaurys: Dantirya Sambail may never have come out this far at all. He may have only pretended to be heading east, allowing us to think he was going toward the Great Sea while actually traveling some other way entirely"

Prestimion kicked angrily at the spongy golden turf. "Exactly as I thought he might from the beginning. Simply feinting a journey into these unknown eastern lands but actually doubling back after a short while toward the Mount, and then on to some western seaport and the voyage to Zimroel."

"It appears that that is what he has done, my lord."

"We'll find him, then, wherever he is. We have a hundred sorcerers to his one. —You're sure he's not somewhere out there ahead of us?"

"I'm sure of nothing, my lord. But the probabilities are against it. The eastward route holds no benefit for him. My own intuitions, which I trust, tell me that he's behind us, and getting further from us every day."

"Yes. While we head the wrong way. This has all been nothing but a wild gihorna chase, I see." And no justification whatever remained now for proceeding on the journey, other than his hunger to explore new lands. That was not sufficient. He clapped his hands together. —"Gialaurys! Abrigant!"

They came running at Prestimion's call. Quickly he set forth for them all that Maundigand-Klimd had just told him.

"Good," said Gialaurys immediately, with a fierce grin of satisfaction. "I'll send word down the line that we're starting back to the Mount."

Abrigant still argued valiantly for his village of blue-tiled cottages sixty miles away. But Prestimion knew that it would be foolish to go searching after what was surely yet another phantom; and—not without some sadness at the thought of giving up the venture here—he gave permission for Gialaurys to sound the order for retreat.

That night they camped in a wooded place where purple mists seeped from the moist ground, so that the gray clouds that moved in at sunset quickly turned deep violet and the sun, as it dropped toward the west, lit the shining leaves of the forest trees to a magical translucent red. Prestimion stood for a long while looking westward into this strange light, until at last the sun disappeared behind the far-off bulk of Castle Mount and darkness came gliding over him out of the east, out of that remote land by the shores of the Great Sea whose immensity, he knew, he would never in this life behold.

Behold it he did, though, just a few hours later, in a dream of exquisite vividness that came to him almost as soon as he had closed his eyes in sleep. In that dream they had not given up the eastward trek, but somehow had ventured on, and on and on and on, past the last outpost of explored territory, the place called Kekkinork, where the blue seaspar with which Lord Pinitor of ancient times had bedecked the walls of Bombifale city was mined. Just beyond Kekkinork lay the Great Sea itself, shielded behind great cliffs that stretched off parallel to the shore as far to north and south as anyone could see, a formidable and seemingly endless barrier of gleaming black stone shot through with dazzling veins of white quartz. But there was a single opening in that unending cliff, a narrow sliver through which the glint of the new day's sunlight came, and in his dream Prestimion went running toward that opening and through it, and onward, down to the waiting sea, and waded out into the gentle pink surf of the ocean that occupied close to half of the planet.

Dreaming, he stood at the brink of the world.

The western coast of Zimroel lay somewhere out there before him, inconceivably far away, lost from view beyond the curve of the horizon. As he stared outward he tried without success to fathom the immensity of the span that lay between him and the other shore. But no mind could encompass it. He saw only water, a soft pink here at the sandy shore, then a pale green, then turquoise and rich deep blue farther on, and beyond that only a realm of unchanging azure gray that blended imperceptibly with the sky.

It was impossible for him to believe that there could be any end to that tremendous ocean, although he knew in some rational corner of his mind that there had to be—far away, so far that the ship had never been built that could survive the journey. The continent of Zimroel was out there somewhere in front of him, and beyond that lay the Inner Sea, which had seemed so huge to him when he had journeyed from Alaisor to Piliplok long ago, but which was only a puddle compared with this one; and far off in the east on the opposite shore of the Inner Sea was Alhanroel, with its thousand cities and its Labyrinth and its Castle; and here he stood at Alhanroel's other edge, looking off toward Zimroel and unable to comprehend the distance between here and there.

"Prestimion?" a soft voice called.

Thismet, it was.

He turned and saw her coming out of that narrow gateway in the black cliff, running toward him across the sand, smiling, extending her arms to him. She was dressed as she had been that day in his tent in the quiet Vale of Gloyn, just before the final battle of the civil war, when she had come to him to confess her error in pushing her brother toward his taking of the crown, and to offer herself to him as his bride: a sheer white gown, was all, and nothing beneath it but her sleek and beautiful self. A dazzling sun-halo glistened about her. "We could swim to Zimroel, Prestimion," she said. "Would you like to? Come. Come." And the gown was gone, and in the bright light of morning her slender dusky-skinned body gleamed in its miraculous nakedness like burnished bronze. He stared at her taut, trim form in a transport of delight, his gaze sweeping downward in wonder to take in the slim shoulders and the high, rounded little breasts and the flat belly that flared outward so startlingly at her hips and the lean, sinewy legs below;

and then, with trembling hands, he reached for her.

She folded his hand into hers. But instead of coming to him she pulled him toward her, pulled with a strength that he could not have resisted had he wanted to, and led him onward into the sea. The water, enveloping him easily, was warm and soothing. Surely the womb itself could not have been more comforting than this. With swift, strong strokes they swam eastward, Thismet just a little way ahead of him, her black lustrous hair glinting in the new day's light; and for hours they went on that way, heading ever toward the continent on the far shore, she turning now and then to smile and wave and beckon him on.

He felt no fatigue whatever. He knew he could swim for days like this. For weeks. Months.

But then, after a while, he looked toward Thismet and became aware that he could not see her anywhere, and indeed realized that it was some time since he had, that he could not actually remember when she had last been there ahead of him. "Thismet?" he called. "Thismet, where are you?" But there was no answer, only the gentle lapping of the waves, and after a time he knew himself to be entirely alone in the vastness of that great ocean.

In the morning Prestimion said nothing to anyone, simply washed his face by a limpid little stream that ran alongside their campsite and dressed and found some cold meat from last night's meal for his breakfast; and a little while afterward they broke camp and began their long trek back to the Castle, no one speaking of the dreams that had come in the night, or of the failure of the quest for Dantirya Sambail.

3

IT WAS ONLY MID-MORNING, but already at least ten assassins with drawn swords had come bursting into the Coronal's official suite so far that day, and Septach Melayn had despatched them all with his usual efficiency. Usually they

arrived in groups of two or three, but the most recent bunch
had been a foursome. That had been half an hour ago. He
had given them a very fine lesson in swordsmanship indeed.

Now, slumped in a gloomy slouch behind Prestimion's
desk with the latest thick stack of governmental documents
in front of him awaiting his signature, he felt a most powerful urge to get up and wipe out a few more. It was not
just a matter of keeping his reflexes sharp, though that was
important enough, but of preserving his sanity. Septach Melayn had sworn long ago that he would serve Prestimion in
all tasks that were required of him, yes. But he hadn't bar-
gained on being cooped up here in Prestimion's office at the
Castle for weeks on end, handling all the dreary tasks that
a Coronal was required to deal with, while the real Coronal
was off roaming about in the mysterious east country, not
merely hunting for Dantirya Sambail but also encountering
excitements of all kinds along the way, a whole great host
of strange monsters and marvels.

Let someone else be regent the next time Prestimion feels
like going on a trip, Septach Melayn thought. Gialaurys, or
Navigorn, or Duke Miaule of Hither Miaule, or anyone else
at all—Akbalik, Maundigand-Klimd, even that new boy
Dekkeret. Anyone. Just not me, he thought. I have had more
than a sufficiency of this. I am a man for action, not desks
and papers. You have been unfair to me, Prestimion.

He turned to the top document on the stack.

Resolution No. 1278, Year 1 Pont. Confalume Cor. Lord
Prestimion. Inasmuch as the municipal council of the City
of Low Morpin has demonstrated conclusively that a need
exists for renovation of the municipal sewage line that runs
from Havilbove Way in central Low Morpin to the boundary
of the Siminave district in the adjacent city of Frangior, and
the municipal council of Frangior is in agreement that the
aforesaid renovations are not objectionable to it, be it
herewith resolved that—

Yes. Be it resolved. Whatever they were resolving, let it
herewith be resolved: the dumping of both cities' sewage
into the central plaza of Sipermit, for all Septach Melayn
cared at this point. What business was it of his? Why should

it even be the Coronal's affair, for that matter? His eyes were beginning to glaze with boredom and fatigue. Quickly he scrawled his signature on the resolution without reading the rest of it and shoved it aside.

Next: Resolution No. 1279, Year 1 Pont. Confalume—

He could bear it no longer. Half an hour of this at a time was all he could take. His soul rebelled.

"What?" he bellowed, looking up. "More murderers? Ha! Is there no respect for high office in the world any more?"

There were five of them this time, lean sharp-nosed men with the sun-darkened skin of southerners. Septach Melayn leaped to his feet. His rapier, which remained just beside him at the desk at all times, was in his hand and already in motion. "Look at you," he said, with a disdainful edge to his voice. "Those dirty boots! Those ragged leather jerkins! Spots of grease all over them! Don't you know how to dress when you come calling at the Castle?" They had arrayed themselves in a semicircle from one side of the big room to the other. I will start at the end closest to the window, thought Septach Melayn, and work my way across.

And then he stopped thinking and became pure motion, a mere machine of death, dancing on the tips of his toes in perfect balance, his long right arm extending, thrusting, withdrawing, extending again, parrying, thrusting, withdrawing. His blade moved with the speed of light.

Let them keep pace with him if they could. They would be the first who had ever managed it.

"Ha!" he cried. "Yes!" So, so, so: with a little grunting sound of delight he skewered the scar-faced one by the window through the throat, then whirled neatly and put the tip of his blade deep into the belly of the one next to him with the red bandanna, who was kind enough to topple heavily athwart the third, the stunningly ugly one, thus forcing him to turn his back on Septach Melayn just sufficiently long for Septach Melayn to take him in the heart from the side. "Ah! There! So!" One, two, three. This was mere dancing; this was good simple play. The two surviving killers now attempted to charge Septach Melayn at the same time, but he was much too fast for them: a hard lunge to the right carried

his blade all the way through the midsection of the first, and
by lowering his left shoulder and flexing his left knee he
was able to dodge under the thrust that came from the other
attacker while simultaneously pulling his sword from the
body of the first, and then with a triumphant cry of "Ha!
Ha!" he pivoted sharply and—

A knock at the door. A voice from the hallway. "My lord
Septach Melayn! My lord, is everything all right with you
in there?"

Damn. It was doddering old Nilgir Sumanand, Prestimion's aide-de-camp and major-domo. "Of course everything's all right!" Septach Melayn told him. "What do you
think?" Hastily he returned to the desk and tucked his sword
out of sight by his feet. He brushed a vagrant lock of his
hair back into place. Reaching for Resolution No. 1279, he
made a devout pretense at studying it intently.

Nilgir Sumanand peered in. "I thought I heard you speaking to someone, though I knew no one was there," he said.
"And there were some outcries, or so it seemed to me; and
other sounds. Footsteps, as if someone was moving quickly
about the room. A scuffle, perhaps? —But there's no one
here except yourself, I see. The grace of the Divine be on
you, my lord Septach Melayn! I must have been imagining
things."

No: I was, thought Septach Melayn wryly, glancing about
the empty room. He could still see the bloody heaps of dead
assailants, although he knew the other man could not.

"What you heard," he said, "was the regent of the realm
at his exercise. I'm not used to such a sedentary kind of
life. I get up from this desk every hour or so and indulge
in some calisthenics, do you follow? To keep myself from
rusting away. A quick bit of feint and slash, a little tuning-
up of wrist and arm and eye. —What is it you want, Nilgir
Sumanand?"

"Your noontime appointment is at hand."

"And what appointment is that?"

Nilgir Sumanand looked a little taken aback. "Why, the
transmuter of metals, my lord. You sent word three days
past that you would meet with him here today at noon."

"Ah. So I did. I do recall it now."

Damn. Damn damn damn.

It was the alchemist, the man who claimed to be able to manufacture iron from charcoal. Another bit of infernal bother, Septach Melayn thought, scowling. This was Abrigant's project, not Prestimion's. It wasn't sufficient to be doing the Coronal's job; they wanted him to handle Abrigant's business as well. Abrigant too was off in the east with Prestimion, though. Since no one knew when they were going to return, all manner of strange things were falling to Septach Melayn in their absence. And this one seemed the wildest fantasy, this conjuring of valuable metal out of useless charcoal. But he had promised to give the man a little of his time.

"Let him come in, Nilgir Sumanand."

The major-domo stepped aside to allow someone to enter. "I hail the great lord Septach Melayn," his visitor said obsequiously, and executed a profound, if clumsy, bow.

Septach Melayn felt a wince of distaste. The man who stood before him was a Hjort! That was something he hadn't anticipated: a big-bellied stubby-legged Hjort with gleaming bulgy eyes like those of some unpleasant fish and dull gray skin that was erupting everywhere with smooth rounded protrusions as big as good-sized pebbles. Septach Melayn did not care for Hjorts. He knew that was wrong of him, that Hjorts were citizens too, and usually decent ones, and could not help it that they looked so hideous. There had to be a whole world full of Hjorts somewhere in the universe and its people would surely think he was hideous. But he was uncomfortable in their company, all the same. They irritated him. This one, who was dressed with particular resplendence in tight red trousers, a dark-green doublet with scarlet trim, and a short cloak of purple velveteen, seemed to glory in his own ugliness. He showed no special awe at finding himself in the private office of the Coronal Lord, or in the presence of the High Counsellor Septach Melayn.

As a private citizen of aristocratic background, Septach Melayn could feel any way about outworlders that he pleased. But as regent for the Coronal of Majipoor he knew he must show respect for citizens of every sort, be they Hjorts or Skandars or Vroons or Liimen, Su-Suheris or Ghayrogs or anything else. He bade the Hjort welcome—Taihjorklin was his name—and asked him to fill him in on the details of his researches, since the absent Abrigant had not provided him with much to go on.

The Hjort clapped his pudgy hands and two assistants appeared, both of them Hjorts as well, rolling a large four-wheeled tray on which was stacked a great assemblage of implements, charts, scrolls, and other impedimenta. He seemed prepared for an extensive demonstration.

"You must understand, my lord, that all things are interwoven and become separate again, and that if one can fathom the rhythm of the separation, one may replicate the interweaving. For the sky gives and the land receives; the stars give and the flowers receive; the ocean gives and the flesh receives. The mingling and combining are aspects of the great chain of existence; the harmony of the stars and the harmony of—"

"Yes," Septach Melayn cut in. "Prince Abrigant has explained all these philosophical matters to me already. Be kind enough to show me how you go about making metal out of charcoal."

The Hjort seemed only slightly disconcerted by Septach Melayn's brusqueness. "We have, my lord, approached our task through the use of various scientific techniques, to wit, calcinations, sublimations, dissolutions, combustions, and the joining of elixirs. I am prepared to elaborate upon the specific efficacy of each of these techniques, if it should please you, my lord." Hearing no such request, he went on, choosing relevant exhibits from his tray as he spoke: "All substances, you must realize, are made up of metal and nonmetal in varying proportions. Our task is to increase the proportion of the one by reducing the proportion of the other. In our processes we employ both waters corrosive and waters ardent as our catalysts. Our chief reagents are green vitriol, sulfur, orpiment, and a large group of active salts, primary among them sal hepatica and sal ammoniac, though there are many others. The first step, my lord, is calcination, the reduction of the matters used to a basic condition, This is followed by solution, the action of the liquor distilled from our reactive substances upon the dry substances, after which we induce separation and then conjunction, by which I mean—"

"Show me the metal that your process produces, if you will," said Septach Melayn, not in an unkindly way.

"Ah." Taihjorklin's balloon-like throat membranes expanded in an unsettling fashion. "Of course. The metal, my lord."

The Hjort turned and took from the tray a delicate strand of bright wire, no thicker than a hair and no longer than a finger, which he presented to Septach Melayn with a grand flourish.

Septach Melayn scrutinized it coolly. "I would have expected an ingot, at the least."

"There will be ingots aplenty in good time, my lord."

"But at present, this is what you have?"

"What you see represents no small achievement, your lordship. But the process is only rudimentary at this point. We have established general principles; now we are ready to move on. Much equipment remains to be purchased before we can proceed to the stage of large-scale production. We require, for instance, proper furnaces, stills, sublimatories, scorifying pans, crucibles, beakers, lamps, refluxatory extractors—"

"All of which will cost a large amount of money, I take it?"

"Some considerable funding will be required, yes. But there can be no doubt of success. Ultimately we will draw any required quantity of metal from base substances, in the same way as plants draw nourishment from air and water and soil. For one is all, and all is one, and if you have not the one, then all is nothing, but with proper guidance the highest descends to the lowest and the lowest will rise to the highest, and then the total achievement is within our grasp. We are in command, let me assure you, my lord, of the element that enables all. Which element, I tell you, my lord, is none other than dry water, which has been sought by so many for so long, but which we alone have succeeded in—"

"Dry water?"

"The very same. Repeated distillation of common water, six, seven hundred distillations, removes its moist quality, provided certain substances of great dryness are added to the substratum at particular phases of the process. Permit me to show you, my lord." Taihjorklin reached behind him and took a beaker from the tray. "Here, your lordship, is dry water itself: do you see it? This brilliant white substance, as solid as salt."

"That scaly crust, you mean, along the side of the beaker?"

"None other. It is a pure element: the quality of dryness residing in first matter. From such elements as this can be rendered the elixir of transmutation, which is a transparent body, lustrous red in its emanation, by which—"

"Yes. Thank you," said Septach Melayn, settling back in his chair.

"My lord?"

"I will report the details of today's meeting to the Coronal immediately upon his return. One is all, I will tell him. All is one. You are the master of calcination and combustion, and the mystery of dry water is a mere elementary riddle to you, and with proper governmental funding of a certain considerable scope you assert that you can bring forth from the sands of Majipoor an infinite supply of valuable metals. Do I have it correctly, Ser Taihjorklin? Very well. I will make my report, and the Coronal will deal with it as he sees fit."

"My lord—I have only begun to explain—"

"Thank you, Ser Taihjorklin. We will be in touch."

He rang for Nilgir Sumanand. The Hjort and his assistants were ushered from the room.

Pfaugh, thought Septach Melayn, when they were gone. One is all! All is one!

The whole bizarre swarm of sorcerers and exorcists and geomancers and haruspicators and thaumaturges and warlocks and superstition-mongering seers of all the other kinds that had been spreading across the world since he was a boy had seemed bad enough to him. But one transmuter of metals, it seemed, could generate more nonsense than any seven wizards!

All that was Prestimion's problem, though—when and if Prestimion deigned to come back from the east country. He and Abrigant could hire a thousand transmuters a week, if that was what they cared to do. That would not be an issue for Septach Melayn.

His own problem was that the regency was driving him crazy. Perhaps slaying a few more assassins would help to calm his nerves. He reached for his sword. Glared at the new horde of enemies that had come bursting into the room.

"What, six of you at once! Your audacity knows no limits, vermin! But let me teach you some fine points of the art of swordsmanship, eh? See, this is known as calcination! This is the combustion of sublimation! Ha! My rapier is dipped in dry water! Its merciless tip turns the one into all, and the all into one. So! Thus I transmute you! So! So! So!—"

His afternoon schedule was a busy one. Vologaz Sar was the first caller, his majesty the Pontifex's official delegate at the Castle: a cheerful, airy-spirited man of late middle years, fair-skinned and with a look of fleshy good health about him, who seemed delighted to have escaped the gloomy depths of the Labyrinth after a lifetime in Pontifical service. He came originally from Sippulgar, that sunny city of golden buildings on Alhanroel's distant Aruachosian coast, and like many southerners he had an easy, genial manner that Septach Melayn found pleasing. But today Vologaz Sar seemed troubled to some extent by Lord Prestimion's continued absence from the Castle. He expressed puzzlement over the fact that a newly seated Coronal would spend so much time traveling about, and so little at his own capital.

"I understand Lord Prestimion has gone east this time," he said. "That seems quite unusual. A Coronal would want to show himself to his people, yes, but who is there to show himself to in the east-country?"

They were drinking the smooth blue wine of the south-land, which its makers rarely exported to other provinces. It had been very kind of Vologaz Sar to bring such a delightful gift, thought Septach Melayn. The Pontifical delegate was a man of taste and distinction in every respect. His manner of dress showed as much. Vologaz Sar had chosen impeccable garb, a long cotton robe of brilliant white, elegantly embroidered with abstract patterns in the amusing Stoienzar style, over a rich undertunic of dark purple silk, and hose of a paler purple hue. A black velvet mantle lay across his shoulders. The golden Labyrinth emblem on his breast that marked him as a member of the Pontifical staff was decorated with three tiny emeralds of great depth of color. Septach Melayn found the total effect greatly satisfactory. Such attention to detail of dress always drew his admiration.

He refreshed their bowls and said, choosing his words with care, "His journey east is not exactly a formal processional. He has special business of a delicate kind to handle there."

The Pontifical delegate nodded gravely. "Ah. I see." But did he? How could he? Vologaz Sar was much too polished, of course, to pursue the inquiry in that direction. He simply said, after just the slightest pause: "And when he returns, what then? Does other special business await him that will take him elsewhere again?"

"None that I've been told of. Is it a source of great concern to the Pontifex that Lord Prestimion's been away so much?"

"Great concern?" said Vologaz Sar lightly. "Oh, no, great concern is not quite the right phrase."

"Well, then—?"

For a moment or two there was silence. Septach Melayn sat back, smiling, and waited impassively for his majesty's representative to come to his point.

After a time Vologaz Sar said, with a minute but perceptible intensifying of tone, "Has the notion of Lord Presti-

mion's making a trip to the Labyrinth to offer his respects
to his imperial majesty been discussed yet?"

"We have it on our agenda, yes."

"With any specific date in mind, may I ask?"

"None as yet," said Septach Melayn.

"Ah. I see." Vologaz Sar took a reflective sip of his wine.
"It's custom of long standing, of course, for the new Coronal
to pay a call on the Pontifex fairly early in his reign. To
receive his formal blessing, and to set forth whatever legislative plans he may have in mind. Perhaps this has been
overlooked, it being so many years since the last change
among the Powers of the Realm." Yet again his tone
deepened and darkened ever so slightly, though it remained
cordial and light. "The Pontifex is the senior monarch, after
all, and, of course, is in a technical sense the father of the
Coronal as well. —I understand from Duke Oljebbin that
Confalume has been heard lately to remark on the fact that
he's had rather little contact of any sort with Lord Prestimion thus far."

Septach Melayn began to comprehend.

"Is his majesty displeased, would you say?"

"That might be too strong a term. But he is certainly
perplexed. He has the greatest affection for Lord Prestimion,
you understand. I scarcely need point out that when he was
Coronal he looked upon Prestimion virtually as a son. And
now, to be so completely ignored—the constitutional issues
aside, you understand, it's a matter of simple courtesy, is it
not?"

All very pleasantly put. But they were verging into
regions of high diplomacy, Septach Melayn saw. He refreshed the wine-bowls once again.

"No discourtesies are intended, I assure you. The Coronal's had certain unusually difficult matters to deal with here
at the outset of his reign. He felt that it was necessary to
address them immediately, before allowing himself the pleasure of the ceremonial visit to his imperial father the Pontifex."

"Matters so difficult that he chooses not even to bring
them to the Pontifex's attention? They are supposed to be

ruling jointly, as of course you are aware." It was beyond question a rebuke, but uttered very blandly.

"I'm not in a position to offer illumination here," said Septach Melayn, studiedly matching blandness with blandness, though he understood that combat on the highest level was under way. "This is a matter between Lord Prestimion and the Pontifex. —His majesty is well, I take it?"

"Quite well, yes. He's remarkably vigorous for a man of his years. I think Lord Prestimion can expect a lengthy reign as Coronal before his own time of succession to the Labyrinth arrives."

"The Coronal will be overjoyed to hear that. He feels the greatest fondness for his majesty."

Vologaz Sar's posture shifted in a way that signaled that they were entering the crux of the matter, though there was no further alteration in the honeyed tone of his voice. "I will tell you in all confidence, Septach Melayn, that the Pontifex has been in something of a grim mood these days. I could not tell you why: he seems unable to explain it himself. But he prowls the imperial sector of the Labyrinth in apparent confusion, as though he's never seen the place before. He sleeps badly. I'm told that he brightens greatly when told that he has visitors, but then shows obvious disappointment when the visitors are brought to him, as though he's perpetually expecting someone who never arrives. I'm not necessarily implying that that person is Lord Prestimion. The whole hypothesis is pure guesswork. Obviously it wouldn't be reasonable for him to expect the Coronal to arrive without prior notice. It may simply be that the move from the Castle to the Labyrinth has depressed the Pontifex. After forty years as Coronal, living up here in the bright splendor of the Castle amid crowds of high lords and courtiers, suddenly to find oneself forced into the Labyrinth's dark depths—well, he'd not be the first Pontifex to feel the strain of that. And Confalume such a hearty, outgoing man, as well. He's changed enormously in just these few months."

"A visit from Lord Prestimion might cheer him, then, do you think?"

"No question of it," said Vologaz Sar.

Septach Melayn proffered the last of the blue wine, and he and his guest toasted one another graciously.

The visit was plainly ending, and it had been altogether amiable throughout. But no ambiguities lurked behind Vologaz Sar's suave politeness. Prestimion had been avoiding Confalume—had since the day of his accession been running the government, in fact, as though he were sole monarch of the world—and Confalume was aware of it, and was annoyed. And now commanded—that was the only word, commanded—Prestimion to get himself down to the Labyrinth post-haste and bend his knee to the senior monarch as the law required.

Prestimion was not going to be pleased about that. Confalume, Septach Melayn knew, was the one person in all the world whom Prestimion did not want to face.

Septach Melayn well understood—and Prestimion, when he returned, would also, though Confalume himself did not—what process must be going on in Confalume's mind these days. Prestimion's deliberate shirking of his ceremonial duties at the Labyrinth was only a secondary issue. The visitors for whom Confalume unconsciously longed, and whose perpetual non-arrival brought him such incomprehensible distress, were Thismet and Korsibar, the children of his blood, the children of whose very existence he no longer had any knowledge. Their absence somehow throbbed in him like the pulsations of an amputated limb.

It was a strange kind of misery, and one that would wring Prestimion's heart. Prestimion had scarcely been the cause of the deaths of Korsibar and Thismet in the civil war—their dooms were something that they had brought upon themselves—but beyond any doubt it was Prestimion who had stolen Confalume's memories of his lost son and daughter from him, a theft that Prestimion must surely look upon as a deed of a fairly monstrous sort, and it was that guilty awareness that led Prestimion now to keep his distance from the sad old man that the once-great Confalume had become.

Well, there was no help for it, Septach Melayn thought. All acts have consequences that can never be indefinitely avoided; and Prestimion must live with the thing he had brought about. It was impossible for him to stay away from the Labyrinth forever. Confalume was Pontifex and Prestimion was Coronal and it was high time that the rituals of their relationship were properly observed.

"I'll convey all that you've said today to Lord Prestimion as soon as he returns," said Septach Melayn, as he showed the Pontifical delegate to the door.

"You have his majesty's gratitude for that."

"And you'll have mine," said Septach Melayn, "if you'll share one bit of information with me in return."

Vologaz Sar looked uncertain and just a trifle alarmed. "And that is—?"

Septach Melayn smiled. One could focus on matters of high politics only so long. He was determined to put the tensions of this meeting behind him as quickly as he could. "The name of the merchant," he said, "who provided you with the fabric for that delightful robe."

Two more appointments remained on his afternoon calendar, and then he was free.

The first was with Akbalik, whom Prestimion, just before his departure for the east-country, had named as a special emissary to far Zimroel, with the thought of posting a reliable man in Ni-moya to look out for signs of unrest among the followers of Dantirya Sambail. Akbalik was ready now to begin his journey. He had come to the Coronal's office today so that Septach Melayn, as regent, could sign his official papers of rank.

Somewhat to Septach Melayn's surprise, Akbalik had the new knight-initiate Dekkeret with him, the big, husky protege whom Prestimion had discovered during his trip to Normork. Evidently this was Dekkeret's first visit to this suite of royal power, for he looked about in undisguised wonder at the magnificent central room, the great palisander desk, the huge window looking out into the infinite sky, the marvelous inlaid patterns of rare woods that formed a huge starburst pattern in the floor.

Septach Melayn threw Akbalik an interrogatory frown.

No one had told him that Akbalik would be bringing Dekkeret here. Akbalik said, with a gesture toward the young man, "I'd like to take him with me to Zimroel. Do you think the Coronal would mind?"

Wickedly Septach Melayn said, "Ah, have you two become such good friends so soon?"

Akbalik did not seem amused. "It's nothing like that, and you know it, Septach Melayn."

"What is it, then? Is the boy in need of a holiday already? He's only begun his training here."

"This would be part of his training," said Akbalik. "He's asked if he could accompany me, and I think it might be a good thing for him. It's healthy for a young initiate to acquire some understanding of what it's really like out there beyond Castle Mount, you know. To experience an ocean voyage, to get a feel for the true size of the world. To see such a spectacular place as Ni-moya, also. And to observe how the machinery of the government actually works across such immense distances as we have to deal with."

Turning toward Dekkeret, Septach Melayn said, "Immense distances, yes. Do you realize, boy, that you'll be away nine months, maybe a year? Can you spare that much time from your studies, do you think?"

"Lord Prestimion said in Normork that I was to have accelerated training. A trip like this would surely accelerate it, sir."

"Yes. I suppose it would." Septach Melayn shrugged. Would Prestimion mind, he wondered, if the boy were to vanish into Zimroel for a year? How was he supposed to know? For the thousandth time he cursed Prestimion for having loaded all this decision-making on him. Well, it had been Prestimion's idea to make him regent: so be it, he must act as he saw fit. Why not let the boy go? It would be on Akbalik's head, not his. And Akbalik was right: it was always useful for a young man to learn something of the real world.

Dekkeret was staring at him in earnest supplication. Septach Melayn found something charmingly innocent and sweet about that eager imploring look. He could remember

a time when he had been eager and earnest himself, long
ago, before he had chosen instead to mask himself in an air
of lazy debonair frivolity that by now was no mask, but the
very essence of his character. As he looked at the boy it
was easy enough to see those qualities of seriousness and
strength that had attracted Prestimion's interest.

So be it, he thought. Let him go to Zimroel.

"Very well. Your papers are ready, Akbalik. I'm adding
the name of the knight-initiate Dekkeret here—so—and in-
itialing the page."

Already he found himself envying the boy. To get away
from the Castle—to go roving off into the far regions of the
realm—to escape all this politicking for a while and get the
good fresh air of some other place into your lungs—!

He glanced toward Dekkeret and said, "And allow me,
if you will, to offer a small suggestion. If you're not kept
too busy in Ni-moya all the time, you and Akbalik should
allow yourself a little excursion up north into the Khyntor
Marches while you're over there, and do a bit of steetmoy-
hunting. —You know about steetmoy, don't you, boy?"

"I've seen garments made from their fur, yes."

"Wearing a stole made of steetmoy fur's not quite the
same thing as looking a living steetmoy in the eye. Most
dangerous wild animal in the world, so far as I know, the
steetmoy. Beautiful thing: that thick fur, those blazing eyes.
Went hunting them myself, once, the time Prestimion and I
went to Zimroel. You hire yourself some professional hunters in Ni-moya and you head far up north, into the
Marches—cold, snowy place, like nothing you've ever seen,
all misty forests and wild lakes and a sky like an iron plate,
and you track down a pack of steetmoy, not an easy thing,
white animals against the white ground, and go for them at
close range, a poniard in one hand and a machete in the
other—"

The boy's eyes were aglow with excitement. But Akbalik
seemed less delighted.

"You were worried, I thought, that he would be skimping
on his training by going with me to Zimroel. Now, suddenly,
you've got him running up to Khyntor and chasing after

steetmoy in the snow. Oh, my friend, you never can manage to be serious very long, can you?"

Septach Melayn reddened. He had, he realized, allowed himself to be carried away. "That will be part of his training too," he said huffily, and stamped his seal onto Akbalik's papers. "Here. A good journey to you both. And let him go to Khyntor for a week, Akbalik," he added, as they went out. "What harm could it do?"

Prince Serithorn of Samivole was the only one left for him to see, now, and then he could go to the gymnasium over in the east wing for his daily late-afternoon fencing-match with one of the officers of the guard. Septach Melayn practiced a different weapon each day—rapier, two-handed sword, basket-hilt saber, Narabal small-sword, singlestick baton, Ketheron pike—and each with a different partner, for he learned a man's basic moves so quickly that it was a dull business for him to fence with anyone more than two or three times. His opponent today was a new young guards-man from Tumbrax, Mardileek by name, said to be a good man with the saber, who came with a recommendation from Duke Spalirises himself. But there was Serithorn to deal with first.

The prince had added himself to Septach Melayn's appointments list only that morning. Ordinarily one could not get to see the regent on such short notice; but Serithorn, as the senior peer of the realm at the Castle, was an exception to that rule as to all others. Besides, Septach Melayn, like everyone else, found Serithorn a congenial and appealing character, and never mind that after much to-ing and fro-ing he had eventually thrown his support to Korsibar in the civil war. It was hard to hold a grudge against Serithorn for anything for long. And the war was not even ancient history, now: it was no history at all.

Usually Serithorn was late for appointments. But today, for some reason, he was precisely on time. Septach Melayn wondered why. As usual, Serithorn was simply and unostentatiously dressed, a plain russet cloak of many folds over a somber purple tunic, and simple leather boots lined with red fur. The wealthiest private citizen of Majipoor did not need to trumpet his wealth. Where another man might have chosen as his headgear some showy wide-brimmed deep-felted hat trimmed with metal braid and scarlet tiruvyn feathers, Prince Serithorn was content to wear an odd stiff-sided yellow cap, high and square, that a Liiman sausage-peddler would have spurned. He took it off now and tossed it on the desk—the Coronal's desk—as casually as if he were in his own sitting-room.

"I understand that my nephew's just been here. A splendid fellow, Akbalik. A credit to the family. Prestimion's shipping him off to Zimroel, I hear. Whatever for, I wonder?"

"Simply to get some notion of how the Zimroelu feel about their new Coronal, I'd imagine. It's a good idea, wouldn't you say, for Prestimion to keep himself up to date on the general run of sentiment over there?"

"Yes. Yes, I suppose it is." Then, indicating the tall stack of documents piled by the edge of the desk, Serithorn said, "You've been working hard, haven't you, for such a light-hearted fellow? Laboring away mightily at all this dreary paper! I commend you for your newfound industriousness, Septach Melayn."

"The compliment's undeserved, Prince Serithorn. These documents are all still in need of attention from me."

"But nevertheless you'll give it, I'm sure you will! Only a matter of time. —How very admirable you are, Septach Melayn! I have, you know, a light spirit very much like yours; but here you are toiling heroically at your regency day after day, whereas I've never been able to force myself to deviate into seriousness for any span of time longer than three minutes running. My congratulations are sincere:"

Septach Melayn shook his head. "You overestimate me, I think. And much underestimate yourself. Some men are secretly foolish, and conceal their flaws behind an air of great gravity, or much bluster. But you are secretly deep, affecting frivolity. And have had vast influence in the realm.

I happen to know that it was you who induced Lord Confalume to pick Prestimion as his successor."

"I? Ah, you're deceived in that, my friend. Confalume spotted Prestimion's ability all on his own. I merely added my approval when he asked." Serithorn lifted an eyebrow. A blithe smile crossed his smooth face. —"Secretly deep, you think? Flattering of you to say so, very flattering. But entirely untrue. You may have secret depths, dear friend: quite likely you do. But I'm frivolous through and through. Always have been, always will be." Serithorn's wide, clear eyes contemplated Septach Melayn in a mordant way that seemed to negate everything that he had just said. There were layers upon unfathomable layers of wiliness here, thought Septach Melayn.

But he refused to offer any challenge. With an ingratiating little laugh he replied, "The fact is, I think, that each of us overestimates the other. You're frivolous through and through, you say? Very well: I consent to accept your opinion of yourself. As for me, I propose to stipulate that I'm a mere idle-spirited mocker, lazy and gay of heart, overly fond of silks and pearls and fine wines, whose only worthwhile qualities are a certain skill at swordplay and a deep loyalty to his friends. Can we agree with that evaluation also? Do we have a treaty on this, Serithorn?"

"We do. You and I are of one sort, Septach Melayn. Piffling frothy triflers, both of us. And so you have my deepest sympathy for having been forced by Prestimion to cope with all this bureaucratic nonsense. Your soul's far too sprightly and buoyant for this sort of work."

"This is true. Next time the Coronal goes traveling, I'll go with him and you can be regent."

"Me? But I invoke our treaty! I'm no more qualified for sitting behind that desk than you are. No, no, no, let some more solid citizen of the realm have the post. If I had wanted to do the sweaty work of a Coronal, I'd have seen to it long ago that I had the glory and homage that goes with it. But never for a moment did I crave the crown, Septach Melayn, and that mountain of papers on this desk is exactly the reason why."

He was, Septach Melayn knew, being completely serious
now. Serithorn was by no means the lightweight he claimed
to be; but he had ever been content to exercise his will at
one remove, standing close to the throne but never seated
upon it. The blood of many kings ran in his veins: no one
in the world had loftier lineage, not that that in itself could
have made him Coronal. Intelligence and shrewdness were
different matters, though, and Serithorn had those in abundance. He was of kingly quality in all respects but one,
which was his utter and wholehearted desire not to bear the
burden of power.

According to Prestimion, who had heard the story from
his mother, Lord Prankipin decades ago had actually asked
Serithorn to be his successor as Coronal when he became
Pontifex, but Serithorn had said, "No, no, give the job to
Prince Confalume." The tale had the ring of truth to it. There
could be no other reason why Serithorn had not had the
throne. And here they all were, so many years later, and
Confalume was Pontifex himself after a long and splendid
run as Coronal and Serithorn had never been anything more
than a private citizen, welcome in all the halls of power but
wielding none himself, a cheerful, easy-hearted man whose
unlined features and easy stance made him appear twenty
or thirty years younger than he really was.

"Well," said Septach Melayn, after a time. "Now that
that's settled, will you tell me whether there's some special
reason for this visit? Or is it purely social?"

"Oh, your company's pleasant enough, Septach Melayn.
But this, I think, is a matter of business." A quick lowering
of his brows furrowed Serithorn's forehead, and a slight
darkening was evident in his tone. —"Could you be kind
enough to supply me, do you think, with some sort of sum-
mary of whatever it is that has been taking place in recent
months between Prestimion and the Procurator of Ni-
moya?"

Septach Melayn felt a band of muscles go tight across
his midsection. A blunt question like that was very far indeed from Serithorn's customary brand of frivolity. Caution
seemed appropriate.

"I think," he said, "that you had better take that matter up with Prestimion himself."

"I would do just that, if only Prestimion happened to be here. But he's chosen to go wandering around interminably in the east-country, hasn't he? And you sit here in his place. —I've got no desire to be troublesome, Septach Melayn. In fact, I'm trying to be helpful. But I lack so much basic information that I can't properly evaluate the nature of the crisis, if 'crisis' is the proper term for what we have. For instance, during the coronation week a story was going around that Dantirya Sambail was, for some reason, being held prisoner in the Sangamor tunnels."

"I could provide you with an official denial of that, I suppose."

"You could, but don't put yourself to the bother. I had the story direct from Navigorn, who said Prestimion had made him the Procurator's special custodian. Navigorn was pretty puzzled about that assignment, I can tell you. As were we all. —Shall we agree to accept it as a legitimate fact that Prestimion was in fact keeping Dantirya Sambail in the tunnels during the coronation and shortly afterward as well, presumably for some good and proper reason about which I am not at present making inquiries?"

"Be it so stipulated, Serithorn."

"Good. Note that I used the past tense. Was keeping. The Procurator's free now, isn't he?"

"I do wish you'd address all these questions to Prestimion," said Septach Melayn uncomfortably.

"Yes, I'm sure that you do. —Please, Septach Melayn. Stop trying to parry me at every step: this isn't a duel. The fact is that Dantirya Sambail has escaped. And Prestimion's somewhere between here and the Great Sea, yes, he and Gialaurys and Abrigant and a whole troop of soldiers, wandering around in the hope of recapturing him. Yes. Yes. I know that that's so, Septach Melayn. No need to deny it. Now: forget that I ever asked you for details of the quarrel between Prestimion and the Procurator. Only confirm for me that there is a quarrel. They are in fact bitter enemies, is that not so?"

"Yes," Septach Melayn said, with a nod and a slow sigh of resignation. "They are."

"Thank you." Serithorn took a folded paper from his robe. "If Prestimion hasn't learned it already, I think it would be helpful to him for you to get word to him that he's almost certainly looking in the wrong place."

"Is he, now?" said Septach Melayn, eyes widening, though only for a moment.

Serithorn smiled. "I am, you know, a landowner of some considerable extent. I constantly receive reports from my estate managers in various parts of the world. This one comes from a certain Haigin Hartha, in Bailemoona city in the province of Balimoleronda. A very odd business, actually. A party of strange men—Haigin Hartha doesn't say how many—was discovered poaching the gambilak herds on my lands outside Bailemoona. When my gamekeeper objected, one of the poachers told him that the meat was wanted on behalf of Dantirya Sambail, the Procurator of Nimoya, who was making a grand processional in this region. Another of the poachers—am I boring you, Septach Melayn?"

"Hardly."

"You seemed inattentive."

"Thoughtful, rather," said Septach Melayn.

"Ah. To continue, then: another of the poachers then struck the first one in the face, and said to my gamekeeper that the first man's story was completely untrue, a sheer fantasy that the gamekeeper should wipe from his mind immediately, and that they were simply taking the meat on their own account. He offered my man fifty crowns in payment, and, since the alternative appeared to be to be murdered on the spot, the gamekeeper accepted the offer. The poachers went off with their catch. Later in the day, Haigin Hartha—he is my estate manager in Bailemoona, you will recall—heard from a friend that someone with the highly distinctive features of Dantirya Sambail had been seen that morning traveling with a group of men on the outskirts of Bailemoona city. My manager's friend wondered whether Haigin Hartha might be expecting a formal visit from the

Procurator at our estate, which, as you might expect, Haigin Hartha found a very unsettling idea. And then, no more than ten minutes later, the gamekeeper came in with his account of the poachers and the bribe. What do you make of all this, Septach Melayn?"

"It all seems clear enough. I wonder about the poacher who struck the other one, though. Whether he might have been tall and lean, with a death's-head sort of face, all angles and planes and mean murderous dark eyes."

"The Procurator's poison-taster, is that the man you're speaking of? A disagreeable piece of work, that one."

"Mandralisca, yes. He'd be traveling with Dantirya Sambail. —Is there more to the story?"

"Nothing else. Haigan Hartha concludes his message by saying that he never heard from the Procurator one way or the other about a visit, and inquires as to whether he is supposed to expect one. Naturally, he is not. Why, I wonder, would a Procurator of Ni-moya be making a grand processional through Balimoleronda province, or any other place in Alhanroel?"

"Grand processional's the wrong term, of course. He's simply traveling privately through Balimoleronda on his way back from the Castle to Zimroel, I suppose."

"From his imprisonment at the Castle?" asked Serithorn mildly. "He is, am I to understand, a fugitive on the run?"

"Terms like 'imprisonment' and 'fugitive' are ones that I wish you'd reserve for your conversations with Prestimion. But I can tell you, at least, that the Coronal is indeed trying to locate Dantirya Sambail. And, since Bailemoona is, as I recall, south of Castle Mount, Prestimion's evidently not going to find him by going due east. I thank you on his behalf. Your report has been very useful."

"I do try to be of help."

"You have been. I'll see to it that the Coronal is told of all this as quickly as possible." Rising to his full considerable height, Septach Melayn stretched first his arms and then his legs, and said to Serithorn, "You'll forgive me, I hope, for seeming restless. This has been a taxing day for me. Are there any other matters for us to discuss?"

"I think not."

"I'm to the gymnasium, then, to work off the day's stresses by belaboring some hapless new guardsman from Tumbrax with my saber."

"A good idea. I'm going in that direction myself: shall I accompany you?"

They went out together. Serithorn, ever the soul of affability, provided Septach Melayn with a series of diverting gossipy tidbits as they made their way through the maze of the Inner Castle, past such ancient structures as the Vildivar Balconies and Lord Arioc's Watchtower and Stiamot Keep, toward the Ninety-Nine Steps that led downward into the surrounding regions of the great amorphous conglomeration that was the Castle.

Their route brought them after a while near the awesomely unsightly pile of black stone that Prankipin, early in his days as Coronal, had inflicted on the Castle to serve as the office of the Ministers of the Treasury. As they approached it Septach Melayn caught sight of a curiously ill-matched pair coming toward the building from the opposite direction: a tall, strikingly handsome dark-haired woman, accompanied by a much shorter and stockier man who was elaborately overdressed in what seemed like a glittering parody of appropriate court costume, all sequins and flash and grotesquely intricate brocaded fabric. He, too, was of striking appearance, but in a very different way—inordinately ugly, with his most notable feature being the carefully coiffed mountain of silver hair rising upright from his wide forehead.

It was no great task for Septach Melayn to recognize these two instantly: they were the financier Simbilon Khayf, no doubt on his way toward some maneuver of chicanery involving the Treasury, and his daughter Varaile. The last time he had seen them, some months back, it had been in Simbilon Khayf's grand mansion in Stee, that time when he had been decked out in the coarse linen robes of a merchant, and had worn a brown wig and a false beard over his own golden hair, and had played the role of a country bumpkin to help Prestimion penetrate the mystery of that other and

insane Lord Prestimion who was harassing the shipping of
Stee. Septach Melayn was more grandly dressed today, in
his true capacity of High Counsellor of the Realm. But after
all the other complicated transactions of this day, he had no
wish now to deal with the coarse and vulgar Simbilon
Khayf. "Shall we turn to the left here?" he said quietly to
Serithorn.

Too late. They were still fifty feet from Simbilon Khayf
and his daughter, but the banker had spied them already and
was shouting his greetings.

"Prince Serithorn! By all that's holiest, Prince Serithorn,
how splendid it is to see you again! And look! Look, Varaile, this is the great Septach Melayn, the High Counsellor
himself! Gentlemen! Gentlemen! What a pleasure!" Simbilon Khayf came rushing toward them so hastily that he
nearly tripped over his own brocaded robe. "You surely
must meet my daughter, gentlemen! It's her first visit to the
Castle, and I promised her the sight of greatness, but I never
imagined that we would so swiftly encounter this evening a
pair of lords of the magnitude and significance of Serithorn
of Samivole and the High Counsellor Septach Melayn!"

He thrust Varaile forward. Her eyes rose, up and up, toward those of Septach Melayn, and a little gasp of surprise
escaped her lips. Softly she said, "Ah, but I believe we have
already met."

An awkward moment. "It is not the case, my lady. There
must be some mistake!"

Her eyes did not leave his. And now she smiled. "I think
not," she said. "No. No. I know you, my lord."

4

"AND THERE WE WERE," Septach Melayn said, "right out in
front of Lord Prankipin's Treasury, her and me and Serithorn and that impossible simpering father of hers. Of course
I denied any possibility that she and I could have had a
previous meeting. It seemed the only thing to do."

"And how did she react to that?" asked Prestimion.

They were in Prestimion's private apartments in Lord Thraym's Tower. It was Prestimion's first day back from the east country. The long and fruitless journey had left him very weary; and he had barely had time to bathe and change his garments before Septach Melayn had come rushing in with his report on all that had taken place here in his absence. What a lot of stuff it was, too! This Hjort wizard of Abrigant's who claimed to be able to turn trash into precious metal, for one, and then the alleged sighting of Dantirya Sambail down by Bailemoona, and Confalume apparently complaining that his Coronal was snubbing him, and new tales of widespread unrest and cases of greatly disturbed minds in this city and that.

Prestimion was hungry for more details on all of those things right away. And yet Septach Melayn seemed to be obsessed with this trivial episode involving the daughter of Simbilon Khayf.

"She knew I was lying," he said. "That was easy enough to see. She kept staring at my eyes, and measuring my height against her own, and it was obvious that she was thinking, Where have I seen eyes like that before, and a man as tall and thin as this one is? Her mind could easily supply the wig and the false beard, and she'd have her answer. I thought for a moment she was going to hold her ground and insist that she knew me from somewhere. But her father, who may be coarse and vulgar but who's very far from stupid, realized what was about to happen and obviously didn't want his daughter to get involved in contradicting the High Counsellor to his face, and so he called her off. She was wise enough to take the hint."

"For the moment, yes. But she suspects the truth, and that's bound to lead to further complications."

"Oh, she doesn't just suspect the truth," said Septach Melayn lightly. He smiled and made a graceful little two-handed flourish of his wrists. Prestimion knew that gesture of Septach Melayn's very well. It meant that he had taken some unilateral action for which he was asking to be excused, but which he did not regret in any way. "I sent for her the next day and told her the tale of the whole masquerade straight out."

Prestimion's jaw gaped. "You did?"

"I had to. One simply can't lie to a woman of that quality, Prestimion. And in any case she definitely hadn't been fooled at all by my denials."

"You told her who your two companions were also, I suppose?"

"Yes."

"Oh, well done, Septach Melayn! Well done! What did she say, then, when she found out that she had entertained the Coronal of Majipoor, and the High Counsellor and the Grand Admiral too, in her father's sitting-room?"

"Say? A little murmur of surprise. Turned very red. Looked quite flustered. And, I think, also amused and rather pleased about it all."

"Was she, now? Amused! Pleased!" Prestimion rose and paced about, pausing by the window overlooking the airy bridge of shining pink agate, reserved for the Coronal's use alone, that led across the Pinitor Court to the royal offices and the adjacent ceremonial rooms of Inner Castle. "I wish I could say the same. But I tell you, Septach Melayn, I find nothing very agreeable about the thought that Simbilon Khayf has been made aware that I was secretly sniffing around in Stee wearing some kind of comic-opera disguise and pretending to be a thick-headed peddler of business machines. What sort of use, I wonder, is he going to put that bit of information to?"

"None, Prestimion. He doesn't know a thing about it, and he's not going to find out."

"No?"

"No. I made her promise not to tell her father a word."

"And she'll keep that promise, of course."

"I think she will. I gave her a good price for her silence. She and Simbilon Khayf are going to be invited to the next court levee and formally presented to you. At which time he'll be decorated with the Order of Lord Havilbove, or some such meaningless honor."

A croaking sound of disbelief escaped from Prestimion.

"Are you serious? You're actually asking me to permit that loathsome clown to set foot in the royal chambers? To let him come before the Confalume Throne?"

"I am always serious, Prestimion, in my way. Her lips now are sealed. The Coronal and his friends were having a little adventure in Stee, and no one needs to know about it, and she will abide by her part of the agreement if you abide by yours. As you sit upon the throne they'll approach you reverently and make starbursts to you, and you'll smile and graciously acknowledge their homage, and that will be that. For the rest of his life Simbilon Khayf will glow with rapture over having been received at court."

"But how can I—"

"Listen to me, Prestimion. It's a shrewd arrangement on three counts. The first is that you want our prank in Stee covered up, and this will accomplish that. The second is that Simbilon Khayf has been lending money to half the princes of the Castle, and sooner or later one of them looking for easier terms or an extension of a loan is going to feel impelled to wangle a court invitation on his behalf, which you will grant, even though you think Simbilon Khayf's a despicable boor, because the request will come from somebody influential and useful like Fisiolo or Belditan or my cousin Dembitave. This way, at least, you give Simbilon Khayf the access to court that he's bound to get anyway, eventually, under terms that are advantageous to yourself."

Prestimion threw Septach Melayn a black look. But Septach Melayn's argument had some logic to it, he conceded grudgingly, repugnant though it all was to him. —"And the third count? You said there were three."

"Well, you want to see Varaile again, don't you? Here's your chance. She might as well be a million miles away, living down there in Stee. You may never visit Stee again in your life. But if she's right here in residence at the Castle as one of the royal ladies-in-waiting, a position which you could readily offer her while chatting with her after the throne-room reception—"

"Wait a moment," said Prestimion. "You move along a

little too quickly, my friend. What makes you think I'm so eager to see her again?"

"But you do, isn't that so? You found her very attractive while we were in Stee."

"How would you know that?"

Septach Melayn laughed. "I'm not blind to such things, Prestimion. Or deaf, either. You couldn't stop staring at her. The sound of your pupils dilating could be heard halfway across the room."

"This is exceedingly impertinent, Septach Melayn. She's a good-looking woman, yes. That's obvious to anyone, even you. But for you to leap from there to the assumption that— that I'm—"

His voice trailed off into an incoherent sputter.

"Ah, Prestimion," said Septach Melayn, smiling warmly at him from across the room. "Prestimion, Prestimion, Prestimion!" The look in his eyes was sly and knowing, and his tone was certainly not that of subject to monarch, nor even that of a High Counsellor to the Coronal he served, but the gentle, intimate one used between two friends who had seen in many a midnight together.

Prestimion felt the light-hearted rebuke. There was no way he could refute it. For he had stared at Varaile, that time in Stee, with intense fascination. Had responded to her beauty with an undeniable quiver of approbation. Of desire, even.

Had dreamed of her, and more than once.

"We are getting into a region," said Prestimion after a considerable while, "where I'm uncertain of the meaning of my own feelings. I pray you, Septach Melayn, put this subject aside for now. What we need to discuss is this tale of Serithorn's that has to do with the whereabouts of Dantirya Sambail."

"Navigorn will give you the latest news of that. He's on his way over right now. —You'll permit Simbilon Khayf and his daughter to be received from the throne? I gave my word you would, you know."

"Yes, Septach Melayn! Yes. Yes. So be it. Where's Navigorn, now?"

*   *   *

"This is the district where he's most likely to be," said
Navigorn. He had brought a map with him to the meeting,
a hemiglobe of fine white porcelain overpainted in blue,
yellow, pink, violet, dull green, and brown to indicate major
geographical features. It was the sort of map that was
equipped to display special information in bright patterns of
light, and Navigorn brought that function to life now with
a touch of his hand.

Points of red fire, connected by lines of brilliant green,
sprang up on its face along the lower quadrant of the continent of Alhanroel. "Here's Bailemoona, south of the Labyrinth and very slightly to the east," he said, indicating the
brightest of the red dots. "The sighting there was incontrovertible. Not only was someone who looks just like Dantirya
Sambail seen in the vicinity of Serithorn's estate around the
time of the game-poaching, but one of the Procurator's men
told Serithorn's gamekeeper that the meat he was stealing
was being taken for the benefit of Dantirya Sambail."

"There were plenty of incontrovertible sightings of him
in the east country, too," Abrigant pointed out. "All over
the place, as a matter of fact. They were all planted by the
Procurator's sorcerers to fool us. What makes you think that
this isn't the same wizardy sort of stuff?"

Navigorn merely scowled. Prestimion looked in appeal
toward Maundigand-Klimd, who said, "There's no question
the Procurator was in the east country for a time. I believe
that he actually was seen by villagers in the Vrambikat district. But most of the reports that drew us onward were
illusions born of enchantments and dreams, not genuine eye-
witness sightings. While we ran hither and thither after
them, he was doubling back into central Alhanroel, leaving
us to chase fantasies of his making all over the wilderness
area. The Bailemoona report, I think, is different: authentic."

Abrigant looked unconvinced. "This is assertion without
demonstration. You simply tell us that one set of reports
was illusion and this other one is real. But you offer no
proof."

It was the left head of the Su-Suheris that had spoken before. Now the other head said calmly, "I have a certain gift of second sight. The Bailemoona reports have the ring of truth to me, and so I choose to give them credence. You are not obligated to agree."

Abrigant began to make some grumbling reply; but Navigorn said, with a sharp note of testiness in his voice, "May I continue?" He traced a line with his hand over the illuminated places on the map. "There have been additional sightings, some of them more trustworthy than others—here, here, here, and here. You'll note that the general direction is southerly. That's the only sensible direction for him to go in anyway, because he's got nothing to his north or west except the desert that surrounds the Labyrinth, not a useful choice, and he wouldn't have anything to gain by going back into the east-country. But there's a clear line of march here that's taking him toward the southern coast."

"What cities are those?" Abrigant asked, indicating the red dots strung like glowing beads along the lines of green that stretched southward across the land.

"Ketheron up here," said Navigorn. "Then Arvyanda. This is Kajith Kabulon, where the rain never ceases falling. Once he makes his way through its jungles, he emerges on the southern coast, where he can get a ship heading toward Zimroel in any one of a hundred ports."

"Which are the main ones?" Gialaurys asked.

"Due south of the rain-forest country," Navigorn said, "we have Sippulgar, first. Continuing on westward along the coast from there, he would come to Maximin, Karasat, Gunduba, Slail, and Porto Gambieris—this, this, this, this, and this." He spoke in a brusque, commanding tone. He had prepared himself well for this meeting: a way of atoning, perhaps, for his negligence in allowing Dantirya Sambail to slip free in the first place. "Aside from Sippulgar, none of these has direct shipping connections with Zimroel, but in any of them, or their neighbors farther along the north shore of the Stoienzar peninsula, he could book a passage on a coasting vessel that would carry him up to Stoien city, to Treymone, even to Alaisor. In any of those he'd be able to arrange for the voyage across to Piliplok, and from there upriver to Ni-moya."

"No, not so easily," said Gialaurys. "You may recall that I've placed all ports from Stoien to Alaisor under close surveillance. There's no way that anyone as unusual-looking as he is could slip past even the dullest-witted customs official. We'll extend the blockade eastward now as far as Sippulgar. Farther, even, if you want me to, Prestimion."

Prestimion, studying the map with care, made no immediate reply. "Yes," he said, after a good deal of time had gone by. "I also think that we'd do well to set up military patrols along a line beginning just north of Bailemoona and running westward as far as Stoien city."

"That is to say, along the route of the klorbigan fence," said Septach Melayn, and began to laugh. "How very appropriate. For that's what he is, isn't he? Ugly as a klorbigan, and five times as dangerous!"

Prestimion and Abrigant began to laugh also. Gialaurys, looking vexed, said, "I pray you, what are you talking about here?"

"Klorbigans," said Prestimion, still chuckling, "are fat, lazy, clumsy burrowing animals of south-central Alhanroel with great pink noses and enormous hairy feet. They live on bark and tree roots, and in their native district they eat only certain wild species that are of no use to anyone but themselves. About a thousand years ago, though, they began migrating north into the areas where the farmers grow stajja and glein, and they discovered that they liked the taste of stajja tubers every bit as much as we do. Suddenly there were half a million klorbigans digging up the stajja crop all over the middle of Alhanroel. The farmers couldn't kill the beasts fast enough. Whoever was Coronal at that time finally hit on the idea of a special kind of fence that runs right along the middle of the continent. It's just a couple of feet high, so any animal that's even slightly less sluggish than a klorbigan can step right over it, but it goes down six or seven feet underground, which apparently keeps them from burrowing beneath it."

"Lord Kybris, it was, who built it," Septach Melayn said.

"Kybris, yes," said Prestimion. "Well, we'll build a klor-bigan fence of our own, a patrol line without any breaks in it, so that if Dantirya Sambail decides to swing around once again and go north, he'll be picked up in—" He paused in mid-sentence. "Navigorn? Navigorn, what's the matter?"

Everyone stared. Big black-bearded Navigorn had turned away suddenly from his map and was doubled into a crouch, head bowed and arms clutching his middle, as if in some terrible racking spasm of pain. After a moment he raised his head, and Prestimion saw that Navigorn's features were contorted into a horrifying grimace. Appalled, Prestimion signaled for Gialaurys and Septach Melayn, who were closest to him, to go to his aid. But Maundigand-Klimd acted first: the Su-Suheris lifted one hand and inclined his two heads toward each other, and something invisible passed between him and Navigorn, and within a moment the entire strange episode appeared to have ended. Navigorn was standing upright as though nothing at all had occurred, blinking the way one might after having dropped into an unexpected doze. His face was calm. —"Did you say something, Prestimion?"

"A very singular expression came over you, and I asked you what the matter was. It seemed you were having a seizure of some sort."

"I was? A seizure?" Navigorn looked bewildered. "But I have no recollection of any such thing." Then he brightened. "Ah! Then it must have happened again, without my knowing it!"

"Then this is something frequent with you?" asked Septach Melayn.

"It has occurred more than once," said Navigorn, looking a little sheepish now. Plainly he was abashed to be making this admission of weakness. But he plunged forward even so. "Along with great headaches, yes, that come and go suddenly, so that I think my skull will split open. And terrible dreams, very often. I have never had dreams of such a sort before."

"Will you tell us of them?" asked Prestimion gently.

It was a delicate thing, asking someone—a nobleman, a warrior at that—to reveal his dreams in such a group. But

Navigorn said unhesitatingly, "I am on a battlefield, again and again, a great muddy field where men are dying on all sides and streams of blood run underfoot. Who among us has ever fought a pitched battle, my lord? Who ever will, on this peaceful world? But I am there, armed and armored, laying about me with my sword, killing with every stroke. I kill strangers and I kill friends too, my lord."

"You kill me, perhaps? Septach Melayn?"

"No, not you. I don't know who they are who fall to my sword. They are not people whose faces I can identify when I awaken and think back upon my dream. But as I lie dreaming I know that I am killing dear friends, and it sickens me, my lord. It sickens me." Navigorn shivered, though the room was very warm. "I tell you, lordship, this dream comes to me over and over, sometimes three nights running, so that by now I fear closing my eyes at all."

"How long has this been going on?" Prestimion asked.

Navigorn said, shrugging, "Days? Weeks? It's not something I can easily reckon up. —May I be excused for a few minutes?"

Prestimion nodded. Flushed now and glossy with sweat, Navigorn went from the room. Prestimion said quietly to Septach Melayn, "Did you hear? A battle in which he kills his friends. This is one more thing for which I bear the guilt."

"My lord, what guilt there is in this is Korsibar's," said Septach Melayn.

But Prestimion merely shook his head. Grim thoughts assailed him. Yes, the battle itself where so many had died had been of Korsibar's making. Navigorn's baffling dreams, though, his spasms of agony, his inner confusion long after the event, all of that was part of the new madness, and who was responsible for that if not Prestimion himself? This madness was something that his sorcerers had conjured upon the world at his behest, though he had not known it would happen.

Abrigant broke suddenly into Prestimion's meditation while they waited for Navigorn to return. "Brother, will you

be going down yourself into the south-country to look for
the Procurator, as you went east?"

Prestimion was startled at that, because the thought had
only just been forming in his own mind. But they were of
one flesh, he and Abrigant, and often of the same mind as
well. He said with a grin, "I might very well do that. It will
need discussion before the full Council, of course. But his
majesty the Pontifex has requested my presence at the Labyrinth, and he is right to so request; and as long as I've gone
that far south, I'll probably continue on toward Stoien in
the hope of finding—"

"You speak of the full Council," said Septach Melayn.
"While Navigorn is out of the room, let me ask this, Prestimion: suppose some member of the Council—Serithorn,
say, or my cousin Dembitave—demands from you outright
to know why it is that Dantirya Sambail happens to be a
fugitive whom you're hunting from one end of Alhánroel to
another? What would you say to him, then?"

"Simply that he has given grave offense against the law
and against the person of the Coronal."

"And you will offer no explanatory details of any sort?"

"I remind you, Septach Melayn, he is Coronal," said Gialaurys irascibly. "He can do as he pleases."

"Ah, no, good friend," said Septach Melayn. "He is king,
yes, but not a tyrant absolute. He's subject to the decrees of
the Pontifex as are we all, and he is accountable in some
degree to the Council as well. Decreeing a great potentate
like Dantirya Sambail to be a criminal, and giving no reason
for it to his own Council—not even a Coronal can do that."

"You know why he must," Gialaurys said.

"Yes. Because there is one great fact that has been with-
held from all the world, excepting only the five of us who
are here, and Teotas who is not." And Septach Melayn nodded toward Maundigand-Klimd and Abrigant, the two late-
comers to the truth of what had happened that day at
Thegomar Edge. "But we get deeper and deeper into equiv-
ocation and evasion and downright lying the longer we
clutch that secret to our bosoms."

"Let it be, Septach Melayn," Prestimion said. "I have no

answers for these questions of yours, except to say that if the Council presses me too far on the subject of Dantirya Sambail's unspecified crimes, I will equivocate and evade. And, if necessary, lie. But I like none of this any better than you do. —And now Navigorn's coming back, so put an end to it."

Abrigant said, just as Navigorn was entering, "One further thing, brother: if you are going south into Aruachosia, I ask permission to accompany you part of the way."

"Only part?"

"There is the place called Skakkenoir, which we discussed not long ago, where one can recover useful metals from the stems and leaves of the plants that grow there. It's in the south, somewhere east of Aruachosia, perhaps even east of Vrist. While you hunt for Dantirya Sambail down there, I would go in search of Skakkenoir."

In some amusement Prestimion said, "I see that nothing will turn you from this quest. But the metal-bearing plants of Skakkenoir are a wild fantasy, Abrigant."

"Do we know that, brother? Allow me but to go and look."

Again Prestimion smiled. Abrigant was a relentless force. "Let's speak of this later, shall we, Abrigant? This is not the time. —Well, Navigorn, are you recovered? Here, have a bit of this wine. It'll soothe your soul. Now, as I was just about to say at the moment when Navigorn became ill: the Pontifex Confalume has reminded me that I am long overdue to call upon him in his new residence, and therefore—"

That evening, just the two of them dining alone in the Coronal's apartments, Septach Melayn said to Prestimion, "I see you wrestling with the matter of the great secret we keep, and I know how much anguish it gives you. How are we going to deal with this thing, Prestimion?"

They sat face-to-face in Prestimion's private dining-alcove, a seven-sided elevated room separated from its surroundings by an ascent of seven steps made of solid beams of black fire-oak, and bedecked by embroidered hangings a thousand years old, silks of many colors interwoven with gold and silver threads, that depicted the sports of hunting and hawking.

"If I had an answer for that," said Prestimion, "I would have given it to you this afternoon."

Septach Melayn stared for a time at the grilled kaspok in his plate, a rare delicacy—a white fish of the northern rivers, with meat as sweet as fresh berries—that he had scarcely tasted. He took a sip of his wine, and then drank again, not a sip this time. "You wanted to heal the world's pain, you told me, by wiping clean its memory of the war. To allow everyone a chance at a fresh start. Yes, all well and good. But this general madness that seems to have followed upon it—"

"I never anticipated that. I would never have called for the obliteration, if I could have seen that that would happen. You know that, Septach Melayn."

"Of course I do. Do you think I'm holding you at fault?"

"You seem to be."

"Not at all. Quite the opposite. The thing has happened, and I see you taking personal responsibility for it, and I see the effect that it's having on you. Well, I say once again: what's done is done. Leave off expending energy in guilt, and deal only with the challenges that we now face. You'll harm yourself otherwise. When Navigorn had that fit today—"

"Listen to me," Prestimion said. "I am responsible for the madness. And for everything else that has befallen the world since I took the throne, and everything that will happen throughout my life. I am Coronal, and that means, above all else, the burden of responsibility for the world's destiny. Which I am prepared to bear."

Septach Melayn attempted to speak, but Prestimion would not have it. "No. Hear me out. —Did you think I imagined that wearing the crown meant nothing more than grand processionals and splendid banquets and sitting here in the Castle's opulent rooms amidst ancient draperies and statuary? When I made the decision at Thegomar Edge to cleanse the world of all awareness of the war, it was a hasty thing, and I see now that it may have been a poor choice. But it was my own decision for which I had valid reasons at the time and which still seems to me not altogether a misguided idea. Does that sound like a statement of a man tormented by guilt?"

"You used the word yourself only today. Do you remember? 'This is one more thing for which I bear the guilt.' "

"A passing fancy, nothing more."

"Not so passing. And not such a fancy, Prestimion. I see into your soul as readily as any magus. Each new report of the madness racks you with pain."

"And if it does, is it worth ruining this fine dinner to tell me so? Pain fades with time. This kaspok was brought by swift couriers from the shores of Sintalmond Bay for your delectation and mine, and you allow that dainty piece of fish to turn to old leather in your plate while you belabor me with all this. Eat, Septach Melayn. Drink. I assure you, I'm ready to live with whatever discomfort the consequences of my decision at Thegomar Edge will bring me."

"All right," said Septach Melayn. "Permit me to come to my true point, then. If you must live in pain, why do you condemn yourself to bearing that pain alone?"

Prestimion looked at him without comprehension. "What are you talking about? How am I alone? I have you. I have Gialaurys. I have Maundigand-Klimd to offer me wisdom and consolation, both heads of him. I have my two sturdy brothers. I have—"

"Thismet will not come back to life, Prestimion."

Septach Melayn's bold words struck Prestimion like a slap across the face.

"What?" he asked, after a stunned moment. "Does the madness have hold of you, now, that you talk such idiocy? Yes, Thismet is dead, and always will be. But—"

"Are you going to spend the rest of your life in mourning for her?"

"No one but you, Septach Melayn, would dare speak so close."

"You know me well. And speak close I do." There was no way to deflect the singleminded force of Septach Melayn's intensely focused blue gaze. "You live in terrible solitude, Prestimion. There was a time, in those few weeks before Thegomar Edge, when you seemed full of new life and joy, as though some piece of you that long was missing had at last been put into place. That piece was Thismet. It was plain to us all at Thegomar Edge that we were destined to smash Korsibar's revolt that day, because you were our leader, and you had taken on an aura of invincibility. And so it befell; but in the hour of victory Thismet was slain, and nothing has been the same for you ever since."

"You tell me nothing that I do not already—"

Coronal or no, Septach Melayn coolly overspoke him. "Let me finish, Prestimion. Thismet died, and it was the end of the world for you. You wandered the battlefield as though you were the one that had lost the war, not as though you had fought your way through to the throne. You called for the memory-obliteration, as if you needed to hide the dark circumstances surrounding your ascent from all the universe, and who could speak against you in that moment? On the very day of your coronation I came upon you in despair in the Hendighail Hall, and you said things to me that no one would have believed if I had repeated them beyond us two: the kingship meant nothing to you, you said, except years and years of hard joyless work, and then some time in the grimness of the Labyrinth while waiting for your death. All this despair I credit to the loss of Thismet."

"And if that's so, what then?"

"Why, you have to put Thismet from your mind, Prestimion! By the Divine, man, don't you see that you must give her up? You'll always love her, yes, but loving a ghost brings chilly comfort. You need a living consort, one who will share the glories of your reign when all is going as it should, and hold you in her arms in the darkness of the other times."

Septach Melayn's fair skin was flushed now with the excitement of his own oratory. Prestimion stared at him in astonishment. This was presumption indeed. Septach Melayn was a uniquely privileged friend; only he in all the world could speak to him like this. But what he was saying now came near a breach of that privilege.

Containing himself with no little effort, Prestimion asked, "And you have a candidate in mind for the post, I suppose?"

"It happens that I do. The woman Varaile, of Stee."

"Varaile?"

"You love her, Prestimion. —Oh, don't start fulminating at me with protests! I saw it plain as day"

"I've met her just once, for no more than an hour, while going under an assumed name and wearing false whiskers."

"It took five seconds, no more, for the thing to happen between you. She struck as deep into your soul as a woodsman's axe, and struck such sparks from you that it lit the entire room."

"You think I'm made of metal within, then, that an axe will strike sparks against me? Or stone, perhaps."

"There could be no mistaking it: she for you, and you for her."

Prestimion found nothing here that he could deny. And yet it was outrageous to be invaded so intimately, even by Septach Melayn. He reached for the flask of wine that sat between them and held it contemplatively a long while with both his hands before refilling their bowls. At last he said, "What you propose is impossible. Varaile is a commoner, Septach Melayn, and her father is a gross and boorish beast."

"You wouldn't be marrying her father. —As for her, Coronals have married commoners many a time. I will get the history books and quote you examples, if you like. In any case, all aristocrats spring from common families, if only you go back far enough. I mean no offense, Prestimion, but is it not true that the princely family of Muldemar itself sprang from a line of farmers and vinters?"

"Ages ago, long before Lord Stiamot's day, Septach Melayn. By the time he began to build this Castle we were already ennobled."

"And you will hold your nose and make Simbilon Khayf a count or an earl—not the first grubby vulgar moneylender to be granted such a dignity, I think—and by so doing, you'll be able to make his daughter a queen."

It was a struggle now not to order Septach Melayn from the room. Prestimion fought for inner calmness, and found some, and his tone was a level one as he replied, "You amaze me, my friend. I concede the point that grieving forever over Thismet would be folly, and a Coronal does well to provide himself with a consort. But would you really marry me to a woman I've known less than an hour? The question of her common birth completely aside: I remind you again, Septach Melayn, that she and I are complete strangers to each other."

"Which can readily be repaired. She's in the Castle this very hour. Next week she comes before you at the royal reception. As has already been pointed out, if you ask her to join the ladies-in-waiting of the Castle, she'll have no way to refuse. And then there'll be ample opportunity for you and her to—"

The anger that had been not very far from the surface in Prestimion a moment before dissolved now in laughter. "Ah, I see it all! You've contrived the whole thing very carefully, haven't you, by dangling that offer of a royal reception before them?"

"It was necessary to buy her silence, or Simbilon Khayf would have known who those three merchants were who came to him for a loan that day in Stee."

"So you've said. I wonder if there might not have been some simpler way to manage all that. —In any case, Septach Melayn, let us make an end of this. I want you to understand that at the present time the idea of marriage is extremely distant from my mind. Is that clear?"

"All I ask is that you take the opportunity to get to know her a little better. Will you do that much?"

"It's important to you that I do, I see."

"It is."

'Well, then. For your sake, Septach Melayn, I will. But don't arouse any false hopes in her, my good friend. However much you may want me to, I'm not about to take a wife. If you yearn so much for there to be marriage festivities at the Castle, you can marry her."

"If you choose not to," said Septach Melayn airily, "then I will."

5

IT HAD BEEN LORD Confalume's custom, and Lord Prankipin's before him, to hold invitational royal receptions on the second Starday of each month. Various prominent citizens of the realm were brought before the Coronal and honored with a moment or two of his attention. Prestimion, though he found the custom fatuous and even distasteful, was aware of its usefulness in forging the ties through which governance was achieved. A moment spent in the presence of a Coronal was something that would remain with a citizen for a lifetime; that person would always think of himself as affiliated in some way with the grandeur and power of that Coronal, and would feel enhanced by that, and profoundly grateful, and eternally loyal.

This was only the third such reception that Prestimion had been able to find time to hold since his accession. Since it was primarily an act of political theater, the royal levee needed careful staging and thorough rehearsal. Among other things, he had to spend an hour or two, the night before, going over the list of events with Zeldor Luudwid, the chamberlain in charge of such events, memorizing some flattering fact about each honoree. Then, on the day of the ceremony, at least an hour more was required for proper robing. He must look overwhelmingly regal. That meant not merely some costume in the traditional green and gold, the colors that symbolized to any viewer the office and the power of the Coronal. It meant elaborate overembellishment: varying combinations of fur mantles, silken scarves, stiff flaring epaulets, diadems and gems, all manner of frills and furbelows, this bit of trimming and that one being put on him and removed and put on him again until just the right mix of grandiosity was attained.

Today the basic costume was a high-waisted loose-fitting golden velvet doublet, paned at the chest in front and back to reveal the green silk shirt beneath. The doublet's wide winged sleeves, similarly paned to the elbow, then close-fitting to the wrists, ended in turned-back lace cuffs partly concealed by handsome gauntlet gloves of crimson leather. His boots, of the same leather, were turned down to reveal green silk stockings.

The boots caused trouble, because they were padded in the sole to add two inches to his height. Prestimion had long ago come to terms with the fact that he was not as tall as many other men, and that mattered not at all to him. Indeed, he rarely gave it a thought. The artificial boosting that these boots provided was offensive to him, and he asked for them to be taken away and replaced by a normal pair. Only after a fifteen-minute delay was it determined that no unpadded boots of a color appropriate to the rest of his costume existed in his closet, and therefore he would have to begin the robing all over again with a doublet of a different shade of gold. Which brought a hot burst of anger from him, because it was too late to start doing that; and in the end he wore the padded boots, although it made him suddenly self-conscious to find himself looking at the world from a height two inches greater than usual.

On his brow, of course, was the grand starburst crown of Lord Confalume, that preposterous intricate confection of emeralds and rubies and purple diniabas and dazzling metal chasings, a thing that announced in a voice of thunder that its wearer was the properly anointed incarnation of the majesty of the realm. And on his chest rested the golden medallion that Confalume had given him at his coronation, with the signet seal of Lord Stiamot in its center. It was, ostensibly, a modern reproduction of the medallion that the Coronals of antiquity had worn. But in fact it was no such thing. Prestimion himself, in conspiracy with Serithorn and the late and no longer remembered Prince Korsibar, had invented the tale of the medallion out of thin air and designed a plausible-looking "reproduction" of the supposedly long-lost original as a gift for Lord Confalume to celebrate his fortieth year as Coronal. Now it had been passed onward to Prestimion himself, and would, he supposed, go marching on down through the centuries from Coronal to Coronal, revered and cherished. After a couple of hundred years it would probably be an unquestioned article of faith that the half-legendary Stiamot himself had worn this very one, an eon and a quarter ago. In such ways, he thought, are potent traditions born.

Lord Confalume also had bedecked the throne-room with the tripods and censers and astrological computing-machines of his court wizards, not because these devices played any part in the official ceremonies of the court, but simply because in his later years he had come to like having such things about him. But Prestimion was a less credulous man than Confalume. He was well enough aware, in a calculating way, of the value and uses of sorcery in modern-day Majipoor, but he had never managed to arrive at a completely comfortable acceptance of the way the public had embraced so much that was mere superstition and chicanery.

Therefore he had banned all of Confalume's implements of magic from the room. But he did permit a magus or two to be on hand for his receptions, if only to gratify public taste. If they needed to believe that he ruled not just by the grace of the Divine but also with the aid of whichever demons, spirits, or other supernal powers the people of Majipoor currently held in high esteem, he would not deny that to them.

Maundigand-Klimd was the magus on duty today—a Su-Suheris was always valuable for instilling awe—and, at Septach Melayn's special request, so also were two geomancers from Tidias, complete with their tall brass helmets and shining metallic robes. Lord Confalume had brought them to the Castle in his time, along with a great host of others of their profession, and they all still seemed to be here and on the public payroll, although they had no official function in the administration of the new Coronal. Apparently these two had complained of their idleness to Septach Melayn, a man of Tidias himself; and so they were here, standing sternly on either side of Maundigand-Klimd, impressive brass-helmeted symbols of the realm of supernatural forces that existed side by side with the visible world that was everyday Majipoor. They were not, though, permitted to utter invocations or draw their invisible lines of power on the floor or burn their colored powders of mystic virtue. They were mere decorations, like the clustered masses of moonstones and tourmalines and amethysts and sapphires that Lord Confalume, when he had this room built, had caused at enormous expense to be inserted into the gigantic gilded beams of the ceiling.

"Your lordship," said the major-domo Nilgir Sumanand. "It's time for the reception."

So it was. Prestimion left his robing-chamber and made his way, awkward in his thick-soled boots, through the hallways of the ancient myriad-roomed Castle that he had inherited from his multitude of royal predecessors. He would, he knew—eventually, in the fullness of his years—place his own imprint on the Castle of the Coronal. It was the tradition, after all, for each ruler to make his own additions and modifications.

The series of minor rooms that lay between the robing-chamber and the Confalume throne-room, for instance, seemed like a poor employment of the space they occupied. He had it in mind to clear them all away and construct a great judgment-hall next to the throne-room itself, something huge and grand, with crystal chandeliers and windows of frosted glass. An austere but imposing chapel nearby for the private reflections of the Coronal might be worthwhile, too. The present one was an awkward little afterthought of a room with no architectural merit whatever. And outside the central core, perhaps over by the watchtower of lunatic design that Lord Arioc of long ago had built, Prestimion wanted to erect a museum of Majipoori history, an archive containing memorabilia of the world's long past, where future Coronals could study the achievements of their predecessors and contemplate their own high intentions. But all that was for the future. His reign had only just begun.

Unsmiling, looking neither to left nor right, walking stiffly in an attempt to avoid tripping over his own trouble-

some boots, he entered the throne-room, solemnly inclined
his head as his subjects greeted him with starbursts, and
ascended the many steps of the mahogany pedestal atop
which the throne itself was set.

Solemnly. That was the key. He knew better than anyone
what empty mummery such a spectacle as this really was.
Its prime and perhaps only purpose was to awe the credulous. Yet for all his intelligence and sophistication and that
touch of irreverence that he hoped he would never lose,
Prestimion was more than somewhat awed by it too. A Coronal must believe his own mummery, he knew, or the people
never would.

And that faith in the grandeur and might of the Coronal
Lord, rooted in this very pageantry, this showy business of
robes and thrones and crowns, had had much to do, he was
certain, with the general tranquility and prosperity of this
great world over the thirteen thousand years since humans
first had come to settle on it. The Coronal was the embodiment of the whole world's hopes and fears and desires. All
of that had now been entrusted to the care of Prestimion of
Muldemar, who understood only too well that he was human
and mortal, but must nevertheless conduct himself as though
he were much more than that. If for the sake of the public
good he must don ornately fanciful green-and-gold robes
and sit with solemn face upon a gigantic gleaming block of
black opal shot through with veins of blood-scarlet ruby, so
be it: he would play his part as he was expected to do.

To his left, as he took the throne, stood the chamberlain
Zeldor Luudwid, with a table beside him on which the decorations to be handed out today were piled. A little farther
on was Maundigand-Klimd, who was flanked to right and
left, as though they were bookends, by the two Tidias geomancers. On the other side of the throne were a couple of
secondary chamberlains—two massive Skandars who were
huge even as Skandars went—carrying great staffs of office.
Prestimion caught sight of Septach Melayn in the shadows
just beyond, studying him thoughtfully. For the High Counsellor to attend a levee was a bit unusual; but Prestimion

had a good idea of why Septach Melayn had showed up here today.

For there was Simbilon Khayf out there, plainly visible among the multitude of citizens who would be presented to the Coronal this day—that rigid pile of glittering silver hair was unmistakable—and there was the lady Varaile, tall and stately and beautiful, at her father's side. And Septach Melayn—damn him!—was here, Prestimion realized, to supervise her meeting with the Coronal.

"His lordship the Coronal Prestimion welcomes you to the Castle," Zeldor Luudwid intoned grandly, "and bids you know that he has studied your attainments and achievements with care and regards each of you as an ornament of the realm."

It was the standard greeting. Prestimion, only half listening, nevertheless adopted a pose of seeming attentiveness, sitting staunchly upright and looking serenely outward at the waiting crowd. He took care, though, not to let his eyes fasten on anyone in particular. He aimed his gaze well above their heads, so that it rested on the glowing tapestry on the far wall, the one depicting Lord Stiamot receiving the homage of the conquered Metamorphs.

Idly he wondered, not for the first time, how many thousands of royals Confalume had expended while he was Coronal in the course of creating the fabulous throne-room that bore his name. Prestimion made a mental note to search the archives some day for the exact amount. Probably it was more than Stiamot had spent to build the original Castle in the first place. It had taken years to construct this high-vaulted room, with its gem-encrusted beams covered with hammered sheets of pale-red gold, its spectacular tapestries, its floor of costly yellow gurnawood. The throne alone must surely have cost a fortune—not just for that colossal block of black opal of which it was fashioned, but for the stout silver pillars beside it and the great canopy of gold, inlaid with blue mother-of-pearl, that those pillars supported, and for the starburst symbol above all the rest, made of white platinum tipped by spheres of purple onyx.

But of course the money had been there for Confalume

to spend. Majipoor had never known such a time of affluence and general well-being as it had in his reign.

Much of that was due to good luck: a general absence, for many decades now, of droughts, floods, great storms, and other natural disasters. But also the former Coronal—building on the work of his predecessor, Lord Prankipin—had promulgated a sharp cut in taxation, with immediate benefits, and had gone to great lengths to seek out and extirpate ancient and foolish trade restrictions that were holding back the free flow of goods from one province to another. He had acted in many other ways to eliminate all manner of unneeded regulatory impediments, also. In this he had had the valuable support of Dantirya Sambail, who as Procurator of Ni-moya had come over the years to rule the lesser continent of Zimroel virtually as a king in his own right. Many of those ancient trade regulations had originally been enacted to protect the interests of Zimroel against the older and more fully developed continent of Alhanroel. But Dantirya Sambail understood that all those obsolete restrictions were by now doing more harm than good and had raised no objection to striking them from the books. As a result there had been an enormous worldwide increase in productivity and in the general welfare of all.

From Prestimion's point of view that was both good and bad. He had been given the throne of a wondrously thriving realm, and though it was necessary now to cope with the damage that the civil war had done and the fact that Dantirya Sambail had ceased to be an agent for the general good and had become an obstacle to its continuation, Prestimion was confident that both of those problems could be dealt with quickly enough. They had better be. His name would be cursed forever if during the years ahead he failed to sustain the level of prosperity that had been reached in the time of Lord Confalume.

One by one the day's chosen ornaments of the realm, whose attainments and achievements the Coronal had stud-

ied with such care, were summoned to the throne to be acknowledged for all that they had done.

No members of the titled nobility were here today. The
aristocracy received its rewards in other ways. The group
now gathered before the Coronal was made up of humbler
folk: elected officials of cities or provinces, and an assortment of businesspeople, and farmers who had in one note-
worthy fashion or another advanced the state of agriculture;
and also artists and writers, stage performers, athletes, even
a scholar or two.

Usually Prestimion was able to call from his memory the
reason why each of them was being honored in this day's
ceremony, or to guess it from some phrase of the introductions that Zeldor Luudwid provided. Where he could not
come up with anything specific, he was always able, at least,
to make some general remark that passed as appropriate.
Thus, when the mayor of Khyntor in Zimroel came forward
to be acclaimed for some undoubtedly significant municipal
accomplishment, Prestimion had no recollection at all of
what it was the good woman had done, but it was not a
difficult matter for him to hold forth with great vigor on the
famous bridges of Khyntor, those remarkable engineering
feats, miraculously spanning the stupendous width of the
River Zimr, that any child on Majipoor would have known
something about. When a soul-painter from Sefarad who
had done a celebrated series of canvasses depicting the tide-
pools of Varfanir approached the throne, Prestimion realized
that he had confused the man with another soul-painter famous for his portraits of ballerinas, and was not sure which
was the tide-pool man and which the connoisseur of the
dance. He offered, instead, a brief discourse on the marvels
of soul-painting itself, speaking of the fascination he had for
that medium, in which artists imprinted their visions on cunningly prepared psychosensitive fabric, and expressed his
hope to do a little soul-painting himself one day when the
cares of government permitted him the leisure to master the
art. And so forth: one deft little speech after another, graceful, well turned, kingly, after which Zeldor Luudwid presented the honoree with the appropriate insignia of

distinction, a bright riband or sparkling medallion or something of the like, and gently sent him back to his seat, pleasantly dazed by his encounter with greatness.

Simbilon Khayf was one of the last to be presented. For him, of course, Prestimion had no problems of memory. He spoke first of the importance of such private banks as Simbilon Khayf's in stimulating the growth of entrepreneurial industry on Majipoor, and then turned easily to a synopsis of Simbilon Khayf's own great achievement in rising from the humble ranks of the factory-workers of Stee to his present eminence in the world of finance. Simbilon Khayf's eyes did not leave Prestimion's as the Coronal delivered his encomium; and once again Prestimion wondered whether this shrewd, unpleasant man might somehow have succeeded in linking the crowned king high atop the throne before him with the bewhiskered merchant who had come to him at his mansion in Stee seeking a loan.

But Simbilon Khayf betrayed no such awareness. Throughout the entire time of his audience with the Coronal his face wore an unvarying expression of frozen humility and awe; and when he accepted from Zeldor Luudwid the golden wreath of the Order of Lord Havilbove and muttered his thanks, his voice was thick and husky with emotion and his hands were trembling, as though he was barely able to withstand the immense importance of the honor that had been bestowed upon him.

After the ceremony the Coronal always held a more casual reception in one of the adjacent rooms for the recipients of the more important decorations. Here, now, Prestimion knew, would come the triumphal moment of Septach Melayn's stage-managing. For those who had been awarded the Order of Lord Havilbove were entitled to attend the second reception. Inevitably Prestimion would find himself confronting Simbilon Khayf and his daughter once again, in circumstances where conversations of an extended sort would be hard to avoid. Impossible, actually.

Which must have been precisely what Septach Melayn had had in mind.

*   *   *

Smoothly and swiftly Prestimion moved through the crowded room, exchanging a brief word with each of his guests. The unnaturally thick soles of his boots hampered him only a little, though it was odd to feel so tall. After a time he could see the uncouth spire of Simbilon Khayf's hair just ahead of him in his direct path. Varaile, oddly, did not seem to be anywhere near her father; but then Prestimion caught sight of her on the other side of the room, speaking with Septach Melayn.

The merchant banker still seemed overwhelmed by it all: He barely managed to make sense as he blurted out a little stammering speech of gratitude for the Coronal's kindness in inviting him here today, which turned, after a moment or two, into a rambling and disjointed speech, accompanied by much heavy breathing and floridity of face, in praise of his own accomplishments. All perfectly in character, a flustered combination of high self-approbation and extreme insecurity. The banker's wayward performance bolstered Prestimion's feeling that the likelihood of Simbilon Khayf's having guessed the connection between his bearded visitor in Khayf and the Coronal before whom he now stood was not very great. And plainly Varaile had not violated her promise to Septach Melayn to keep the truth about that to herself.

Simbilon Khayf's huffing and puffing went on and on and on. Prestimion detached himself finally and moved along through the throng; but it was ten minutes more before he came to Varaile.

Their eyes met and for him it was just as it had been before, that other time in her father's house in Stee: that disquieting tingle of electric connection, that quiver of excitement, of uncertainty, of confusion. And for her, too, of that he was certain: he saw the quick flaring of her nostrils, the brief quirking of the corners of her mouth, the sudden darting of her eyes from side to side, the flush slowly spreading over her flawless features.

This is no illusion, he thought. This is something very real.

But it passed quickly. In a flash, she was cool and calm and self-possessed again, the very model of a well-bred young woman who has no doubt of how to conduct herself in the presence of her king. As poised and proper as her father had been gauche and jumpy, she hailed him with the appropriate deference, making the starburst gesture to him and thanking him simply but warmly, in that deep, wondrously musical voice of hers that he remembered so well from Stee, for the great honor he had conferred upon her father. By the nature of the occasion nothing further was called for in this situation. It would have been easy enough now for Prestimion to acknowledge her gratitude with a quick impersonal word or two and move along to the next guest.

But he saw Septach Melayn standing to one side with folded arms, watching keenly, smiling slyly, and knew that his friend occupied the position of power in this. The master duelist had backed him into a corner. Septach Melayn did not intend to permit him any sort of facile and cowardly escape.

Varaile was waiting, though. Prestimion searched his mind for the right words—something that would bridge the immense gap between Coronal and subject that separated him from her now and transform this into a normal conversation between a man and a woman. Nothing came. He wondered if such a conversation would even be possible. He had no idea of what to say. He had been trained since boyhood to conduct himself effectively in any kind of diplomatic situation; but his training had not prepared him for anything like this. He stood before her mute and incapable.

And in the end it was Varaile who rescued him. In the midst of his frozen silence her cool and formal pose of reverent deference began to give way, ever so subtly, to something warmer and less stiff: a hint of amusement in her eyes, the merest trace of a playful smile on her lips, a tacit affirmation that she saw the comic nature of their present predicament. That was all it took. Immediately there was that unquestionable current of connection running between them again, sudden, startling, intense.

Prestimion felt a flood of relief and delight.

It was difficult for him to maintain his own sternly regal posture while all of that was passing through him. He allowed a certain softening of his stance, a relaxation of his official face, and she took her cue from it. Quietly she said, looking straight into his eyes as she had not dared to do a moment before, and speaking in the most casual, informal tone, "You're taller now than you were in Stee. Your eyes were on a level with mine, then."

It was a gigantic leap across the boundaries that separated them. And instantly, as though recoiling in consternation at her own boldness, she drew back with a little gasp, pressing her fingertips to her mouth. They were monarch and subject once again.

Was that what he wanted? No. No. Absolutely not. So now it was Prestimion's turn to put her at her ease, or the moment would be lost. "It's these idiotic boots," he said, smiling. "They're supposed to make me look more imposing. You won't ever see me in them again, I assure you."

At once the mischief was back in her eyes. "The boots, no. But will I ever see you again?"

Septach Melayn, against the wall a dozen feet behind her, was nodding and beaming in delight.

"Do you want to?" Prestimion asked.

"Oh—my lord—oh, yes, my lord—"

"There's a place for you at court if you want it," said Prestimion. "Septach Melayn will arrange for it. I'll have to pay a visit to the Labyrinth soon, but perhaps we can dine together after I return to the Castle. I'd like to get to know you much better."

"That would give me great pleasure, my lord." The tone this time was a mixture of formality and eagerness. A slight tremor in it betrayed her confusion. For all her innate poise, she had no real idea of how to handle what was unfolding now. But neither did he. Prestimion wondered what it was, exactly, that Septach Melayn had said to her about his intentions. He wondered, too, just what those intentions were.

And this present conversation had gone on much too long. Septach Melayn was not the only one watching them now.

"My lord?" she said, as he bade her a formal farewell and began to move away.

"Yes, Varaile?"

"My lord, was that really you, that time at our house in Stee?"

"Do you have any doubt of that?"

"And just why was it, may I ask, that you came?"

"To meet you," he said, and knew there would be no turning back from there.

6

THE LABYRINTH OF MAJIPOOR was a joyless place at best: a huge underground city, level upon level descending into the depths of the planet, with the hidden lair of the Pontifex at its deepest point, at the level farthest from the warming rays of the sun.

Prestimion had experienced some of the blackest moments of his life here.

It was in the great hall of the Labyrinth known as the Court of Thrones that Korsibar, in the moment of the announcement of the death of the Pontifex Prankipin, had carried out his astounding seizure of the starburst crown that was to have been Prestimion's, right before Prestimion's eyes and those of the highest figures of the realm.

And it was in the suite of rooms set aside for the Coronal's use at the Labyrinth that Prestimion had come before Korsibar's father, Lord Confalume, who had now become the Pontifex Confalume, to demand of him the throne that Confalume had promised to him; and had heard from the bewildered and broken Confalume that nothing could be done, that the usurpation was an irrevocable act, that Korsibar was Coronal now and Prestimion must slink away to make whatever he could out of his life without further hope of attaining the throne. Confalume had wept, then, when

Prestimion had pressed him to take action against this outrage—Confalume, weeping! But the Pontifex was paralyzed by fear. He dreaded a bloody civil war, which would certainly be the outcome of any challenge to Korsibar, too greatly to want to set himself in opposition to his son's amazing and unlawful act. The thing is done, Confalume had said. Korsibar holds the power now.

Well, the thing that had been done had now been undone, and Korsibar had been blotted from existence as though he had never been, and Prestimion was Lord Prestimion now, returning in glory to this place from which he had crept away in shame and defeat. No one but he and Gialaurys and Septach Melayn knew anything of the dark events that had taken place in the subterranean metropolis in the days immediately after the death of the Pontifex Prankipin. But the Labyrinth was full of painful memories for him. If he could have avoided this journey, he would have. He had no wish to see the Labyrinth again until the day—let it be far in the future, he hoped!—when Confalume at last was dead and he himself must take up the title of Pontifex.

Staying away from the Labyrinth entirely, though, was impossible. The new Coronal must present himself, early in the reign, to the Pontifex from whom he had received his throne.

Here he was, then.

Confalume awaited him.

"Your journey was a pleasant one, I hope?"

"Fair weather all the way, your majesty," Prestimion said. "A good breeze carrying us southward down the Glayge."

They had had the introductory formalities, the embraces and the feasting, and now it was just the two of them together in quiet conversation, Pontifex and Coronal, emperor and king, nominal father and adoptive son.

The river route was what Prestimion had taken to get here: the usual one for a lord of the Castle who was making a visit to the Labyrinth. He had traveled aboard the royal barge down the swift, wide Glayge, which rose in the foot-

hills of the Mount and made its way south through some of
the most fertile provinces of Alhanroel to the imperial
capital. All along the river's banks the populace had been
assembled to cheer him on his way: at Storp and Mitripond,
at Nirnivan and Stangard Falls, Makroposopos and Pendiwane and the innumerable towns along the shores of Lake
Roghoiz, and the cities of the Lower Glayge beyond the
lake, Palaghat and Terabessa and Grevvin and all the rest.
Prestimion had made this journey in reverse not many years
before, returning from the Labyrinth to the Castle after the
usurpation, and a far more somber trip it had been, too, with
banners portraying the newly proclaimed Lord Korsibar fluttering in his face at every port. But that was then, and this
was now, and as he went past each city the cry of "Prestimion! Prestimion! All hail Lord Prestimion!" echoed in his
ears.

There were seven entrances to the Labyrinth; but the one
that Coronals used was the Mouth of Waters, where the
Glayge flowed past the huge brown earthen mound that was
the only part of the Labyrinth visible aboveground. Here, a
line so sharp that a man could step across it in a single stride
marked the division between the green and fertile Glayge
Valley and the lifeless dusty desert in which the Labyrinth
lay. Here Prestimion knew he must put behind him the sweet
breezes and soft golden-green sunlight of the upper world
and enter into the mysterious eternal night of the underground city, the sinister descending coils of its densely populated levels, the hermetic and airless-seeming realm far
below that was the home of the Pontifex.

Masked officials of the Pontificate were on hand to greet
him at the entrance, with the Pontifex's pompous white-
haired cousin, Duke Oljebbin of Stoienzar, at the head of
the group in his new capacity as High Spokesman to the
Pontifex. The swift shaft reserved only for Powers of the
Realm took Prestimion downward, past the circular levels
where the Labyrinth's teeming millions of population
dwelled, those who served the Pontifical bureaucracy and
those who simply performed the humble tasks of any great
city, and onward to the deeper zones where the Labyrinth's

famed architectural wonders lay—the Pool of Dreams, the mysterious Hall of Winds, the bizarre Court of Pyramids, the Place of Masks, the inexplicable gigantic empty space that was the Arena, and all the rest—and with breathtaking swiftness delivered him to the imperial sector, and to the Pontifex. Who immediately dismissed his entire entourage from the room, even Oljebbin. Prestimion's meeting would be with Confalume alone.

Nor was the Confalume who faced him now the Confalume that Prestimion was expecting to see.

He had feared that he would find the feeble ruined hulk of a man, the sorry and dismal remnant of the great Confalume of yore. The beginning of that collapse had already been in evidence at their last meeting. The Confalume with whom he had that fruitless, despondent meeting in the grim aftermath of the thunderbolt force of Korsibar's power-grab, the man who had wept and trembled and begged most piteously to be left in peace, had been only a shadow of the Confalume whose forty-year reign as Coronal had been marked by triumph after triumph.

Although the later obliteration of specific knowledge of the usurpation and the civil war that had ensued would have spared Confalume from the grief he felt over his son's actions, there was no reason to think he would ever recover from the damage that had been inflicted on his spirit. Even at Prestimion's coronation, with the whole Korsibar event now relegated to oblivion, Confalume had seemed little more than an empty shell, still physically strong but befuddled of mind, haunted by phantoms whose identity he could not begin to understand. And, according to Septach Melayn, who had met with the legate Vologaz Sar during Prestimion's absence in the east-country, the Pontifex now was still a greatly troubled man, confused and depressed, plagued by sleeplessness and nebulous free-floating distress.

And so Prestimion had thought that that charismatic Confalume of old surely would be gone, that he would meet a frail trembling man who stood at the edge of the grave. It was frightening to think that Confalume might not have much longer to live, for Prestimion himself had hardly commenced his own reign. He was far from ready to be pulled away from the Castle prematurely in order to immure himself in the dark pit that was the Labyrinth, although that was a risk that any Coronal faced when he succeeded one who had held his Castle throne as long as Confalume had.

But it was a Confalume reborn and revivified to whom Prestimion presented himself now in the Court of Thrones, that hall of black stone walls rising to pointed arches where Pontifex and Coronal were meant to sit side by side on lofty seats—the very place in which Korsibar had staged his coup-d'etat. Here before him was Confalume, and he seemed to be the robust and forceful man Prestimion remembered from former days: jaunty and erect in the scarlet-and-black Pontifical robes, with a miniature replica of the ornate Pontifical tiara glittering bravely on one lapel and the little golden rohilla, the astrological amulet that he was so fond of wearing, mounted on the other. Nothing about him had the aspect of imminent death. When they embraced, it was impossible not to be impressed by the strength of the man.

Confalume was himself again, rejuvenated, thriving. He had always been a man of tremendous physical vigor, not tall but powerfully built, with keen gray eyes and a full thick sweep of hair that had maintained its chestnut hue far into his later years. In any gathering at the Castle, the former Lord Confalume had automatically been the center of attention, not solely because he was Coronal, but because there emanated from him such personal magnetism, such a potent pull of inherent force, that you could not help but turn toward him. And clearly more than a vestige of that Confalume still remained. That innate vigor of his had pulled him through the crisis. Good, Prestimion thought. He felt a tide of immense relief go flooding through him. But at the same time he realized that he would be dealing now not with a shattered, weary old man to whom he could say whatever he thought most useful, but rather with one who had spent better than forty years on the Coronal's throne, and who understood the wielding of high power better than anyone else in the world.

*   *   *

"You look well, majesty. Remarkably well!"

"You seem surprised, Prestimion."

"I had heard rumors of a troubled mood—restlessness, difficulty sleeping—"

"Pah! Rumors, nothing more. Fables. I had a few hard moments at the beginning, perhaps. There's a necessary period of adjustment, coming down from the Castle to live in this place, and I won't pretend that that part's easy. But it passes; and then you feel quite at home here."

"Do you, then?"

"I do. And you should take comfort from it. There's never been a Coronal yet who hasn't been appalled by the necessity of moving along eventually to the Labyrinth. And why not? To wake each morning in the Castle, and look out at that great airy expanse all around, and to be able to descend from the Mount whenever you please to go wherever you like, Alaisor or Embolain or Ketheron if the whim takes you, or Pidruid or Narabal, for that matter—all the while knowing that one of these days the old emperor's going to wake up dead, and when that happens they're going to come for you and ship you down the Glayge to this place and point nine miles straight down and say, Here's your new home, Lord So-and-So—" The Pontifex smiled. "Well, it's not all that terrible to be here, let me assure you. It's different. Restful."

"Restful?" That hardly seemed the word for this sunless cheerless place.

"Oh, yes. There's definitely something to say for the seclusion, for the peace and quiet of it. No one can even speak to you directly, you know, no one but your Spokesman and your Coronal. No pestilent petitioners plucking at your sleeve, no crowds of ambitious lordlings flocking around hoping for favors, no backbreaking journeys to undertake across thousands and thousands of miles because your Council has decided that it's time to show your face in some distant province. No, Prestimion, you sit down here in your cozy underground palace, and they bring you legislation to read and you glance at it and say yes or no or maybe, and they take it away and you no longer have to give it a thought. You're young and full of vitality, and you can't begin to comprehend the merits of being sequestered in the Labyrinth. I admit that I felt the same way, thirty years ago. But you'll see. Have yourself forty-odd years as Coronal, as I did, and I promise you you'll be more than ready for the Labyrinth, and no anguish about it at all."

A forty-year reign as Coronal? Well, there was no probability of that, Prestimion knew. Confalume was past seventy already. A decade or so at the Castle was about the best the new Coronal could hope for, and then he would find himself Pontifex. But the older man seemed sincere in what he was saying, and there was great comfort in that.

"No doubt all you tell me about life in the Labyrinth is true," Prestimion said, smiling. "I'm quite willing to wait forty years to find out, though."

Confalume looked pleased. His return to something approaching his old strength was neither a pretense nor an illusion, Prestimion realized. Confalume seemed rejuvenated, brimming with life, settling in for a long stay in his strange new home.

He filled their wine-bowls with his own hand—for once, no oversolicitous servants were lurking about—and swung around in his seat to face Prestimion. "And you?" he said. "Not overwhelmed, are you, by all your new tasks?"

"So far I hold my own, your majesty. Although it's been a busy time."

"It must have been, yes. I hear so little from you. You leave me in the dark, you know, about all the affairs of the realm, and that's not so good."

It was said very pleasantly, but there was no mistaking the implicit sting of the words.

Prestimion's reply was a cautious one. "I realize, sir, that I've been remiss in reporting to you. But there's been a great many problems to take care of all at once, and I wanted to be able to come to you with some evidence of real progress to show."

"Problems such as what?" the Pontifex asked.

"Dantirya Sambail, for one."

"The bloody Procurator, yes. But he's all noise and no push, is that not so? What's he been up to?"

"Contemplating setting up a separate kingdom for himself in Zimroel, apparently"

Confalume's hand leaped as if of its own accord to the rohilla in his lapel and rubbed it in a counterclockwise way. He gave Prestimion an incredulous stare. "Are you serious? And is he? Where is he now? Why haven't I been told of any of this?"

Prestimion stirred uneasily in his seat. They were entering into perilous territory here. "I was waiting, sir, until I could interrogate the Procurator myself about his intentions. He was at the Castle for a time"—that was true enough—"but then he left, supposedly on a journey into the east country."

"Why would he go there?"

"Who can know any reason for anything Dantirya Sambail does? At any rate, I gathered a small force and went out there after him."

"Yes," said the Pontifex tartly. "So I understand. You might have informed me of that, too."

"Forgive me, sir. I've been remiss in many ways, I see. But I assumed your own officials would notify you of my departure from the Castle."

"As they did, yes. —Dantirya Sambail eluded you in the east-country, apparently."

"He's in southern Alhanroel now, and intends, I assume, to take ship shortly for his homeland. When I leave here, I'll be going down toward Aruachosia to try to seek him out." Prestimion hesitated a moment. "The Grand Admiral has blockaded the ports."

Confalume's eyes flashed surprise. "What you're telling me, then, is that you regard the most powerful man in the world, other than yourself and me, as a dangerous threat to the integrity of the realm. Am I correct? That he has eluded your attempts to take him into custody. That he is currently a fugitive running hither and thither around Alhanroel as he seeks to get back overseas. What is it we have here, Prestimion, a civil war in the making? Over what? Why should the Procurator suddenly be talking about setting up an independent government? He's been content with the present power-sharing arrangements all these years. Is it that he looks upon the new regime as weak, and feels safe in making his move? By the Divine, he won't succeed at it! —You're his kinsman, Prestimion. How can he dare think of launching an uprising against his own kin?"

He already has launched one, Prestimion thought, which has been fought and settled at a terrible cost, and the world will never be the same for it. But it was impossible for him to speak of that in any way. And Confalume's face had grown troublesomely red with rage.

This topic had to be put quickly to rest.

Calmly Prestimion said, "These rumors may all be overblown, sir. I need to find Dantirya Sambail and discover from him myself whether he feels that his present high position is insufficiently eminent. And if he does, I'll convince him, I assure you, that he's mistaken. But there'll be no civil war."

The Pontifex appeared to be satisfied by that reply. He busied himself with his wine for a time; and then he began to question Prestimion quickly about other matters of state, moving with great efficiency from one subject to another, the rebuilding of the dam on the Iyann, the problem of inadequate harvests in places like Stymphinor and the valley of the Jhelum, the puzzling reports of outbreaks of insanity in many cities across the land. It was obvious that this man was no feeble and ill-informed recluse huddled away here in the dark recesses of the Labyrinth to wait out the final years of his life: plainly Confalume intended to be an active and dynamic Pontifex, very much the strong emperor to whom the Coronal would be the subordinate king, and even in the absence of detailed reports from Prestimion he had managed to keep abreast of much of what was taking place in the world. More, probably, Prestimion suspected, than he was bringing up for discussion now. It was common knowledge when Confalume was in his prime that underestimating him was a dangerous game to play; Prestimion knew that it would be rash to underestimate him even now.

The meeting, which Prestimion had hoped would be brief and even perfunctory, proved to be a lengthy one. Prestimion replied to everything in great detail, but always choosing his words with extreme care. It was a tricky thing to tell Confalume how he proposed to go about solving the current spate of problems, when he could not allow himself even to reveal to Confalume any knowledge of why these problems happened to exist in their happy and harmonious world at all.

The shattering of the Mavestoi Dam, for example. That had been the doing of Confalume's own son Korsibar, at Dantirya Sambail's suggestion: one of the most frightful calamities of the civil war. But how could he ever explain that to Confalume, who no longer knew even of Korsibar, let alone of the war? There was famine in places like the Jhelum Valley and Stymphinor because great battles had been fought there, thousands of soldiers quartered on the land, granaries emptied to feed them, whole plantations trampled underfoot. The battles were forgotten; the consequences remained. And the madness? Why, there was every likelihood that that was the result of the vast witchery called down upon the world by Heszmon Gorse and his crew of sorcerers at Prestimion's own order! But any attempt to explain that would also entail speaking of the war, and of its bloody conclusion, and then of his decision—which now looked so reckless even to him—to blot the whole thing from the minds of billions of people.

A deep longing arose in him to reveal the truth to Confalume here and now: to share the terrible burden, to throw himself on the older man's mercy and wisdom. But that was a temptation he dared not yield to.

He did have to give the Pontifex some sort of answers to his questions, or he would risk seeming incompetent in the eyes of the one who had nominated him for the throne. But there was so much that simply could not be spoken. All too often it seemed that he could respond to Confalume either by telling outright lies, which he most profoundly hoped to avoid doing, or else by revealing the unrevealable.

Somehow though, by dint of half-truth and subterfuge, he succeeded in threading his way through the maze of the Pontifex's queries without speaking of that which could not be told, and yet without resorting to any truly shameful deception. And Confalume appeared to accept what he had been told at face value.

Prestimion hoped so, anyway. But he was much relieved when the meeting reached its apparent end and he could take his leave of the older man without further cause for uneasiness.

"You won't be so long in coming the next time, will you?" Confalume asked, rising, letting his hands rest on Prestimion's shoulders, looking squarely into Prestimion's eyes. "You know what pleasure it gives me to see you, my son."

Prestimion smiled at that phrase, and at the warmth of the Pontifex's tone, though he felt a sharp pang also.

Confalume went on, "Yes, 'my son,' is what I said. I always wanted a son, but the Divine would never send me one. But now I have one—after a manner of speaking. For by law the Coronal is deemed the son-by-adoption, of course, of the Pontifex. And so you are my son, Prestimion. You are my son!"

It was an uncomfortable, even painful moment. The Divine had sent Confalume a son, a fine noble-looking one at that. But he was Korsibar, who now had never been.

Worse was to come.

For then, even as Prestimion was edging uneasily toward the door, Confalume said, "You should marry, Prestimion. A Coronal needs a partner for his labors. Not that I did all that well myself with my Roxivail, but how was I to know how vain and shallow she was? You can manage it better. Surely there's a woman somewhere who'd be a fitting consort for you." And once again Thismet's image blazed in Prestimion's mind, and brought him the unfailing stab of agony that came with any thought of her.

Thismet, yes. Confalume had never known of the late-blooming romance that had sprung up between Thismet and him on the battlefields of western Alhanroel.

But what did that matter now? It would have been lawful for Prestimion to marry Confalume's daughter, yes, despite the technicalities of the adoptive relationship. Only Confalume had no daughter. Her name itself had been canceled from the pages of history. Prestimion's brief and swiftly extinguished alliance with Thismet was simply one thing more of which he could say nothing. Now there was Varaile; but she and he were still strangers. Prestimion had no way of knowing whether the promise of their early meetings would ever be fulfilled. He was oddly unwilling, besides, to mention Varaile at all to Confalume for another reason: out of some perverse and, he realized, wholly ridiculous fidelity to the memory of the murdered daughter of whose existence Confalume had no clue.

So he smiled and said, "Surely there is, and may it be that I find her, some day. And if and when I do, I'll marry her quickly, you can be sure of that. But let us say no more on that subject now, shall we, father?" And saluted and hastily took his leave.

7

DEKKERET HAD LEARNED ABOUT Ni-moya when he was a boy at school, of course. But no geography lesson could possibly have prepared him for the reality of Zimroel's greatest city.

Who could believe, after all, that the other continent could have any city so grand? As far as Dekkeret knew, Zimroel was mainly an undeveloped land of forests and jungles and enormous rivers, with much of its central region given over to the impenetrable wilderness to which the aboriginal Metamorphs had been banished by Stiamot, and where they still had their largest concentration of population. Oh, there were some cities out there, too—Narabal and Pidruid and Piliplok and such—but Dekkeret imagined them

to be muddy backwaters inhabited by hordes of coarse, ignorant yokels. As for Ni-moya, the continental capital, one
heard impressive population figures, yes—fifteen million
people were said to be living there, twenty million, whatever
the number was. But many cities of Alhanroel had reached
such proportions hundreds of years ago, so why get excited
over the size of Ni-moya when Alaisor and Stee and half a
dozen other cities of the older continent were at least as big,
or bigger? In any event, population size itself was no guar-
antee of distinction. You could readily cram twenty million
people into one area, or fifty million, if you cared to, and
create nothing better than an enormous squalid urban mess,
noisy and dirty and chaotic and close to intolerable for any
civilized person who had to spend more than half a day in
it. And that was what Dekkeret was expecting to find at his
journey's end.

He and Akbalik had sailed from Alaisor, the usual
port of embarkation for travelers bound to the western continent from central Alhanroel. After an uneventful but
interminable-seeming sea journey they made their landfall
at Piliplok on Zimroel's eastern coast.

Which proved to be a city that lived up in every way to
Dekkeret's expectations of it: he had heard that Piliplok was
an ugly place, and ugly it was, brutal and rigid of design.
People often said of his own native city of Normork that it
was dreadfully dark and somber, a city that only someone
born there could love. Dekkeret, who found Normork's appearance quite pleasing, had never understood that criticism
before. But he understood it now: for who could possibly
love Piliplok except someone native to the place, to whom
Piliplok's brutal and rigid look was the norm of beauty?

One thing that it wasn't, though, was a muddy backwater.
A backwater, maybe, but not at all muddy; Piliplok was
paved, every last inch of it, a hideous metropolis of stone
and concrete with barely a tree or a shrub to be seen. It was
laid out with mathematical and indeed almost maniacal precision in eleven perfectly straight spokes radiating outward
from its superb natural harbor on the Inner Sea, with curving
bands of streets crossing the axis of the spokes in disagree-

ably exact rows. Each district—the mercantile quarter close to the waterfront, the industrial zone just beyond it, the various residential and recreational areas—was uniform throughout itself in architectural style, as though fixed by law, and the buildings themselves, clumsy and heavy, were not much to Dekkeret's taste. Normork was an airy paradise by comparison.

But their stay there was blessedly brief. Piliplok was not just the main harbor for the ships that sailed between Alhanroel and Zimroel, and for the fleet of sea-dragon hunters that plied the waters of the Inner Sea in quest of the gigantic marine mammals that were so widely prized for their meat. It was also the place where the River Zimr, the greatest of all Majipoor's rivers, reached the sea after its seven-thousand-mile journey across Zimroel; and so, by virtue of its position at the huge river's mouth, Piliplok was the gateway to the whole interior of the continent.

Akbalik bought passage for them aboard one of the big riverboats that plied the Zimr between Piliplok and the river's source at the Dulorn Rift in northwestern Zimroel. The riverboat was enormous, far larger than the ship that had carried them across the Inner Sea; and whereas the oceangoing vessel had been simple and sturdy of design, intended as it was to bear up under the stresses involved in crossing thousands of miles of open sea, the riverboat was an ungainly and complicated affair, more like a floating village than a ship.

What it was, actually, was a broad, squat, practically rectangular platform with cargo holds, steerage quarters, and dining halls belowdecks, a square central courtyard bordered by pavilions and shops and gaming pavilions at deck level, and, at the stern, an elaborate many-leveled superstructure where the passengers were housed. It was decorated in an ornate and fanciful way, a jagged scarlet arch over the bridge, grotesque green figureheads with painted yellow horns jutting out like battering-rams at the bow, and a bewildering abundance of eccentric ornamental woodwork, a whimsical host of interlacing joists and scrolls and struts sprouting on every surface.

Dekkeret stared in wonder at his fellow passengers. The largest single group of them were humans, of course, but also there were great numbers of Hjorts and Skandars and Vroons, and a handful of Su-Suheris in diaphanous robes, and some scaly-skinned Ghayrogs, who were reptilian in general appearance although in fact they were mammals. He wondered if he would see Metamorphs too, and asked Akbalik about that; but no, Akbalik said, the Shapeshifter folk rarely left their inland reservation, even though the ancient prohibition against their traveling freely through the world had long since ceased to be firmly observed. And if there were any on board, he added, they would probably be wearing some form other than their own, to avoid the hostility that Metamorphs aroused whenever they mingled with other folk.

The Zimr, at Piliplok, was dark with the silt it had scoured from its bed in the course of its long journey east, and where it met the sea the river was some seventy miles across, so that it hardly looked like a river at all, but rather like a gigantic lake beneath which a vast stretch of the coast lay drowned. Piliplok itself occupied a high promontory on the river's southern bank; as they set out on their journey Dekkeret could just barely make out the uninhabited northern bank, plainly visible even across that great distance because it was a massive white cliff of pure chalk, a mile high and many miles long, brilliant in the morning light. But soon, as the riverboat left Piliplok behind and began to make its way upriver, the Zimr narrowed somewhat and took on more a riverlike appearance, though it never became truly narrow.

For Dekkeret this was like a journey to another world. He spent all his time on deck, staring out at the round-topped tawny hills and busy towns that flanked the river, places whose names he had never heard before—Port Saikforge, Stenwamp, Campilthorn, Vem. The density of population along this stretch of the river astonished him. The riverboat rarely traveled more than two or three hours before pulling into some new port to discharge passengers, pick up new ones, unload cargo crates, take new cargo on. For a time he jotted the names of them in a little notebook he carried—Dambemuir, Orgeliuse, Impemond, Haunfort Major, Salvamot, Obliorn Vale—until he realized that if he kept on writing down all these towns, there would be no room left in the book for anything else long before he reached Ni-moya. So he was content simply to stand by the rail and stare, drinking in the constantly changing sights. After a time they all blurred pleasantly together, the unfamiliar landscape started to look very familiar indeed, and he no longer felt such a sense of overwhelming strangeness. When dreams came to him in the night, though, they very often were dreams in which he was flying through the endless midnight of space, moving in utter ease from star to star.

There were two disturbing events during the voyage, both of them occurring within a few days after the departure from Piliplok, one comic, the other tragic.

The first involved a red-haired man just a few years older than Dekkeret, who seemed to spend much of his time wandering the decks muttering to himself, or chuckling unaccountably, or pointing at some spot in the empty air as if it held mysterious significance. A harmless lunatic, Dekkeret thought; and, remembering that other madman, not at all harmless, who had killed his beloved cousin Sithelle in the course of a crazed attempt to assassinate the Coronal, he made a point of keeping his distance from the man. But then, on the third day, as Dekkeret stood near the starboard rail looking out at the passing towns, he suddenly heard maniacal laughter coming from his left—or perhaps they were frantic shrieks; there was no way of telling—and looked about to see the red-haired man run wildly across the riverboat's central concourse, arms flailing, and mount the steps that led to the upper decks, and stand for a moment at the edge of the observation portico up there, and then, uttering a cascade of grotesque giggles and cackles, hurl himself over the side and into the river, where he began to thrash about in a frantic, frenzied way.

Immediately a loud cry of "Man overboard!" went up, and the riverboat halted and swung around in its path. Two burly crewmen went out in a dinghy and without much difficulty hauled the hapless lunatic from the water. They brought him back on board, dripping and spuming, and took him down belowdecks. That was the last Dekkeret saw of him until the riverboat pulled in, a day later, at a town called Kraibledene, where the fellow was put ashore and, so it appeared, turned over to the local authorities.

A day later came an even stranger thing. In early afternoon of a clear, warm day, as the riverboat was traversing a stretch of the river without settlements, a gaunt stern-faced man of about forty in a stiff, thickly brocaded robe descended from the passenger deck carrying a large and obviously heavy suitcase. He set the suitcase down in an unoccupied section of the main deck, opened it, and drew from it a series of odd-looking instruments and implements, which he proceeded to arrange with meticulous care in a perfect semicircle in front of him.

Dekkeret nudged Akbalik. "Look at all that weird stuff! It's sorcerer's equipment, isn't it?"

"It certainly looks like it. I wonder if he's going to cast some sort of spell right here in front of us all."

Dekkeret knew little about sorcery and had even less liking for it. Manifestations of the supernatural and irrational made him uncomfortable. "Is that anything we need to worry about, do you think?"

"Depends on what kind of spell it is, I suppose," Akbalik said, with a shrug. "But maybe he's just planning to hold a bargain sale for amateur wizards. Nobody would ever use all those different things in a single spell." And he began to point out and identify the different implements for Dekkeret. That triangular stone vessel was called a veralistia: it was used as a crucible in which powders were burned that permitted a view into things to come. The complex device with metal coils and posts was an armillary sphere, which showed the positions of the planets and stars so that horoscopes might be cast. The thing made of brightly colored feathers and animal hair woven closely together—Akbalik could not recall its name—was employed to facilitate conversations with the spirits of the dead. The one next to it, an arrangement of crystal lenses and fine golden wires, was called a podromis: wizards used it in restoring sexual virility.

"You seem to be quite the expert," said Dekkeret. "You've had personal acquaintance with all of this, I take it?"

"Hardly. I don't often have occasion to converse with the spirits of the dead, and I haven't had much need of podromises, either. But you hear about these things wherever you turn, nowadays. —Look, he's still got more! I wonder what that one is supposed to do. And that, with all the wheels and pistons!"

The suitcase was finally empty. A good-sized crowd had gathered by now. Word must be getting around the ship, Dekkeret thought, that some kind of demonstration of magic was about to get under way. You could always draw a big crowd for that.

The gaunt magus for that was surely what he was, a magus—took no notice of his audience. He was seated crosslegged now before his neat semicircular row of strange glittering apparatus and appeared to be off in some other realm of consciousness, eyes half closed, head rocking rhythmically from side to side.

Then, abruptly, he rose. Raised his foot and brought it down with savage force on the fragile instrument that Akbalik had called a podromis. Mashed it flat, and went on to trample the armillary sphere, and the device of wheels and pistons, and the small, delicate machine of interlocking metallic triangles just beyond it. The onlookers gasped in amazement and shock. Dekkeret wondered if it might be blasphemous to destroy such things as these, whether doing so would bring down the vengeance of the supernatural spirits. If indeed such spirits existed at all, he added.

The magus now had systematically destroyed almost his entire collection of magical equipment. Those that he could not smash, like the veralistia, he hurled overboard. Then, calmly, purposefully, he walked to the rail and in a single smooth movement surmounted it and leaped into the river.

This time there was to be no rescue. The man had gone straight under, vanishing instantly from sight as though the pockets of his robe were filled with stones. Once again the riverboat came to a halt and crewmen went out in a dinghy, but they found no trace of the jumper, and returned after a time, grim-faced, to report their failure.

"Madness is everywhere," Akbalik said, and shivered. "The world is turning very strange, boy."

After that, members of the crew patrolled the deck two by two at all hours to guard against further such incidents. But there were no others.

The two bizarre events left Dekkeret in a somber, brooding mood. Madness was everywhere, yes. He could not now keep the memory of Sithelle's incomprehensible terrible death, which for months he had worked hard to repress, from flooding back into his mind in all its full horror. That wild-eyed lunatic—those clotted, unintelligible cries of rage—Sithelle stepping forward—the flashing blade—the sudden startling spurt of blood—

And now a giggling clownish fellow jumps overboard in mid-river, and then a magus who has evidently reached the end of his tether. Could it happen to anyone at any time, the onset of irresistible madness, the utter unstoppable flight of all reason from the mind? Could it happen even to him? Worriedly Dekkeret searched his soul for the seeds of insanity. But they did not seem to be present within him, or, at any rate, he could not find them; and after a time his normal high spirits reasserted themselves, and he went back to his pastime of peering at the passing cities of the riverbank without fear that he would without warning be seized with the unconquerable urge to hurl himself over the rail.

When the splendor of Ni-moya burst abruptly upon him he was utterly unprepared.

For several days, now, the river had been growing wider. Dekkeret knew that a second great river joined the Zimr just south of the city—the Steiche, it was, coming up out of the wild Metamorph country—and where the two rivers flowed together, their union would of necessity form one much larger than either of its components. But he had not expected the joining of the rivers to create such a vast body of water. It made the mouth of the Zimr at Piliplok look like a trickling stream. Crossing that great confluence was much like being on the ocean again. Dekkeret was aware that Ni-moya was somewhere to the north; there were other great cities over on the other shore; but it was hard for his stunned mind to take in the immensity of the scene, and all he could see was the dark breast of the water stretching to the horizon, dotted everywhere by the bright pennants of the hundreds of local ferries that crossed it constantly in all directions.

He stared for what seemed like hours. Then, as he stood gaping, Akbalik took him by the elbow and turned him to one side.

"There," he said. "You're looking in the wrong direction. That's Ni-moya up yonder. Some of it, anyway."

Dekkeret was astounded. It was a magical sight: an endless backdrop of thickly forested hills, with an enormous city of shining white towers in the foreground, each one seeming taller than its neighbor, row upon row of titanic structures descending right to the shore of the river.

Was this a city? It was a world in itself. It went on forever, following the river's course as far as he could see, and continuing onward, obviously, for a long distance beyond—hundreds of miles, maybe. Dekkeret caught his breath. So much! So beautiful! He felt like dropping to his knees. Akbalik began to speak like a tour guide of Ni-moya's most famous sights: the Gossamer Galleria, a mercantile arcade a mile long that hovered high above the ground on nearly invisible cables; and the Museum of Worlds, where treasures from all over the universe were on display, even, so it was said, things from Old Earth; and the Crystal Boulevard, where revolving reflectors created the brilliance of a thousand suns; and the Park of Fabulous Beasts, full of wonders from remote and practically unknown districts—

There was no end to the recitation. "That's the Opera House, there on the hill," said Akbalik, indicating a many-faceted building gleaming so brightly that it made Dekkeret's eyes ache to look at it. "With a thousand-instrument orchestra, creating a sound you can't begin to imagine. That big glass dome over there with the ten towers sprouting from it, that's the municipal library, which holds every book that's ever been published. Over there, that row of low buildings right at the water's edge, with tiled roofs and turquoise and gold mosaics on their fronts, the ones you might think are the palaces of princes, those are the customs buildings. And then, just above and to the left of them—"

"What's that one?" Dekkeret broke in, pointing toward a structure of great size and transcendent beauty, a good way down the shore, that rose above everything else in supreme majesty, imperiously summoning the attention of every eye even amidst this phenomenal concatenation of architectural wonders.

"Oh, that," said Akbalik. "That's the palace of the Procurator Dantirya Sambail."

It was a white-walled building of unthinkable splendor and grace: not of such prodigious size as Dekkeret knew Lord Prestimion's Castle to be, but quite large enough to meet almost any prince's requirements, and of such wondrous elegance that it dominated the waterfront by its sheer perfection.

The Procurator's palace appeared to hover in mid-air, floating above the city, although in actuality, Dekkeret saw, it was situated atop a smooth white pedestal of stupendous height—a more modest version, in its way, of Castle Mount itself. But instead of sprawling off in all directions, as the Castle did, this building was a relatively compact series of pavilions and colonnaded porticos that made ingenious use of suspension devices and cantilevered supports to give the appearance of complete defiance of gravity. The uppermost floor was a series of transparent bubbles of clearest quartz, with a row of many-balconied chambers below it, and a wider series of galleries in the next level down, reached by a cascading series of enclosed staircases that bowed outward like knees and swung sharply back inward again in a manner that seemed to defy all geometry. Squinting into the glare of Ni-moya's radiantly white towers, Dekkeret could make out hints of other wings flanking the building on both sides below. At its gleaming base a single sturdy octagonal block of polished agate, at least as big as an ordinary person's house, jutted from the facade like an emblazoned medallion.

"How can any one person, even the Procurator, be allowed to live in anything so grand?"

Akbalik laughed. "Dantirya Sambail is a law unto himself. He was only twelve, you know, when he inherited the procuratorial fief of Ni-moya. Which had always been an important fief, you understand, the most important one in Zimroel, but that was before Dantirya Sambail took control of it. Everyone assumed there would have to be a regency, but no, not at all, he disposed of his cousin the regent in about two minutes and took power in his own right, and then, thanks to at least three marriages and half a dozen informal alliances and a lot of very desirable inheritances from an assortment of powerful kinsmen, he put together what amounts to a private empire. By the time he was thirty he held direct rule over a third of the continent of Zimroel and indirect influence over just about all the rest of it except the Metamorph reservation. If he could have figured out some way of taking that over too, he probably would have done it. As it is, he rules Zimroel pretty much as its king. A king needs a decent palace: Dantirya Sambail has spent the last forty years improving the one he inherited into what you see before you now."

"What about the Pontifex and the Coronal? Didn't they have any objections to all this?"

"Old Prankipin's main concern, at least before he fell in with the sorcerers, was always commerce: constant economic expansion and the free flow of goods from one region to another, with everybody making a nice profit and the money going around and around. I think he saw the rise of Dantirya Sambail as a favorable contributing factor. Zimroel was a pretty fragmented place, you know, so far from the centers of government across the sea that the local lords mostly did whatever they pleased, and when the interests of the Duke of Narabal clashed with the interests of the Prince of Pidruid, it wasn't always healthy for the regional economy. Having someone like Dantirya Sambail in charge, capable of telling all the local boys what they should do and making it stick, played right into Prankipin's plan. As for Lord Confalume, he was even more enthusiastic about the unification of Zimroel under Dantirya Sambail than the Pontifex. Neither of them liked Dantirya Sambail, you understand—who could?—but they saw him as useful. Indispensable, even. So they tolerated his power grab and in some ways even encouraged it. And he was smart enough not to tread on their toes. Traveled often to the Labyrinth and the Castle, he did, paid his respects, loyal subject of his majesty and his lordship, et cetera, et cetera."

"And Lord Prestimion? Is he going to go along with the arrangement also?"

"Ah. Prestimion." A cloud appeared to cross Akbalik's face. "No, things are different now. There's some trouble between Lord Prestimion and the Procurator. Fairly serious trouble, in fact."

"Of what sort?"

Akbalik looked away. "Not of any sort that I'm able to discuss with you right now, boy. Serious, is all. Extremely serious. Perhaps we'll have an opportunity to go into the details some other time. —Ah: we're landing in Ni-moya, it seems."

The section of the city where the riverboat came to shore was called Strelain, which Akbalik told him was the name of Ni-moya's central district. A government floater was waiting for them; it took them up and up through the hilly streets of the great city, and deposited them at last at the tall building that was to be their home for the next few months.

Dekkeret's little apartment was on the fifteenth floor. That a building could have so many floors was something that had never occurred to him. Standing by the wide window, peering out at the tops of the buildings below, and at the river farther on, and the dark line of the Zimr's southern shore so far off that he could barely make it out, he had the

giddy feeling that the building might at any moment pitch
forward purely of its own unsustainable height and tumble
down the hill, scattering its component bricks far and wide
as it fell. He turned away from the window, shuddering. But
the building stood firm.

The next day he began work at the Office of Documentary Appeal. That was a subdivision of the Bureau of the
Treasury, housed in a back wing of the rambling thousand-
year-old governmental complex of blue granite known as
the Cascanar Building, in south-central Strelain.

It was meaningless work. Dekkeret had no illusions about
that. He was supposed to interview people who had had
important documents—important to them, anyway—garbled
somehow by the bureaucracy, and help them straighten out
the confusion. From his first day he found himself attempting to unravel disputes about erroneous listings of birth-
dates, improper delineation of property boundaries, muddied
self-contradictory statements inserted into legal depositions
by careless stenographers, and a host of other such things.
There was no reason in the world why it had been necessary
to ship him thousands of miles to handle such drab and
trifling matters, which any career civil servant already working here could be dealing with.

But the point, he knew, was that everyone in the government, from the Pontifex and Coronal on down, was a career
civil servant. And every prince of Castle Mount who had
any ambition toward high office was required to put in time
doing routine work of just this sort. Even Prestimion, who
had been born to the rank of Prince of Muldemar and might
have spent a life of pleasant idleness puttering in his vineyards, had had to go through a round of chores like this by
way of gathering the practical experience that had carried
him to the throne.

Dekkeret, a salesman's son, had never had such grandi-
ose ambitions. The starburst crown was no part of his plan;
to be a knight of the Castle seemed as bold an aspiration as
he could allow himself. Well, he was that, now, thanks to
the happenstance of his having been standing close by the
Coronal at the time of the assassination attempt: a knight-

initiate, anyway. And therefore he found himself behind this
desk at the Office of Documentary Appeal in Ni-moya, plodding through day after day of foolish dreary work and hoping eventually to move on to grander things, closer to the
summit of power. But this had to be done first.

Akbalik, whom he never saw during his working hours
and only occasionally in the evenings, was someone who
already had gone on to grander things, though Dekkeret was
not sure just what they were. Plainly Akbalik was a model
worth patterning oneself after. He was very close to the Coronal's inner circle, apparently, if not actually a member of
it himself just yet. He was quite friendly with the High
Counsellor Septach Melayn; he had the respect of the gruff
and businesslike Admiral Gialaurys; he seemed to have easy
access to Lord Prestimion. Surely he was destined to have
a swift ascent to the highest reaches of the government.

Of course, Akbalik was the nephew of the wealthy and
powerful Prince Serithorn, and that surely helped. But although high birth could get you fairly easily to high places
in the Castle hierarchy, Dekkeret knew that ultimately it was
merit, intelligence, character, perseverance, that brought you
to the top. Fools and sluggards didn't become Coronals,
although they might, by good luck and the accident of family connection, attain illustrious lesser posts despite their
blatant deficiencies. Count Meglis of Normork was a good
example of that.

Nor did great riches or noble birth suffice to get one to
the throne, or else Serithorn, descended from half the great
Coronals of antiquity, would have had it. Prince Serithorn,
though, was not the kind of man who was suited for the
job. He lacked the necessary seriousness. Septach Melayn,
the High Counsellor, would never be Coronal either, it
seemed, for the same reason.

But Lord Prestimion, obviously, had proven himself fit
for the post. So had Lord Confalume before him. And Akbalik, too, that calm, steady-minded, quick-witted, hard-
working, reliable man, might have the stuff of Coronals in
him. Dekkeret admired him inordinately. It was much too
early even to speculate about who might succeed Prestimion

as Coronal when he became Pontifex; but, Dekkeret thought, how splendid if it turned out to be Akbalik! And how good that would be for Dekkeret of Normork, too, for he could plainly see that Akbalik looked upon him favorably and regarded him as a highly promising young man. For a moment, just a moment, Dekkeret allowed himself the wild fantasy of picturing himself as High Counsellor to the Coronal Lord Akbalik. And then it was back to correcting misspelled names on deeds of trust, and sorting out conflicts in land titles that went back to Lord Keppimon's day, and authorizing refunds for taxes that had been levied in triplicate by overenthusiastic revenue inspectors.

Two months went by in this fashion. Dekkeret grew enormously restless at his job, but he plodded gamely onward and allowed no hint of discontent to pass his lips. In his free time he roamed the city, bowled over again and again by the splendors he found everywhere. He made a few friends at the office; he met a couple of pleasant young women; once or twice a week Akbalik joined him at a local tavern for an evening's amiable exploration of the excellent Zimroel wines. Dekkeret had no idea what sort of assignment it was that had brought Akbalik to Ni-moya, and he did not ask. He was grateful for the older man's company, and wary of seeming to probe matters that obviously did not concern him.

One night Akbalik said, "Do you remember that time when we were in the Coronal's office and Septach Melayn spoke about our going on a steetmoy-hunting expedition while we were here?"

"Of course I do."

"You're bored silly with the work you've been doing, aren't you, Dekkeret?"

Dekkeret reddened. "Well—"

"Don't try to be diplomatic. You're supposed to be bored silly with it. It was designed to bore you. But you weren't sent here to be tortured. I'm about ready for a break in my own work: what say we take ten days up north, and see how the steetmoy are running this time of year?"

"Would I be able to arrange a leave of absence?" Dekkeret asked.

Akbalik grinned. "I think I could manage to get one for you," he said.

8

THE COUNTRYSIDE CHANGED VERY quickly once they were north of Ni-moya. The climate of most of Majipoor was subtropical or tropical, except along such high mountain ridges as the Gonghar mountains of central Zimroel and atop Mount Zygnor in far-northern Alhanroel. Castle Mount itself, where the weather-machines devised by the ancients eternally fended off the bitter night of the stratospheric altitude, enjoyed an endless springtime.

But one sector of northeastern Zimroel reached far up toward the pole and therefore had a cooler climate. In the high, mountain-bordered plateau known as the Khyntor Marches, snow was not at all uncommon during the winter months; and beyond that, walled off behind the tremendous peaks known as the Nine Sisters, there was an unknown polar land of perpetual storm and frost where no one ever went. In that grim and virtually inaccessible region, so legend had it, a race of fierce fur-clad barbarians had dwelled for thousands of years in complete isolation, as unaware of the comfort and warmth and prosperity enjoyed by Majipoor's other inhabitants as the rest of Majipoor was of them.

Akbalik and Dekkeret had no intention of going anywhere near that myth-shrouded land of constant winter and unyielding ice. But even just a short distance back of Ni-moya, its stark influence on the territories bordering on it was quickly apparent. Lush green subtropical forests yielded to vegetation more typical of a temperate climate, dominated by curious angular deciduous trees with bright yellow trunks, set very far apart from one another in stony meadows of scruffy pallid grass. And then, as they entered the foothills of the Khyntor Marches, a further increment of bleakness became evident. The trees and grass were far sparser,

now. The landscape here was a gradually rising terrain of
flat gray granite shields with swift cold streams slicing down
out of the north. In the hazy distance the first of the Nine
Sisters of Khyntor was visible: Threilikor, the Weeping Sister, whose dark facade was glossy with a multitude of riv-
ulets and streams.

Akbalik had hired a team of five hunters, March-men,
lean leathery-skinned mountaineers of the northlands who
dressed in rough, crudely stitched robes of black haigus-
hide, to guide them into the Marches. Three of them seemed
to be male, two female, although it was not easy to tell, so
thoroughly were they engulfed in their bulky robes. They
said very little. When they talked to each other, it was in a
harsh mountain dialect that Dekkeret found practically impossible to understand. In addressing their two Castle lordlings they took care to use conventional speech, but he had
trouble with that too, because the thick-tongued mountaineers spoke with heavy accents tinged with the rhythms of
their own tongue, and also Dekkeret was often unfamiliar
with the Ni-moyan idioms that peppered their speech. He
let Akbalik do most of the talking.

The mountain folk appeared to regard their city-bred
charges with amusement verging on scorn. They definitely
had no great respect for Dekkeret, who had never been in
wilderness country before, and who was obviously uncertain
of himself despite his size and strength. They looked upon
him, he was sure, as an inept and useless boy. But they
seemed not to have much esteem even for Akbalik, whose
aura of competence and capability usually won quick rec-
ognition anywhere. Whenever he asked them something
they would reply in curt monosyllables, and sometimes
could be seen to turn away with sardonic smiles, as though
barely able to suppress their contempt for any city man who
needed to ask about something so self-evident that any child
would know it.

"The steetmoy are forest creatures," Akbalik told him.
"They don't like it much out here on the open tundra. That's
their home territory down there, that dark place in the
shadow of the mountain. The hunters will scare up a pack

of them for us in the deep woods and drive them into a
stampede. We select the ones we want to go after and chase
them through the forest until we have them cornered." Akbalik glanced at Dekkeret's oddly short legs, heavily knotted
with muscle. "You're a good runner, aren't you?"

"I'm no sprinter. But I can manage."

"Steetmoy aren't especially fast either. They don't need
to be. But they have plenty of stamina and they're better
than we are at barreling through thick underbrush. It's easy
for one to make his way into dense cover and get away
from you. The problem then is that they sometimes come
slipping around behind you and attack from the rear. They
live primarily on berries and nuts and bark, but they don't
mind eating meat, you know, especially in winter, and
they're very adequately equipped for killing."

Turning to his pack, he began to draw weapons from it
and lay them out in front of Dekkeret.

"These are what we'll take with us. The hooked machete
is for cutting your way through the brush. The poniard is
what you use for killing your steetmoy."

"This?" Dekkeret asked. He picked it up and stared at it.
Its blade was impressively sharp but no more than six inches
in length. "Isn't it a little short?"

"Did you expect to be using an energy-thrower?"

Dekkeret felt his face going hot. He remembered, now,
that Septach Melayn had talked about how steetmoy are
hunted with poniard and machete. Dekkeret hadn't given it
much thought at the time. "Well, of course not. But with
this thing I'd have to be right on top of the steetmoy for the
kill."

"Yes. You would, wouldn't you? That's the whole point
of the sport: hunting at close range, great risk for high reward. And also, doing as little damage to the valuable fur
as possible. If it comes down to a matter of your life or the
steetmoy's, you can use your machete, but that's not considered very sporting. Imagine Septach Melayn, for instance,
hacking away at a steetmoy with his machete!"

"Septach Melayn has the quickest reflexes of any man

who ever lived. He could kill a steetmoy with an ivory toothpick. But I'm not Septach Melayn."

Akbalik seemed unworried. Dekkeret was big and strong; Dekkeret was determined; Dekkeret would look after himself quite satisfactorily down there in the steetmoy forest.

Dekkeret himself was less confident. He had never asked for this adventure. It had all been Septach Melayn's idea originally. He had been eager enough to undertake it, yes, back there in the Castle, but that was without any real awareness of what hunting steetmoy in their native territory might involve. And, though he had heard plenty of exuberant hunting tales from other young knight-initiates during his first few months at the Castle, and had envied them greatly, he realized now that it was one thing to roam the walled hunting preserves of Halanx or Amblemorn in search of zaur or onathils or bilantoons, but it was something else entirely to be roaming around in a cold northern forest looking for a ferocious steetmoy that you planned to kill with a tiny dagger.

Cowardice, though, was no part of Dekkeret's makeup. What lay ahead sounded like a tough assignment, but perhaps the hunt wouldn't turn out to be as risky as it seemed just now, with his imagination leading him to anticipate the worst. So he picked up his poniard and his machete and hefted them and took a few fierce swipes through the air for practice, and told Akbalik cheerfully that on second thought the poniard seemed more than adequate for the job and he was ready for the steetmoy hunt whenever the steetmoy were ready for him.

Akbalik had a new surprise in store for him as they followed the five March-men down a long boulder-strewn slope into the dark glade where the steetmoy lived. Reaching into his pack, he drew forth two blunt-nosed metal tubes, stuck one into his belt next to his poniard, and handed the other one to Dekkeret.

"Energy-throwers? But you said—"

"Lord Prestimion's orders. We want to behave like

proper sportsmen, yes, but I'm also supposed to bring you back from here alive. The poniard is the prime weapon, and if you get into difficulties you use the machete, and if you get into real difficulties you blast the damned animal with the energy-thrower. It's not the elegant way, but it's a sensible last resort. An angry steetmoy can rip a man's guts out with three slashes of his claws."

Feeling more ashamed than relieved, Dekkeret tucked the energy-thrower into one of the loops of his belt, wishing there were some way of pushing it down out of sight to keep the March-men guides from noticing it. But that hardly mattered. They had already made it quite clear that they looked upon Dekkeret and Akbalik as a pair of shallow self-indulgent fops so doltish that they could find nothing better to do with their time than take themselves off into the forests of the north and hunt dangerous animals for no motive more worthy than their own amusement. It could scarcely lessen them in the March-men's eyes if one of them suddenly happened to pull out an energy-thrower and blaze away at an inconveniently rambunctious steetmoy. All the same, Dekkeret quietly vowed that he would not use the weapon even as a last resort. The poniard and—if necessary—the machete would have to do the job.

It had snowed during the night. Though the temperature was a little above freezing now, the ground was white everywhere. A few solitary flakes still were coming down. One of them struck Dekkeret's cheek, causing a little burning sensation. A strange feeling, that. The whole concept of snow was new to him, and very curious.

The trees in this glade had yellow trunks like those farther to the south, but they carried heavy growths of blackish-brown needle-like leaves rather than showing bare deciduous branches, and instead of having their trunks and branches contorted into odd angles these trees stood tall and straight, with their thick crowns meeting far overhead. Underneath, a dense darkness prevailed. A stream dotted by big boulders flowed past on one side, and on the other, the one closest to the mountain, the land dropped sharply away into a swooping valley.

The five hired hunters led the way, with Dekkeret and Akbalik close behind, following in the tracks that the March-men left in the snow. Gradually the pace picked up until they were trotting through the forest, moving in easy loping bounds along the bank of the stream. Hardly ever did the hunters look back toward them. When one of them did— it was one of the women, a flat-faced, wide-mouthed one with big gaps between her teeth—it was to give Dekkeret a mocking grin that seemed to say, In five minutes you will be frightened entirely out of whatever wits you may have. Perhaps he was wrong about that. Perhaps she was just trying to look encouraging. But it was not a pretty grin.

"Steetmoy," Akbalik said suddenly. "Three of them, I think." He pointed off to the left, into a dark grove where the yellow-trunked trees stood particularly close together and the snow lay thick on the ground. At first Dekkeret noticed nothing unusual. Then he glimpsed a zone of whiteness in there that was different from the whiteness of the snow: softer, brighter, with a lustrous gleam instead of a hard glitter. Large furry white animals, moving about. The sound of their low muttering growls came toward him on the wind.

The hunters had paused by the edge of the grove. A few unintelligible muttered words passed among them; and then they began to move toward the trees, fanning out in a wide arc as they did so.

Quickly Dekkeret came to understand what was happening. The steetmoy—three of them, yes—had picked up the scent. They were moving slowly about amidst the trees, as if working out their strategy. Dekkeret could see them clearly now, thick-bodied beasts built low to the ground, with long jutting black snouts and flat triangular heads out of which golden eyes, rimmed with red, were staring intently. They were about the size of very large dogs, but heavier and sturdier. They looked graceless but powerful: their thighs and haunches were massive, their forearms plainly held great strength. Long curving claws, black and shiny, jutted from their paws. Dekkeret could not believe that he would be expected to kill one of these creatures with a mere handheld dagger. But that was what was done, sup-posedly. It seemed improbable. He hadn't forgotten Septach Melayn's words: "Beautiful thing: that thick fur, those blaz-ing eyes. Most dangerous wild animal in the world, so far as I know, the steetmoy "

The gap-toothed mountain woman was gesturing at him.

"First one's yours," Akbalik said.

"What?"

Dekkeret had expected the older, more experienced Ak-balik to go first. But the meaning of those gestures was not at all ambiguous. The woman was beckoning to him.

"They've decided it," Akbalik said. "They usually know the best match of hunter and prey. You'd better go ahead. I'll be right behind you."

Dekkeret nodded. He stepped forward, still apprehensive and uneasy. But with his first step toward the dark glade an astonishing thing happened. All uncertainty dropped away. A strange cool calmness settled over him. Fear and doubt were utterly absent from his mind. He found himself entirely ready, primed for the kill, utterly focused on his objective.

And an instant later the hunt was on.

The March-men now had positioned themselves across a lengthy curving front that spanned the place where the three steetmoy were moving about and extended well beyond it on both sides. The woman who seemed to be Dekkeret's guide was at the center of the line. She led the way forward, with Dekkeret close behind her. The two hunters at farthest left and right were moving inward at a sharp angle, pulling the line in toward the animals. They started now to set up a terrible din with brass hunting-horns that they had drawn from their packs, while the other two March-men began to clap their hands and shout.

The idea, Dekkeret saw, was to separate the animals, driving two of them away to give him a clear path to the third. And the noise was having its intended effect. The steetmoy, puzzled and bothered by the strident blaring sounds, were up on their hind legs, raking trees with their claws in what seemed to be a reflexive expression of irritation, and their growls no longer were low rumbling mutters but reverberating bellows of anger.

The March-men continued to close in. The steetmoy, showing no apparent fear, but only annoyance and perhaps disgust at being harassed in this fashion in their own domain, turned slowly and began to lope away in different directions—each heading, perhaps, for its own den. The five hunters ignored the two biggest ones, allowing them to slip away undisturbed into the deeper woods. They gave their attention to the remaining one, a female, perhaps, smaller than the other two but still a formidable beast. They were advancing on it in high-kicking strides as though on parade, and making noise for all they were worth.

The animal seemed befuddled by the uproar for a moment or two. Then, blinking and grumbling, the steetmoy swung around and headed at a slow but steadily accelerating pace toward the cover of a clump of shrubbery a few hundred yards away.

The gap-toothed woman stepped aside. Dekkeret knew that this was his moment.

He went rushing forward, machete in one hand, poniard in the other.

At the fringe of the glade the trees were fairly far apart, but they quickly became more dense, with saplings and brush occupying the spaces between them and semi-woody vines dangling from their lower branches. Before long Dekkeret was moving through one difficult thicket after another, chopping away furiously with the machete as he scrambled through. He drove himself onward in a kind of frenzy, heedless of obstacles. And yet for all his frenetic exertions he was losing ground. He could still see the retreating steetmoy up ahead. But the beast, slow-moving though it was, seemed easily able to clear a path for itself with its powerful forearms, leaving a tangled trail of shattered underbrush and torn vines behind it that only made Dekkeret's task harder. Very gradually it was widening the distance between itself and its pursuer.

And then it disappeared entirely. He was all alone.

Where had it gone? Into a hidden burrow? Had it wrig-

gled under some impenetrable pile of brush? Or, Dekkeret
wondered, maybe it had simply stepped behind some thick-
trunked tree up ahead, and was at this very moment wending
its way back toward him, slinking from one clump of brush
to the next, moving into position for the lethal counterattack
that Akbalik had said they sometimes made.

Dekkeret looked around for the mountain woman. No
sign of her. Somehow in his pell-mell race through the
woods he had left her behind.

Clutching his two weapons tightly, he turned in a full
circle without moving from the spot, staring warily into the
dimness, listening desperately for the sound of ripping underbrush, of falling saplings. Nothing. Nothing. And now
thick mist had begun to rise from the snowy ground to veil
everything in white. Should he call out for the woman? No.
Possibly her disappearance was deliberate; perhaps it was
always the custom to leave the huntsman alone with his prey
in the final moments of the chase.

After a few moments he began to move cautiously off to
his left, where the mist seemed a little thinner. His plan was
to traverse a circular arc back to his starting point, searching
for the steetmoy's hiding-place as he went.

In the forest, all was still. It was as if he had gone into
it on his own.

Then, as he came around past a copse of straight-trunked
young trees that had sprouted just inches apart from one
another so that they formed a tight palisade, everything
changed in a hurry. On the far side of the copse he found
himself looking into a little clearing. The woman stood at
the center of it, peering around in all directions as though
searching for the steetmoy, or, perhaps, for him. Dekkeret
called out to her; and in the same instant the steetmoy came
bounding out of the woods on the other side.

The gap-toothed woman, already turning toward Dekkeret, swung around swiftly to face the angry animal. The
steetmoy, rising on its hind legs, swatted her aside with one
swipe of its forearm. She went sprawling to the ground.
Without a pause the steetmoy went pounding on past the
astonished Dekkeret toward the nearest group of trees.

It took him a moment to break from his stasis. Then he too was in motion, running after the steetmoy once more, knowing only that this was his final chance, that if he let the beast get away from him a second time he would never see it again.

Knots were forming in his thighs and calves. He could feel the muscles writhing. As he made a sharp turn he stepped on a slick snow-covered slab of rock, and slipped, twisting his ankle and sending a jolt of fire running up his left leg. But he kept on going. The steetmoy no longer seemed to be trying to take evasive action; it was simply trotting ahead of him, moving now through a sector of the forest that was open enough for both of them to move readily through it. That gave an advantage to Dekkeret, who, slow runner that he was, should have been able in open terrain to move a bit faster than the steetmoy.

But he was unable to close the space between him and his prey. He had plenty of stamina left, but there appeared to be no way that he could compel the rebellious muscles of his legs to drive him onward any more quickly. It began to become clear to him that the steetmoy would elude him once more.

Not so. The beast fetched up against a thickly snarled mass of brush and vines and came to a halt there, unaccountably choosing to swing about and stand its ground instead of ripping its way through. Had it decided to halt for a showdown with its bothersome foe? Or was it simply tired of running? Those were questions that Dekkeret would never be able to answer. He had no time to pause for thought at all. Before he even realized fully what had happened, his own momentum brought him virtually up against the animal, which was standing erect with its back to the tightly woven underbrush. He heard the creature's angry growling. A massive paw swung toward him. Instinctively Dekkeret ducked around it and brought the poniard upward and inward. The steetmoy roared in pain. Dekkeret stepped back, thrust forward again, found his target a second time. Brilliant crimson blood spurted over the soft white fur of the steetmoy's breast.

He stepped back, breathing hard. Would a third blow be necessary? Did he need to use the machete?

No and no. The steetmoy, looking confused, remained upright for a moment, rocking slowly from side to side, as its bright red-rimmed eyes slowly began to glaze. Then it toppled. Dekkeret stood over it, hardly believing what had happened. The animal did not move.

Turning, then, he cupped his hands and yelled. "Hoy! Akbalik, where are you? I got it, Akbalik! I got it!"

A muffled reply came to him through the mist from far away. He was unable to make it out.

He tried again. "Akbalik?"

This time, no call came in return. There was no response from any of the hunters either. Where was everyone? If he left the steetmoy lying here, would scavenging beasts tear it apart before he could return to it? For that matter, would he even be able to locate it again in this mysterious misty forest?

Some minutes passed. Swirls of new snow descended. Dekkeret realized that he could not continue to remain where he was. Slowly he began to make his way back in the direction from which he thought he had come, searching for his own tracks in the snow as he went. After a time he saw the tight-grown copse again; and on the far side of it he came upon a scene that would remain in his mind to the end of his days.

Akbalik and four of the March-men hunters were standing in the middle of the clearing back of the copse. A bloody machete dangled from Akbalik's hand and there was more blood all over the snow. The March-men, farther to the rear, stared stonily at Dekkeret as he came into view. The gap-toothed woman lay on her back, motionless, her entire midsection torn apart, a terrible wound. Five or six feet away from her was the dead body of some squat thick-snouted beast that had been cut practically in half by Akbalik's machete. It had bloodstains on its muzzle as well.

"Akbalik?" Dekkeret asked, bewildered. "What's happened here? Is she—?"

"Dead? What do you think?"

"Is this the animal that killed her? What is it, anyway?"

"A tumilat, they said. A scavenger, a carrion-feeder. They
live in underground burrows around here. It'll kill, sometimes, if it finds a dying or unconscious animal. But what I
can't understand is why a scavenging animal would attack
someone who isn't—"

"Oh," said Dekkeret, in a very small voice, and put his
hand over his mouth. "Oh. Oh. Oh."

"What is it, Dekkeret? What are you trying to say?"

"Not the tumilat," Dekkeret murmured. "The steetmoy.
It came out of nowhere and ran right into her and knocked
her down with its paw. And kept on going. So did I. I went
right after it and caught up with it and killed it, Akbalik. I
killed it. But I didn't stop to think about the hunter woman.
She was lying here—wounded, maybe, unconscious—oh,
Akbalik! I never even gave her a thought. And then, while
she was lying here all alone, the scavenging animal came
up to her, and—oh—" He stared into the gathering whiteness all about him, appalled at what he had done. "Oh, Akbalik," he said again, feeling numb. "Oh!"

9

WHEN PRESTIMION AND HIS companions emerged from the
Labyrinth's southernmost mouth they saw the broad reaches
of Alhanroel stretching before them like an endless ocean.
The land was flat here, and the horizon was a gray hazy line
that seemed to be a million miles off. Every day brought
new landscapes, new kinds of vegetation, new cities. And
somewhere ahead of them in that unending vastness was
Dantirya Sambail, slipping steadily away.

The royal party halted first in Bailemoona, that lovely
city of the fertile plain southeast of the Labyrinth where the
Procurator's man Mandralisca had had his encounter with
Prince Serithorn's gamekeeper. Kaitinimon, Bailemoona's
new young duke, Kanteverel's son, met them outside the
city's bright claret-hued walls and gave them a royal welcome.

He had his late father's round-faced easy-going look, and, like Kanteverel, preferred simple loose-flowing tunics to more glittery formal garb. But Kanteverel had rarely been anything other than cheerful and jovial, and there was a barely hidden tension about this man, a poorly concealed rigor of spirit, that showed him to be of a different sort entirely. Still, it was a long while since a Coronal had visited Bailemoona, and Kaitinimon displayed nothing but delight at Prestimion's arrival, staging an appropriately splashy festivity for him, a host of musicians and jugglers and cunning conjurers and a grand display of the famed cuisine of the region, with local wines to match each dish. And, of course, he provided a visit to Bailemoona's legendary golden bees.

Nearly every city of the realm had its special item of distinction. The golden bees were Bailemoona's. Once, long ago, in the days when only sparse bands of Shapeshifters had lived in this part of Alhanroel, such bees had been far from uncommon throughout the entire province and the adjacent territories. But the spread of human civilization had sent them into a long decline that brought them eventually to the brink of extinction, and now the only ones that remained were those that the Dukes of Bailemoona kept sacrosanct in the celebrated apiary on the grounds of the ducal palace.

"We open the apiary to the general public just three times a year," Duke Kaitinimon said, as he led Prestimion through the palace garden to the bee-house. "On Winterday, on Summerday, and on the duke's birthday. Admission is by lottery, a dozen visitors an hour for ten hours, and tickets change hands at high prices. At other times no one is permitted to visit them except their regular keepers and members of the ducal family. But, of course, when the Coronal comes to Bailemoona—"

The apiary was a building of startling beauty: a huge lacy structure of radiant metallic mesh, held upright by smooth tubular struts of some gleaming white wood that crossed and crossed again in an intricate way baffling to the eye, the entire thing seemingly so insubstantial that a puff of wind would hurl it into ruin. Within it Prestimion was able to make out a myriad bright bursts of light winking on and off with a rapidity that made the mind reel, like semaphore signals so swift that no one could possibly decipher their message. "What you're seeing," said the duke, "is sunlight glancing off the bodies of the bees as they move about. But come: come inside, if you will, my lord."

A long entryway leading to a series of small chambers, each with a door at both ends, admitted Prestimion and his party to the apiary proper. Which was a gigantic dome four or five times the size of the Confalume throne-room, and so artfully woven that the mesh of which it was made was only faintly visible when beheld from within, a mere faint film against the open sky.

A high-pitched droning sound enveloped the visitors like a thick veil. There were bees everywhere overhead. Hundreds of them. Thousands.

They were in ceaseless motion, endlessly crossing and recrossing the upper reaches of their home in a bewildering airborne ballet. Prestimion was amazed by their numbers, and by the speed at which they moved, and the brilliance of the light that rebounded from their glossy sides and wings as they flitted quickly about. He stood for a long moment at the entrance, staring upward in wonder, marveling at the rapidity of the bees' movements and the dizzying beauty of the patterns that they created.

Gradually he began to focus on individual bees instead of simply following the movements of the group, and it started to dawn on him that the bees seemed very large, as insects went. But Septach Melayn voiced the question first. Turning to the duke, he said, "Are these really bees, your grace? For as I track them about this cage with my eyes they appear as big as birds to me."

"Your eyes are not deceiving you," replied the duke. "As if ever they could. But bees are truly what they are. Here: let me show you."

He walked out into the middle of the floor and took up a pose with outstretched arms and upturned hands. Within moments half a dozen of the apiary's inhabitants had swooped down to settle on him as though they were his pets flocking to their master, and a dozen more, just after, descended and took up orbit around his head.

The duke remained motionless. Only with his eyes did he signal to his guests. "Come close, now. Look at them. Slowly—slowly—take care not to frighten them—" Prestimion carefully advanced, and Septach Melayn, and then big Gialaurys, who was most careful of all, walking as though on a carpet of eggshells.

But Maundigand-Klimd, for whom the bees seemed to hold no interest, remained by the entrance. Abrigant, likewise, stayed at the apiary's edge, his face darkened by a perpetual scowl. Since their arrival in Bailemoona he had scarcely bothered to veil his impatience to be on his way, off to Skakkenoir somewhere to the south and east, where the metal-bearing plants supposedly were to be found. The quest for Dantirya Sambail was only an irritating distraction to him; an hour spent among flittering bees, however beautiful they might be, an unutterable waste of time.

When he was close enough to Duke Kaitinimon to have a clear view of the gleaming little entities that were crawling over his palms, Prestimion emitted a low whistle of surprise. The golden bees of Bailemoona were creatures several inches in length, with plump little bodies, very birdlike indeed.

What actually were they, he wondered, small birds or very large insects?

Insects, Prestimion decided, when he had moved another few steps nearer. Now he was able clearly to make out their three pairs of furry legs. Their bodies were segmented, head and thorax and abdomen. They were covered everywhere, wings and body both, with a sleek reflective armor that could easily be mistaken for a fine coating of gold, and which accounted for the dazzling light-effects that their movements caused.

"Even closer," said the duke. "Close enough to see their eyes."

Prestimion obeyed. And gasped. Their eyes!—those strange eyes!—he had never seen such eyes.

Not the cold faceted eyes of insects, no, not at all. Nor

the beady glittering ones of birds, for that matter. Their eyes were disproportionately large and had an oddly mammalian look to them, the warm, soft, liquid eyes of some little creature of the forest. But there was a burning intelligence in them, also, that set these creatures apart from the chattering droles and mintuns of the woods. It was almost frightening to look into those knowing eyes.

"Stand as I'm standing," the duke said. "Stay very still, and they'll come to you also."

Neither Septach Melayn nor Gialaurys cared to make the experiment. But Prestimion thrust his arms outward with his palms facing up. A moment or two went by. Then a pair of the bees came out of the air and flew inquisitive circles around his head; and, after another minute or so, one of them cautiously lit on Prestimion's left hand.

He felt an odd tickling sensation as it moved about on him. Very slowly he turned his head toward the left for a better view, and found himself staring into the insect's huge solemn eyes. It was watching him closely.

There was intelligence there, beyond any doubt.

A tiny mind, but keen, penetrating. To what end, though? What kind of thoughts circulated in the brains of these little creatures, the last of their kind, as they flew their endless sparkling loops around the great apiary that was their only refuge in the world?

"Our ancestors kept them in little cages as pets," Kaitinimon said, after a time. "They'd fly around for a month or two at most, and then would sicken and die. They could not abide the cages, you see. But no one who had ever had bees even a few days could resist their beauty: when your bees died, you felt you must immediately replace them, although those would die also, just as quickly. Once there were millions of them in this province. They turned the whole sky golden when they flew overhead in great masses. Now I alone have the privilege of keeping bees in Bailemoona; and this cage, as you see, is quite large. They would never survive in anything smaller. —If you carefully turn your hands over, like this, my lord, the bees will leave you. Unless, of course, you wish to extend the experience a little longer."

"Just a few minutes more, I think," Prestimion said. Two more bees arrived on his left hand, and then a third, landing on the other one. He stood transfixed, unable to take his eyes from theirs, lost in contemplation of the small intelligences that now quite placidly were traversing his hands. There were five of them on him, now. Six. Seven. He must seem safe. He wondered if they were looking somehow into his mind.

Abruptly he found himself wishing most intensely that Varaile had been here to see the bees with him today.

The thought startled him: that Varaile had taken Thismet's place in his mind already, that he should be longing for this new woman whom he barely knew, and wishing that he had her by his side as he rode on and on through the world. And he did. It amazed him that he should feel her absence so strongly. But Thismet was gone forever, and Varaile awaited him at Castle Mount. By virtue of his power and his responsibilities, he was destined to spend his life traversing the world, and suddenly, with a degree of passion that astonished him, he yearned to share it all with Varaile, to show her everything that he would be privileged to see himself, the golden bees of Bailemoona, the vanishing lake of Simbilfant, the midnight market of Bombifale, the surging colors of Gulikap Fountain, the gardens of Tolingar—everything. Everything.

"You find our bees interesting, my lord?"

Caught off guard, Prestimion gave the duke a hasty glance. "Oh, yes," he said quickly. "Yes! How extraordinary they are! How remarkable!"

"I could send a few to you at the Castle," Kaitinimon said. "But they would only die, like all the rest."

That night, as they dined on delicacies of the region in the ducal palace, Prestimion's thoughts still were fixed on the golden bees, and on the longing for Varaile that they had so unexpectedly kindled in him. The bright glow of their enigmatic eyes would not release him, nor the pretty dazzle of the myriad flitting fliers swiftly moving through the upper reaches of their immense apiary. Those knowing eyes—that look of inexplicable intelligence—that beautiful golden gleam winking on and off—

This wondrous world, he thought, this place of miracles, that held enough surprises to last one for ten lifetimes—

But to see the famous golden bees had not been the primary purpose of the Coronal's visit here, and it was Gialaurys, finally, who brought matters around to the essential topic.

"There was a report," he said to the duke, "that the Procurator Dantirya Sambail and one or two of his men had passed this way not long ago. The Coronal has reason to speak with him and wishes to locate him. We wonder if you've had any contact with him."

The duke showed no sign of surprise. Very likely word had reached him and no doubt many others, by this time, that Lord Prestimion was trying to locate the Procurator of Ni-moya and that a continent-wide manhunt was under way.

Which was, of course, news of the most sensational kind. But Duke Kaitinimon knew better than to raise whys and wherefores with Prestimion in such an affair. He asked no questions and offered only the most straightforward kind of response, telling the Coronal that he too had heard of the Procurator's presence in the area, but had not been visited by him. That had puzzled him, that the Procurator would pass this way and not trouble to pay a call. He was certain, though, that Dantirya Sambail was no longer to be found anywhere in Balimoleronda province. More than that he could not say. And when Septach Melayn asked him whether he thought it more likely that the fugitive Procurator would have gone south or west from Bailemoona, Duke Kaitinimon could only shrug. "Plainly he's trying to get home. What he seeks, I suppose, is the sea. He could reach it either way. Who am I to try to comprehend the mind of Dantirya Sambail?"

Prestimion decided on the southward route out of Bailemoona. There was never any such thing as a short journey on Majipoor, but the Procurator would have a shorter time of it reaching the sea by going to the south than toward the

west; and, though the ports were supposed to be blockaded,
Prestimion knew only too well how easy it would be for
someone as wily as Dantirya Sambail to bribe his way
through any blockade. He had, after all, bought his way out
of the Sangamor tunnels. What challenge could it be for him
to find some lazy and venal customs official in a southern
port who would look the other way while he and Mandralisca put themselves aboard a freighter heading toward Zimroel?

Southward, then, for Prestimion. Toward Ketheron and
its Sulfur Desert.

It was a logical choice, and an alluring one. The Sulfur
Desert was neither a desert nor a place where sulfur was to
be found; but from all reports it was one of the most striking
sights in the world. Prestimion was grateful to Dantirya
Sambail for having given him a pretext to visit it.

One more place that he would go without Varaile. He
could not get her out of his mind.

Two days' journey out of Bailemoona they began seeing
the first outcroppings of yellow sand. At first there were
only stray streaks and tailings of the stuff, mixed with ordinary dark soil that diluted the brilliance of its hue. But
gradually the prevalence of it intensified until all the hillsides and valleys seemed stained with it; and then, when the
travelers came to the Sulfur River itself, yellowness was all
about them as though it were the only color in the universe.

It was easy to see why the first explorers of this district
had believed they had stumbled upon a vast trove of sulfur.
Surely there could be no other substance that had that same
bright warm hue. But indeed there was; for the "sulfur" of
the Sulfur Desert was nothing but powdery yellow sand, a
fine calcareous sand given its striking pigmentation by
grains of quartz and minute fragments of feldspar and horn-
blende. It had been formed, apparently, in some incalculably
ancient era when much of central Majipoor had been a desert of the most arid kind, and great yellow mountains occupied the territory west of the Labyrinth. The potent action

of hard winds over many millennia had scoured those mountains down into powder and carried it thousands of miles, depositing it finally in the region over the Gaibilan Hills behind Ketheron, where the Sulfur River had its source; and the river had done the rest, sweeping enormous quantities of the sand down out of the hills and distributing it across the entire broad valley where the travelers from Castle Mount now stood, a valley that had been known since time immemorial as the Sulfur Desert.

In most parts of it these unique yellow sands formed a superficial layer that rarely exceeded twenty or thirty feet in thickness. But there were some places where it had a depth of half a mile or more and had solidified under the pressure of the eons into a soft, porous rock that readily formed lofty vertical cliffs. It was in that zone of flat-faced yellow cliffs that the towns and cities of the Ketheron district had been built.

There were those who thought that Ketheron had a fairyland loveliness about it; but to others, the region was a grotesque and bizarre place, something one might imagine in a nightmare. Erosion had cut a network of sharp-sided gullies deep into the cliffs' topmost strata, and weathering had created gnarled tapering spires of a hundred fanciful shapes in the exposed areas. By hollowing those spires out and punching tiny slit-windows through the soft rock of their walls, the Ketheron folk had transformed them into dwelling-places, dreamlike and odd, whole towns made up of tall narrow yellow buildings that looked like the pointed caps of witches.

The strangeness of Ketheron made it a favorite site for soul-painters, who had flocked here for centuries, unfurling their psychosensitive canvases and letting impressions of what they saw filter onto them through their trance-enhanced minds. Hauntingly atmospheric soul-paintings showing Ketheron's twisted yellow towers were standard items in the houses of the newly rich who had not yet learned to shun the commonplace. Even in the Castle Prestimion had seen five or six Ketherons hanging in odd places about the premises, and they had so thoroughly accustomed him to the look of this place that he was afraid he might take the actuality of it for granted when he finally beheld it.

But the soul-paintings, he quickly came to see, had not prepared him in any way for Ketheron itself. That yellow landscape, with the muddy yellow river flowing serenely through its heart, and the skewed and contorted ogre-houses of Ketheron city rising spikily from the tops of the cliffs— how mysterious it all looked, how much like a piece of some alien world that had been set down here on Majipoor between Bailemoona and the Aruachosian coast!

Of course, Prestimion thought, any place you did not know had to be regarded as a place of mystery. And how much knowledge did you ever have, really, even of the places you thought you knew?

What he saw here, though, was truly strange. Ketheron city, which extended for some miles along the northern bank of the river in the heart of the valley, was the capital of the Ketheron district. It was small as the cities of Majipoor went, half a million people at best. Prestimion stared in wonder at the oddly shaped houses, at the unfamiliar faces of the townspeople who came out to peer at their Coronal as he rode past. Yes, Ketheron was unusual-looking to an extreme. The people themselves had a yellow cast to their features, or so he imagined, and they favored billowing baggy clothing and long floppy caps that gave them a gnomish look perfectly in keeping with the weirdness of their district.

But even if Ketheron had been as familiar to him in its contours and textures as Muldemar or Halanx or Tidias, Prestimion realized that he would be deceiving himself if he believed that he knew it. Every city was a world in itself, a world in miniature, with thousands of years of history locked up in its walls—more secrets than you could ever learn if you spent the rest of your life there. And Ketheron was just one city of all the multitudinous cities of this vast world that had been given into his care, a place that he would pass through this day, and never see again, and its essence would be as much of a riddle to him tomorrow as it had been the day before yesterday.

This was farming territory—the soft yellow ground was phenomenally fertile—and the people seemed like simple folk, by and large, unaccustomed not only to visiting Coronals but to aristocrats of any sort. The mayor of Ketheron city appeared almost to be trembling as he came out of the town hall, a spindly, warped three-story tower at the very edge of the cliff, to greet Prestimion and lead him within. He was protected by a formidable armamentarium of superstition: his purple-and-yellow cloak of office was bedecked with so many talismans and amulets that it was a wonder the poor man could stand upright beneath their weight, and he had brought two mages with him for moral support, a plump little oily-skinned man and a tall gaunt scarecrow of a woman, who carried the holy implements of what was apparently a purely local cult, since not even Maundigand-Klimd had ever seen their like before. The Su-Suheris seemed amused by the earnest clodhopping conjurations by which the pair drove lurking dark spirits from the cavernous, musty-smelling room where the meeting was taking place, rendering it safe for the Coronal and his party. Or was it for the mayor's own benefit that these rites were being performed?

Gialaurys conducted the inquiry, while Prestimion and the rest stood to one side. Clearly the mayor was too thoroughly intimidated by the mere proximity of Prestimion to be able to carry on a conversation with him, and Septach Melayn's airy insouciance did not seem likely to put the poor man any more at ease. But Gialaurys, massive and fearsome though he looked, had the art of speaking with plain folk, for he came of plain stock himself.

Had the mayor or any of the townsfolk seen or heard aught of Dantirya Sambail in these parts? he asked. No, they had not. The mayor did seem aware, at least, of who Dantirya Sambail was. But he could not imagine why the awesome Procurator of Ni-moya would have been traveling hereabouts. That so mighty and terrifying a personage could have had any reason whatever for entering this picturesque but unimportant region was a concept that left the poor man looking baffled and dismayed.

"We have chosen the wrong route, I think," Prestimion murmured to Septach Melayn. "If he'd been heading straight for the Aruachosian coast, he'd have had no choice but to pass through here, wouldn't he? We should have gone west from Bailemoona instead of south."

"Unless the mayor's somehow been magicked into forgetting that Dantirya Sambail ever came by," said Septach Melayn. "The Procurator knows how that game's played, now."

But nothing so devious had been necessary. When Gialaurys produced a sketch of Mandralisca that they were carrying with them, the mayor recognized the poison-taster's bleak face instantly. "Oh, yes, yes," he said. "He was here. Traveling in a rusty old floater, he was, and stopped in town to buy provisions—three weeks ago, five, six, somewhere back then. Who could ever forget a face like that?"

"Traveling alone, was he?" Gialaurys asked.

The mayor had no idea. No one had taken the trouble to investigate the floater, which had been parked by the bank of the river. The hatchet-faced man had bought what he needed and returned to his floater and continued onward. Nor could the mayor say which way he had gone.

Here, at least, his mages were of some use. "We could see that this stranger would bring no luck to our city," the gaunt woman volunteered. "And so we followed along his floater's trail for half a mile or so, and planted dragon-wax candles every hundred yards to ensure that he'd not return."

"And the direction he was going—?"

"South," the little oily-faced man said immediately. "Toward Arvyanda."

10

"THEY WERE GLAD TO get rid of us," Prestimion said, chuckling. The royal caravan was crossing something called Spurifon Bridge, a weatherbeaten, disturbingly creaky wooden span that could well have been five thousand years old. It was just barely possible to see the silt-choked Sulfur

River far below them, moving at the sluggish pace of a
sleepy serpent, a tawny yellow line against the brighter yellow of the valley through which it flowed. "How terrifying
we must have seemed! I hope they didn't just make up the
first story that came into their minds for the sake of moving
us on out of town."

"It takes courage to lie to a Coronal," Abrigant said.
"Was there so much as one atom of courage in that whole
town?"

"They told the truth," said Maundigand-Klimd. "I detect
the trail of their incantation-candles along our path. Look:
there, and there. Burned to stumps, but there are the stumps.
We go the right way."

"These Ketherons are harmless timid people caught up
in matters too deep for them, and we have badly frightened
them," Prestimion said. "We should do something for
them." He looked toward Septach Melayn. "Make a note of
it. We'll build them a new bridge, at least. This one belongs
in a museum."

"It's the responsibility of the Pontifex to build bridges,"
grumbled Septach Melayn. "That's what the title means:
builder of bridges. An ancient word, millions of years old."

"Nothing's millions of years old," said Abrigant. "Not
even the stars."

"Well, thousands, then."

"Peace, both of you," Prestimion snapped. "Let the appropriate department be notified, a new bridge for Ketheron,
and so be it, with no further quibbling." What was the use
of being Coronal, he wondered, if he had to utter a decree
twice, even among his closest associates, in order to make
it effective?

South of the river the prevailing yellowness of the countryside soon began to thin out, reversing the pattern of the
north, streaks of darker soil becoming more and more common until everything was normal again. It was something
of a relief to be leaving it behind. The brilliant color, strange
as it was, numbed and deadened the mind after a time by
its very intensity, and the monotony of the sulfureous landscape had begun to become oppressive.

They camped that night in the foothills of a mountain range of moderate size that lay just ahead of them. A sending of the Lady of the Isle came to Prestimion as he slept.

It was uncommon for Coronals to receive sendings, and not only because the Lady customarily was his own mother. Sendings were meant as guidance for the soul; and one Power of the Realm ordinarily did not presume to advise another. But sometimes when a Coronal stood at a point of decision and crisis the Lady would take it upon herself to intervene with her wisdom. This night, sleep overcame Prestimion almost as soon as he had closed his eyes. He felt himself going down into the trance state that betokened a sending. Then he heard the soft music of the Lady's domain, and glided easily into a low pavilion of pure white marble set all about with pots of flowering shrubs, fragrant alabandinas and tanigales and the like. And there before him was the Princess Therissa, Lady of the Isle, his mother and mother to all the world, smiling and holding out her hands to him.

She looked as young as ever, for she was one of those women whom age seemingly could not touch. Her thick dark hair had lost none of its gleam since she had taken up her new duties. The silver headband of her office lay lightly on her brow. On the bosom of her robe, as always, rested the Muldemar Ruby, that wondrous jewel that had been in the family four thousand years, a deep red stone with a purple flush, set in a golden hoop.

Thismet was standing beside her.

Or so it seemed at first to Prestimion. That small, delicately formed woman of the mischievous sparkling eyes could only be Thismet; but even as his spirit reverberated with surprise and unease—for why would Thismet be here with the Lady in this sending, when he thought he had begun to make his final peace with the tragedy of her death, and was moving onward in his life?—everything shifted in the smooth way that things often shift in dreams, and he was plainly able to see that the woman next to his mother was not Thismet at all, had never been Thismet, could not have been Thismet. She was Varaile. How strange, he thought, that he had mistaken her for Thismet. For each was beautiful and compelling in her own way, but tall robust full-bodied Varaile looked nothing at all like the tiny fragile-seeming woman whom Prestimion had loved and lost so long ago.

He became aware that his mother was speaking. But there seemed to be some barrier between her and him that kept him from comprehending her words. It was as if the air was too dense in this pavilion, or the fragrance of the flowers too strong. And still she spoke, smiling throughout, gesturing gently toward him, toward Varaile, toward herself. He strained to hear. And at last he understood. "Do you know this woman, Prestimion?" the Lady was saying. "Her name is Varaile, and she lives in Stee."

"I know her, yes, mother. Yes."

"She has the bearing of a queen."

"A queen is what she will be," said Prestimion. "My queen, who will live beside me at the Castle."

"Do you mean that, Prestimion? Tell me that you do."

"Oh, yes, mother. Yes, I do. Yes!"

When he woke in the morning the dream was still burning in his mind, as true sendings always do. Septach Melayn, who was the first to come upon him, looked at him strangely and laughed, and said, "You appear to be in another world today, my friend."

"Perhaps I am," said Prestimion.

It was necessary, though, for him to return to this one. They were still many days' journey from the southern coast, and there was no time to waste if he hoped to overtake Dantirya Sambail.

The last of the yellow sand now lay behind them. So was the desert aridity of Ketheron. The air was soft and moist here, warm and velvet smooth, the hills thick with greenery that had a waxy sheen, the sky often darkened by rain-clouds, though the showers were always brief. They were moving now toward the tropical regions.

Three singular landmarks marked the point of transition.

The first, in a place where the road veered upward suddenly out of the flat plain and delivered them into a country of craggy hills, was what seemed initially to be a solitary mountain that loomed to their left, but which quickly revealed itself to be an entire mountain range, a long gray wall that rose with surprising abruptness from the terrain surrounding it. Atop the great base rose a host of smaller rounded peaks, each one the exact image of its neighbor, that swarmed along its elongated summit in chaotic and bewildering profusion.

"It is the Mountain of the Thirteen Doubts," said Maundigand-Klimd, who had made himself the custodian of their maps during this journey. "Its many peaks look just like each other, and one pass leads only into another, so that a traveler attempting to cross the mountain must invariably get lost."

"And will that happen to us?" asked Prestimion, wondering if the Procurator might at this moment be wandering around amidst those identical stone humps.

The Su-Suheris shook both his heads in that unnerving way of his. "Ah, no, lordship: we go past these mountains, not over them. But their presence to the east of us tells us that we have taken the correct road. We must look now for the Cliff of Eyes, which will be coming upon us very soon."

"The Cliff of Eyes," said Septach Melayn. "What in the name of the Divine can that be?"

"Wait and see," said Maundigand-Klimd.

When they found it—and sharp-eyed Septach Melayn was the first to spy it—there could be no doubt of its identity. It was a stately mountain of some whitish stone that stood by itself, rising conspicuously above the highway just to their right; and its entire face was bespeckled with a multitude of large, deeply inset oval-shaped boulders of some dark shining mineral, scattered across it like raisins in a pudding. The effect was of a thousand stern black eyes peering down at passers-by from the mountain's white face. Gialaurys made a flurry of holy signs at the sight of it, and even Prestimion felt a shiver of something like awe, or even fear.

"How did this happen?" he wanted to know. But no one offered an answer, and he knew better than to expect one. Who could say what force had shaped the world, or for what reason? One did not inquire into the nature and motives of the Divine. The world was the world: it was as it was, a place of eternal delight and mystery.

The Cliff of Eyes seemed to watch them for hours as they rode past its eerie flank.

"And soon," said Maundigand-Klimd, bending over his map, "we will be at the Pillars of Dvorn, which mark the boundary between the central sector of Alhanroel and the south."

It was just before dusk when they reached them: two great blue-gray rocks, ten times the height of a man and tapering upward to sharply pointed tips. They stood facing each other with the road running straight as an arrow's flight between them, so that they formed a kind of ceremonial gateway to the lands beyond. The rocks were rough and convoluted on their outer faces but smooth and flat on the inner ones, which made it seem as if they were the two severed halves of a single great structure.

"There is magic here," Gialaurys muttered restively, and offered another swarm of holy signs.

"Ah, yes," said Septach Melayn, with a playful lilt to his voice. "There's a curse on the place. Every twenty thousand years the rocks come crashing together, and woe betide the wayfarers who happen to be passing through the gateway just then."

"So you know the old legend, do you?" asked Maundigand-Klimd.

Septach Melayn swung around to face him. "Legend? What legend? I was only having a little sport with Gialaurys."

"Then you reinvent what already was," said the Su-Suheris. "For indeed there was an ancient Shapeshifter tale that said just that, that these were clashing rocks, which had moved before and someday would move again. And, what is worse, that the next time they did, it would be a great king of the human folk that perished here between them."

"It would, would it?" said Prestimion, smiling jauntily and letting his gaze travel quickly from one great rock face to another. "Well, then, I suppose I'm safe, because, although I'm certainly a king, no one yet would call me a great one." And added, with a wink at Septach Melayn, "But perhaps we should look for some other route south anyway, eh? Just to be absolutely safe."

"The Pontifex Dvorn, my lord, caused magical plates of brass to be installed on each side of the road, inscribed with runes to protect against just such a thing," Maundigand-Klimd said. "Of course, that was thirteen thousand years ago and the plates have long since vanished. You see those shallow square indentations high up on the walls? That was where they were, or so it's said. But I think our chances of passing through safely are excellent."

And indeed the Pillars of Dvorn remained in place as the royal caravan went past them. There was a distinct change in the look of the land on the far side, a greater density of foliage in response to the increase in warmth and humidity, and the hills there were smooth, rounded humps instead of hard jagged crags.

Maundigand-Klimd's maps showed no settlements within fifty miles of the Pillars. But the travelers had gone no more than ten minutes' journey when they came upon the ghost of a road leading off the main highway toward a cluster of low hills to the west, and Septach Melayn, fastening his keen vision on those hills, announced that he could make out a row of stone walls midway up, half buried beneath thickets of strangling vines. Prestimion, his curiosity piqued, sent Abrigant off with a couple of men to investigate. They returned fifteen minutes later with the report that a ruined city lay hidden in there, deserted except for a family of Ghayrog farmers who made their home amidst the ancient buildings. It was, so one of the Ghayrogs had told them, all that remained of a great metropolis of Lord Stiamot's time, whose people were massacred by Shapeshifters during the Metamorph Wars.

"This cannot be," said Maundigand-Klimd, shaking both his heads at once. "Lord Stiamot lived seventy centuries ago.

In this climate the jungle would long since have swallowed up any such abandoned city."

"Let's have a look at it," said Prestimion, and they made a side jaunt down the western road, which after a few hundred yards became nothing more than a dirt track that climbed steadily into the hills at a gentle grade. Soon the wall of the ruined city came into view. It was a substantial stone structure, at least fifteen feet high in most places, but nearly overwhelmed by shrubs and vines. Just to the left of the entrance to the city proper stood an immense many-buttressed tree with pale-gray bark, whose myriad arms, flattening as they embraced the stone of the wall, seemed to be melting into it so that it was difficult to tell where tree left off and ruin began.

Two sturdy young Ghayrogs came forth to greet them. They were both naked, but it was impossible to tell whether they were male or female, because the sexual organs of male Ghayrogs emerged only when they were aroused, and the breasts of the females were similarly hidden except when they were nursing young. Nor, mammals though they were, was it easy to think that they were other than reptilian. These two had brightly gleaming scales and strong tubular arms and legs; their cold green eyes were unblinking and their forked scarlet tongues flicked constantly in and out between their hard fleshless lips; and masses of fleshy black coils writhed like serpents on their heads in lieu of hair.

They greeted their visitors with a kind of indifferent courtesy and asked them to wait while they summoned their grandfather. He appeared shortly, a venerable Ghayrog indeed, limping slowly up to them. "I am Bekrimiin," he said, with a creaky but effusive gesture of welcome. Prestimion did not offer his own name in return. "We are very poor here, but you are welcome to such hospitality as we can provide," Bekrimiin said, and signaled to his grandchildren, who quickly produced platters that were nothing more than the giant heart-shaped leaves of some nearby tree, on which they had placed some sort of mashed starchy vegetable, evidently fermented, that had a fiercely spicy flavor. Prestimion took some and ate with a determined show of pleasure,

and several of the others followed suit, though neither
Gialaurys nor the fastidious Septach Melayn made even a
pretense of eating. A sweet, mildly bubbly liquid—either
wine or beer; Prestimion was unable to tell which—accompanied it.

Afterward the Ghayrog led them into the heart of the
ruins. Only the merest outlines of the city were visible,
mainly the foundations of buildings, here and there a charred
tower, or a couple of standing walls, propped up by the trees
that stood beside them, of what might once have been a
warehouse or a temple or a palace. Most of the structures
had long since been engulfed by the giant buttressed trees,
whose flattening arms tended to grow together until they
completely encircled and concealed whatever it was that
they had drawn their support from when young. The name
of the city, the old man said, was Diarwis, a name that meant
nothing to Prestimion or his companions.

"It dates from Lord Stiamot's time, does it?" Prestimion
asked.

The Ghayrog laughed harshly. "Oh, no, nothing like that.
These foolish children told you that? They are ignorant.
Whatever I try to teach them of history goes from their
minds before I finish my words. —But no, the city is much
more recent. It was abandoned only nine hundred years
ago."

"Then there was no Metamorph attack here, either?"

"They told you that too, did they? No, no, that is just a
myth. The Metamorphs were long gone from Alhanroel by
then. This city destroyed itself." And the old Ghayrog told
a tale of a cruel and haughty duke, and of an uprising of
the serfs who tilled his fields: the murder of three members
of the duke's family, and the duke's savage reprisal, and
then a further uprising, leading to an even more brutal reprisal, followed by the assassination of the duke himself and
the abandonment of the city by serfs and masters alike, for
by that time not enough people remained alive here to sustain any sort of urban life.

Prestimion listened in brooding silence, stunned by this
bit of unknown history.

Like any prince of the Castle who had been marked for a high role in the government, he had made an extensive study of the annals of Majipoor's history; and, by and large, it was a strikingly peaceful tale, with no significant bloodshed between the time of Stiamot's campaigns against the Metamorphs and Prestimion's own struggle with Korsibar. Certainly he had never come upon any accounts of rebellious serfs and assassinated dukes. The story went against all that he wanted to believe about the basically benign ways of the people of Majipoor, who had learned long ago to settle their quarrels by less violent means. He would rather have been told that the Shapeshifters had been the ones who worked this ruination; at least there already was a well-established history of fierce conflict between humans and Metamorphs, though it had come to an end thousands of years before this city's destruction.

Bekrimiin informed his guests now that they were welcome to stay with him overnight, or for as long as they wished; but Prestimion had already had more than enough of this place, which had begun to weigh heavily on his spirits. To Gialaurys he said, "Thank him and give him some money, and tell him that it is the Coronal who he has entertained this afternoon. And then let's be on our way." To Abrigant he added, "When we are back at the Castle, find me whatever documents you can that exist concerning this place. I'd like to study its history more deeply."

"There may very well be nothing to find in the archives about it," said Septach Melayn. "The suppression of unpleasant facts was perhaps not any invention of ours, my lord."

"Perhaps so," Prestimion said somberly, and went out through the city's gateway, and stood for a time staring at the great tree that held the city wall in its devouring embrace; and he said little to anyone all the rest of the afternoon.

They entered now into the district known as Arvyanda. Whenever anyone spoke of that region, it was always in the phrase, "Arvyanda of the golden hills," which brought to Prestimion's mind the image of the parched tawny hills of some area that had long dry summers, as was common farther to the north. He wondered why hills would be golden in this perpetually green and lush tropical region of frequent rainfall. Or was it that the yellow metal itself was mined in this place?

But the answer came quickly enough, and it was neither of those. A thick-boled tree with wide boat shaped leaves grew in copious quantity on the hillsides of Arvyanda, to the exclusion of nearly everything else; and in the bright tropical sunlight those innumerable leaves, which were stiff and outspread and of a texture that seemed almost metallic, gave back a brilliant golden reflection, as though the entire region had been gilded.

In Arvyanda city they made inquiries concerning Dantirya Sambail, with inconclusive results. Nobody was prepared to claim that they had actually seen the Procurator pass that way, although there were some scattered reports of unpleasant strangers moving swiftly through the outskirts of town some weeks before. Were they being deliberately vague, or were the Arvyanda folk merely stupid and unobservant? There was no easy way to tell; but in any case there was nothing to learn from them.

"Shall we continue?" Septach Melayn asked Prestimion.

"As far as the coast, yes."

On the other side of Arvyanda were the celebrated topaz mines of Zeberged. It was the transparent form of the precious mineral that was found here, clear as the finest glass and, when polished, of an unparalleled brilliance. But so bright was the sun against the rocky terrain of Zeberged that the topaz outcroppings were invisible by day because of the glare; and therefore the miners came out only at twilight, when the topaz could be seen gleaming lustrously by the last rays of the light, and clapped bowls over the shining stones to serve as markers. Early the next morning they would return and cut away the marked pieces of rock, and turn them over to the craftsmen who polished them.

Prestimion watched all this with interest. But the miners

of Zeberged, though they presented him with wondrous slabs of purest topaz, could give him no information about Dantirya Sambail.

Beyond Zeberged the sky grew dark with clouds, hanging heavy in the sky like thick, opalescent gauze. They were entering rainy Kajith Kabulon, where a wedge-shaped mountain formation perpetually caught the fogs that came off the southern seas and transformed them into rain. Indeed it was not long before they reached the zone of precipitation, and once they did they saw no more sunlight for days. The rain came in a steady drumbeat. It was essentially continuous, interrupted only by occasional scant hours of surcease.

The jungles of Kajith Kabulon were green, green, green. Trees and shrubs in exuberant prodigality rose everywhere toward the sky, their trunks striped brilliantly with strands of red and yellow fungi that provided the only splashes of vivid color to be seen and their crowns tied together by an impenetrable tangle of lianas and epiphytes that formed a virtually solid canopy, against which the rain constantly splashed, dripping through to the ground below. The spongy soil was covered by a dense carpet of furry green moss, broken here and there by narrow streamlets and numerous small pools, all of which reflected and refracted the dim greenish light in such complex ways that it often was impossible to tell whether that light came from overhead or rose in spontaneous generation from the forest floor.

There was animal life everywhere here too, bewildering in its abundance. Voracious long-legged bugs; clouds of fleas; droning white wasps with black-striped wings. Blue spiders that hung groundward in lengthy chains from towering trees. Flies with immense ruby eyes. Yellow-spotted scarlet lizards. Flat-headed booming toads. Mysterious small things that lurked in the crannies of rocks without revealing any more of themselves than hairy probing talons. And, now and again, some heavy shaggy beast that never came anywhere near the travelers, but could be seen at a great distance, snorting and snuffling through the jungle as it overturned clods of moss with its fork-like trunk to seek whatever might dwell beneath. In the green darkness, things took on strange borrowed forms: slender chameleons looked like gray twigs, twigs like chameleons, snakes pretended to be vines, certain vines had the unmistakable look of serpents. Rotting logs lying in the streams were easily enough taken for lurking predatory gurnibongs; but once, as Gialaurys knelt by the water's edge to splash his face in the morning, he saw what he was sure was only a log that was lying in the stream a few feet from him rise, grunting, on four stubby legs and move slowly away, snapping its long toothy snout in displeasure at having been disturbed.

Prince Thaszthasz, a supple, olive-skinned man of unknowable age who had governed in Kajith Kabulon as far back as Prestimion could remember, took the unheralded arrival of the Coronal in his province as calmly as he seemed to take everything else. He provided a lavish feast for Prestimion at his wickerwork palace at the heart of the jungle, an open and airy structure that he said was patterned after a style favored by the Metamorphs of Iliryvoyne, far off on the other continent. "I build a new one every year," Thaszthasz explained. "It saves on housekeeping costs." They dined on the sweet fruits and smoked meats of the rainforest, a procession of flavors wholly unfamiliar to the men from Castle Mount, but the wine, at least, was of the north, a touch of home at last. There were musicians; there were jugglers; three sinuous girls wearing next to nothing performed an intricate, provocative dance. Prestimion and the prince discussed the pleasures of the Coronation festivals, the vigorous health of the Pontifex as Prestimion had lately observed it, and the fascinations of the jungle about them, which Thaszthasz unsurprisingly thought the most beautiful district in all of Majipoor.

Gradually, as the night wore on, the talk came around to more serious matters. Prestimion began gradually to move toward the topic of Dantirya Sambail; but before he had quite managed to be specific about his reasons for coming south, Prince Thaszthasz deftly interjected that he had a grave problem on his hands himself, which was the growing incidence of inexplicable insanity among the people of his province.

"We are in general very well balanced folk here, you know, my lord. The unvarying mildness and warmth of our climate, the beauty and tranquility of our surroundings, the steady music of the rain—you have no idea, your lordship, how beneficial all of that is for the soul."

"This is true. I have no idea of it indeed," said Prestimion.

"But now—in the past six months, or eight, perhaps—quite suddenly, there has been a change. We see the most solid citizens suddenly rising up and going off by themselves, entirely unprepared, into the forest. Leaving the main roads, you understand, which is a perilous thing, for the forest is huge—you would call it a jungle, I suppose—and it can be unkind to those who flout its requirements. There have been eleven hundred such disappearances so far. Only a handful of those who have gone have returned. Why did they go? What were they seeking? They are unable to tell us."

"How strange," said Prestimion uncomfortably.

"Then, too, we've had a great many unusual episodes of irrational behavior, even violence, in the city itself—actual fatalities, even—" Thaszthasz shook his head. A look of pain appeared on his smooth, normally serene face. "It goes beyond my understanding, my lord. There have been no changes here that might have brought about such upheavals. I confess I find it distasteful and disturbing. —Tell me, lordship, have you heard similar reports from other districts?"

"From some, yes," said Prestimion, who, distracted by the strange new scenery all about him, had managed to put this entire issue out of mind since leaving the Labyrinth. It was unpleasant to have to confront it once again. "I agree: the situation is troublesome. We are conducting investigations."

"Ah. And no doubt will have important conclusions to share with us shortly. —Can it be some kind of sorcery, do you think, that has caused all this, my lord? That is my theory, and a sound one, I think. What else could have robbed so many people of their reason all at once, if not a

great witchcraft that some dark force has cast across the
land?"

"We are giving it our closest attention," said Prestimion,
this time putting enough sharpness into his tone so that
Thaszthasz, long experienced in the ways of power, could
see that the Coronal wished to end the discussion. "Let me
turn to another matter, now, Prince Thaszthasz, which is in
fact the purpose for which I have ventured into your lovely
forest—"

11

"HE CERTAINLY WAS QUITE cool about it," said Septach Melayn in some dudgeon, as they were making their way out
the southern end of the rain-forest country. "Oh, yes, of
course, the celebrated Procurator," he said, in devastating
high-pitched mimicry of Prince Thaszthasz's bland, unper-
turbable style of speech. " 'What a remarkable person he is!
And what a season this has been for unexpected visits by
the greatest citizens of the realm!' Hadn't he heard a thing
about the coastal blockade? Or the interdiction line that
we've run from Bailemoona to Stoien?"

"He knew," said Abrigant harshly. "Of course he knew!
He just didn't want to get himself into a quarrel with Dantirya Sambail. Who would? But it was his responsibility to
detain the Procurator until—"

"No," Prestimion said. "We were too dainty in our an-
nouncements. We sent word to port officials to detain him
if they saw him, but we never said any such thing to people
like Thaszthasz who hold authority inland across Dantirya
Sambail's most probable route to the sea. And now we see
the result of our delicacy. By failing to name Dantirya Sambail openly as a fugitive from the law, we've made it possible not only for him to slip through to the coast, but for
him to enjoy the hospitality of princes along the route."

But Abrigant persisted. "Thaszthasz should have known
that we wanted him. He should be punished for his negligence in—"

"In what?" Gialaurys demanded. "In inviting the ruler of the entire western continent to sit down and have a meal in his palace? If we don't come out and say that Dantirya Sambail's a criminal who needs to be brought to trial, why should we expect anybody to assume that he is?" Gialaurys shook his head heavily. "Even if he knew, why would he meddle? Dantirya Sambail's big trouble for anyone, and Thasthasz obviously has no stomach for trouble. He may not even have had an inkling of the whole affair. He lives out here in his jungle listening to the lovely rain come down, and nothing else matters to him at all."

"There is still the hope," said Maundigand-Klimd, "that someone has been bold enough to seize Dantirya Sambail at one of the coastal ports." And, since no one cared to deny that possibility, they put the subject aside.

They were entering the territory of Aruachosia, now, along the southern coast of Alhanroel. The sea was only a few hundred miles away, and every breeze brought them its salty tang and sultry warmth. This was a humid, steamy land; great stretches of it, swampy and insect-plagued and covered by tangled thickets of saw-edged manganoza palms, were virtually uninhabitable. But in the western part of the province there was a cone-shaped domain of relatively temperate country leading down to Sippulgar, the main seaport of the southern coast, which lay athwart the boundary between Aruachosia and its neighbor to the west, the province of Stoien.

Golden Sippulgar, it was always called. This has been a golden journey indeed, thought Prestimion: the golden bees of Bailemoona, the yellow sands of Ketheron, the golden hills of Arvyanda, and now golden Sippulgar as well. All very picturesque; but thus far they had little to show for their efforts other than fool's gold. Dantirya Sambail had hopped blithely on and on ahead of them, unhindered in any way, and by now very likely had slipped through the port blockade as well and was on the high seas, heading home for his own private kingdom in Zimroel, where he would be virtually impregnable.

Did this continued pursuit make any sense? Prestimion

wondered. Or should he halt at this point and hasten back to the Castle? The duties of kingship awaited him there. Dantirya Sambail's defiance was not the only problem confronting him; there was a real crisis in the land, evidently, a plague, an epidemic. But the Coronal and his closest advisers were off once again in outlying districts engaged in a fruitless search that might better be carried on by other means.

And then—Varaile—the great unanswered question of his life—

For a moment, then and there, Prestimion resolved to turn at once from his quest for the Procurator. But no sooner had the thought come to him than he thrust it from him. He had followed Dantirya Sambail's track this far, through desert and jungle, through one golden land after another: he would keep going, he decided, at least until he reached the coast, where he might obtain some reliable account of the Procurator's movements. Golden Sippulgar would be the last point on his journey. To Sippulgar it was, then; and then homeward, homeward to the Castle, homeward to his throne and his tasks, homeward to Varaile.

Sippulgar was called "golden" because the facades of its multitude of sturdy two- and three-story buildings were fashioned without exception from the golden sandstone that was quarried in the hills just to its north. Just as the metallic leaves of the trees of Arvyanda, gleaming under the potent tropical sun, turned that region into a realm of brilliant gold, so too did the warm mellow stone of Sippulgar, glinting with bits of micaceous matter, yield a dazzling golden glow in the full brightness of the day.

It was in every way a city of the far south. The air was moist and heavy; the plantings that lined the streets and clustered about the houses were superabundantly lush, and offered up a riot of bewilderingly colorful blooms in a hundred different shades of red, blue, yellow, violet, orange, even dark maroon and a pulsating, shimmering black so intense that it seemed the quintessence of color rather than the total absence of it. The people were black, too, or, at least, dark, their faces and limbs all showing evidence of the sun's hot touch. Sippulgar was beautifully situated, in a curving bay along the blue-green shore of the Inner Sea, crowded with ships from every part of the world. This stretch of southern Alhanroel was known as the Incense Coast, for everything that grew here was fragrant in one way or another: the low plants right along the shore that pro- duced khazzil and the balsam known as himmam, and the forests not far inland of cinnamon trees and myrrh, thani- bong trees, scarlet fthiis. All of these exuded such a pleni- tude of aromatic oils and gums that the air itself about Sippulgar seemed perfumed.

Prestimion's arrival in Sippulgar was not unexpected. He had known from the beginning of this southern journey that no matter which route he took from the Labyrinth, he would eventually have to reach the coast here, unless information were to reach him along the way that led him to follow Dantirya Sambail in some other direction. And so the city's highest official, who bore the title of Royal Prefect, had a majestic suite ready for him in the governmental palace, a substantial building of the local sandstone with a sweeping view of the bay.

"We are, my lord, prepared to meet your every need, both material and spiritual," the Prefect said at once.

Kameni Poteva was his name: a tall, hawk-faced man with not an ounce of fat on him, whose white robe of office was decorated with a pair of jade amulets of the kind known as rohillas and a sewn band of holy symbols. Sippulgar was a superstitious city, Prestimion knew. They worshipped a god who represented Time here, in the form of a winged serpent with the ferocious toothy snout and blazing eyes of the little omnivorous beast called a jakkabole: Prestimion had seen representations of it in several great plazas on his way into the city. There were exotic cults here, too, for Sippulgar was home to a colony of various expatriate beings from the stars, folk whose entire populations on Majipoor were no more than a few hundred all told. One entire street of the Sippulgar waterfront, he had heard, was given over to a row of temples to the gods of these alien people. Prestimion made a mental note to have a look at them before he moved along.

Septach Melayn came to him that evening as he was making ready for the formal dinner that the Prefect was giving in his honor. "A message from Akbalik, in Ni-moya," he said, holding out an already-opened envelope. "Very strange news. Young Dekkeret has signed on with the Pontifical bureaucracy and taken himself off to Suvrael."

Prestimion stared in bewilderment at the paper in Septach Melayn's hand without reaching for it. "What did you say? I don't think I understand."

"You remember, don't you, that we sent Akbalik out to Zimroel to check on whether Dantirya Sambail was fomenting trouble over there? And that at the last moment I suggested that Dekkeret go with him to pick up a little diplomatic experience?"

"Yes, yes, of course I remember. But what's this about his taking a job with the Pontifical people? And why Suvrael, of all places?"

"He's doing it as a penance, apparently."

"A penance?"

Septach Melayn nodded. He gave Akbalik's letter a quick glance. "They went hunting steetmoy up in the Khyntor Marches, apparently—that was my idea too, I have to admit—and there was some sort of accident, a local guide-woman killed during the course of the hunt, through some negligence of Dekkeret's, I gather. Or at least that's what Dekkeret believes is what happened. Anyhow, Dekkeret felt so bad about it that he decided to go off to the most unpleasant place he knew of in the entire world and carry out some difficult task under conditions of extreme physical discomfort, by way of atoning for whatever it was he felt responsible for causing while he was hunting in the northlands. So he bought himself a ticket to Suvrael. Akbalik tried to talk him out of it, of course. But it happened that the Pontifical people in Ni-moya were looking for some young official willing to undertake a ridiculous mission to Suvrael to find out why the Suvraelinu hadn't been meeting their quota of beef exports lately, and when one of Dekkeret's friends who worked for the Pontificate found out that Dekkeret was going to Suvrael anyway, he arranged to get him a temporary commission on the Pontifical staff, and off he went. He's probably landed in Tolaghai by now. The Divine only knows when he'll be back."

"Suvrael," Prestimion said, shaking his head. Fury was mounting in him. "An act of penance, he says. The young idiot! By all the demons of Triggoin, what's wrong with him? He belongs at the Castle, not running around in that blasted desert wasteland! If he felt some need to atone, the Isle of Sleep's the usual place for such things, isn't it? And a much shorter trip, too."

"I suppose the Isle seemed like too tame a place for him. Or maybe going there never occurred to him."

"Then Akbalik should have suggested it. Suvrael! How could he have done that? I had plans for that boy! I'll hold Akbalik responsible for this!"

"My lord, Dekkeret is very headstrong. You know that. If he had his mind made up to go to Suvrael, you could not have dissuaded him yourself."

"Perhaps so," said Prestimion, trying now without much success to get his irritation under control. "Perhaps." Scowling, he swung about and stared out the window. "All right. I'll deal with young Dekkeret when and if he gets back from this mission of penance of his. I'll give him something to be penitent about! Reporting on Suvraelu beef exports for the Pontifex! There's been a drought in Suvrael for years, and the pastures have burned out, and they've butchered all their cattle because they can't feed them, that's why the beef exports have fallen off! What need does the Pontificate have of sending a man all the way down there just to find out about the obvious? The drought is over, anyway, so I understand. Give them two or three years to rebuild their herds, and they'll be shipping as much beef as they ever—"

"The point, Prestimion, isn't what sort of information the Pontificate thought it needed to gather. The point is that Dekkeret has an exaggerated sense of personal honor and felt obliged to expiate what he believed to be a terrible sin by undergoing prolonged personal suffering. There are worse failings for a young man to have, you know. You're being really unfair to him."

"Am I? I suppose you may be right," said Prestimion reluctantly, after a little while. "What about Akbalik? What else does he have to report, and where is he now?"

"He's heading back from Ni-moya by way of Alaisor at the moment, and says he'll rejoin us at any place you care to name. As for the Procurator, there's been no sign of him in Ni-moya, and from what Akbalik's been able to find out he doesn't seem to be anywhere in Zimroel yet."

"I suppose he's somewhere on the high seas, then, between here and there. Well, so be it. We'll deal with him when the time comes. Anything else?"

"No, my lord."

Septach Melayn handed the despatch to Prestimion, who took it without looking at it and tossed it to a nearby table. Turning his back on Septach Melayn once again, he glared toward the water as if he could see all the way to Suvrael from here.

Suvrael! Dekkeret has gone to Suvrael!

Such foolishness, Prestimion thought. He had thought so highly of the boy, too, especially in the immediate aftermath of the Normork assassination attempt, when Dekkeret had seemed so stalwart, so quick, so fundamentally capable. And now this! Well, perhaps it could be chalked off to youthful romanticism. Prestimion almost felt sorry for the young man, off there in the sun-baked southern continent, which from all reports was a miserable arid place of sand dunes and stinging insects and scorching winds.

The memory awoke in Prestimion of his own disagreeable wanderings in the Valmambra Desert of the north after the great defeat at Mavestoi Dam, the darkest hour of the Korsibar war. He had suffered grievously in the Valmambra: had dropped finally into a delirium of fatigue and starvation, and would surely have perished if another two or three days had gone by before he was found. That journey through the Valmambra had been the most arduous event of Prestimion's life.

And yet they said that Suvrael, any part of it, was ten times worse than the Valmambra. If so, then Dekkeret would certainly find there the ordeal that he craved for the sake of purifying his soul. But what if it took him the next five years to get himself out of Suvrael and back to the Castle? What would become of all his youthful promise, then? For that matter, what if he were to die down there? Prestimion had heard tales—everyone had—of inexperienced wayfarers who had strayed from some desert path and, lost without drinking water in Suvrael's blast-furnace heat, met their deaths within just a few hours.

Well, Dekkeret was probably able to look after himself. And Septach Melayn was right: it was a pardonable exploit, at least in one so young. The Suvrael adventure might be the making of him, if he survived it. It would toughen him; it would give him a deeper perspective on life and death, on responsibility and obligation. The best hope Prestimion had was that the boy came quickly to forgiving himself, down there, for his northlands mishap, and returned to the Castle in a reasonable period of time ready to take on the duties that were waiting for him.

The main issue for Prestimion, here in golden Sippulgar, was Dantirya Sambail. And the Prefect Kameni Poteva lost no time sharing such news as he had of the Procurator's whereabouts, although it was, alas, no news at all.

"At your request, my lord, we have raised an embargo against him at every port along the coast. Since we received word from you concerning the emergency, no ship has left Sippulgar bound for Zimroel without a complete check of the entire passenger manifest being undertaken by my port officials. Dantirya Sambail was not seen. We have also run checks on any ship leaving here for other ports along the Alhanroel coast that serve the Zimroel trade. The result was the same."

"What ports are those?" Prestimion asked. The Prefect spread a map of southern Alhanroel before them. "They all lie west of here. We can eliminate the other direction. As

you see, my lord, here is Sippulgar near the provincial border separating us from Stoien, and this, here, is eastern Aruachosia. Running onward still farther to the east lie the
provinces of Vrist, Sethem, Kinorn, and Lorgan. The only
port of any significance along that entire coastal stretch is
Glystrintai, in Vrist, and the only ships that sail out of Glystrintai come here. So if the Procurator had been foolish
enough to go eastward when he reached the coast, he would
only have come back here anyway, and we would have
taken him into custody."

"And to the west?"

"To the west, my lord, is the province of Stoien, devel-
oping into the Stoienzar Peninsula. We find just a few
widely spaced ports along the southern Stoien coast, because
the great heat, the insects, the impenetrable saw-palm jungles, have discouraged settlement. In a span of close to three
thousand miles we have only the towns of Maximin, Karasat, Gunduba, Slail, and Porto Gambieris, none of them of
any consequence. If the Procurator had emerged from Kajith
Kabulon at any of those and attempted to buy passage to
some port farther west, we would certainly have had word
of it; but no one resembling Dantirya Sambail has been seen
in any of them."

"What if he didn't come as far overland as the southern
coast, though?" Septach Melayn wanted to know. "What if
he simply turned in a westerly direction farther up, and
headed for one of the ports on the northern side of the peninsula? Would that have been possible?"

"Possible, yes. Difficult, but possible." The Prefect traced
a line across the map with the tip of one long, bony finger.
"Here is Kajith Kabulon. The only good road that comes
out of the rain-forest is the one going due south, which
brought you here. But there are some country roads, badly
maintained and not easy to use, that might have more appeal
for a man trying to escape justice. This one, for instance,
which leaves Kajith Kabulon at its southwest corner and
passes through north-central Aruachosia heading west toward the peninsula. If he managed things successfully, the
Procurator would have been able to reach any one of a

dozen ports on the peninsula's Gulf side. And from there things would be much easier for him."

"I see," said Prestimion, with a sinking feeling within. He stared at the map. The Stoienzar peninsula, Duke Oljebbin's domain, came thrusting westward out of the lower part of Alhanroel like a gigantic thumb, reaching far out into the ocean. South of the peninsula was the main body of the Inner Sea, leading to Suvrael. On the north side of the peninsula lay the calm, tropical waters of the Gulf of Stoien; and Stoienzar's Gulf coast was one of Majipoor's most heavily populated regions, with a major city every hundred miles and a string of resort towns and agricultural centers and fishing villages occupying nearly all the open territory between them. If Dantirya Sambail had succeeded in reaching any part of the Gulf coast, he might well have been able to find some rogue mariner who would transport him to Stoien city, the most important port along that coast, from which ships traveled constantly back and forth between Zimroel and Alhanroel.

They had, of course, placed an interdiction on Stoien, and on all the other ports of that part of the continent that engaged in intercontinental shipping. But how reliable would that interdiction be? These easygoing tropical cities had always been notorious hotbeds of official corruption. Prestimion, in his years of training at the Castle, had studied the lively case histories. The governor Gan Othiang, who had flourished in the peninsula port of Khuif in the reign before Prankipin's, had been in the habit of imposing a personal levy as well as the regular harbor taxes on all merchants whose ships called there; at his death, his private coffers, laden with ivory, pearls, and shells, held more wealth than the municipal treasury. Up the way at Yarnik, the mayor, one Plusiper Pailiap, had been in the habit of confiscating the property of deceased merchants whose heirs did not file a claim within three weeks. Duke Saturis, Oljebbin's grandfather, had several times been accused of draining off a percentage of all customs revenues for his own benefit, though the governmental inquiries that followed had always been quashed for reasons that no longer were clear. A prefect of

Sippulgar about a thousand years ago had covertly maintained his own fleet of pirate ships to raid local shipping.
And so on. It was as if there was something in the sultry
air down here that eroded rectitude and piety.

Prestimion shoved the map aside. To Kameni Poteva he
said, "How long, do you think, would it have taken Dantirya
Sambail, traveling by floater, to reach the port of Stoien
from—"

The Prefect's demeanor, though, had suddenly become
exceedingly peculiar. Kameni Poteva was a tightly wound
man at his best—that had been obvious from the start but
the inner tension that must perpetually have gripped him
appeared now to have heightened to a degree that was very
close to the breaking point. His lean, sharp-featured face,
from which the tropic sun seemed to have burned away all
superfluous flesh, was drawn so tight that the skin looked
to be in danger of cracking. A muscle was leaping about in
his left cheek and his thin lips were twitching, and his eyes
stood out fiercely, a pair of huge, bulging white orbs, below
his dark forehead. Kameni Poteva's hands were clenched
into taut fists; he held them pressed together, knuckle tight
against knuckle, over the two rohillas on the breast of his
robe.

"Kameni Poteva?" Prestimion said, in alarm.

From the Prefect came a hoarse gasp: "Forgive me, my
lord—forgive me—"

"What is it?"

Kameni Poteva's only reply was a shake of his head,
more like a shudder than anything else. His whole body was
trembling. He seemed to be fighting desperately for control
over it.

"Tell me, man! Do you want some wine?"

"My lord—oh, my lord—your head, my lord—?"

"What about my head?"

"Oh—I'm sorry—so sorry—"

Prestimion glanced about at Septach Melayn and Gialaurys. Was this the madness, striking right at the Coronal's
own elbow? Yes. Yes. Surely it was.

In this moment of mounting strangeness Maundigand-

Klimd stepped forward quickly and extended his hands so that they rested on the Prefect's shoulders; inclining both his heads until they were no more than inches from Kameni Poteva's forehead, the Su-Suheris uttered a few quiet words, unintelligible to Prestimion. A spell, no doubt. Prestimion imagined that he saw a white mist appear in the air between the two men.

A few seconds passed without apparent change in Kameni Poteva's state. Then a low hissing sound came from the Prefect's lips, as though he were a balloon that had been inflated almost to the breaking point, and there was a perceptible easing of his posture. The crisis seemed to be ending. Kameni Poteva looked up for an instant at Prestimion, eyes wild, face livid with shame and shock, and then looked away again.

After a moment he said, in a hollow, barely audible voice, "My lord, this is unbearably humiliating—I humbly ask your pardon, my lord—"

"But what was it? What happened? —Something about my head, you said."

A long anguished pause. "I was hallucinating." The Prefect groped for the wine-flask. Quickly Septach Melayn refilled his bowl for him. Kameni Poteva drank greedily. "These things come, two, three times a week, now. There is no escaping them. I prayed that there would be none while I was with you, but it happened anyway. Your head, sire—it was monstrous, swollen, about to explode, I thought. And the High Counsellor—" He looked at Septach Melayn and shuddered. "His arms, his legs, they were like those of some giant spider!" He closed his eyes. "I must be dismissed from office. I am no longer qualified to serve."

"Nonsense," said Prestimion. "You need a little rest, that's all. By all reports you've been doing a fine job. Are they something new, these hallucinations?"

"A month and a half. Two months." The man was in misery. He was unable now to look directly at Prestimion at all, but sat with his head bowed and shoulders hunched, staring at his feet. "It is like a fit that comes over me. I see the most dreadful things. Nightmare visions, monstrosities, one after another for five, ten, sometimes fifteen minutes. Then they go away, and each time I pray that it will be the last. But there is always another time."

"Look at me," said Prestimion.

"My lord—"

"No. Look at me. Tell me this, Kameni Poteva. You aren't the only one in Sippulgar who's been suffering these disturbances, have you?"

"No. I am not." A very small voice.

"I thought so. Has there been very much of it recently? Normally stable people breaking down, behaving oddly?"

"Some of that, yes. A great deal, I would have to say."

"Deaths?"

"Some, yes. And destruction of property. My lord, I must have sinned very grievously, to have brought this thing upon—"

"Listen to me, Kameni Poteva. Whatever's going on, it isn't your fault, do you understand me? You mustn't take it personally, and you mustn't regard it as a disgrace that the attack happened to hit you in my presence. Just as you're not the only one in town experiencing hallucinations, Sippulgar is not the only city where it's happening. It's everywhere, Kameni Poteva. Bit by bit, it seems, the whole world is going crazy. I want you to know that."

The Prefect, calmer now, actually managed a smile.

"If you mean to comfort me with such a statement, my lord, I must tell you that you are not succeeding."

"No. I suppose not. But I felt you should know. It's an epidemic, a universal phenomenon. At the moment we aren't sure what's causing it. But we are very much aware of the problem and we're working on it, and we intend to solve it."

Prestimion heard a faint forced cough from Septach Melayn. He glared sharply at him to let Septach Melayn know that this was no moment for his usual brand of mockery.

At least some of what he had just said was true, after all. Some. They were aware of the problem. They did intend to solve it. But how, or when, or by what means—well, Pres-

timion thought, one thing at a time. Lord Stiamot himself
could do no more than that.

There seemed no purpose any longer in continuing the
hunt for the escaped Procurator. Prestimion knew that he
could run and run, on and on, farther and farther, but he
was unlikely to find Dantirya Sambail, nor would he ever
escape the demons that were writhing within his own soul
by wandering this way and that across the world. It was
time to get back to the Castle.

Kameni Poteva, the next day, turned over to Prestimion
the file of all the information about the fugitive that he had
been able to glean from his fellow administrators in the
provinces of Aruachosia and Stoien. The whole thing
amounted to nothing whatever: sketchy guesses, untrust-
worthy rumors, and a good many firm denials that Dantirya
Sambail had been anywhere in the vicinity of the domain
of the official in question.

No definite sightings of the Procurator had been reported
since the one that had come by way of Prince Serithorn from
his estate manager Haigan Hartha, many long months ago,
just outside Bailemoona; and that had been a second-hand
report, at that. Aside from that, very little: just Haigan Hartha's own encounter with someone who very likely was
Mandralisca, about the same time, and that second sighting
of Mandralisca some months later, far to the south, in Ketheron. After that the trail gave out.

"There are just two possibilities," said Septach Melayn.
"The first is that they slipped through Arvyanda and Kajith
Kabulon without being noticed at all, found a western road
to Stoienzar as the Prefect suggested, got themselves aboard
a ship heading for Zimroel, and are somewhere on the high
seas between Stoien city and Piliplok at this very minute.
The other, since they obviously didn't come by way of Sippulgar and aren't likely to have taken any route that goes
east of Sippulgar, is that they wandered into some quicksand
bog in the rainforest, were swallowed up, and will never be
seen in this world again."

"The Divine would not be so kind to us," Prestimion said.

"You overlook a third alternative," said Gialaurys, giving Septach Melayn a look of glowering irritation. "Which is that they emerged safely from the Kajith Kabulon jungles, entered Stoienzar, discovered the embargo in the ports, and went into hiding in some pleasant little town on the peninsula, patiently awaiting the arrival of a rescue armada that they have summoned by swift courier from Zimroel."

"There's some sense to that notion, I think," said Abrigant.

"It would be like him, yes," Prestimion said. "He's capable of great patience indeed in pursuing his ends. But we can hardly conduct a village-to-village search from here to Stoien city."

"We could have the Pontifex's officials do it for us, though," suggested Septach Melayn.

"We could, yes. And will. My own feelings, I should add, lean toward the first theory: that he's slipped through our net and is already on the way to Zimroel. In which case, we should hear sooner or later that he's arrived there. Dantirya Sambail's not one to remain silent for long on his own turf. Either way, we should return without further delay to the Castle, where there's much for us to do, I suspect."

Abrigant said, "By your leave, brother, if I may speak to another subject, I wish to raise the question of Skakkenoir once again. You told me that when we were finished in Sippulgar, I could go in search of it."

"Skakkenoir?" Gialaurys said.

"A place said to be somewhere in Vrist, or even farther east," said Septach Melayn with a faint but unmistakable note of scorn in his voice, "where the soil is full of iron and copper that the plants themselves pull up from the ground, atom by atom, so that it can be recovered by burning their branches and leaves. The only problem is that nobody's ever succeeded in finding it, because it doesn't exist."

"It does!" cried Abrigant hotly. "It does! Lord Guadeloom himself sent an expedition to look for it!"

"And failed to find it, I believe, nor has anyone else even bothered to look in the last few thousands of years. You'd do as well trying to fetch iron ore back from your dreams, Abrigant."

"By the Divine, I'll—"

Prestimion raised his hand. "Silence! You two will be coming to blows next!" To Abrigant he said, "Your soul will have no rest until you make this journey, is that not so, brother?"

"So I do feel."

"Well, if you must, then, take two floaters and a dozen men and go in search of the iron of Skakkenoir. Perhaps the Prefect Kameni Poteva has some useful maps for you."

"You jeer at me too, do you, Prestimion?"

"Peace, brother, I meant nothing by it. It was a serious suggestion. For all we know there's information about this place buried in the Sippulgar archives. Ask him, at any rate. And then go. But I put one commandment on you, Abrigant."

"And that is?"

"That if you haven't found Skakkenoir and its metal sands within six months, you turn about and return to the Castle."

"Even if I'm within two days' journey of my goal?"

"How will you know that? Six months, Abrigant. Not an hour more. Swear me that."

"If I have definite information that Skakkenoir lies a day or two before me, definite information, and—"

"Six months exactly. Swear."

"Prestimion—"

"Six months."

Prestimion held out his right hand, the hand on which he wore the ring of kingship. Abrigant looked at it in amazement for a moment or two. Even now he appeared to be of a rebellious mind. But then, as if remembering that he and Prestimion were no longer just brother and brother but also subject and king, he nodded and lowered his head and touched his lips to the ring.

"Six months," he said. "Not an hour more, Prestimion. I'll bring you two floaters full of iron ore when I return."

12

HOMEWARD THE ROYAL PARTY sped, taking only the straightest and swiftest routes, pausing not at all. Couriers preceding them cleared the roads for their passage north. There were no conferences this time with local dukes or mayors, no official banquets, no tours of scenic wonders: just day after day of hard travel through the southern provinces of Alhanroel, past the Labyrinth, up the Glayge valley toward Castle Mount. But to Prestimion the journey seemed to take an eternity and a half. His mind raced with thoughts of all that awaited him once he was at the Castle again.

And then, at last: the Mount filling the sky before him, and the commencement of the familiar ascent by way of Amblemorn of the Slope Cities. The quick eastern road up the mountain by way of Morvole and Dekkeret's Normork, past Bibiroon Sweep and Tolingar Barrier and the wonderful self-maintaining garden that Lord Havilbove had laid out three thousand years ago, past the Free Cities ring to Ertsud Grand, where the upward slope steepened and the Mount became a gray granite shield pointing toward the clouds that lay just below the summit; Minimool; Hoikmar; the cloud zone, cool and moist, of the Inner Cities. Passing the sparkling burnt orange spires of Bombifale, then, and moving on into the realm of eternal sunlight above, with the High Cities just beyond. They were two dozen miles up into the sky by that time, with the thousands of miles of sprawling lowlands of Alhanroel spread out behind them like a map on which the most gigantic cities became mere dots. Here, now, was the summit road, paved with bright red flagstones, to carry them from Bombifale to High Morpin, with the Castle itself in view above them, finally; and round and round the vast mountain's diminishing tip they went, the ten miles of the Grand Calintane Highway, brightened by the splendor of the myriads of flowers that bloomed every day of the year amidst the gnarled and fantastic spearlike peaks of the summit.

A great crowd was waiting for him at the Dizimaule Plaza, an immense reception party gathered on the green porcelain cobblestones, with the Castle in all its bewildering bulk of thirty thousand rooms as the backdrop. Navigorn, who had served as regent in Prestimion's absence, was the first to embrace him. Prestimion's brother Teotas was waiting also, and Serithorn, and the counsellors Belditan and Dembitave and Yegan and the rest of his inner circle of government, and such members of Lord Confalume's regime as still remained at the Castle. But one person was not there.

Prestimion said quietly to Navigorn, as they proceeded through the Dizimaule Arch toward Vildivar Close and the Inner Castle buildings that lay beyond it, "And the lady Varaile, Navigorn? How has she fared in my absence? And why was she not at the gate to greet me now?"

"She is quite well, my lord. As for her not being at the gate today, let her give you her reasons herself. I can only tell you that she was invited, and chose not to come."

"Chose not to come? What does that mean, Navigorn?"

But Navigorn would only say again that the lady Varaile would have to explain that herself.

Which could not be done immediately, much to Prestimion's displeasure. There were rites that had to be performed to mark a Coronal's return to the Castle after a long absence, and then it behooved him to go to his office to receive the most urgent of the accumulated memoranda of state, and after that he had his own report to make to the Council. Only then, then, would he be free to pursue private inquiries.

He hastened through the ritual of return in so casual and cursory a way that even Serithorn looked a little shocked. The memoranda of state—abstracts of the host of piled-up reports from every region of the world—were not so easy to dismiss, but Prestimion cut corners by devoting most of his immediate attention to the summaries that had been prepared by the office of the Pontifex, abstracts of the abstracts: presumably those had been filtered for their significance before being forwarded to the Castle. What he saw there was dismaying, tales of mounting insanity in any number of provinces, bands of addled saints drifting about the land and plenty of addled sinners too, riots and other kinds of civil disturbance, fires, crime, a nightmare of ever-expanding chaos. It was precisely as he had said, in an unguarded moment, to the Prefect Kameni Poteva. Bit by bit, it seems, the whole world is going crazy.

Of Dantirya Sambail there seemed to be no news. Akbalik had returned from Ni-moya and was in the western port of Alaisor, awaiting a new assignment. Dekkeret evidently was still in Suvrael. No report had come from Abrigant thus far concerning his expedition to Skakkenoir. From the Isle of Sleep there was a message from the Princess Therissa, suggesting that he find occasion to pay her a visit as soon as his other duties permitted. That would certainly be an appropriate thing to do, Prestimion agreed. He had not seen her for many months. But for the time being that trip would have to wait.

The Council meeting, which lasted about an hour, came next. Navigorn's report covered much the same material Prestimion had already seen in the papers on his desk. When he was done, the other Council members expressed their concern over the rising incidence of madness across the world, and Gialaurys offered a motion that the high wizards of Triggoin be summoned to the Castle for a consultation that might lead to a remedy. It passed by a powerful margin, despite a protest of sorts from Prestimion. "It was my hope to reduce the influence of superstition in the world, not to hand the government over to the sorcerers," he said. But even he recognized the value of properly harnessed wizardry; and also he knew only too well how effective the incantations of such men as Gominik Halvor and his son Heszmon Gorse could be. After voicing his objections, then, he quickly withdrew them, and gave his assent to Gialaurys's measure.

At that point, pleading the fatigue of travel, he ordered the meeting adjourned, and went to his private chambers.

"Ask the lady Varaile," he said to the major-domo Nilgir

Sumanand, "if she will have dinner with the Coronal this evening."

She was as beautiful as he remembered her to be: more beautiful, even. But she had changed. Something was different about the expression of her eyes and the set of her jaw, and she held her lips now in a tightly compressed way that Prestimion did not recall from before.

Of course she had really been not much more than a girl when he had first met her at the time of his little masquerade in Stee. Now she was moving into her twenties; perhaps all that had happened was that the last vestiges of adolescence were going from her face as she made the transition into full adulthood. But no—no—there seemed to be something else at work—

Perhaps only nervousness, Prestimion decided. She was a commoner, he was the Coronal; and she was a woman, and he a man; they were alone with each other in the Coronal's private chambers. They barely knew each other, and yet, in their last meeting long months ago, they had reached some sort of understanding that neither of them had been willing to voice explicitly, but which clearly had held implications of a future alliance. In all these months they both had had plenty of time to consider and reconsider those few words that had passed between them in the reception hall after the royal levee at which her father had been honored.

To put her at her ease he opened with what he hoped would be a light-hearted approach: "I told you, the last time we met, that we'd have dinner together as soon as I got back from my trip to the Labyrinth. I neglected to add, I suppose, that I would be going on as far south as Sippulgar before I returned to the Castle."

"I did begin to wonder, as the weeks mounted up, my lord. But then my lord Navigorn told me that you would be making a further journey and might not be back for many months. He said it was a mission of the highest importance, one that would take you into a distant part of the continent."

"Did Navigorn tell you just how far I was going, or why?"

She looked startled at that. "Oh, no! Nor did I ask. It's not my place to be privy to the business of the realm. I'm a mere citizen, my lord."

"Yes. So you are. But a lady of the court, also, now. Ladies of the court somehow come to learn of many things that mere citizens never hear of even in their dreams."

It was meant as a joke, if only a feeble one; but it was not received as one. Something was definitely wrong, he thought. A certain degree of tension was only to be expected at such a meeting as this; he felt it himself. But what had impressed him about her whenever he had seen her previously was her remarkable poise, her utter command of self, far beyond her years. She made it seem as if there was no situation, however ticklish, that she would be unable to handle. The unsmiling woman who stood before him now was stiff and uneasy, guarded in her movements, seemingly weighing every word before she spoke.

She said, "Nevertheless, I felt it was inappropriate to inquire after the reason for your journey. Would it be proper to inquire of you whether your trip was a successful one, my lord?"

"It was and it wasn't. My meeting with the Pontifex went well. After that, I visited strange and interesting places, and met the people who govern them. That part of it was fine also. But I had another purpose, which was to locate a certain troublesome lord whose actions threaten the stability of the realm. Do you know who I mean, Varaile? No. Well, you will, eventually. In any case, I wasn't able to find him. He seems to have slipped through my net."

"Oh, my lord, I'm sorry!"

"So am I."

Prestimion noticed now, for the first time, how plainly and soberly she was dressed: a formal robe, yes, suitable for calling upon a Coronal, but of a drab beige tone that seemed inappropriate for her high-colored complexion, and her only ornament was a slender silver bracelet. And she had pulled her splendid hair back in an unflattering way.

This long-awaited reunion was going most unpromisingly. Some wine and food, he thought: perhaps that would relax things. He summoned Nilgir Sumanand.

Who had everything ready in the antechamber, a feast of truly royal quality. But Varaile only picked at her food, sipped desultorily at her wine.

Prestimion said, finally, when the conversation had sputtered out for the third or fourth time, "There's some problem here, Varaile. What is it? You seem six million miles away."

"My lord, do I? Certainly it was most kind of you to ask me to dine with you, and I don't mean to seem—"

"Call me Prestimion."

"Oh, my lord, how can I do that?"

"Easily. It's my name. A long one, perhaps, but not hard to pronounce. Pres-tim-i-on. Try it."

She looked close to tears. "This is not right, my lord. You are the Coronal and I am no one; and in any event we barely know each other. To call you by your name like that—"

"Never mind, then." He began to feel some annoyance, but whether it was with her for her moodiness and distance, or for himself for his clumsiness in leading this conversation, he was not sure. Somewhat brusquely he said, "I asked you a minute ago to tell me what the problem was. You evaded the issue. Are you afraid of me? Or do you think it's wrong, perhaps, for you to be here alone with me? —By the Divine, Varaile, you haven't fallen in love with someone while I was away, have you?" But he could see by her face that that was not it either. "Tell me. You've changed, somehow, in my absence. What's happened?"

She hesitated a moment.

"My father," she said, in a voice so faint he could barely make out her words.

"Your father? What about your father?"

Varaile looked away; and a dozen wild suppositions ran through Prestimion's mind at once. Was Simbilon Khayf seriously ill? Had he died? Gone bankrupt overnight through the catastrophic failure of one of his loathsome speculative schemes? Warned Varaile sternly to ward off any romantic overtures the seductive young Coronal Lord might make?

"He's lost his mind, my lord. The plague—the madness that is sweeping the world—"

"No! Not him too!"

"It was very quick. He was at Stee when it happened, and I was at the Castle, of course. One day he was fine, I was told, working on deals, meeting with his agents and factors, arranging the takeover of some company, all his usual projects. The next day everything was changed. You know his hair, how proud he is of it? Well, his chief clerk, Prokel Ikabarin, is always the first person to arrive at his office every morning. This time, when Prokel Ikabarin came in, he found my father kneeling in front of his desk, cutting off his hair. 'Help me, Prokel Ikabarin,' he said, and handed him the scissors to reach the places he couldn't get to. He had hacked most of it off by then."

A surge of amusement welled up in Prestimion at that. He turned aside to conceal his grin from Varaile. Simbilon Khayf's extravagantly foolish sweep of silver hair, cut down to mere stubble? Why, what more delicious kind of insanity could have stricken him than that?

But there was more. And worse.

Varaile said, "When he was done with his hair, he announced that his life had been a sinful waste, that he repented all his greed, that he must at once distribute his wealth to the poor and take up a life of meditation and prayer. Whereupon he asked Prokel Ikabarin to send for his half-dozen closest advisers, and began signing away his property to whatever charitable organizations happened to come to his mind. He gave away at least half his fortune in ten minutes. Then he put on beggar's robes and went out into Stee to ask for alms."

"This isn't easy for me to believe, Varaile."

"Do you think it was for me, my lord? I know what sort of man my father was. I never had any illusions about him at all; but it wasn't for me to lecture him on his ways, nor was I the sort to turn my back on his wealth myself, I suppose, no matter how I felt about his business practices. But when they came to me here at the Castle—I have been in residence here all the time of your absence, you understand, my lord—when they came to me and said my father was roaming through Stee in a torn and dirty robe, begging for a few copper weights for his next meal—well, I thought it was some black jest at first, of course. And then—then, when other reports came in, and I went down to Stee to see for myself—"

"He's given away everything? The house, too?"

"He didn't remember about the house. Just as well, too, for what would have become of all our servants, turned out into the streets overnight? Did he expect them to become beggars too? No, he didn't manage to give it all away. His mind was too murky to manage that. Thousands of royals went, yes—millions, maybe——but there's plenty left. He still controls dozens of companies, banks all over the world, great estates in seven or eight provinces. But he's completely incompetent now. I had to have a receiver appointed to manage his holdings—it's not something I could do myself, you realize. And he's completely insane. Oh, Prestimion, Prestimion, I was aware of all my father's faults, his vanity, his hunger for money, his coldblooded treatment of anyone who stood between him and what he wanted, but still—still—he's my father, Prestimion. I love him. And what has happened to him is so utterly terrible."

It did not escape Prestimion's notice that she had begun calling him by his name.

"Where is he now?"

"At the Castle. I asked my lord Navigorn to bring him here, because if he stayed in Stee, someone was bound to harm him on the streets. They have him under guard in one of the back wings. I visit him every day, but he hardly recognizes me now. I don't think he quite knows who he is, any more. Or what he once was."

"Take me to visit him tomorrow."

"Do you really think that you ought to see—"

"Yes," he said. "I do. He is your father. And you are—"

There was no need to finish the sentence. The barriers that she had put up between them earlier were gone. She was staring at him now with an entirely new expression in her eyes.

This was the moment, Prestimion thought, to make everything completely clear between them.

"When I invited you here tonight," he said, "it was with the notion of making some sort of speech about how important it was for us to spend more time together, to get to know one another, and so on and so forth. I won't make that speech. I've had plenty of time, all these months roaming around in places like Ketheron and Arvyanda and Sippulgar, to get to know you already."

She seemed apprehensive. "Prestimion—?"

His words came tumbling out helter-skelter. "I've lived alone long enough. A Coronal needs a consort. I love you, Varaile. Marry me. Be my queen. I warn you, it won't be easy, being wife to the Coronal. But you are the one I choose. Marry me, Varaile."

"My lord—?" she said, with astonishment in her voice.

"You were calling me Prestimion a moment ago."

"Prestimion, yes. Oh, yes! Yes! Yes!"

III

*The Book
of Healing*

1

MORE THAN THIRTY YEARS had passed since there last had been a royal wedding at the Castle, that of Lord Confalume and the Lady Roxivail; and no one now attached to the Coronal's staff was old enough to know the proper procedures and protocols for such an event. So a great scurrying about in the archives was initiated by the officials involved, until Prestimion found out about it and made an end to the search. "We're capable of putting on a wedding here without having to turn to the oldsters to find out how we ought to do it, isn't that so?" he asked Navigorn. "Besides, was the marriage of Confalume and Roxivail such a magnificent success that we want to take any aspect of it as a model for anything we do?"

"The Lady Varaile," said Navigorn with diplomatic earnestness, "is nothing at all like the Lady Roxivail, my lord."

No, Prestimion thought. Nothing at all.

Prestimion had seen the vain and willful estranged wife of Lord Confalume only once in his life—at the coronation games in honor of her son Korsibar, when that prince's brief, illegitimate, and disastrous reign as Coronal was just getting under way. Roxivail, a small, dark, strikingly attractive woman, had maintained her looks well into middle age with the aid of wizardry, and Prestimion had been startled by her beauty. As well he might be; for she and her daughter Thismet resembled each other in an extraordinary way, to the degree that Roxivail seemed more like Thismet's elder sister than her mother.

Her surprising appearance at the coronation games, her first visit to the Castle in some twenty years, had revived all the old gossip. Confalume, masterly and potent Coronal that he was, had not been able to govern his own wife; their marriage had been stormy throughout, and had culminated in Roxivail's noisy departure from the Castle to take up life in a luxurious palace on an island in the Gulf of Stoien. She had remained there ever since, excepting only her journey to the Mount at the time of her son's coronation. In her long absence Confalume had had to rule without a consort and to raise their twin children alone—twins whose very existence no one, not even their parents, now remembered at all. Those who had any recollection of the previous Coronal's marriage would think of it, if ever they did, as being barren as well as unhappy. Prestimion had fonder expectations for his own.

In the end it was Prestimion himself, with some help from Navigorn and an immense amount of advice on matters of taste and style of decor from Septach Melayn, who worked out a formal program for the wedding. The usual high princes of Castle Mount would be in attendance, but not, Prestimion decided, anyone from the provinces. For that would mean extending an invitation to Dantirya Sambail along with all the other great provincial lords, and the absence of the Procurator of Ni-moya would be awkward to explain.

Invitations would go to the Lady Therissa, of course, and the Pontifex Confalume. But Prestimion assumed that their own current responsibilities and the great distances they would have to travel would keep them from coming to Castle Mount for a second time in little more than a year, and indeed they sent their apologies and regrets. They would be represented by their official surrogates at the Castle, the hierarch Marcatain for the Lady, and Vologaz Sar for the Pontifex. The Lady Therissa reiterated her hope that Prestimion would come to her at the Isle as soon as his present duties at the Castle permitted, and that he would bring his bride with him.

Some of Varaile's own friends from Stee would be her ladies-in-waiting. Prestimion would be attended at the ceremony by Septach Melayn, Gialaurys, and Teotas. His other brother Abrigant should have been part of the event as well; but there was no telling whether he would return from his quest for the iron ore of Skakkenoir on time, and Prestimion did not propose to delay the wedding on his behalf.

He dealt quickly with the fact that Varaile was a commoner, and that nobody at the Castle could recall an occasion when a Coronal had chosen a commoner as his bride. Summoning Navigorn, he said, "We are creating a new duke today, and I have just drawn up the papers. See to it that the normal procedures are followed."

Navigorn glanced at the document Prestimion handed him and his face turned scarlet with surprise and dismay. "My lord! A dukedom for that abominable, moncy-grubbing, utterly offensive—"

"Gently Navigorn. You're talking about the father of the Coronal's consort-to-be."

Appalled at his own words, Navigorn made a little choking sound and mumbled an apology.

Prestimion laughed. "Not that anything you just said is untrue, of course. But we will ennoble Simbilon Khayf even so, because that will ennoble his daughter as well, and thus we sidestep a certain little problem of protocol. It seems the simplest way to handle it, Navigorn. And, best of all, he won't ever know that it's happened. His mind's completely gone, you know. I could just as easily make him Coronal or Pontifex as give him a dukedom, for all he'd be able to understand."

Which brought up another little difficulty involving the father of the bride, which was that Simbilon Khayf was altogether unfit to appear in public. He was a babbling, pathetic figure now, indifferent to cleanliness or decorum and muttering constantly of a need to atone for his sins. Even at his best, he would have been an embarrassment to Prestimion at the ceremony; but in his present condition there could be no question of it. "We will let it be known that he is too ill to attend," Varaile declared, and so it was done.

Easily enough solved; but hardly a day went by without some new procedural problem arising.

One was the issue of how many mages would be at the wedding other than Maundigand-Klimd, and of which schools of practice, and what roles, if any, they would play. If Prestimion had had his own way, there would have been none. But Gialaurys was able to convince him of the rashness of that position. In the end a full array of wizards was in attendance at the rite, although at Prestimion's insistence they were kept at a circumspect distance from the dais and allowed to utter their incantations only as part of a general preliminary invocation.

Then there was the matter of finding some function for Serithorn, as the senior peer of the realm, to perform, and the question of what to do about preventing another mountain of gifts from flowing toward the Castle when so many of the coronation presents still had not yet been unpacked, and of whether to hold another round of knightly games by way of celebrating the Coronal's nuptials. Prestimion had not anticipated so many little details to deal with. But in a way he welcomed the distraction: for the time being, he was spared the need from fretting about the madness epidemic, or pondering the problem of finding the unfindable Dantirya Sambail, or dealing with any of the thousand routine questions that come before a Coronal in the course of an ordinary week. Everyone about him understood that the royal wedding took precedence, for the moment, over all of that.

And then, finally, he found himself on the high dais of Lord Apsimar's Chapel, which someone had determined was the traditional place for such events, with the hierarch Marcatain standing to his right on behalf of the Lady of the Isle and the representative of the Pontifex Confalume at his left and Varaile facing him, and a host of grandees of the realm in magnificent garb looking on, and Septach Melayn beaming in smug self-satisfaction at the job of matchmaking that he had achieved; and the traditional words were being spoken and the rings were being exchanged and the familiar old wedding anthem that went back to Lord Stangard's day was resounding in his ears.

It was done. Varaile was his wife.

Or would be, in a truer sense of the word, some hours later, when all the night's feasting and celebration was over and they could at last be alone.

There was a lavish suite of rooms adjacent to Prestimion's own that had belonged to the Lady Roxivail in the days of her marriage to Lord Confalume. In accordance with the wish of Lord Confalume it had not been used by anyone since Roxivail's departure from the Castle. The court cham-

berlains, expecting that those rooms would be occupied now
by Varaile and used by the royal couple on their wedding
night, had gone to great effort to restore and refurbish them
after their two decades of neglect.

But Prestimion regarded the Roxivail suite as an unlucky
place for their first night together. He chose, instead, the
apartments in Munnerak Tower, the white-brick building in
the Castle's eastern wing, where he had lived in his days as
one of the many princes of the Castle. Those chambers
lacked the majesty and splendor of the ones set apart for the
use of the Coronal; but Prestimion felt no great need for the
ultimate in majesty and splendor this night, and, he suspected, neither did Varaile. It was a handsome enough suite
in its way, with spacious rooms that had a marvelous downslope view through their curving many-faceted windows of
the abyss known as the Morpin Plunge, and an oversized
bathing-tub fashioned from huge blocks of black Khyntor
marble that had been so cunningly set in place by the arti-
sans that it was impossible to detect the joinings between
one block and the next. To this suite Prestimion brought his
bride; and here he waited, in the little room that had been
his study and library, while she bathed away the fatigue of
the long day of wedding rituals.

What seemed like ten years went by before she summoned him. But then came the call at last.

She was waiting for him in the room where the nuptial
bed had been installed, a magnificent bed of imperial dimensions, carved from the darkest Rialmar ebony and can-
opied with the sheerest lace of Makroposopos. As he went
down the corridor toward it Prestimion felt a sudden maddening burst of terror at the thought that the ghost of Thismet would somehow interpose itself between him and his
bride in this moment of moments; but then he opened the
bedroom door, and saw Varaile standing beside the bed in
the soft golden glow of three scarlet waxen tapers taller than
herself, and Thismet at that instant became only a name, a
cherished but distant memory, the mere ghost of a ghost.

Varaile was clad, after her bath, in a filmy gown of fine
white silk, fastened at her left shoulder by a clasp of woven

gold. Prestimion admired the reticence that had led her to cover herself for his arrival in the bedroom. But he noted also the lush and supple contours of her body glimmering through the gossamer fabric, and knew that modesty was not its only purpose. He caught his breath in delight and stepped toward her.

There was, for just an instant, a look of anxiety, even fear, in her eyes. It vanished, though, as quickly as it came. "The consort of the Coronal," Varaile said, as though in wonder. "Can this be real?" And answered herself before he could speak. "Yes. Yes. It can. Come to me, Prestimion."

She touched a drawstring at her shoulder.

The gown fell away like a cobweb.

2

A THREE-DAY HONEYMOON IN the pleasure-city of High Morpin, an hour's ride by floater below the Castle, was all that he could allow himself. He had been away from the seat of power too much of the time already since attaining the throne.

In his youth Prestimion had come often to that happy glittering playground of a place to go on dizzying juggernaut rides and let himself be catapulted through the power-tunnels and dance on the baffling, challenging mirror-slides. Such amusements were beyond his grasp now. A Coronal could not allow himself to put his body even to the slight risk that such games afforded, nor would the populace be pleased to see him cavorting like a boy in public. That he had become the prisoner of his own royal majesty was a fact beyond all denying.

But there were compensating delights in High Morpin for those whose high place in the realm denied them the freedom to move openly among the populace. Prestimion and Varaile stayed at the Castle Mount Lodge, a knifeblade-sharp slab of white stone set aside for the use of the nobility, and there they occupied the many-chambered penthouse known as the Coronal's Suite, which was not so much a suite as a miniature palace that clung to the upper levels of the towering hotel much as the Castle itself wraps itself about the summit of the Mount.

The uppermost level of their suite was a transparent bubble of clearest quartz, which served as their bedchamber. From it they had a view of the entire sparkling city, all the way across to the immense fountain that Lord Confalume had had built at the city's edge, which constantly hurled thick plumes of water, ever-changing in color, to an enormous height. One floor down was their robing-room, a horn-like excrescence of some shining white metal boldly cantilevered out from the other side of the building to provide a view of the lovely suburb of Low Morpin and the

stupefying dark emptiness of the Morpin Plunge, where the
face of the Mount fell away for a sheer drop of thousands
of feet. Just below that was a room carved from a single
gigantic green globe of jade, where soft musical tones
emerged without apparent source from the air: the harmonic
retreat, that room was called. Then a long white-vaulted passageway led at a steeply descending angle to the private
dining-quarters, a small, elegantly appointed room where the
Coronal and his consort could take their meals. A cascading
series of balconies gave them access to the clear, pure air
of the Mount and a third view, this one of the dark intricate
bulk of the Castle rising high above them.

A second passageway in a different direction opened into
an elaborate pleasure-gallery supported by pillars of golden
marble. Here the residents of the suite could swim in a shimmering pool lined with garnet slabs, or suspend themselves
in a column of warm air and permit streams of unquantified
sensation to flood their senses, or put themselves in contact—through appropriate connectors and conduits—with
the rhythms and sighing pulses of the cosmos. Here also
were kept patterned rugs for focused meditation, banks of
motile light-organisms for autohypnosis, a collection of
stimulatory pistons and cartridges, and a host of other devices for the royal couple's amusement.

From there the structure made an undulating swaybacked
curve and sent two wings back up the building at differing
levels. One contained an array of soul-paintings that had
been collected by various Coronals of the the previous two
centuries, and the other was a gallery for the housing of
antiquities, bric-a-brac, and a miscellany of small sculptures
and decorative vases. Centrally positioned between these
two groups of rooms was the suite's grand dining hall, a
single sturdy octagonal block of polished agate thrusting far
out into the abyss for the delight of such guests as the Coronal and his consort might care to entertain.

But the Coronal and his consort did not care to entertain
anyone, just now, except each other. There would be time
later to carouse with Septach Melayn, to listen to old Serithorn's tales of the court gossip of long ago, to play host to

great princes and dukes. This was a time purely for themselves. They had much still to learn about each other, and this was the finest opportunity they would ever have. Prestimion and Varaile spent their three days moving from room to room, from level to level, examining the curious artifacts with which the place was filled, taking in the glorious views of the gleaming airy city outside, paddling up and down the pool, and, much of the time, exchanging thoughts, memories, ideas, caresses. Meals were brought to them by silent servants whenever they remembered to request them.

On the third day, with the greatest regret, they came forth from their retreat. A royal floater waited outside the building to return them to the Castle; and thousands of people of every rank and station, those who had come to High Morpin on holiday and those whose role it was to serve their needs, sent up a great cry: "Prestimion! Varaile! Prestimion! Varaile! Long live Prestimion and Varaile!"

But then it was back to work. For Prestimion, the million minutiae of government; for Varaile, the weighty task of taking command of the royal household.

It was a busy time. Prestimion had had ample opportunity in recent years, sitting as he had at Lord Confalume's right hand, to see how much work it was to be Coronal. But somehow the reality of it had never sunk in. Confalume, that robust and hearty man, had made it all look easy. To Confalume, the endless routine responsibilities of the throne had always been nothing but mere buzzing interruptions of the real work, which was to express the grandeur of the realm and its monarch by a glorious construction program: fountains, plazas, monuments, palaces, highways, parks, harbors. The lavishly conceived Confalume Throne and the awesome throne-room in which it was set would symbolize the reign of Lord Confalume for centuries to come. Even when he had been Coronal for forty years, and had largely withdrawn from active rule into a private world of mages and incantations, he still managed to keep up an outward show of gusto and vitality. Only those closest to him had any inkling of how weary he actually was toward the end, how relieved he was that the aged Pontifex Prankipin had died and allowed him at last to move on to the quieter life of the Labyrinth.

Prestimion was hardly lacking in vitality himself. But his was of a kind different from Confalume's. Confalume expended his energy in a steady calm radiant outpouring, like the sun itself. Prestimion, a more volatile man, taut and tense within, functioned by bursts of impulsive action, tempered by long periods devoted to the accumulating of strength. That was how he had handled the insurrection of Korsibar: a lengthy period of waitful calculation and planning, and then the sudden launching of the counterstrike that had swept the usurper away.

But you could not reign as Coronal that way. You sat here atop the world, most literally, and the needs and hopes and fears and problems of the fifteen billion people of Majipoor found their way up the slopes of Castle Mount to you day after day after day. And although you delegated as much of the work as you could to others, the ultimate responsibility for every decision was always yours. Everything flowed through you. You were the world incarnate; you were Majipoor, in and of yourself.

Had Korsibar realized that, when he foolishly decided to make himself Coronal? Had he thought that being king was an unending round of tournaments and feasts, and nothing more? Very likely he had, that shallow man.

Prestimion could never have allowed himself to stand to one side and let Korsibar keep the throne: it was as much a matter of his sense of obligation to the world as it was his own desire to be Coronal himself.

And so, when he might have had peace with Korsibar and a place for himself on the Council for the price of a starburst gesture and an oath of allegiance, Prestimion had not been able to do it, and Korsibar had thrown him into the Sangamor tunnels as a traitor, and the war between them had begun. Now Korsibar was forgotten and Prestimion was Coronal Lord of Majipoor; and here he was, plodding through a daily stack of petitions and resolutions and memoranda and acts of the Council so thick it would choke a gabroon. It was enough to make him nostalgic, almost, for the days of the civil war, when he was far from all this paperwork, living a life of pure action.

Not that everything that crossed his desk was stultifyingly routine, of course.

There was the madness plague, for one. Gibbering vacant-eyed victims roamed the streets of a thousand cities, most of them harmless, some not. Hospitals everywhere were filling with screaming lunatics. There were accidents, collisions, fires, even murders. What was causing it? Prestimion feared that he knew, but it was not something he could speak of to anyone. Nor could he see a solution. The constant reports of chaos out there weighed heavily on his spirit. But there was nothing he could do.

Nothing he could do, either, about the dangers posed by his distant cousin Dantirya Sambail: the great adversary, the ever diabolical foe, malevolent and unpredictable, still at large. Where was he? What was he up to? All these months, and no one had seen or heard from him.

It was easy and tempting to think that he had perished, that he and his demonic man Mandralisca lay dead and rotting in some roadside ditch in southern Alhanroel. But that was too easy; and it strained Prestimion's imagination to believe that fate could so conveniently have removed Dantirya Sambail from his list of problems without the slightest effort on his part. Still, a network of spies on two continents had produced no information.

The Procurator should surely have reached his headquarters in Ni-moya by now, but his throne there sat empty. Nor had he surfaced anywhere in southern or western Alhanroel. It was all very unsettling. Dantirya Sambail would reappear when least expected, Prestimion knew, and would cause maximum trouble when he did. But here, again, all that he could do was wait, and do his daily work, and wait. And wait.

*   *   *

Maundigand-Klimd came to him and said, "Look at these, my lord." The Su-Suheris magus had a cloth sack with him, bulging as though he had brought three pounds of ripe calimbots straight from the marketplace.

It was Threeday morning, the day of the week when Prestimion customarily went down to the exercise-hall to engage in a little singlesticks contest with Septach Melayn. That was always an unequal match, for Septach Melayn had the reach on him by eight or ten inches, and had unparalleled mastery of any kind of hand-wielded weapon besides. But it was essential for the two men, bound now as they were to their desks so much of the time, to work at keeping their bodies in tune; and so on Threedays they dueled with batons, and on Fivedays they tested each other on the archery course, where the advantage lay with Prestimion.

"What do you have here, and is it necessary for me to see it at just this moment?" Prestimion asked, in some impatience. "I have an appointment with the High Counsellor."

"It will take only a minute or two, my lord."

Maundigand-Klimd up-ended his bag and what looked like three dozen tiny severed heads fell out onto Prestimion's desk.

They were ceramic, he realized, after the first startled glance. But modeled in an extremely vivid and realistic manner, with terrifying grimacing faces—mouths gaping wide, eyes staring wildly, nostrils flaring—and a convincing swath of gore at the neck-stumps: cunning simulations of people who had died in the most frightful agony.

"Very pretty," Prestimion said bleakly. "I've never seen anything like them. Is this the latest fashion of jewelry among the ladies of the court, Maundigand-Klimd?"

"I bought them last night at the sorcerers' market in Bombifale. They are amulets, my lord, to guard one against the madness."

"The sorcerers' market, as I recall, is open only on Seadays, and not even all of those. Yesterday was Twoday."

"The sorcerers' market at Bombifale is open every night of the week now, lordship," said the Su-Suheris quietly. "These things are sold at many of the booths. Five crowns apiece, they are: stamped from molds in great quantity. But exceedingly well done."

"So I see." Prestimion poked at them with the tip of one finger. They were grisly things, all too convincingly real despite their miniature size. He saw the faces of men and women both, a few Ghayrogs, a couple of Hjorts, even a single Su-Suheris head that sent a particularly severe tremor of repulsion through him. Small metal fasteners were attached to them in back. "Magic against magic, is that it? One wears them, does one, for the sake of counteracting whatever witchcraft is causing the insanity plague?"

"Exactly. It is what we call in the trade a cloaking-magic. The little image sends a message indicating that the person who wears it is already afflicted with the madness—screaming, wild-cyed, mutilated of soul, altogether deranged—and so there is no need for the agent that brings the malady to act on them."

"And do they work?"

"I doubt it, my lord. But people have faith in them. Nearly everyone I saw in the market was wearing one. There are other devices available, too, for the same purpose, at least seven or eight sorts, all of them guaranteed by their vendors to provide complete security. Most of them are crude, primitive things that make me embarrassed for my profession. They are what you might expect savages to use. But the fear is very widespread. —Do you remember, my lord, in the days when Prankipin was dying and dire omens were being read into every cloud and every bird that passed overhead, how all manner of strange new cults sprang up in the world?"

"I do remember, yes. I saw the Beholders dancing the Procession of their Mysteries in Sisivondal once."

"Well, they dance it again. All the masks and idols and holy implements of an unholy kind are being brought forth. These little amulets here are but a sample of the whole. My lord, sorcery is my profession, and I do not doubt the existence of the powers of the invisible world, as I know that you often do. But to me these things are abominations. They bespeak an insanity of a sort themselves, as troublesome as the one they pretend to cure."

Prestimion nodded somberly. He prodded the little heads again, turning over two or three of them that had landed upside-down, and was stunned to find himself looking at his own face.

"I wondered when you would notice that one, my lord," said Maundigand-Klimd.

"Astonishing. Absolutely astonishing!" Prestimion picked it up and examined it closely. It gave him the shudders. A likeness of great fidelity, it was: a miniature screaming Lord Prestimion, hardly bigger than the ball of his thumb. "I suppose there's a Septach Melayn somewhere in the batch, too, and a Gialaurys, and maybe a Lady Varaile, eh? And is this Su-Suheris here supposed to represent you, Maundigand-Klimd? What do they think: that our faces will be more powerful in warding off the madness than those of ordinary folk?"

"It is a reasonable expectation, lordship."

"Ah. Maybe so." Septach Melayn was here, yes. They had rendered him very well, down to the insouciant grin— even in the midst of a madman's scream—and bold, flashing blue eyes. He saw no Varailes, though, and was very glad of that. He pushed the pile of amulets away from him. "How I hated all this credulous foolishess, Maundigand-Klimd! This pathetic faith in the worth of magic, in talismans and images, in spells and powders, exorcisms, abracadabras, the conjuring up of fiends and demons, the using of rohillas and ammatepilas and veralistias and all of that. What a waste of time, and money, and hope! I saw Lord Confalume utterly devoured by these follies, so befuddled by the whisperings of this magus and that that when a real crisis came upon him, he was completely unable to deal with—" He halted, unwilling even with Maundigand-Klimd to speak of the Korsibar revolt. "Well, I know as well as you do that some of it works, Maundigand-Klimd. But most of what passes for magic among us is nothing more than simple idiocy. I had hoped that the tide of superstition would begin to recede a little during my reign. And instead—instead—a new wave of this nonsense sweeping up over us, just when—" He paused again. "I'm sorry, Maundigand-Klimd: I know that you're a believer. I've given you offense."

"You've given none, my lord. I am no more of a 'believer,' as you put it, than you are yourself. I live not by faith but by empirical test. There are things that are self-evidently true, and other things that are false. What I practice is the true magic, which is a form of science. I have as much contempt for the other sort as you do, which is why I brought you these things today."

"Thinking that I'll issue an ordinance prohibiting them? I can't do that, Maundigand-Klimd. It's never wise to try to legislate against people's irrational beliefs."

"I understand that, lordship. I only wanted to call to your attention the fact that the madness is bringing forth a secondary level of insanity, which in itself will have harmful consequences for your reign."

"If I knew what needed to be done, I'd be doing it."

"Beyond doubt that is so."

"But what—what? Is there anything you can suggest?"

"Not at this moment, my lord."

Prestimion detected a curious inflection in Maundigand-Klimd's voice, as though he might be leaving something of significance unspoken. Prestimion stared up at the two heads, at the four opaque green eyes. The Su-Suheris was an invaluable counsellor, and even, to a degree, a cherished friend. There were times, though, when Prestimion found Maundigand-Klimd unreadable, incomprehensible, and this was one of them. If there was some hidden subtext here, he was uncertain of what it was.

But then one possibility presented itself to him. It was a disagreeable one, but it needed to be pursued.

He said, "You and I have already discussed Septach Melayn's notion that the madness has been caused by the world-wide obliteration of memory that I imposed, the day of the victory over Korsibar at Thegomar Edge. I think you know that I'm reluctant to accept that theory."

"Yes, my lord. I do."

"I can tell from the way you say it that you don't agree

with me. What are you holding back, Maundigand-Klimd? Do you have certain knowledge that I did bring the madness on that way?"

"Not certain knowledge, my lord."

"But you think it's very probable, do you?"

All this while it had been Maundigand-Klimd's left head, usually the more loquacious of the pair, that had been speaking. But it was the other one that replied now:

"Yes, my lord. Very probable indeed."

Prestimion closed his eyes a moment, drew in his breath sharply. The blunt statement came as no surprise. In recent weeks he had been veering more and more, in his own thoughts, toward the likelihood that he and he alone was responsible for the new darkness that had begun to descend upon the world. But it stung him deeply, all the same, to have the shrewd and capable Maundigand-Klimd lend his support to that idea.

"If the madness was caused by magic," he said slowly, "then it can only be healed by magic, would you not say?"

"That could be so, my lord."

"Is what you're telling me, then, that one possible way to fix things is to call Heszmon Gorse and his father down out of Triggoin, and all the rest of the mages who took part in casting the spell that day, and have them cast a reverse spell that would restore everyone's knowledge of the civil war?"

Maundigand-Klimd hesitated, something that Prestimion had rarely seen him do.

"I am not sure, my lord, that such a thing would be effective."

"Good. Because it's never going to happen. I'm not happy about the apparent consequences of what I did, but it's a safe bet that I'm not going to try anything like it again. Among other things, I don't have any desire to let everyone know that their new Coronal began his reign by hoodwinking the entire planet into thinking his accession had been peaceful. But also I see great risks in suddenly restoring the old sequence of events. People have spent the past couple of years living with the false history that I had my mages instill in their minds at the end of the civil war. For better or worse, they accept it as the truth. If I take all that away now, it might just cause an upheaval even worse than what's going on now. What do you say about that, Maundigand-Klimd?"

"I agree completely."

"Well, then: the problem remains. There's a plague loose in the world, and a lot of bad magic is springing up as a result, a mess of chicanery and fraud which you and I both despise." Prestimion, glowering at the little ceramic heads that Maundigand-Klimd had spilled all over his desk, began to scoop them back into their sack. "Since the plague was brought on by magic, it needs to be dealt with by a counter-magic—good magic, true magic, as you say. Your kind of magic. Very well. Please work something out, my friend, and tell me what it is."

"Oh, Lord Prestimion, if only it were that easy! But I will see what I can do."

The Su-Suheris went out. Prestimion, when he was gone, fished about in the sack until he had found the Lord Prestimion head and the Septach Melayn, and dropped them in a pocket of his tunic.

Septach Melayn was waiting for him in the gymnasium, restlessly pacing up and down and flicking his baton through the air, bringing an ominous hum from the slender wand of nightflower wood at every motion of his supple wrist. "You're late," he said. He pulled a second baton from the rack and tossed it to Prestimion. "A lot of important decrees to sign this morning, was it?"

"A visit from Maundigand-Klimd," said Prestimion, laying the baton aside and drawing the little heads from their pocket. "He brought me these. Charming, aren't they?"

"Oh, indeed! Your portrait and mine, if I'm not mistaken. What are they meant for?"

"Amulets to conjure with. To keep the madness away, supposedly. Maundigand-Klimd tells me that the midnight market's full of stuff like this, all of a sudden. They're selling the way sausages would in the middle of the Valmambra. He bought a whole bag of them. Not just your face and mine, but all sorts, even a Ghayrog and a Hjort and a Su-Suheris. Something for everyone. All the old cults are starting up again, too, he says: big business all over again for the whole magus crowd."

"A pity," said Septach Melayn. He took the portrait of himself from Prestimion and balanced it in the palm of his hand. "A little on the grisly side, I'd say. But so cleverly done! Look, I'm grinning and shrieking at one and the same time. And I seem to be winking a little, too. I'd love to meet the artist who designed it. Perhaps I could get him to do a full-scale portrait, you know?"

"You are a madman," said Prestimion.

"You may very well be right. May I keep this?"

"If it amuses you."

"It certainly does. And now, please, my lord, pick up your baton. Our exercise hour is long overdue. On your guard, Prestimion! On your guard!"

3

AT THE BEGINNING OF the week following, word was brought to Prestimion as he breakfasted that his brother Abrigant had returned to the Castle from the south-country in the middle of the night, and was requesting immediate audience.

Prestimion had arisen at dawn. The hour was not much past that now. Varaile still slept; Abrigant must not have been to bed at all. Why such urgency?

"Tell him that I'll meet with him in the Stiamot throne-room in thirty minutes," Prestimion said.

Hardly had he settled into his seat there when Abrigant came bursting in, looking as though he had not taken the trouble even to change his clothing since his arrival. He was bronzed and weatherworn from his travels, and the brown cloak that he wore above threadbare green leggings was patched and soiled. Over his left cheekbone there was a bruise of considerable size, plainly not a recent one but still quite livid.

"Well, brother, welcome back to—" Prestimion began, but he got no further along than that with his greeting.

"Married, are you?" Abrigant blurted. His expression was fierce and challenging. "For that is what I hear, that you've taken a queen. Who is she, Prestimion? And why didn't you wait until I could attend the ceremony?"

"These are very straightforward words when spoken to a king by his younger brother, Abrigant."

"There was a time once when I made a grand starburst to you and a deep bow, and you told me that that was much too much obeisance between brother and brother. Whereas now—"

"Now you go too far in the other direction. We haven't seen each other for many months; and here you are, charging in like a wild bidlak, not even a smile or a friendly embrace, immediately asking me to explain my actions to you as though you were Coronal and I a mere—"

Again Abrigant cut him off. "The groom who received me when I arrived told me that you have a consort now, and that her name is Varaile. Is this true? Who is this Varaile, brother?"

"She is the daughter of Simbilon Khayf."

If Prestimion had struck him across the face, Abrigant would not have looked more astounded. He recoiled visibly. "The daughter of Simbilon Khayf? The daughter of Simbilon Khayf? That puffed-up arrogant fool is a member of our family now, Prestimion? Brother, brother, what have you done?"

"Fallen in love, is what I've done. What you've done is to behave like a belligerent boor. Calm yourself, Abrigant, and let's begin this conversation again, if you will. The Coronal Lord welcomes the Prince of Muldemar to the Castle after his long journey, and bids him be seated. Sit there, Abrigant. There. Good. I don't like to have people looming up over me, you know." Abrigant seemed totally nonplussed, but Prestimion could not tell whether it was from the rebuke or from his bland admission of having married Simbilon Khayf's daughter. "You look as though you've had an arduous trip. I hope it was a fruitful one."

"Yes, it was. Very much so." Abrigant's words came as if through clenched teeth.

"Tell me about it, then."

But Abrigant would not be turned from his course. "This marriage, brother—"

Summoning all the patience he could manage, Prestimion said, "She is a splendid queenly woman. You'll not doubt the wisdom of my choice when you meet her. As for her father, I assure you that I'm no more enamored of him than you are, but there's no cause for dismay. He's caught the madness that's running about the world, and has been locked away where he can't offend anyone with his vulgar ways. In the matter of my not holding the wedding off until you got back here, I shouldn't have to justify that to you; but I ask you to bear in mind that I had no assurance you'd keep your promise about giving up your quest for Skakkenoir within six months. For all I knew, you'd be gone two or three years—or forever."

"You had my solemn pledge. Which I kept to the very letter of the word. It was six months exactly from the day we parted that I began my homeward trip:"

"Well, you have my gratitude for that, at least. The expedition was successful, you say?"

"Oh, yes, Prestimion. Quite successful. I have to tell you that it would have been a far greater success if you hadn't sworn me to that six-month limit, but there's much to report even so. —He's really gone mad, has he? A raving imbecile, eh? What a perfect fate for him! I hope you've got him chained up among all those hideous beasts Gialaurys brought back from Kharax for you."

"You said there was much to report," Prestimion reminded him. "It would be kind of you to begin, brother."

He had commenced the trip, Abrigant said—still obviously thunderstruck by the news of Prestimion's marriage, but making a visible effort to put it out of mind—by heading eastward from Sippulgar along the Aruachosian coast of the Inner Sea. But that was such a vile sweltering place, where the air was so wet and thick that one could hardly breathe, and the wasps and ants were the size of mice and the very worms had wings and jaws, that they were driven inland soon after crossing over into the province of Vrist. The last glimpse of the sea that they had was at the dreary Vristian port of Glystrintai; after that, they found themselves in much less humid country, largely uninhabited—a hot, primordial-looking plateau of wrinkled crags and congealed lava, of pink lakes in which gigantic snakes lay coiled, of turbulent rivers inhabited by monstrous sluggish mud-colored fish, bigger than a man, that seemed to have wandered out of a much earlier era.

In this sun-baked prehistoric land of broad vistas and distant horizons a terrible silence prevailed day after day, broken only by the occasional skreeking cries of sinister-looking predatory birds, bigger even than the khestrabons or surastrenas they had seen in the east-country, that went soaring by high overhead. The travelers felt almost as though they were the first explorers of some virgin planet.

But then they spied smoke on the horizon—campfires— and they came the next day to a land of jet-black hills laced with dazzling outcrops of brilliant white quartz, where thousands of Liimen living in the middle of nowhere were mining gold. "True gold this time?" said Prestimion. "After golden bees and golden hills and walls of golden stone, a place where the actual metal itself is found?"

"The metal itself," Abrigant said. "These are the mines of Sethem province, where naked Liimen work like slaves under the murderous sun. Here. See for yourself." And he reached into a burlap knapsack that he had brought into the throne-room with him and pulled forth three square thin plates of gold, each about the size of the palm of his hand, on which geometric symbols had been marked with punches. "They gave me these," said Abrigant. "I don't know what they're worth. The miners didn't seem to care. They just do their work, as though they were machines."

"The mines of Sethem," Prestimion said. "Well, the stuff had to come from somewhere. I never gave it a thought."

The image came to him of long lines of Liimen at work

in that barren stony landscape: strange uncomplaining
rough-skinned beings, with broad flat heads shaped like
hammers and three fiery eyes glowing like smouldering
coals in the craters of their deeply recessed eye-sockets.
Who had assembled them and brought them there? What
thoughts went through their minds as they plodded through
their days of unthinkable toil?

The gold lay hidden in the quartz, the merest dusting of
it scattered thinly through the rocky veins. The Liimen
mined it, Abrigant said, by building fires on the black stony
outcrops and hurling cold water and vinegar against the
heated rock to fracture it so that the ore could be extracted
from the fissures thus created. Some worked on the surface
of the hills, others in deep tunnels that were too low-roofed
for them to stand in, so that they had to writhe along the
ground, seeing their way with lamps fastened to their foreheads. Eventually great mounds of ore-bearing rock were
collected. Then a different group would set to work with
stone sledgehammers to break that up into smaller pieces,
which yet other workers took and ground down in mills
operated by great handles, two or three Liimen to a handle,
until it came to the consistency of flour.

The final phase was to spread the processed quartz out
on slanting boards and pour water over it to flush away the
dross, a task repeated again and again until only pure par-
ticles of gold remained. This then was smelted for days on
end in a kiln, along with salt and tin and hoikka bran, and
eventually pure gleaming nuggets came forth, which were
beaten into the thin plates that Abrigant had been given.

"It is miserable work in a miserable place," he said. "But
they toil every hour of the day, handling an immense
amount of rock to produce very little gold. And all that labor
just for the sake of gold! If only there were more of the
stuff, perhaps we could find some way to convert it into
useful iron or copper. But as it is, we have just this, suited
only for trifling decorative purposes."

"And after Sethem," Prestimion said, "where did you go
then?"

"Eastward still," replied Abrigant, "into the province of

Kinorn, which was not quite a land of deserts but far from pleasant, having been folded again and again by ancient movements of the land so that crossing it was like crossing a giant griddle. We went on and on, ridge after ridge, and there was always the next steep ridge to climb, and we were tossed about in our floaters as though in a storm at sea. This bruise, Prestimion—I struck my head once when our car overturned and thought it would be my death. Some villages had been founded here, too, the Divine only knew why, where the people lived by farming and seemed to have very little knowledge of the great world beyond. They spoke a dialect that was difficult to understand. Zimroel was only a myth to them, and its demonic Procurator unknown; they claimed to know of such places as the Fifty Cities of Castle Mount, and Alaisor and Stoien and Sintalmond and Sisivondal, but it was obvious that their information went no farther than those cities' mere names. I asked of Skakkenoir, though, and they smiled at that, and said, yes, yes, Skakkenoir, and pointed east. They pronounced the name in a barbarous way that I could never get my tongue to imitate; but the soil there, they said, was bright red. The red of iron, Prestimion."

"Of course, the six-month limit expired precisely at that point," said Prestimion lightly, "and therefore you turned back without investigating any further."

"You knew it, brother! That is what happened. But in fact we were actually a few days short of the six months, so we went on a little way. And look, Prestimion!" He put his hand into the knapsack again, taking from it three little glass vials of red sand, and a fourth that contained the dried and crumbling leaves of some plant. "Have this sand analyzed, and I think you'll find them rich with iron, as much as one part in ten thousand. And the leaves: can these be from the metal-bearing plants of Skakkenoir? I think they are, Prestimion. It was only a small strand of red earth, twenty feet wide at most and soon petering out—one little accidental tongue jutting forth out of the land of Skakkenoir, I think. And half a dozen scraggly little plants growing on that red soil. The real wealth lay still to the east, of that I was sure. But of course I was sworn to turn back on the day the seventh month began, and that day had now arrived, and so I did. I came very close, I believe. But I was sworn to turn back."

"All right, Abrigant. You've made your point."

Prestimion opened the vial of leaves and lifted one out. It looked like nothing more than a dried leaf, such as one would use as a cooking herb. There was nothing metallic about it: one might do better, perhaps, trying to extract gold from the shining shrubs on the hills of Arvyanda that reflected the gold of the sunlight than to get iron from this little wrinkled brown scrap of vegetation. But he would have it analyzed, all the same.

"There you are," said Abrigant. "The mines of Skakkenoir are yours for the taking. It is such ugly country, Prestimion, and so forbidding in its heat and its up-and-down landscape: I can see why other explorers gave up too soon. But perhaps they weren't as eager as I was to find the land of iron. The great prosperity of the age of Prestimion, brother, is in those four vials."

"May that truly be so. I'll have them examined this very day. But even if they prove to bear iron, what then? A bit of red sand and a few leaves won't take us very far. Skakkenoir itself remains undiscovered."

"It lay just beyond the next hill, Prestimion! I swear it!"

"Ah, but did it, though?"

Abrigant gave him a stormy look. "I would go again and see. With bigger floaters and a great many more men. And no six-month deadlines, this time. It's a ghastly land, but I would go, if only you'll authorize a second expedition. And I'll bring back all the iron you would ever want to possess."

"First the chemical analysis of these little samples of yours, brother. And then we'll discuss a new expedition."

Abrigant seemed to be on the verge of some hot retort; but just then came a knock at the door, the little rat-tat-tat pattern that Prestimion recognized as Varaile's. He held up his hand to silence his brother before he could speak and crossed the room to admit her.

She greeted him with a warm hug; and only after they

stepped back from each other did she notice that there was someone else in the room.

"Forgive me, Prestimion. I didn't know that you were—"

"This is my brother Abrigant, newly among us again after a difficult journey to the far south, questing after the land of iron. It took him very much by surprise, apparently, to discover that I had married in his absence. Abrigant: here is my consort Varaile."

"Brother," she said unhesitatingly. "How happy I am to know that you've returned safely!" And went instantly to him and enfolded him in an embrace nearly as warm as the one she had given Prestimion.

Abrigant seemed taken aback for a moment by the immediate openhearted fondness of her greeting, and returned it stiffly and awkwardly at first. But then he took her more wholeheartedly into his arms; and when he released her his eyes were shining in a new way and his fair-skinned face was reddened with confusion and pleasure. It was plain to see that Varaile had won him over in an instant, that he was overwhelmed by the beauty and poise and imposing presence of his brother's new wife.

"I was just telling Lord Prestimion," Abrigant said, "how greatly I regretted missing your wedding. I am the brother nearest to him in age; it would have been my great pleasure to stand beside him when he spoke his vows."

"He too regretted it that you could not be there," said Varaile. "But it was possible you'd be gone a very long while, and no one was sure how long. We both thought it best not to wait."

"I quite understand," Abrigant said, with a little bow. He could not have been more courtly, now. The angry man of a few moments before had utterly vanished. Looking toward Prestimion, he said, "I think we've finished our business for now, brother. —I'll go to my rooms, if I may, and leave you with your lady."

His eyes were glowing, and the meaning of that glow was as unmistakable to Prestimion as if it were possible for him to read his brother's thoughts. *You have done well for yourself, brother. This woman is truly a queen!*

"No, no," Varaile said, "I was just passing by. I wouldn't want to interrupt your meeting. Surely you two still have much to tell each other." She blew Prestimion a kiss and started toward the door. "Will we be lunching in the Pinitor Court as usual, my lord?"

"I think we will. And perhaps Abrigant will join us."

"I would like that," she said pleasantly, and made gestures of farewell to them both, and left the room.

"How altogether splendid she is," Abrigant said, still aglow. "I comprehend everything now. —Does she call you 'my lord' all the time?"

"Only when she's among people unfamiliar to her," Prestimion said. "A little touch of formality, is all. She's a very well-bred woman, you know. But we're on more intimate terms when we're alone."

"I would hope so, brother." Abrigant shook his head in amazement. "Simbilon Khayf's daughter! Who would ever believe it? That squalid little man, bringing into the world a woman like that—"

4

AND NOW IT WAS summer in the Alhanroel midlands where Castle Mount rose to the heavens, though there was no sign of a change of seasons at the Castle itself, favored as always by its perpetual gentle springtime.

A deceptive calm had settled there. For the moment, at least, there were no crises to deal with. Prestimion, accustoming himself now to his role as Coronal, met with delegations from far-off lands, paid occasional visits to the neighboring cities of the Mount, presided over the deliberations of the Council, conferred with the representatives of the Pontifex and the Lady on such matters of government as required his cooperation. The plague of madness continued to claim new victims, but not quite so voraciously as before, and the populace at large seemed to have accepted it as a fact of life, like unduly heavy rainfall that flooded the fields at harvest time, or lusavender blight, or the sandstorms that sometimes ravaged southeastern Zimroel, or any of the other little flaws of existence that made Majipoor something other than a perfect paradise.

As for Dantirya Sambail, he seemed to have vanished from the face of the world. That he had lost his life somehow in the course of his wanderings through Alhanroel struck Prestimion as being much too good to be true; but he was coming reluctantly to accept the possibility that that might have been what had occurred. The mere thought of a world without Dantirya Sambail caused wondrous serenity and ease to steal over him. At moments of high stress or great fatigue during the course of his daily tasks Prestimion would sometimes pause and think, I am rid forever of Dantirya Sambail, simply for the sake of savoring the tranquility that the words brought to his spirit.

Varaile, too, had adapted well to the change in her circumstances that marrying Prestimion had brought. The Coronal's wife had tasks of her own, a full daily round of them. One, though, was self-imposed: a visit to Simbilon Khayf in his comfortable captivity in the guest-house in the northern wing of the Castle near Lord Hendighail's Hall, every morning before going on to that day's regular chores.

The man who once had been the richest citizen of Stee, and whose grand mansion in that city had been the object of universal envy and admiration, now lived in just five modest rooms far from the center of Castle life. But he did not seem to care, or even to notice. Simbilon Khayf's days of striving were over. He gave no indication even of remembering the power that had been his, or the fierce driving ambition that had led him to it, or the multitude of little vanities by which he had announced to the world that Simbilon Khayf was a force to be reckoned with.

Each day now he was born anew into the world. Yesterday's experiences, such as they had been, had been washed from his mind as completely as the tracks that birds make at low tide along the sandy shore of the Inner Sea. His morning nurse awakened him and bathed him and dressed

him in a simple white robe, and gave him his breakfast, and
took him for a short walk along Lord Methirasp's Parapet,
the broad cobblestoned terrace behind his residence. Usually
Varaile arrived just as he was returning from that.

This morning, as every morning, Simbilon Khayf seemed
relaxed and happy. He greeted her, as ever, with a courteous
if absent-minded kiss on the cheek and a brief, fleeting
handclasp. Though he remembered little of his former life,
he did, at least, generally recall that he had a daughter, and
that her name was Varaile.

"You look well this morning, father. Did you have a good
rest?"

"Oh, yes, very good. And you, Varaile?"

"It would have been nice to sleep a little longer, but of
course I couldn't do that. We were up very late last night:
another banquet, it was, the Duke of Chorg here from Bibiroon, and he's a great connoisseur of wines. And since
Prestimion's family is famous for its wine, naturally it was
necessary to have a whole case of rarities shipped up from
Muldemar for the banquet, and the duke, wouldn't you
know, wanted to have a sip from every single bottle—"

"Prestimion?" said Simbilon Khayf, smiling vaguely.

"My husband. Lord Prestimion, the Coronal. You know
that I'm the Coronal's wife, don't you, father?"

Simbilon Khayf blinked. "You've married old Confalume, have you? Why would you have wanted to do that?
Isn't it strange, being married to a man older than your
father?"

"But I'm not," she said, laughing despite the gravity of
the situation. "Father, Confalume isn't Coronal any longer.
He's gone on to become Pontifex. There's a new Coronal
now."

"Yes, of course: Lord Korsibar. How silly of me! How
could I have forgotten that it was Korsibar who became
Coronal after Confalume? —So you've married Korsibar,
have you?"

She stared at him, puzzled and saddened. His damaged
mind wandered in the strangest ways. "Korsibar? No, father.
Wherever did you get that name from? There isn't any Lord

Korsibar. I've never heard of anyone by that name."

"But I was sure that—"

"No, father."

"Then who—"

"Prestimion, father. Prestimion. He's the Coronal now, the successor to Lord Confalume. And I'm his wife."

"Ah. Lord Prestimion. Very interesting. The new Coronal's name is Prestimion, not Korsibar. What could I have been thinking of? You're his wife, you say?"

"That's right."

"How many children do you and this Lord Prestimion have, then?"

Varaile said, reddening a little, "We haven't really been married all that long, father. We don't have any children yet."

"Well, you will. Everybody has children. I had one myself, I think."

"Yes. You did. You're speaking with her right now."

"Oh. Yes. Yes. The one who married the Coronal. What's his name, this Coronal you married?"

"Prestimion, father."

"Prestimion. Yes. I knew a Prestimion once. Smallish man, blond hair, very quick with a bow and arrow. A clever sort. I wonder what ever became of him."

"He became Coronal, father," said Varaile patiently. "I married him."

"Married the Coronal? Is that what you said: you married the Coronal? How very unusual! And what a step upward in the world for us, my dear. No one in our family has ever married a Coronal before, isn't that so?"

"I'm sure that I'm the first," Varaile said. It was about this time, each visit, when her eyes would begin welling with tears and she would have to turn briefly away, for it was bewildering and upsetting to Simbilon Khayf to see her cry. That happened now. She flicked her fingers across her face and turned back to him, smiling valiantly.

In recent weeks it had become quite clear to her that she had never actually loved her father in the days when his mind was intact: had not, in fact, even liked him very much.

She had accepted the nature of their life together without
ever questioning any aspect of it: his hunger for money and
glory, his embarrassing social pretensions, his arrogance, his
many foolishnesses of dress and speech, his enormous
wealth. A prank of the Divine had made her his daughter;
another, her mother's early death, had made her the mistress
of Simbilon Khayf's household when she was still just a
girl; and Varaile had accepted all that and had simply gone
about the responsibilities that had fallen to her, repressing
whatever rebellious thoughts might surface in her mind. Life
as Simbilon Khayf's daughter had often been a trying business for her, but it was her life, and she had seen no alternative to it.

Well, now the horrid little man who had happened to be
her father was a shattered thing, an empty vessel. He too
had been the victim of a prank of the Divine. It would be
easy enough for her to turn her back on him and forget that
he had ever existed; he would never know the difference.
But no, no, she could not do that. All her life she had looked
after the needs of Simbilon Khayf, not because she particularly wanted to, but because she had to. Now that he was
in ruins and her own life had been immensely transformed
for the better by yet another of the Divine's little jokes, she
looked after him still, not because it was in any way necessary, but because she wanted to.

He sat there smiling uncomprehendingly as she told him
of yesterday's Castle events: the meeting in the morning
with Kazmai Noor, the Castle architect, to discuss the preliminary plans for the historical museum that Prestimion
wanted to build, and then her lunch with the Duchess of
Chorg and the Princess of Hektiroon, and in the afternoon
a visit to a children's hospital downslope at Halanx and the
dedication of a playground in nearby Low Morpin. Simbilon
Khayf listened, ever smiling, saying now and then, "Oh,
that's very nice. Nice indeed."

Then she drew some papers forth and said, "I also had a
few matters of private business to deal with yesterday. You
know, father, that I've been signing all the family enterprises
over to the employees, because someone has to run those

companies and neither you nor I would be capable of doing that now, and in any case it would never do for the Coronal's wife to engage in commerce. We transferred seven more of them yesterday."

"Oh, very nice," said Simbilon Khayf, smiling.

"I have their names here, if you're interested, though I don't think that you are. Migdal Velorn was at the Castle—you know who he is, father? The president of your bank in Amblemorn?—and I signed all the papers he brought me. They involved Velathyntu Mills, and the shipping company in Alaisor, and two banks, and—well, there were seven. We have just eleven companies left, now, and I hope to be rid of them in another few weeks."

"Indeed. How good of you to take such care of things."

His constant smile was unnerving. These visits were never easy. Was there anything else she needed to tell him today? Probably not. What difference did it make, anyway? She rose to leave. "I'll be going now, father. Prestimion sends his love."

"Prestimion?"

"My husband."

"Oh, you're married now, Varaile? How very nice. Do you have any children?"

On a fine golden morning toward the end of summer Prestimion went downslope to his family estates in Muldemar to attend the great annual festival of the new wine. Every year at that time, by ancient tradition, the newly made wines of the previous autumn's vintage were brought out for their first tasting, and a lively day-long celebration was held in Muldemar city, capped by a grand banquet at Muldemar House, the residence of the Prince of Muldemar.

Prestimion had presided over a dozen or so of these events in his time as prince. Then, for two years running, there had been the distraction of the civil war to keep him from being present. Now he was Coronal and Abrigant had succeeded him at Muldemar. But last year there had been no banquet either, because he and Abrigant had been off in the east country chasing after Dantirya Sambail at the customary time of the festival. So this would be Abrigant's first festival since becoming Prince of Muldemar; and he would regard it as a high honor if Prestimion were to attend. The Coronal did not ordinarily attend the Muldemar festival. But no member of Prestimion's family had ever gone on to become Coronal before, either. Prestimion felt obligated to be there. It would mean an absence of three or four days from the Castle altogether.

Varaile, though, was a little unwell, and begged off attending. Even the short trip down to Muldemar seemed a little too much for her to deal with just now, she told him, and she certainly had no eagerness to take part in a lavish dinner where rich food and strong wines would be served far into the night. She asked Prestimion to bring Septach Melayn along as his companion instead. Prestimion was reluctant to go without her; but he was even more reluctant to disappoint Abrigant, who would be deeply hurt if he failed to appear. And so it happened that when the majordomo Nilgir Sumanand arrived at the Coronal's residence with word that a young knight-initiate named Dekkeret had just returned to the Castle after a long absence overseas and was seeking an audience with Lord Prestimion on a matter of extremely great importance, it was to Varaile and not the Coronal to whom he delivered the message.

"Dekkeret?" Varaile said. "I don't think I know that name."

"No, milady. He has been away since before the time you came to live here."

"It isn't usual for knight-initiates to request audiences with the Coronal, is it? How extreme is the importance of this extremely important matter, anyway? Important enough for you to send him down to Prestimion at Muldemar, do you think?"

"I have no idea. He said it was quite urgent, but that he must deliver his report to the Coronal himself, or else to the High Counsellor, or, if neither of them is here, to Prince Akbalik. However, the Coronal is in Muldemar today, as you know, and the High Counsellor is down there with him,

and Prince Akbalik has not yet returned from his own travels—he is in Stoienzar, I think. I hesitate to disturb Lord
Prestimion's holiday in Muldemar without your permission,
milady."

"No. Quite right, Nilgir Sumanand." And then, somewhat
to her own surprise, for she had been feeling queasy all
morning: "Send him here to me. I'll find out from him myself whether it's something worth bothering the Coronal
about."

There was something generous and open-spirited about
Dekkeret's features and the straightforward gaze of his eyes
that made Varaile take an immediate intuitive liking to him.
He was obviously highly intelligent, but there did not seem
to be anything sly or scheming or crafty about him. He was
a big, ruggedly built young man, perhaps twenty years old
or a year or two more, with wide, powerful shoulders and
a general look of tremendous physical strength held under
careful control. The skin of his face and hands had a tanned,
almost leathery look, as though he had spent a great deal of
time outdoors lately in some hot, harsh climate.

The Coronal, she told him, would be away from the Castle for several days more. She made it quite clear that she
would not intrude on her husband's visit to Muldemar except for very good cause. And asked him what it was, exactly, that Knight-Initiate Dekkeret wished to bring to the
Coronal's attention.

Dekkeret was hesitant at first in his reply. Perhaps he was
disconcerted at finding himself in the company of Lord Prestimion's consort instead of Lord Prestimion, or perhaps it
was the fact that Lord Prestimion's consort was so very
close to his own age. Or else he was simply unwilling to
reveal the information to someone he did not know: a
woman, moreover, who was not even a member of the
Council. He made no attempt, at any rate, to disguise his
uncertainty about how to proceed.

But then he appeared to decide that it was safe to tell her
the tale. After some awkward false starts he began to offer

her a long, rambling prologue. Prince Akbalik, he said, had taken him with him some time back on a diplomatic mission to Zimroel. He had not been entrusted with any important responsibilities himself, but was brought along only to gain a little seasoning, since he had only a short while before joined the Coronal's staff. After spending some time in Nimoya he had arranged, for reasons that he did not seem to be able to make very clear, to be transferred temporarily to the service of the Pontifex, and had gone off to Suvrael to investigate a problem involving cattle exports.

"Suvrael?" Varaile said. "How awful to be sent there, of all places!"

"It was at my own request, milady. Yes, I know, it is an unpleasant land. But I felt a need to go someplace unpleasant for a time. It would be very complicated to explain." It sounded to Varaile almost as though he had deliberately been looking to experience great physical discomfort: as a sort of purgation, perhaps, a penitential act. That was hard for her to comprehend. But she let the point pass without attempting to question him on it.

His task in Suvrael, Dekkeret said, had been to visit a place called Ghyzyn Kor, the capital of the cattle-ranch country, and make inquiries there about the reasons for the recent decline in beef production. Ghyzyn Kor lay at the heart of a mountain-sheltered zone of fertile grazing lands, six or seven hundred miles deep in the torrid continent's interior, that was entirely surrounded by the bleakest of deserts. But upon his arrival at the port of Tolaghai on Suvrael's northwest coast, he quickly learned that getting there was not going to be any easy matter.

There were, he was told, three main routes inland. But one of these was currently being ravaged by fierce sandstorms that made it impassable. A second was closed to travelers on account of marauding Shapeshifter bandits. And the third, an arduous desert road that ran across the mountains by way of a place called Khulag Pass, had fallen into disuse in recent years and was in a bad state of repair. No one went that way any more, his informant said, because the route was haunted.

"Haunted?"

"Yes, milady. By ghosts, so I was told, that would enter your mind at night as you slept and steal your dreams, and replace them with the most ghastly terrifying fantasies. Some travelers in that desert had died of their own nightmares, I heard. And by day the ghosts would sing in the distance, confusing you, leading you from the proper path with strange songs and eerie sounds, until you drifted off into some sandy wasteland and were lost forever."

"Ghosts who steal your dreams," said Varaile, marveling. Her innate skepticism bridled at the whole idea. "Surely you aren't the sort to let yourself be frightened by nonsense like that."

"Indeed I'm not. But setting off by myself into that miserable desert, ghosts or no ghosts, was a different matter. I began to think my mission was doomed to end in complete failure. But then I came across someone who claimed that he often went inland by way of Khulag Pass and had never had any problems with the ghosts. He didn't say that the ghosts weren't there, only that he had ways of withstanding their powers. I hired him to serve as my guide."

His name, Dekkeret said, was Venghenar Barjazid: a sly, disreputable little man, very likely a smuggler of some sort, who extorted a formidable price from him for the job. The plan was to reverse the usual patterns of wakefulness, traveling by night and making camp during the burning heat of the day. They were accompanied by Barjazid's son, an adolescent boy named Dinitak, along with a Skandar woman to serve as porter and a Vroon who was familiar with all the desert roads. A dilapidated old floater would be the vehicle in which they traveled.

The journey out of Tolaghai and up into the hills leading to Khulag Pass was uneventful. Dekkeret found the landscape startling in its ugliness—dry rocky washes, sandy pockmarked ground, spiky twisted plants—and it grew even more forbidding once they had gone through the pass and began their descent into the Desert of Stolen Dreams beyond. He had never imagined that the world held any such fearsome place, so stark and grim and inhospitable. But, he

said, he simply took that cruel, barren wasteland as it came,
without feeling a flicker of dismay. Perhaps he even liked
it in some perverse way, Varaile supposed, considering that
he had gone to Suvrael in the first place in search of whatever gratification there might be in hardship and suffering.

Then, though, the nightmares began. Daymares, rather.
He dreamed that he was floating toward the benevolent embrace of the Lady of the Isle, at the center of a sphere of
pure white light; it was a vision of peace and joy, but gradually the imagery of his dream changed and darkened, so
that he found himself marooned on a bare gray mountain-
side, staring down at a dead and empty crater, and awakened
trembling and weak with fear and shock.

"Did you dream well?" Barjazid had asked him, then.
"My son says you moaned in your sleep, that you rolled
over many times and clutched your knees. Did you feel the
touch of the dream-stealers, Initiate Dekkeret?"

When Dekkeret admitted that he had, the little man
pressed him for details. Dekkeret grew angry at that, and
asked why he should allow Barjazid to probe and poke in
his mind; but Barjazid persisted, and finally Dekkeret did
provide a description of what he had dreamed. Yes, said
Barjazid, he had felt the touch of the dream-stealers: an invasion of the mind, a disturbing overlay of images, a taking
of energy.

"I asked him," Dekkeret told Varaile, "if he had ever felt
their touch himself. No, he said, never. He was apparently
immune. His son Dinitak had been bothered by them only
once or twice. He would not speculate on the nature of the
creatures that caused such things. I said then, 'Do the
dreams get worse as one gets deeper into the desert?' To
which he replied, very coolly indeed, 'So I am given to
understand.' "

When they moved on at twilight, Dekkeret imagined he
heard distant laughter, the tinkling of far-off bells, the
booming of ghostly drums.

And the next day he dreamed again, a dream that began
in a green and lovely garden of fountains and pools but
quickly transformed itself into something terrible in which

he lay naked and exposed to the desert sun, so that he felt
his own skin charring and crackling. This time, when he
awakened, he discovered that he had wandered away from
camp in his sleep and was sprawled out in the midday heat
amid a horde of stinging ants. Nor could he find his way
back to the floater, and he thought he would die; but eventually the Vroon came for him, bearing a flask of water, and
led him to safety. There had been suffering aplenty in that
adventure, more, in truth, than he was looking for; but the
worst of it, he told Varaile, had been neither the heat nor
the thirst nor the ants, but the anguish of being denied the
solace of normal dreaming, the terror of having that cheerful
and soothing vision turn to something gruesome and frightful.

"So there really is some truth to these travelers' tales,
then?" asked Varaile. "This haunted desert actually does
have deadly dream-stealing ghosts in it."

"Of a sort, yes, milady. As I will shortly explain."

They were almost out of the desert, now, following the
bed of a long-extinct river through a violent terrain that had
often been fractured by earthquakes. The land here rose
gradually toward two tall peaks in the southwest, between
which lay Munnerak Notch, the gateway to the cooler,
greener lands of the cattle-country beyond. In another few
days he would be at Ghyzyn Kor.

But the worst dream of all still lay ahead for him. He
would not describe it in any specific way to Varaile, saying
only that it brought him face to face with the one evil deed
of his life, the sin that had sent him on his voyage of penance to Suvrael in the first place. Stage by stage he was
forced to re-enact that sin as he slept, until the dream culminated in a scene of the most horrific intensity, one that
made him shiver and blanch even to think of it now; and at
its climax he experienced a sudden piercing pain, an intolerable sensation as of a needle of searing bright light slash-
ing down into his skull. "I heard the tolling of a great gong
far away," said Dekkeret, "and the laughter of some demon
close at hand. When I opened my eyes I was almost insane
with dread and despair. Then I caught sight of Barjazid,

across the way, half hidden behind the floater. He had just taken off some kind of mechanism that he was wearing around his forehead, and was trying to hide it in his baggage."

Varaile gave a little start. "He was causing the dreams?"

"Oh, you are quick, milady, you are very quick! It was he, yes. With a machine that enabled him to enter minds and transform thoughts. A much more powerful machine than those used by the Lady of the Isle; for she can merely speak to minds, and this Barjazid's device could actually take command of them. All this he admitted, not very willingly or gladly, when I demanded the truth from him. It was his own invention, he said, a thing that he had been working on for many years."

"And carrying on experiments with it, is that it, using the minds of the travelers that he took into the desert?"

"Exactly, my lady."

"You did well to come to the Coronal with this, Dekkeret. This device is a dangerous thing. Its use needs to be stopped."

"It has been," said Dekkeret. A broad smile of self-satisfaction spread across his face. "I succeeded in taking Barjazid and his son prisoner then and there, and seized the machine. They are here with me at the Castle. Lord Prestimion will be pleased, I think. Oh, lady, I surely hope that he is, for I tell you, lady, nothing is more important to me than pleasing Lord Prestimion!"

5

"HIS NAME IS DEKKERET," Varaile said. "A knight-initiate, very young and a little rough around the edges, but destined, I think, for great things."

Prestimion laughed. They were in the Stiamot throne-room with Gialaurys. It was only an hour since his return to the Castle and Varaile had greeted him with this tale as though it were the most important thing in the world. "Oh, I know Dekkeret, all right! He saved my life in Normork long ago, when some lunatic with a sharp blade came charging out of a crowd at me."

"Did he? He didn't say anything to me about that."

"No. I'd be very surprised if he had."

"The story that he told me was absolutely astonishing, Prestimion."

He had listened to it with no more than half an ear. "Let me see if I have it straight," he said, when she was done. "He was with Akbalik on an assignment in Zimroel, that much I know, and then for some reason that was never made clear to me he went on by himself to Suvrael, and now, you tell me, he's come back from there bringing what sort of thing?"

"A machine that seizes control of people's minds. Which was invented by some shabby little smuggler, Barjazid by name, who offers to guide travelers through the desert, but who actually—"

"Barjazid?" Prestimion, frowning, glanced at Gialaurys. "It seems to me I've heard that name before. I know I have. But I don't recall where."

"A shady fellow who originally came from Suvrael, with squinty eyes and skin that looked like old leather," Gialaurys said. "He was in the service of Duke Svor for a couple of years: a very slippery sort, this Barjazid, much like Svor himself. You always detested him."

"Ah. It comes back to me now. It was right after that little trouble we had at Thegomar Edge, when we caught hold of that smarmy Vroon wizard, Thalnap Zelifor, who made all those mind-reading devices and had no hesitations about selling them both to us and to our opponents as well—"

Gialaurys nodded. "Exactly so. This Barjazid happened to be standing right there at the time, and you told him to pack up the Vroon and his whole workshop of diabolical machines and escort him into permanent exile in Suvrael. Where, no doubt, he got rid of the wizard at the first possible opportunity and appropriated the mind-control devices for his own use." To Varaile he said, "Where did you say this man Barjazid is now, lady?"

"The Sangamor tunnels. He and his son, both."

Hearty laughter came from Prestimion at that. "Oh, I like that! A nice closing of the circle! The tunnels were the very place where I first encountered Thalnap Zelifor, that time when he and I were prisoners chained side by side." Which brought a puzzled glance from Varaile. Prestimion realized that all this discussion of episodes of the civil war had left her baffled. "I'll tell you that story some other time," he told her. "As for this gadget of his, I'll give it a look when I have the chance. A machine that controls minds, eh? Well, I suppose we can find some use for it, sooner or later."

"Better sooner than later, I think," she said.

"Please. I'm not minimizing its importance, Varaile. There are many other things to deal with right now, though." He smiled to soften the tone of his words, but he did not try to conceal his impatience. "I'll get to it when I get to it."

"And Prince Dekkeret?" Varaile said. "He should have some reward for bringing this thing to your attention, shouldn't he?"

"Prince Dekkeret? Oh, no, no, not yet! He's still a commoner, just a bright boy from Normork who's making his way up the ladder here. But you're quite right: we ought to acknowledge his good services. —What do you say, Gialaurys? Promote him two levels, shall we? Yes. If he's second level now, which I think he is, let's up him to fourth. Provided he's recovered from whatever strange fit of conscience it was that sent him racing off to Suvrael."

"If he hadn't gone there, Prestimion, he'd never have captured the mind-control machine," Varaile pointed out.

"True enough. But the thing may not turn out to have any value. And this whole Suvrael exploit of his bothers me a little. Dekkeret was supposed to be working for us in Nimoya, not going off on mysterious private adventures, even ones that turned out to be worthwhile. I don't want him doing that again. —Now," Prestimion said, as Gialaurys, excusing himself, saluted and left the room, "let's turn to another matter, shall we, Varaile?"

"And that is?"

"A new journey that has to be undertaken."

A flicker of displeasure crossed Varaile's face. "You'll be traveling again so soon, Prestimion?"

"Not just me. Us. This time you'll be accompanying me."

She brightened at that. "Oh, much better! And where will we be going? Bombifale, perhaps? I'd love to see Bombifale. Or Amblemorn, maybe. They say that Amblemorn's very strange and quaint, narrow winding roads and ancient cobblestoned streets—I've always wanted to see Amblemorn, Prestimion."

"We'll be going farther than that," he told her. "A great deal farther: to the Isle of Sleep, in fact. I've not seen my mother since my coronation, and she's never seen my wife at all. We're long overdue for a visit. She wants to meet you. And she says she has important matters to discuss with me. We'll go by riverboat down the Iyann to Alaisor and sail to the Isle from there. This time of year that's the best route."

Varaile nodded. "When do we leave?"

"A week? Ten days? Will that be all right?"

"Of course." Then she smiled: a little ruefully, perhaps, Prestimion thought. "The Coronal never does get a chance to stay home at the Castle for long, does he, Prestimion?"

"There'll be all the time in the world for staying home later on," he replied, "when I am Pontifex, and my home is at the bottom of the Labyrinth."

In the city of Stoien, at the tip of the Stoienzar Peninsula in far southwestern Alhanroel, Akbalik sat before a thick sheaf of bills of lading and cargo manifests and passenger lists and other maritime documents, wearily leafing through them in search of some clue to the location of Dantirya Sambail. He had done the same thing every day for the last three months. A copy of every scrap of paper that had anything to do with vessels traveling between Alhanroel and Zimroel found its way to the intelligence-gathering center that Akbalik, by order of Septach Melayn, had set up here in Stoien. By now he knew more about the price of a hun-

dredweight of ghumba-root or the cost of insuring a shipment of thuyol berries against klegworms than he had ever
imagined he would learn. But he was no closer to finding
out anything about Dantirya Sambail than he had been the
day he arrived.

The despatches he was sending back to the Castle each
week were becoming increasingly terse and cranky. Akbalik
had been away in the provinces for months, passing what
had begun to seem like an endless skein of pointless days
among all these dreary strangers, first Ni-moya, now here.
He was a famously even-tempered man, but even he had his
limits. He was beginning to miss his life at the Castle tremendously. Nothing was being accomplished out here; it
was time, he thought, and well past time, for him to be
transferred back to the capital, and in the last couple of
despatches he had made explicit requests to that effect.

But no answers came. Septach Melayn was probably too
busy keeping his dueling skills polished to bother reading
his correspondence. Akbalik had written once to Gialaurys,
but that was like writing to Lord Stiamot's statue. As for
the Coronal, Akbalik had heard that he had decided to make
a pilgrimage to the Isle of Sleep to introduce his new wife
to his mother, and was somewhere on the River Iyann, midway between the Mount and Alaisor, just now. So there was
no hope at all of arranging a recall order, it seemed. Akbalik
had no choice but to go on sitting here day after day, interminably sifting through his mountains of shipping documents.

At least Stoien city was a cheery enough place to be
stranded, if you had no alternative but to be stranded in
some provincial outpost. Its climate was perfect, summer-
time warmth throughout the year, sweet air and cloudless
skies, pleasant sea breezes from mid-morning through mid-
afternoon, mild evenings, a delicious cooling sprinkling of
rain every night precisely at midnight. The city itself was a
thin strand spilling out for more than a hundred miles along
the sweeping curve of its great harbor, so that a population
of better than nine million was accommodated without any
sense of crowding. And the place was a joy to look at. Be-

cause the whole of the Stoienzar Peninsula was entirely flat, never rising more than twenty feet above sea level at any point, the people of the port of Stoien had introduced topographical variety into their city by requiring that every building had to be erected atop a brick platform faced with white stone, and by decreeing wide variation in the dimensions of the platforms. Some were no more than ten or fifteen feet high, but others, farther back from the shore, were impressive artificial hills that rose to heights of hundreds of feet.

Certain buildings of special importance stood in splendid isolation far above street level atop individual foundations; elsewhere, whole neighborhoods covering a square mile or more shared a single giant pedestal. The eye was kept in constant motion, faced as it was by pleasing alternations of high and low in every direction. And the effect of so much brick was softened by an abundance of bushes and vines and plants growing with tropical extravagance at the base of every platform, along the ramps that led to the higher levels, and clambering up the loftier walls. Those lush plantings afforded a brilliant show of color, not only the myriad different greens of their leaves, but the splendid indigo and topaz and scarlet and vermilion and violet of their innumerable flowers.

A pretty place, yes. And Akbalik's own office high up in the customshouse at the harbor afforded him a delightful view of the Gulf of Stoien, pale blue here, and smooth as glass. He was able to look northward for hundreds of miles, thousands, maybe, until the horizon intersected the planet's great curve and turned everything to a thin gray line. But he longed for home all the same. He began to compose yet another missive to Septach Melayn in his head:

"Esteemed friend and revered High Counsellor. Four months have passed, now, since I came to Stoien city at your behest, and in that time I have loyally and diligently labored at the task of—"

"Prince Akbalik? Your pardon, prince, sir—"

It was Odrian Kestivaunt, the Vroon who served as his secretary here. The little creature stood by the door, fidgety as always, his multitude of dangling tentacles coiling and uncoiling nervously in a way that Akbalik had had to train himself to tolerate. He was carrying yet another stack of papers.

"More things for me to read, Kestivaunt?" said Akbalik, and made a sour face.

"I have already looked these over, Prince Akbalik. And have discovered something quite interesting in them. They were taken from freighters departing from various Stoienzar ports for Zimroel in the past two weeks. If you will allow me, prince, sir—"

Kestivaunt carried the papers to the desk and began to lay them out as though they were playing-cards in a game of solitaire. They were cargo manifests, Akbalik saw, long lists of commodities interspersed with some sea-captain's comments on their condition as of the day they were taken on board, the quality of their packaging, and other such matters.

Akbalik glanced over the Vroon's sloping shoulders as the small being dealt the sheets out. So many quintals of honey-lotus, so many sacks of madarate gum, so many pounds of orokhalk, so many adzes, awls, axe-handles, pack-saddles, sledgehammers—

"Is it really necessary for us to be doing this, Kestivaunt?

"One moment more, I entreat you, good prince. There. Now: I call your attention to the seventh line of the first manifest. Do you see what is entered there?"

" 'Anyvug ystyn ripliwich raditix,' " Akbalik read, mystified. "Yes. I see it. But I don't make any sense out of it. What is it, something in Vroonish?"

"It's more like Skandar than anything else, I would say. But not very much like Skandar. This is not, I think, any language spoken on Majipoor. But to continue, sir, if you will: line ten of this second manifest."

" 'Emijiquk gybpij jassnin ys.' —What is this gibberish, man?"

"A coded message, perhaps? For look, look here, sir, line thirteen of the next paper: 'Kesixm ricthip jumlee ayviy' And line sixteen of the next: 'Mursez ebumit yumus ghok.'

The nineteenth line of the next an orderly progression from sheet to sheet, is that not so?" The Vroon shuffled the papers excitedly, holding one and then another under Akbalik's nose. "This nonsense is interpolated in otherwise ordinary texts at progressive intervals of three lines. We are missing, I think, the first two lines of the message, which would be on the first and fourth lines of documents we do not seem to have here. But it goes on and on: I have found forty lines of it so far. What could it be, if not a code?"

"Indeed. It sounds too absurd to be anyone's language. But there are codes and codes," Akbalik said. "This could all be nothing but some merchant's way of hiding trade secrets from his competitors." He glanced at another sheet. Zinucot takttamt ynifgogi nhogtua. What if that meant, Ten thousand troops setting out next week? He felt a sudden quiver of excitement. "Or, on the other hand, what we have here might well be some sort of communication between Dantirya Sambail and his allies."

"Yes," said the Vroon. "It might well be that. And codes are readily enough broken by those who are expert in that art."

"Are you referring to yourself, perhaps?" Vroons, Akbalik knew, had many divinatory skills.

There came a writhing of tentacles in a gesture of negation. "Not I, sir. This is beyond me. But an associate of mine, a certain Givilan-Klostrin—"

"That's a Su-Suheris name, isn't it?"

"It is, yes. A man of unimpeachable honor, to whom such texts as these would be readily accessible."

"He lives here in Stoien?"

"In Treymone, sir, the city of the tree-houses. That's just a few days' voyage up the coast from here, by way of—"

"I know where Treymone is, thank you." Akbalik paused in thought a moment. In these months of working together he had developed a good deal of trust in this Odrian Kestivaunt, but involving some unknown Su-Suheris in such an explosive affair was another matter entirely. A little behind-the-scenes research would be in order first. The double-headed folk all seemed to know one another. He would ask

Maundigand-Klimd for an opinion before bringing in Givilan-Klostrin.

Geenux taquidu eckibin oeciss. Emajiqk juqivu xhtkip ss.

Akbalik pressed the tips of his fingers to his aching temples. Did this mumbo jumbo, he wondered, conceal the secret plans of Dantirya Sambail? Or was it merely the private lingo of some shaggy Skandar merchant mariner?

Zudlikuk. Zygmir. Kasiski. Fustus.

Off to Castle Mount went a query to the magus Maundigand-Klimd. Back from the Castle, in due course, came Maundigand-Klimd's reply. Givilan-Klostrin, he said, was well known to him: a person in whom prince Abrigant could have absolute faith. "I vouch for him," said Maundigand-Klimd, "as though he were my brother."

A sufficiently impressive recommendation, Akbalik decided. He sent for Odrian Kestivaunt. "Tell your Su-Suheris friend," he said, "to get himself down to Stoien city right away."

But the sight of the actual Givilan-Klostrin made Akbalik wonder about the merit of Maundigand-Klimd's endorsement.

Maundigand-Klimd himself, for whom Akbalik had the highest respect, was a person of great dignity of bearing, indeed, of considerable personal grandeur, which was heightened by the monastic simplicity of his dress. Tastes in clothing at the Castle generally ran to the flamboyantly bright and bizarrely original, but Maundigand-Klimd mainly favored austere robes of black wool, or sometimes one of dark-green linen, with only a red sash to provide a bit of vivid color.

This Givilan-Klostrin, though, arrived at Akbalik's office clad in a grotesque patchwork outfit of gold-embroidered brocade decked with squares of blazing silk in half a dozen clashing colors, and his two long-crowned heads were topped with a pair of towering five-pointed hats whose tips reached almost to the ceiling of the room. Half a dozen huge round staring eyes with great swirling brows were painted on each of the hats, three in front, three behind. Rigid up-jutting epaulets rose eight or ten inches from each of the oracle's shoulders: they too were tipped with eyes, and narrow scarlet banners streamed downward from them.

The whole effect was probably intended to be awesome, but Akbalik found it absurdly comical. It was something that a mendicant fakir might wear, a wandering beggar who told fortunes in the marketplace for a couple of crowns. The Su-Suheris was horrifyingly cross-eyed, besides, the left eye of his right head peering over toward the right eye of the left head in a way that made Akbalik's insides squirm.

I vouch for him as though he were my brother, Maundigand-Klimd had said. Akbalik shrugged. He would not have wanted a brother anything like Givilan-Klostrin; but, then, he was not a Su-Suheris.

"I am the house of Thungma," Givilan-Klostrin declared portentously, and waited.

The Vroon had explained that part already. Thungma was the invisible spirit, the demon, the whatever-it-was, with whose consciousness Givilan-Klostrin made contact when he entered his divinatory trance. Givilan-Klostrin functioned as the "house" of the being during the time of his summoning.

The Su-Suheris, who stood with feet planted wide and arms folded across his chest, seemed to fill the room. He stared icily at Akbalik.

"The fee comes first," Odrian Kestivaunt whispered. "This is extremely important."

"Yes. I understand that. Tell me, Givilan-Klostrin: what will this consultation cost?" Akbalik asked, feeling almost seasick as he struggled to make eye contact somehow with the magus.

"Twenty royals," the left head said immediately. His voice was deep and rumbling.

It was a preposterous amount. Most people worked all year for less. An hour's visit with a dream-speaker would cost no more than a couple of crowns; this was a hundred times as much. Akbalik began to protest, but a quivering of tentacles from the Vroon, and a whispered, "Sir—sir—"

caused him to subside. The magus's fee, Odrian Kestivaunt had told him several times already, was an essential part of the process. Any attempt to bargain would ruin the entire enterprise.

Well, they weren't his twenty royals. Akbalik took four gleaming five-royal pieces from his purse, the new ones showing Confalume in the Pontifex's robes with Prestimion's handsome profile on the reverse, and laid them on the desk. Givilan-Klostrin snatched them up smoothly and lifted them to his faces, pressing the coins against his outer cheekbones and holding them there a moment as though to satisfy himself that they were genuine.

"Where are the documents?" the magus asked.

Kestivaunt had prepared a page-long transcript of the coded lines he had found in the group of cargo manifests. Akbalik handed that to the Su-Suheris. He shook both of his heads at once, an effect that Akbalik found dizzying, and demanded the originals. Akbalik looked toward Kestivaunt, who went scurrying out, tentacles thrashing in agitation, and returned a few moments later with the papers. Givilan-Klostrin took them from him. Akbalik had to fight back laughter at the sight of the seven-foot-tall Su-Suheris solemnly reaching far down toward the tiny Vroon, who was barely eighteen inches high.

Givilan-Klostrin now opened a case he had brought with him and began to set his conjuring apparatus out on a bench. Akbalik felt some surprise at that, for he knew that Maundigand-Klimd performed his own divinations without the aid of a lot of gadgetry, and in fact had often expressed scorn for such devices. Perhaps this was all part of the show, he thought, a justification for that staggering twenty-royal fee. He watched as Givilan-Klostrin put out five cones of incense and lit them, instantly filling the room with clouds of cloyingly sweet smoke. Next the magus brought forth a little metal dome and tapped a projection at its tip, which caused it to emit a steady bell-like tone. A second such device placed beside the first produced the deep, low sound of far-off chanting; a third yielded an eerie, reverberant sound that might have been created by blowing into conical sea-shells.

Givilan-Klostrin handed a fourth such dome to Akbalik, and a fifth to the Vroon. "You will touch their triggers," he said gravely, "at the appropriate moment. You will know when that moment has arrived."

Akbalik was beginning to feel a little uncomfortable. The sickening aroma of the incense, the hypnotic music of the bells and shells, the chanting—it was all rapidly getting to be too much for him.

But there was no turning back. The process, the very expensive process, was under way.

Givilan-Klostrin was holding Kestivaunt's stack of cargo manifests clasped between the outspread fingers of his hands, one hand above, one below. All four of his eyes were closed. From both his throats came a strange, unsettling gargling sound, its doubled rhythms and eerie harmonies coordinated in a weird way with the distant chanting. He seemed almost to have fallen asleep. Then, gradually, his body began to sway and his legs started to quiver. He leaned a long way backward, inclining his heads so that they pointed toward the floor behind him, and stood straight again, and leaned once more, repeating the movement over and over.

Suddenly Odrian Kestivaunt, without having received any perceptible cue, tapped the jutting tip of the little metal dome he was holding. From it there came the sonorous blast of giant trumpets, a sound that expanded through the room with a force that seemed capable of bending the walls. To his own surprise Akbalik felt himself impelled then by some powerful inner force to touch the trigger of his own dome, and, when he did, it gave off a series of tremendous deafening cymbal-clashes. The hubbub all around them was astounding. He felt as though he had somehow been whisked off into the very midst of the thousand-instrument orchestra of the Ni-moya opera house.

Rivers of sweat flowed down Givilan-Klostrin's faces. Akbalik had never seen a Su-Suheris perspire before: he hadn't known they even were capable of it. The magus's

breath was coming in harsh huffing gasps. Blood had begun
to ooze from his nose and mouth. He was clutching the
documents, now, tightly against his chest.

As the sounds emanating from the five metal domes
mounted in intensity, Givilan-Klostrin went reeling drunk-
enly around the room, flinging his heads back and lifting
his knees almost to his chest with every lurching stride.
Savage growling sounds came from him. He went crashing
into tables and chairs without appearing to notice. When one
sturdy chair in particular seemed to draw his anger—he had
stumbled into it three times—he raised one foot and brought
it crashing down with such astonishing force that the chair
went flying into a host of splintered pieces. It was an extraordinary feat. Truly he was a man possessed, Akbalik
thought.

The room now was utterly filled with the sounds of trumpets, bells, gongs. Givilan-Klostrin had come to a halt by
the window, and stood there now, leaning forward,
breathing heavily, his whole body shaking convulsively. He
rocked from side to side, again and again lifting one foot
and carefully putting it down, then lifting the other. His
heads shot outward on their shared neck, moved rapidly inward until they seemed almost to strike each other, shot
outward again. His cheeks were puffed; his tongues were
outthrust; he made frightful blowing noises. Then he opened
his eyes a moment. They were rolling wildly in their sock-
ets.

One minute, two, three, five: it went on and on. The
rhythm was building toward a tension that could only end
in some awesome eruption. But would this terrifying seizure
ever end?

Suddenly there was a startling silence in the room as all
five metal spheres ceased their noisemaking at the same instant. Givilan-Klostrin seemed deep in trance.

His shaking and rocking and foot-lifting all had ceased.
Now he stood statue-still, utterly frozen in place, the right
head dangling limply as though its neck-stalk were broken
and the left one staring unblinkingly forward at Akbalik.
The stasis held for a minute or more. Then from the droop-

ing right head there began to come a low moaning wordless sound, a kind of rumbling whine that wandered up and down over five or six octaves, gradually cohering into a series of unaccented syllabic phrases as unintelligible to Akbalik as the coded lines on the cargo manifest.

After a moment the upright left head began to speak as well: slowly declaiming a translation, apparently, of the oracular sounds coming from the other one, everything uttered clearly and precisely and understandably:

"The man whom you seek," said the left head of Givilan-Klostrin, "is here in this very province. These are messages from his hidden camp in the southern part of the province of Stoien to his companions in another land. He has spent many months gathering an army in a far-off place; he will soon bring his forces together here; it is his desire to overthrow the king of the world."

As he uttered the last of those words the Su-Suheris fell forward in exhaustion, collapsing with a tremendous crash almost at Akbalik's feet. For a long moment he lay face down, trembling. Then he lifted each of his heads in turn and stared at Akbalik in a dazed, groggy way, as if uncertain of where he was or who the man might be that was standing before him.

"Is it over?" Akbalik asked.

The Su-Suheris nodded feebly.

"Good." Akbalik made a brusque chopping gesture with one hand held sideways. "You will forget everything that was spoken here today."

A look of bafflement appeared on both of Givilan-Klostrin's icy-hued faces. In a weak voice the left head said, "Was anything spoken? By whom? I remember nothing, my lord. Nothing. The house of Thungma is empty."

"This is true," the Vroon murmured. "They carry no memories away from their trances. As I explained, they are vehicles, merely, for whatever the demon chooses to reveal."

"I hope that's really so," Akbalik said. "Get him out of here as fast as you can." He felt shaken and weak himself, as if it were he and not the Su-Suheris who had just been through the spasms and convulsions of that eerie seizure.

His head ached from the unrelenting sound of those gongs
and trumpets. And the slow, precise, stunning words of the
oracle reverberated ceaselessly in his mind: *The man whom
you seek is here. He has spent many months gathering an
army in a far-off place. It is his desire to overthrow the king
of the world.*

The usual route from Castle Mount to the port of Alaisor
on Alhanroel's western coast was by river: downslope by
floater by way of Khresm and Rennosk to Gimkandale,
where the River Uivendak had its source, and then by riverboat down the Uivendak past the Slope Cities of Stipool
and Furible and the foothills of-the Mount via Estotilaup
and Vilimong into the great central plain of the continent.
The Uivendak, which after a thousand miles changed its
name to the Clairn, and a thousand miles farther on became
the Haksim, eventually was joined by the potent Iyann,
which came flowing down out of the moist green country
northwest of the Valmambra Desert and met the Haksim at
a place known as Three Rivers, though no one knew why,
since there were only two rivers there. From there to the
coast the united rivers took the name of the Iyann.

That final stretch of the Iyann had once been famous for
its sluggishness, and travelers heading westward on it had
needed to resign themselves to an unhurried final leg of their
journeys; but since the breaking of the Mavestoi Dam upriver from the joining with the Haksim the waters of the
western Iyann were far more vigorous than they had been
in previous centuries, and the riverboat that carried Prestimion and Varaile moved along toward Alaisor at a speed
that Prestimion would have found more heartening if it did
not constantly remind him of the infamous tragedy of the
breaking of the dam.

Now they were just a few days' journey from the coast,
passing swiftly through warm, green, fertile agricultural
lands whose inhabitants lined the shore, waving and cheering, shouting his name and sometimes Varaile's also, as the
Coronal's ship went by. Prestimion and Varaile stood side

by side at the rail, acknowledging the greeting with waves of their own.

Varaile seemed amazed by the strength and depth of the outpouring of affection that came from them. "Listen to it, Prestimion! Listen! You can practically feel their love for you!"

"For the office of the Coronal, you mean. It has nothing much to do with me in particular. They haven't had time to learn anything more about me than that Lord Confalume picked me to succeed him, and therefore I must be all right."

"There's more to it than that, I think. It's that there's a new Coronal, after all those years of Confalume. Everybody loved and admired Lord Confalume, yes, but he'd been there so long that everyone had come to take him for granted, the way you would the sun or the moons. Now there's a new man at the Castle, and they see him as the voice of youth, the hope of the future, someone fresh and full of vitality who'll build on Lord Confalume's achievements and lead Majipoor into a glorious new era."

"Let's hope they're right," said Prestimion.

They were silent for a time after that, looking out toward the west, where the golden-green sphere of the sun had begun to slip toward the horizon. The land was flat, here, and the river very wide. Fewer people could be seen along the shore.

Then Varaile said, "Tell me something, Prestimion. Is it possible under the law for a Coronal's son ever to become Coronal after him?"

The question astounded him. "What? What are you talking about, Varaile?" he said sharply, whirling about to face her with such a furious glare in his eyes that she backed away, looking a little frightened.

"Why, nothing! I was only wondering—"

"Well, don't. It can never happen. Never has, never will! We have an appointive monarchy on Majipoor, not a hereditary one. I could show you historical records going back thousands of years to prove it."

"You don't need to do that. I believe you." She still looked alarmed at the vehemence of his reaction. "But why do you seem so angry, Prestimion? I was simply asking a question."

"A very strange one, I have to say."

"Is it? I didn't grow up at the Castle, you know. I'm not an expert on constitutional law. I do know that the new Coronal usually isn't the son of the one before. But then I found myself wondering, well, what if—"

The question, Prestimion realized, had been entirely innocent. She had no way of knowing of Korsibar and his ill-fated revolt. He tried to calm himself. She had found him off his guard, that was all, seeming to probe into a sensitive, even a forbidden, area but in fact meaning nothing of the kind.

"Well," she said, "if he can't be Coronal—and not Prince of Muldemar either, I guess, because Abrigant's bound to have children of his own some day and they'll inherit that title—well, then, maybe he can be a prince of something else, I suppose."

"He?" Prestimion was completely bewildered now.

"Oh, yes," Varaile said, patting her stomach. "Definitely a he, Prestimion. I knew that weeks ago. But I had Maundigand-Klimd do a divination, all the same, and he confirmed it."

He stared. Suddenly this all made sense.

"Varaile?"

"You look so amazed, Prestimion! As if it's never happened before in the history of the world."

"Not to me, it hasn't. But that's not the thing, Varaile. You told Maundigand-Klimd about it weeks ago, and not me? And told Septach Melayn too, I suppose, and Gialaurys, and Nilgir Sumanand, and your ladies-in-waiting, and the Skandar who sweeps the courtyard in front of—"

"Stop it, Prestimion! You mean you hadn't figured it out?"

He shook his head. "It never occurred to me at all."

"I think that you really ought to pay closer attention, then."

"And you ought not to wait so long before telling me important news like this."

"I waited until now," she said, "because Maundigand-Klimd told me to. He cast my horoscope and said that it would be more auspicious for the child if I mentioned nothing about him to you until we were west of the ninetieth meridian. We are west of the ninetieth meridian, aren't we, Prestimion? He said it was where the land flattened out and the river got very wide."

"I'm not the captain of the ship, Varaile. I haven't really been keeping track of the latitude."

"I was speaking of longitude, I believe."

"Latitude—longitude—what difference does it make?" Were they really past the ninetieth meridian yet? he wondered. Probably so. But either way what difference did it make, eightieth meridian, ninetieth, two hundredth? She should have told him long ago. But it seemed to be his destiny, he thought, to find himself entangled with some sort of wizardry at every turn. His head was throbbing with anger. "Sorcerers! Mages! They're the ones who rule this world, not me! It's outrageous, Varaile, completely outrageous, that this information has been circulating all over the Castle for weeks, and it's been kept from me all this time simply because—because some magus happened to tell you—" He was practically sputtering with indignation. She was looking at him, wide-eyed with amazement. A smile crossed her face, and gave way to a giggle.

Then Prestimion began to laugh as well. He was being very foolish, he knew. "Oh, Varaile—Varaile—oh, I love you so much, Varaile!" He slipped his arms around her and drew her close against him. After a long while he released her, and smiled, and kissed the tip of her nose. —"And no, Varaile, no, he can't possibly become Coronal after me, and don't ever even think about such an idea. Is that understood?"

"I was just wondering, that's all," she said.

6

AT ANY OTHER TIME it would have been appropriate for Prestimion to spend at least a week at Alaisor. As Coronal, he certainly would have to be guest of honor at a banquet with Lord Mayor Hilgimuir in the famous Hall of Topaz and make the obligatory visit to the celebrated temple of the Lady on Alaisor Heights. And if he still had been only Prince of Muldemar, there would be a meeting with the great wine-shippers with whom his family had had commercial connections for so many generations; and so on.

But these were not ordinary times. He had to get quickly to the Isle. And so, although he would meet with the lord mayor, it would be only for an hour or two. He would skip the visit to the hilltop temple, since he would be seeing the Lady herself soon enough. As for the wine-merchants, they were irrelevant now that he was Coronal and no longer could be concerned with the family wine business. A single night in Alaisor was all that he could allow himself, and then they would be on their way.

The lord mayor had provided Prestimion and Varaile with the sumptuous four-level penthouse suite reserved exclusively for Powers of the Realm atop the thirty-story tower of the Alaisor Mercantile Exchange. All of Alaisor could be seen from its windows. Maundigand-Klimd and the rest of the Coronal's entourage had been given lesser but still quite luxurious quarters nearby.

It was a city of high imperial grandeur, the greatest metropolitan center of the western coast. A line of massive towering cliffs of black granite ran parallel to the shore here. The Iyann had carved a deep canyon through that wall of black cliffs long ago in order to reach the sea; and Alaisor lay outspread like a giant fan at their base, spreading far along the shore to north and south, with the bay created by the Iyann's mouth forming the city's magnificent harbor. Grand boulevards ran on great diagonals through Alaisor city from its northern and southern extremities, converging in a circle at the waterfront. At that meeting-point stood six gigantic obelisks of black stone, marking the place where Stiamot, the conqueror of the Metamorphs, had been buried seven thousand years before. Prestimion pointed the monument out to Varaile from the balcony on the west side of the building, which gave them a view that overlooked the harbor.

The story was, he told her, that Stiamot, after becoming Pontifex, had decided in extreme old age to undertake a pilgrimage to Zimroel, to the Danipiur, the Metamorph high chieftain, for the sake of begging her forgiveness for the conquest. But his journey had ended here at Alaisor, where he fell ill and could not continue; and as he lay dying, looking outward toward the sea, he had asked to have his body laid to rest here instead of being carried thousands of miles eastward to the Labyrinth.

"And the temple of the Lady?" Varaile asked. "Where is that?"

They were on the uppermost floor of their suite. Prestimion led Varaile to the great curving eastern window, which faced the dark vertical wall of the cliffs. At this hour of the afternoon the westering sun bathed them in a bronzy-green sheen. "There," he said. "Right below the rim—do you see?"

"Yes. Like a white eye staring at us out of the forehead of the hill. Have you ever been there, Prestimion?"

"Once. I visited Zimroel about a dozen years ago and spent a couple of weeks in Alaisor on the way, and Septach Melayn and I went up there. It's a wonderful building, a slender curve of white marble one story high that seems to be hanging from the face of the cliff. You see the entire city laid out like its own map before you, and the sea beyond it, on and on halfway to the Isle."

"It sounds marvelous. Couldn't we go there just for a little while tomorrow?"

Prestimion smiled. "The Coronal can't go anywhere 'just for a little while.' That building up there's the second most sacred site on Majipoor. If I visited it at all, I'd have to stay overnight at the very least and meet with the Hierarch and her acolytes, and there'd be ceremonies and such, and all manner of other—well, you see how it is, Varaile. Whatever I do has heavy symbolic importance. And the ship to the Isle can't wait: the winds are favorable to the west, and we need to leave tomorrow. Once the wind turns against you here, it can cause delays of many months, and I can't risk that now. We can visit the temple the next time we're in Alaisor."

"And when will that be? The world is so big, Prestimion! Is there time for us ever to see the same place twice?"

"In four or five years," he said, "when things are a little more settled in the world, it'll be appropriate for me to make a grand processional, and we'll go everywhere. I mean everywhere, Varaile. Even over to Zimroel: Piliplok, Ni-moya, Dulorn, Pidruid, Til-omon, Narabal. We'll come through Alaisor again then, and we'll stay longer. I promise you we will. Whatever we've missed on this trip we'll see then."

" 'We,' you say. Does the Coronal's wife go with him on the grand processional? Lord Confalume's wife didn't, when he came to Stee on his last processional."

"Different Coronal. Different sort of wife. You'll be at my side, Varaile, wherever I go."

"That's a firm promise?"

"A solemn vow. I swear it by Lord Stiamot's whiskers. Here in the very shadow of his tomb."

She leaned forward and kissed him lightly. "I guess it's settled, then," she said.

He had never been to the Isle of Sleep. Indeed in his days as a prince of the Castle it had never occurred to him to go there. One did not ordinarily go to the Isle unless one had some special need to undergo a rite of purification. It was not even customary for Coronals to visit it unless they were making a grand processional, and it was too soon in his reign for that.

But now the Isle was rising before him on the horizon

like a wondrous white wall, and the sight of it set strange
excitement churning within him.

"You will be surprised at how big it is," everyone who
had been there constantly said. And so, having been duly
warned, Prestimion expected not to be surprised; but he was,
all the same. An island, he had always thought, was a body
of land that was completely surrounded by water, and is-
lands were usually fairly small. The Isle of Sleep was a big
island, everyone said, and he interpreted that to mean a very
large body of land that was completely surrounded by water.
But he still visualized it as something whose borders could
be perceived as curving away on all sides to the ocean. In
fact, though, the Isle was immense, so big that on any other
world it would have been called a continent. Seen from out
here in the sea, it certainly seemed to have a continent's
vast extent. It was only by comparison with Alhanroel, Zimroel, and Suvrael, the three officially designated continents
of Majipoor, that anyone could have thought of giving the
Isle any lesser designation.

One of the many wonderful stories that they told about
the Isle was that in distant ancient times—millions of years
ago, before there had been Shapeshifters, even, on Majipoor—it all had lain far below the surface of the sea, but
had been thrust upward into the air in a single day and a
single night by some awesome convulsion of the world's
interior. Which was why it was so sacred a place: the hand
of the Divine had taken hold of it and brought it forth from
the waters.

The undersea origin of the Isle could not be doubted. It
was attested to by the fact that the entire place was a single
enormous mass of chalk many hundreds of miles across and
more than half a mile high, having the form of three giant
circular tiers set one atop the next; and chalk is a substance
made up of the shells of microscopic creatures of the sea.

Those great chalk ramparts gleamed now with overpowering whiteness in the bright blaze of the sun, filling all
the sea before them like an impassable barrier. Varaile and
Prestimion stood staring in wonder. "I think I can make out
two of the three levels from here, and maybe just a hint of

the third," he said. "The big one that forms the base of the
island is called First Cliff. There's a forest along its rim,
hundreds of feet above sea level. Do you see? And that must
be Second Cliff that begins there, set back a goodly way
from the one below. If you follow the white wall up and
up, you'll see a second line of green—that's the boundary
between Second Cliff and Third Cliff, I suppose. Third Cliff
itself begins several hundred miles inland. You can't really
see it from below, except perhaps a suggestion of its summit. That's where Inner Temple is: the place of the Lady."

"It dazzles my eyes. I knew the Isle was made of white
stone, but I never thought it would shine like that! Will we
be going all the way to the top?"

"Probably. The Lady rarely descends to meet her son;
it's always the other way around. The custom is for her
hierarchs to meet the Coronal at the harbor and take him
first to the lodge they maintain for him there. He's the representative of the world of action, you see, all noise and
masculine bluster, and he needs to go through some transi-
tional rituals before he can be admitted to his mother's con-
templative domain. Then they conduct him upward to her
through the various terraces of the three cliffs. Eventually
we'll arrive at Inner Temple itself, up at the top, where my
mother will receive us."

So steeply did the Isle's tremendous white rampart rise
from the sea that there were only two harbors where ships
could land, both of them difficult of access: Taleis on the
Zimroel side, and Numinor here, facing Alhanroel. To these,
at certain specified times of the year, came pilgrims from
the mainland, some merely to retreat from the world for a
year or two of meditation and ritual cleansing, others to join
the Lady's realm and spend the rest of their lives in her
service.

The swift vessel that had carried Prestimion and Varaile
across from Alaisor was too big to enter Numinor harbor.
It had to anchor well out at sea, where its passengers were
transferred to a waiting ferry whose pilot knew the secrets
of the narrow channel, much beset by swift currents and

treacherous reefs, through which the shore could be approached.

Three tall, slender elderly women of great dignity and gravity of bearing, clad identically in golden robes trimmed with red, were waiting at the pier when the ferry arrived. They were hierarchs of the Isle, lieutenants whom the Lady Therissa had sent to greet him. "We are instructed to conduct you first," the senior one told them, "to the house called Seven Walls."

Prestimion was expecting that. Seven Walls was the traditional guesthouse for newly arrived Coronals. It turned out to be a low, sturdy building of dark stone that stood atop the rampart of Numinor port, at the very edge of the sea. "But why is it called Seven Walls?" Varaile asked, as they were shown to their chambers within it. "It looks perfectly square to me."

"No one knows," Prestimion replied. "This place is as old as the Castle itself, and most of its history is lost in legend. They say that the Lady Thiin, Lord Stiamot's mother, had it built for him when he came to the Isle to give thanks for his victory at the end of the Metamorph Wars. Supposedly seven Metamorph warriors were entombed in its foundations—warriors that Lady Thiin killed with her own hands while defending the Isle against an army of Shapeshifter invaders. But the building's foundations have often been reconstructed and nobody's ever found any Metamorph skeletons down there. Then there's a notion that Lord Stiamot had a seven-sided chapel constructed in the courtyard while he was here, but there's no trace of that, either. I've also heard it said that the name's just our version of ancient Shapeshifter words meaning 'the place where the fish scales are scraped off,' because there was a Metamorph fishing village here in prehistoric times."

"I like that one the best," said Varaile.

"So do I."

Certain rituals of purification were required of him before he could proceed higher on the Isle, and he spent several hours that evening performing them under the instruction of one of the hierarchs. He and Varaile slept that night in a splendid chamber overlooking the sea, amidst dark weavings of a style so antique that Prestimion found himself wondering whether Lord Stiamot himself had selected them. He imagined that the ghosts of all the kings of bygone years who had slept in this room would be crowding around him in the night, offering anecdotes of their reigns, or advice on how to deal with the problems of his own, but in fact he dropped almost instantly into the deepest of sleeps, and the dreams that came to him were peaceful ones. The Isle was a place of tranquility and harmony: all anxiety was banished here.

In the morning began the journey upward to the Lady. Varaile and Prestimion alone would go, not any of the others who had made the journey with them from the Castle. Permission to ascend to Third Cliff and the Inner Temple was not ordinarily granted to those who had not passed through the full rite of initiation.

The hierarchs led them to the terminal along the waterfront from which the floater-sleds in which they would make their ascent departed. Looking up at the glittering white wall of First Cliff, rising skyward virtually in a straight line, Prestimion was unable to see how it could be possible to traverse it. But the sled rose silently and easily, making the steep climb without effort, and nestled into its landing pad at the summit of the cliff like a great gihorna folding its wings. When they looked back, they could see Numinor port like a toy town below them, and the two curving arms of its stone breakwater jutting out into the sea like a pair of fragile sticks.

"We are at the Terrace of Assessment, where all novices come first. They are evaluated there, and their destinies are decided," one of the hierarchs explained. "Beyond it, a short distance inland, is the Terrace of Inception, where those who will be allowed to continue to a higher level undergo their preliminary training. After a time—weeks, months, sometimes years—they go on to the Terrace of Mirrors, where they are brought into confrontation with their own selves, and make their preparations for what lies ahead."

A floater-wagon was waiting to carry Prestimion and

Varaile onward. Quickly they left the pink flagstone streets of the Terrace of Assessment behind and journeyed across a seemingly endless realm of cultivated fields to the Terrace of Inception, whose entrance was marked by pyramids of dark blue stone ten feet high. Here they saw some novices working at menial farming tasks, and others gathered in outdoor amphitheaters receiving holy instruction. There was no time to pause for a closer look, though, for the distances here were great, and Second Cliff's formidable white bulk, standing large in the sky before them, still was very far away.

Indeed, the afternoon was beginning to wane before they reached the cliff's base. They halted for the night at the third of First Cliff's terraces, the Terrace of Mirrors, which lay right below the mighty facade of the new wall that reared up over them. At this terrace huge slabs of polished black stone were set edgewise into the ground all about, so that wherever you turned you saw your own image looking back at you, transformed and intensified by the mysterious light of this place. And in the early hours of morning it was upward for them once again, a second dizzying floater-sled climb to the rim of the next level.

There atop Second Cliff they could still see the sea, but it seemed very far away, and Numinor itself lay tucked out of sight, hidden from view just beyond the perimeter of the Isle. They could barely make out the pink rim of First Cliff's outermost terrace. The Terrace of Mirrors, directly below them, seemed to be aglow with green flame wherever its monumental stone slabs were struck by the morning sun. "The outer terrace where we stand now," a hierarch told them, "is known as the Terrace of Consecration. From here we will come to the Terrace of Flowers, the Terrace of Devotion, the Terrace of Surrender, and the Terrace of Ascent." Prestimion felt a touch of awe as he contemplated the complexity and richness of the system by which the realm of the Lady was constructed. He had never suspected so elaborate a structure of preparation for the tasks that were carried out here.

But there was no time to linger and learn. The holiest

sanctuary of all, Third Cliff, the abode of the Lady of the
Isle, still had to be attained.

One more breathtaking vertical sled-ride and they were
there. Prestimion was struck at once by the singular quality
of the air up here, thousands of feet above the sea. It was
cool and amazingly clear, so that every topographic detail
of the Isle below them stood out as though magnified in a
glass. The unfamiliar quality of everything—the light, the
sky, the trees—so enthralled him that he paid no attention
as the hierarchs called off the names of the terraces through
which they were passing, until at last he heard one say,
"And this is the Terrace of Adoration, the gateway to Inner
Temple."

It was a place of low, rambling buildings of whitewashed
stone, set in gardens of surpassing beauty and serenity. The
Lady, they were informed, awaited them; but first they must
refresh themselves from their journey. Acolytes conducted
them to a secluded lodge in a garden of venerable gnarled
trees and arbors of serpentine vines laden with many-petaled
blue flowers. A sunken tub lined with cunningly interwoven
strips of smooth green and turquoise stone seemed irresistible. They bathed together, and Prestimion, smiling, ran his
hand lightly over the swelling curve of Varaile's abdomen.
Afterward they dressed themselves in soft white robes that
had been provided for them, and servitors brought them a
meal of grilled fish and some delectable blue berries, which
they washed down with chilled gray wine of a kind Prestimion was unable to identify; and then, only then, did one
of the hierarchs who had accompanied them on their ascent
tell them that they were summoned to the presence of the
Lady. It was all very much like a dream. So solemn and
majestic had the entire process been, and so beautiful, that
Prestimion found it almost impossible to realize that what
he was actually doing was paying a visit to his own mother.

But she was much more than just his mother, now. She
was mother to all the world: mother-goddess, even.

They reached Inner Temple, where she was waiting for
them, by crossing a slender arch of white stone that carried
them over a pond of big-eyed golden fish into a green field

where every blade of grass seemed to be of precisely the
same height. At its far end was a low flat-roofed rotunda,
its facade completely without ornamentation, that had been
fashioned from the same translucent white stone as the
bridge. Eight narrow wings, equidistantly placed, radiated
from it like starbeams.

The hierarch gestured toward the rotunda. "Enter.
Please."

The simple room at the heart of the rotunda was octagonal in design, a white marble chamber without furnishings
of any kind. In its center was a shallow pool, also eight-
sided. The Lady Therissa stood beside it, smiling, holding
out her hands in welcome.

"Prestimion. Varaile."

She seemed, as ever, miraculously youthful, dark-haired
and graceful and smooth of skin. Some said that all that was
achieved through sorcery, but Prestimion knew that that was
untrue. Not that the Lady Therissa had ever shown any disdain for the services of sorcerers: she had long had a magus
or two in her employ at Muldemar House. But she kept them
there to predict the fortunes of the grape harvest, not to cast
spells that would guard her from the ravages of age. Even
now she had a magical amulet about her wrist, a golden
band inscribed in emerald shards with runes of some kind,
but that too, Prestimion was certain, was there for some
reason other than vanity's sake. He was unshakably convinced that it was by her own inner radiance and not any
kind of wizardry that his mother had preserved her beauty
so far into her middle years.

But her ascent to the Ladyship had given her a new kind
of lustre, an unfamiliar queenly aura that enhanced and
deepened her great beauty. The silver circlet about her forehead that was the Lady of the Isle's badge of office en-
shrined her in a wondrous glowing aura.

He had heard tales of that, how the silver circlet inevitably transformed its wearer, and thus it must have happened
to the Lady Therissa. Plainly this was the role she had

waited all her life to play. Her chief claim to distinction, once upon a time, had been that she was the wife of the Prince of Muldemar, and when that title passed to Prestimion she had been known for being the mother of the Prince of Muldemar; but now at last she had become someone of distinction in her own right, holder of the title of Lady of the Isle, one of the three Powers of the Realm. A position for which, Prestimion thought, she had quietly been preparing herself all the time that he had been heir-presumptive to Confalume's throne, and which now provided her with the duties that she had been born to perform, for years not in any way knowing that she had been born for them, but born for them all the same.

She embraced Varaile first, a long warm enfolding of her in her arms, several times calling her "daughter," and tenderly stroking her cheek. She had never had a daughter of her own, and Prestimion was the first of her sons to marry.

Varaile's pregnancy seemed to be no surprise to her: she spoke of it at once, and referred to the child as "him," as though there could be no doubt of that. Prestimion stood to one side a long while as the two women spoke.

Then at last she turned to him and embraced him also, but much more quickly, though at her touch he was able to feel the tingling power of her office, the force that marked her off from all other beings in the world. As she stepped back from him Prestimion saw that her demeanor was different now from what it had been with Varaile a moment before, her warm smile fading away, the expression of her eyes darkening. She was turning to the true business of the visit. "Prestimion, what has happened to the world? Do you know what I see, whenever I send my mind outward into it?"

He had been certain it was going to be this. "The madness, you mean?"

"The madness, yes. I find it everywhere. I encounter bewilderment and pain wherever I look. It is, of course, the task of the Lady and her acolytes to go up and down the world reaching out to those who are suffering and offering them the comfort of kind dreams, and we do what we can;

but what's going on now is beyond the scope of our abilities here. We work day and night to heal those who need us; but there are millions, Prestimion. Millions. And the number grows daily."

"I know. I've seen it in one city after another as I travel. The chaos, the pain. Varaile's own father has been taken by it. And—"

"But have you seen it, Prestimion? Have you? Not as I have, I think. Come with me."

7

SHE TURNED AND WENT from the room, beckoning him to follow her. Prestimion hesitated, frowning, and glanced at Varaile, not sure whether the invitation extended to her; but then he gestured to her to accompany him. The Lady Therissa could always send Varaile away if she was not meant to see whatever it was that the Lady Therissa meant to show him.

Already she was far down the hallway, moving past one and then a second of the spoke-like wings that spread outward from the core of the temple. Glancing in, Prestimion saw acolytes and perhaps hierarchs seated at long tables, heads bowed in what looked like meditation. Their eyes were closed. All wore silver circlets much like the Lady's own around their foreheads. The mysteries of the Isle, he thought: they are casting their minds outward, searching for those in need, bringing dreams of healing to them. Was it sorcery or science by which their questing spirits roved the world? There was a difference between the two, he knew, although the means by which the Lady and her people went about their tasks here seemed every bit as magical to him as the spells and incantations of the mages.

She had gone into a small room brightly illuminated by natural light pouring through carved lacy tesselations in the marble ceiling. It appeared to be her private study. In it were a desk made of a single brilliantly polished slab of some colorful mottled stone, a low couch, a couple of small tables.

Three alabaster vases against the far wall held a lovely display of cut flowers, scarlet and purple and yellow and cobalt blue.

It did not seem to trouble her that Varaile had come to this room with him. But all her attention was turned toward Prestimion. From a shallow, elegantly inlaid wooden box on her desk she took a slender silver circlet similar to the one she wore and handed it to him.

"Put this on, Prestimion."

He obeyed without questioning. He could barely feel that it was there, so finely made and slight was it.

"And now," she said, setting two little wine-flasks on the table before him. She pushed one toward him. "This is no wine of our vineyard, but perhaps you'll recognize the flavor. Drink it down all at once."

Now he did question, at least with a puzzled glance. But she opened her own flask and drained it at a single draught, and after a moment he did the same with his. It was a dark wine, thick and pungent, and sweet with an aftertaste of spices. He had tasted something like it before, he knew, but where? And then Prestimion realized what it was: the wine that dream-speakers employed in consultations, so that the minds of those who came to them for help would be open to them. There was a drug in it that dissolved the barriers between one mind and another. It was years since he last had been for a speaking—he preferred to puzzle out his own dreams rather than have a stranger help him with their meaning—but he was sure that this was the wine.

"You know what this is?" she asked.

"Speaking-wine, yes. Shall we lie down now?"

"This is not a speaking, Prestimion. You will be awake for this, and you will see things you've never seen before. Frightening things, I'm afraid. Give me your hands." He extended them toward her. "Ordinarily one must have months of training in the technique before one is permitted to do this," she said. "The power of the vision is simply too great: it can burn out an unprepared mind in a moment. But you will not be traveling on your own. You'll merely be accompanying me on my own voyage, the one I take every

day across the world. You'll see, through my eyes, the
things I see on those voyages. And I will protect you from
overflow effects."

Gently she took his hands in hers. Then she laced her
fingers between his and tightened her grasp with sudden and
surprising force.

It was like being struck in the forehead by a hammer.

He could no longer focus his eyes. Everything was
blurred. He lurched backward and thought he might fall, but
she held him upright, seemingly without effort. The room
churned and wheeled about him: Varaile, his mother, the
desk, the flower vases, everything in motion, swinging diz-
zyingly in wild orbits around his head. His mind was swirling as it would have been if he had put away five flasks of
wine in half an hour.

Then came calmness again, a blessed moment of balance
and stability, and he felt himself rising wraithlike from the
floor, passing easily through one of the carved lacework
openings in the ceiling, drifting upward and upward into the
sky like an untethered balloon. It reminded him of the drug-
vision he had had long ago in the sorcerers' city of Triggoin,
when by the use of magical herbs and the uttering of powerful Names he had risen beyond the kingdom of the clouds
and looked down on Majipoor from the edge of space.

But the effect was very different now.

That other time he had viewed the world from on high
with the cool objectivity of a god. He had seen the whole
giant planet as nothing more than a little ball turning slowly
in the sky, a toy model of a world, with its three continents
standing out as dark wedges no bigger than one of his fin-
gernails, and he had carefully taken that little ball upon the
palm of his hand and, gently, curiously, touched it with his
finger, examining it with fascination and love, all the while
standing outside it, at a distant remove from the lives of its
people.

Now, though, he was at one and the same time far above
the world and inextricably enmeshed in the inner reality of
what lay below him. He looked down upon it from on high

and yet was intimately linked to the broiling, turbulent energies of its billions of people.

He perceived himself soaring at infinite speed through some region of the upper air, and in the darkness below the myriad cities and towns and villages of Majipoor blazed like beacons, each distinct and easily identifiable: there was the immense Mount, with its Fifty Cities and its Six Rivers, there was the Castle clinging to the tip of that great rock and sprawling far down its sides, and there, limned in the same wondrous clarity, were Sisivondal and Sefarad and Sippulgar, Sintalmond, Kajith Kabulon, Pendiwane and Stoien and Alaisor, and all the rest of Alhanroel as well, and Zimroel's cities just as clear, Ni-moya and Piliplok and Narabal and Dulorn and Khyntor and their many neighbors; and there was the Isle beneath him now, and Suvrael coming up to the south with cities he had not seen even in dreams, Tolaghai and Natu Gorvinu and Kheskh. He recognized each one now by sight, intuitively, as though they bore labels.

But also it seemed to him that he was traveling just above the rooftops of all these places, so close that he could touch the souls of their inhabitants the way he had touched the little turning ball of the world that time in Triggoin.

Potent psychic emanations were coming upward to him like heat out of a chimney, and what he felt was terrifying. No protective membrane separated him from the lives of the swarming billions of people who lived in those cities. Everything reached him in a mighty rush. He felt the outcries that told of pain and sorrow and utter despair; he felt the anguish of souls so isolated from their fellow beings that they might well have been encased in blocks of ice; he felt the bewildered throb of minds that moved in fifty directions at once and therefore could not move at all. He felt the stabbing agony of those who were struggling to make sense of their own thoughts and failed to comprehend. He felt the nightmare dread of those who looked into their minds to find their own pasts, and discovered only gaping canyons.

Over and over he experienced the terror that inner anarchy brings. He felt the desperate turbulence of the wounded spirit. He felt the horror of heart-blindness and the shame of heart-deadness. He felt the bleakness of irrevocable loss.

He felt chaos everywhere.

Chaos.

Chaos.

Chaos.

Madness.

Madness, yes, an irresistible river of it, spilling out across the land like some hideous tide of sewage set free. A great blight, an overwhelming unstoppable disaster, a juggernaut of calamitous pandemonium wheeling through the world, a scourge far greater in scope than anything he had imagined.

"Mother—" he gasped. "Mother!"

"Drink this," Varaile said softly, and offered him a goblet. "Water, that's all it is. Just water."

His eyes fluttered open. He was, he saw, seated on the couch in his mother's study, leaning back against the pillow. The white robe they had given him to wear was drenched with perspiration, and he was trembling. He gulped the water. It made him shiver. Varaile touched her hand lightly to his forehead: her fingers felt cold as ice against his feverish brow. He saw his mother across the room, standing with arms folded beside her desk, watching him calmly.

She said, "Don't worry, Prestimion. The effects will pass in another moment or two."

"I fainted, didn't I?"

"You lost consciousness. You didn't actually fall, though."

"Here. Take this back," he said, reaching for the silver circlet. But it was already gone from his forehead. He shuddered. "What a nightmare it was, mother!"

"Yes. A nightmare. I see these things every day. I have for months, now. So have the people of my staff. This is what the world has become, Prestimion."

"All of it?"

She smiled. "Not all, no, not yet. Much is still healthy. What you felt was the pain of those who were most vulnerable to the plague, the first victims, the ones who had no way of defending themselves against the attack that came in the night. Their cries are the ones that rise to find me as I move through the night above them. What dreams can I send, do you think, that can heal such pain as that?"

He was silent. He had no answer to that. He had never, so it seemed to him then, felt such despair in his life: not even in the moment when Korsibar had seized the crown that he and everyone else had expected to go to him.

I have destroyed the world, he thought.

Looking toward Varaile, he said, "Do you have any idea of what I was experiencing when I was wearing that thing?"

"Some. It must have been very bad. The look on your face—that stunned, terrible expression—"

"Your father is one of the lucky ones," he said. "He isn't able to comprehend what's happened to him. At least I hope he can't."

"You were looking right into people's minds?"

"Not into individual ones, no. At least, it didn't seem that way. It isn't possible, I think, to see into individual minds. What you get is general impressions, broad waves of sensation, the aggregate of what must be hundreds of minds all at once."

"Thousands," the Lady said.

She was studying him very closely, he realized, from her place across the room. Her gaze was warm and compassionate and motherly, but it was a penetrating one, also, cutting deep into the interior of his soul.

After a while she said, very quietly, "Tell me what has occurred, Prestimion, that has brought this thing about."

She knows, he thought.

There can be no doubt of that. She knows. Not the details, but the essence. That I am somehow responsible, that some action of mine is at the bottom of all this.

And she was waiting now to learn the rest of it. It was clear to him that he could hide it from her no longer. She wanted a confession from him; and he was willing, now—eager, even—to pour it all forth.

What about Varaile, though? He cast an uncertain glance

toward her. Should he ask her to leave? Could he say what
he had to say in front of her, and thus make her a party to
his own immense crime? I am the one responsible, he would
have to say, for what has happened to your father, Varaile.
Did he dare tell her that?

Yes, he thought.

Yes, I do. She is my wife. I will have no secrets from
her, king of the world though I be.

Slowly, carefully, Prestimion said, "It is all my doing,
mother. I think you already know that, but I admit it all the
same: I am the cause of the catastrophe, I alone. It was never
my intention to make such a thing happen, but I did, and
the guilt is entirely mine."

He heard Varaile inhale sharply in astonishment and bewilderment. His mother, watching him as calmly and keenly
as before, said nothing. She was waiting for the rest.

"I will explain it from the beginning," he said.

The Lady, still silent, nodded.

Prestimion closed his eyes a moment, steadying himself.
Begin at the beginning, yes. But where was the beginning?

The obliteration first, the reasons for it afterward, he
thought. Yes.

He took a deep breath and plunged in. "The course of
recent world events that you think you know is not the one
that the world actually followed," he said. "A vast deception
has taken place. Great things have happened, things unprec-
edented in the history of the world, and no one knows of
them. Thousands have died, and the reasons for their deaths
have been concealed. The truth has been blotted out and we
have all been living a lie, and only a handful of people are
aware of the real story—Septach Melayn, Gialaurys, Abrigant, two or three others. None besides those. I offer it now
to you; but you will see, I hope, that it must not go beyond
you."

He paused. Looked toward his mother, and then to Varaile. They still did not speak. Their expressions were unreadable, remote. They were waiting to hear what he had to
say.

"You, mother: you had four sons, and one is dead, Taradath, who was so very clever, a poet, one who loved to play games with words. You think he died while swimming in one of the rivers of the north-country. Not so: he died by drowning, yes, but it was in the course of a terrible battle along the River Iyann, when the Mavestoi Dam broke. Does that startle you? It is the truth: that is how Taradath died. But you have believed a lie all this time, and I am responsible for that."

Her only reaction was the merest flicker of the corner of her mouth. Her self-control astounded him. Varaile simply looked mystified.

"To continue: Lord Confalume had two children also. Twins, a son and a daughter. I see you look surprised at that. Yes, the children of Confalume are unknown today, and I am accountable also for that. The daughter's name was Thismet: she was small, delicate, very beautiful, an extremely complex woman full of great ambition. She took after her mother Roxivail, I think. As for the son, he was strong and handsome, a tall, dark-haired man of lordly bearing, an athlete, a skilled hunter. Not particularly intelligent, I must say. A simple soul, but good-hearted, in his fashion. His name was Korsibar."

From Varaile came a little cry of surprise as he spoke that name. Prestimion was puzzled by her reaction; but he chose not to interrupt the flow of his story to ask for an explanation. The Lady Therissa seemed far away, lost in thought.

"The Pontifex Prankipin grew ill," Prestimion said. "Lord Confalume, contemplating the imminent change of Powers, fastened upon me as the one to follow him as Coronal. He said nothing publicly about that, of course, while Prankipin still lived. We gathered at the Labyrinth, all the lords and princes of the realm, to await the Pontifex's death. And in that time of waiting certain villainous folk came to Prince Korsibar and whispered in his ear: 'You are the Coronal's son, and you are a great princely man. Why should little Prestimion be Coronal when your father becomes Pontifex? Take the throne for yourself, Korsibar! Take it! Take it!' Two scoundrelly brothers, Farholt and Farquanor, were

among those who urged him most strongly in that: they are
forgotten now too, and good riddance. Another conspirator
was a Su-Suheris magus, chilly and evil. And there was also
the Lady Thismet, the most powerful influence of all. They
pushed, and Korsibar was too weak and simple to resist. He
had never imagined himself as Coronal. But now they made
him think that the throne was his due. The old Pontifex died;
and we gathered in the Court of Thrones for the passing of
the crown, and Korsibar's magus cast a spell to cloud our
minds, and when we were ourselves again we saw Korsibar
sitting beside his father on the double throne, and the starburst crown was on Korsibar's head and Confalume, who
had had a spell of acquiescence placed upon him, took no
steps to halt his son's seizure of power."

"This is not easy to believe," said the Lady Therissa.

"Believe it, mother. Oh, I urge you, believe it. It happened."

Speaking rapidly now, Prestimion sketched an account of
the civil war for them. Korsibar's proclamation of power
and his own refusal to accept the takeover. The new Coronal's naive invitation to Prestimion to take a seat on the
Council, which was also refused, and with such anger and
contempt that Korsibar had had him arrested and chained
up in the Sangamor tunnels. His release from the tunnels
through a compromise engineered by the tricky Dantirya
Sambail, who hoped to play Korsibar and Prestimion off
against each other to his own advantage; his raising of an
army to challenge the illegal ascent of Korsibar to the
throne; the first battle, outside the foothill city of Arkilon,
which ended in a defeat for Prestimion's rebel forces at the
hands of Korsibar's general Navigorn; the retreat into central Alhanroel, and a great victory for Prestimion over Navigorn at the Jhelum River; other battles, victories and
defeats, his long march northwestward across Alhanroel
with the armies of Korsibar in steady pursuit. And then the
great disaster in the valley of the Iyann, when Dantirya Sambail, who now had allied himself with Korsibar, persuaded
the usurper to blow up the Mavestoi Dam and bring the
entire reservoir down on Prestimion's forces.

"That was when Taradath died, mother, and many another loyal comrade with him, and all the valley was flooded. I was swept away by the waters myself, but managed somehow to swim to safety, and made my way northward into the Valmambra Desert, alone, and nearly died. Septach Melayn and Gialaurys found me there, and Duke Svor, whom you may remember; and the four of us went on to Triggoin, where we spent some months in hiding among the sorcerers, and I learned a few of their skills." Prestimion smiled an oblique smile. "My tutor was Gominik Halvor. That was the beginning of my alliance with him and with his son Heszmon Gorse."

Again Prestimion paused. His mother looked very pale. She was plainly much shaken by all this, and struggling hard to encompass it with her mind. Varaile did not even appear to be trying. Most of these names and places were unfamiliar to her; the tale was incomprehensible; she seemed utterly lost.

He moved on now to the climax of his story. He told of how in Triggoin he had come close to despair, but had undertaken a visionary quest in which he had seen that it was his destiny to overthrow Korsibar and heal the world. He described his coming-forth from Triggoin, his gathering of a new army at Gloyn in west-central Alhanroel, his march eastward toward Castle Mount, culminating in the great final battle against Korsibar and his forces at Thegomar Edge.

Prestimion said nothing of Thismet's decision to change sides; nor of her coming before him in his camp at Gloyn and offering herself to him as his wife—and his consort, once he had attained the throne. He had sworn to have no secrets from Varaile; but here, now, as the episode of his love for Thismet and hers for him reached its proper place in the narrative, he could not bring himself to tell of it. What purpose would be served? It was something that had happened and then had been unhappened, and it had no bearing now on anything pertaining to the present condition of the world: a purely private interlude, buried now in unhistory. Let it remain there, Prestimion thought. The only thing that was important just now was to render an unvarnished account of the events at Thegomar Edge.

"They had the high position," Prestimion said. "We were down below, in a marshy place called Beldak. At first the battle went against us; but as we retreated, Korsibar's infantry foolishly came down the hill to give us chase, and once they broke their formation, we were able to bring reinforcements in from the side and catch them between two fronts. The tide turned in our favor. It was then that I deployed the mages who were my ultimate weapon."

"Mages, Prestimion?" said the Lady Therissa. "You?"

"The fate of the world was at stake, mother. I was resolved to use any force I could to bring Korsibar's reign to an end. Gominik Halvor and his son came forth, and a dozen more of the high wizards of Triggoin with them, and they cast a spell that turned bright noon into moonless night, and in the darkness we destroyed the usurper's army. Korsibar was killed by his own magus, the Su-Suheris Sanibak-Thastimoon. The magus slew the Lady Thismet also, and then lost his life to Septach Melayn. Dantirya Sambail, who had fought against us that day, found me in the confusion and offered to fight me for the throne; but I defeated him and had him put under arrest. Then Navigorn came to me to surrender, and the war was over. The good Earl Kamba, who taught me the art of the bow, died that day, and Kanteverel of Bailemoona, and my dear little sly Duke Svor, and many another great lord, but the war was over, and I was Coronal at last."

He looked toward his mother. The full impact of the story had reached her now. She was stunned into silence.

Then she said, gathering herself a little, "This truly happened, Prestimion? It seems more like some fantastic tale out of some ancient epic poem. The Book of Changes, it could be."

"This truly happened," he said. "All of it."

"If that is so, then why is it that we know nothing of it?"

"Because," he said, "I stole it from your minds." And told them then the last of the story: how he stood amidst the dead at Thegomar Edge feeling no joy for his victory,

but only grief at the sundering of the world, the irreparable
division into two irreconcilable factions. For how could
those who had fought for Korsibar, and seen their comrades
die for him, accept the rule of Prestimion now? And how
could he forgive those who had turned against him, often
treacherously, as Prince Serithorn had, and Duke Oljebbin,
and Admiral Gonivaul, and Dantirya Sambail, after pledging
their support? What, also, of the surviving kin of those who
had perished in those bloody battles? Would they not hold
grudges against the victorious faction forever? "The war,"
Prestimion said, "had left a scar upon the world. No, worse:
a wound that could never heal. But suddenly I saw a way
of repairing the irreparable, of healing the unhealable."

And so the summoning one last time of Gominik Halvor
and his fellow mages, and the giving of the order for the
tremendous incantation that would wipe the war from the
world's history. Korsibar, and his sister also, would never
have been; those who had died as a result of Korsibar's
usurpation would be shown to have died in some way other
than on the field of battle; no one would remember that there
ever had been a war, not even the sorcerers who had brought
about its obliteration from memory—no one but Prestimion
himself, and Gialaurys, and Septach Melayn. And Lord
Prestimion would have succeeded to the starburst crown immediately upon the end of Prankipin's reign, with no Lord
Korsibar intervening.

"There you have it all," Prestimion said. He was trembling again, and his brow was hot as if with fever. "I thought
I was healing the world. Instead I was destroying it. I
opened the gateway for this madness that consumes it now,
the full dimensions of which have only become apparent to
me today."

Varaile said, speaking for the first time in a long while,
"You? But—how, Prestimion? How?"

"Do you know how it is, Varaile, when the hot sun beats
down and warms the air, so that it rises, as warm air will,
and creates a vacant zone behind it? Turbulent cool winds
come rushing in to fill that void. Well, I created such a void
in the minds of billions of people. I lifted a great slice of

reality from their recollection and gave them nothing to re-place it. And, sooner or later, turbulent winds came rushing in. Not to everyone, no, but to many. And the process is not done working yet."

"My father—" she said softly.

"Your father, yes. And all too many others. The guilt for all that is mine. I meant only to heal, but—but—"

He faltered and could not go on.

The Lady said, after a time, "Come here, Prestimion." She held forth her hands.

He went to her and knelt, and laid his cheek against her thigh and closed his eyes, and she held him and stroked his forehead, as she had years ago when he was a small boy and some cherished pet of his had died, or he had done badly at his archery, or his father had spoken too harshly to him. She had always been able to soothe him then and she soothed him now, taking his anguish from him not only as a mother does, but also with the power invested in her as Lady of the Isle, the power to absolve, the power to forgive.

"Mother, I had no choice but to act as I did," he said, his voice muffled and thick. "The war had left great resent-ments. They would have stained my reign forever and ever."

"I know. I know."

"And yet—look what I've done, mother—"

"Shh. Shh." She held him closer. Stroked his brow. He felt the force of her love, the strength of her soul. He began to grow calm. She gently signaled him, after a little while more, to rise. She was smiling.

Varaile said, "You told us at the outset that this has to remain a secret. But do you still feel that way? I wonder if you should let the world know the truth, Prestimion."

"No. Never. It would only make things worse." He was steadier now, purged by his confession, the trembling and the feverishness gone from him now, his head beginning to clear, though the impact of the vision he had had while wearing the Lady's circlet would not leave him. He doubted that he would ever be free of it. But what Varaile was sug-gesting seemed impossible to him. "Not because it would make me look bad," he said, "although it certainly would.

But pile one confusion atop another—take away what little sense anyone may still have of where reality really may lie—I can't, Varaile! You see that, don't you? Don't you, mother?"

"Are you certain?" Varaile asked. "Perhaps, if you spoke out about it at last, your doing it would drive away the nightmares and the fantasies and would establish everyone on solid ground once more. Or else, calling the mages down again, getting them to cast a second spell—"

He shook his head and looked in appeal toward the Lady.

Who responded, "Prestimion's right, Varaile. There's no undoing it now, neither by any public action of the Coronal nor by more wizardry. We've already seen the kind of unintended consequences that an entirely benevolent act has had. We can't risk having that happen again."

"Even so, mother, now we have to deal with those consequences," said Prestimion. "Only—how, I wonder? How?"

8

THEY REMAINED FOR A time at the Isle, and Prestimion made no immediate plan for leaving. The winds were still westerly out of Alhanroel, so that the return voyage would be slow and difficult if he were to set out now.

But also he felt weary and drained by his steadily increasing comprehension of the catastrophe he had caused and the likelihood that there would be no way of repairing the damage. The stain of that, he feared, would darken his name for all time to come.

It had gradually dawned on him, years ago, that it might be possible for him to become Coronal, and that he would be capable of handling the job if he did; and he had then begun to yearn for it with all his heart. And—despite the small interruption created by Korsibar—he had indeed attained the starburst crown, even as Stiamot and Damlang and Pinitor and Vildivar and Guadeloom and all the rest of those whose names were inscribed on the great screen in front of the House of Records in the Labyrinth had done before him. They had ascended to the throne and reigned, more or less gloriously, and each had made his mark on the world's history and had left visible evidence of his moment of power by adding something tangible to the Castle: the Stiamot throne-room, Vildivar Close, the Arioc watch-tower, whatever; and then they had gone on to be Pontifex for a while, and in the fullness of time they had grown old and died. But had any of them ever brought about a disaster such as he had achieved? His place in history would be unique. He had wanted the reign of Lord Prestimion to go down in history as a golden age; and yet he had contrived to lose his throne before he ever had had it, and had fought a war for it that caused the deaths of uncountable and un-thinkable numbers of fine men, along with a few worthless ones—and then, then, when the crown was finally his, he had in a moment of folly done a thing to heal the world of its wound that had made matters infinitely worse than they already were. Oh, Stiamot! he thought. Oh, Pinitor! What a pitiful successor I am to your greatness!

Prestimion drew great comfort in these dark hours from the proximity of the Lady. And so he told her that he had decided to stay at the Isle a little while longer, and a suite of rooms was provided for him and Varaile at Inner Temple.

Ten days passed quietly. Then news reached Third Cliff of the arrival at Numinor of a pilgrim-ship from Stoien. There was nothing unusual in that, in this season of westerly winds. But soon after came a second message from the har-bor. An important dispatch for the Coronal had been carried from Stoien aboard that ship, and a courier was hastening up to Inner Temple with it now.

"It's from Akbalik," Prestimion said, as he severed the thick waxen security-seal. "He's been in Stoien all year, you know, running a data-gathering operation, trying to turn up some sort of definite information on the location of Dantirya Sambail. Why would he bother to write to me here, I won-der, unless he's—oh, Varaile! For the love of the Divine, Varaile—"

"What is it, Prestimion? Tell me!"

He jabbed his finger against the page. "The Procurator's alive, Akbalik says. And still in Alhanroel. He's been hiding out all this time somewhere along the southern shore of Stoien province, skulking among the saw-palms and the swamp-crabs and the animal-plants. Making that his base, it seems, for a new civil war!"

Varaile was instantly aflutter with questions. Prestimion raised his hand for silence. "Let me finish reading," he told her. "Mmm. Coded dispatches intercepted.... A Su-Suheris magus going into some sort of a trance to decipher them.... Full text attached herewith...." He rummaged through the sheaf of papers that Akbalik had sent.

He found it impossible, of course, to make any meaning out of the coded messages themselves, which apparently had been surreptitiously slipped into otherwise innocent cargo manifests. *Emijiquk gybpij jassnin ys.? Kesixm ricthip jumlee ayviy?* It would take a Su-Suheris with three heads, Prestimion thought, to find any sense in that. But Akbalik evidently had picked the right man for the job; for after his wizard had declared that the secret camp of Dantirya Sambail was located along the lower Stoien coast, Akbalik had sent agents to comb that entire region, and they had indeed come upon the Procurator's camp in the very place where the decoded messages indicated it to be.

"But why do you think it's gone unnoticed so long?" Varaile asked.

"Do you know what the southern Stoien coast is like? No, why should you? No one in his right mind goes there. No one ever thinks about it. Which is why he has chosen it for his hiding-place, I suppose. They say it's hot as a steambath there. Your very bones will melt in that heat within an hour. There is a tree there, the manganoza, with sharp-bladed leaves—the saw-palm, they call it—that forms thickets so dense they're impossible to enter. And then, giant insects wherever you walk, and enormous crabs that can snap an unwary man's ankle in half with one bite. Was there ever a more appropriate place for Dantirya Sambail to take up lodgings?"

"You must hate that man very much," Varaile said.

Prestimion was surprised by that. Hate? He didn't think of himself as a hater. The word wasn't an active part of his vocabulary.

Was there anyone, he wondered, whom he had ever hated? Korsibar, perhaps? No, certainly not him. He could make allowances for Korsibar. Korsibar's astonishing grab for power had angered him greatly, yes, but nevertheless Prestimion had never seen him as anything but a big stupid good-natured blockhead of a prince who had been thrust into a situation far beyond his depth by a pack of sinister self-seeking companions.

And Farquanor and Farholt, then, Korsibar's vile henchmen, whom the world was so much better off without? Had he hated them? he wondered.

Not really. Farquanor had been a nasty little schemer, and Farholt a great swaggering bully. Prestimion had disliked them very much. But hatred was not what he had felt for them. He doubted even that he had hated Sanibak-Thastimoon, whose dark conjurations had made so much trouble for the world, and who, in fact, was the one who had taken Thismet's life. But there had been a sword in Thismet's hand when she died. Would Sanibak-Thastimoon have killed her if she had not attacked him?

That hardly mattered now. But one did not hate people for being stupid, as Korsibar had been, or sly like Farquanor, or a blustering fool like Farholt. And Sanibak-Thastimoon had believed he was serving his master Korsibar's best interests: should he have hated the Su-Suheris for that? One did not hate people at all, ideally: one simply disagreed with them, and prevented them from doing harm to you and yours, and went on about one's business.

What about Dantirya Sambail, though, the real author of so many of the world's misfortunes? Did the word apply to him?

"Yes," Prestimion said. "That one I do hate. He's evil through and through, that man. You can see it just by looking at him: those amazingly beautiful deceitful eyes, softly glowing at you out of that fat ugly face. He should never have been born. In a moment of idiotic foolishness I spared his life at Thegomar Edge, and in another I allowed his blotted-out memory of the war he waged against me to be restored; but I would gladly call both those decisions back, now, if only I could."

He paced back and forth in mounting agitation. Merely thinking about the Procurator set him into a furious frenzy.

The treacheries of Dantirya Sambail had provided fresh support again and again for the Korsibar faction, when otherwise the usurper might have fallen through his own ineptitude. At every turn in the civil war, there Dantirya Sambail had been, devilishly engineering some new betrayal or defection. It was the Procurator who had sent his own two loathsome brothers, the drunken Gaviad and the great ugly Gaviundar, to lead armies on Prestimion's side, covertly instructing them to transfer their allegiance at a critical moment. It was Dantirya Sambail who had incited Korsibar to the breaking of the Mavestoi Dam. It was he who—

"The man is a monster," Prestimion said. "I might be able to understand it if he had rebelled out of simple greed, out of the crude and blatant hunger for power. But he already rules a whole continent; he has wealth beyond anyone's comprehension. Nothing drives him except motiveless hatred, Varaile. He seethes without reason with an inner venom that poisons his every act. And he forces us to meet hatred with hatred. It's hardly even two years since we've emerged from the civil war, and we still suffer the aftereffects of that; and here he is making ready for a second one! What else can one feel but hatred for such a man as that? I will destroy him, that I vow, Varaile, if ever I get the chance again."

He was shaking with the force of his anger. Varaile poured wine for him, sweet golden wine of Dulorn, and pressed her fingertips against his temples until he grew more calm.

"You'll be going to this Stoien place, then, won't you, to make war on him?" she asked.

Prestimion nodded. "Akbalik's sent a copy of these dispatches to Septach Melayn at the Castle by now. I don't doubt that he and Gialaurys are already assembling an army to march down into the south-country. In any case I'll have orders to that effect going off to them this very day."

Already the strategy was taking form in his mind.

"One army coming in from the northwest by way of Stoien city, going down on a diagonal across the peninsula, and a second one south through Ketheron and Arvyanda and Kajith Kabulon to the Aruachosian coast, the route we took last year, and then westward from Sippulgar into Stoien province—yes. Yes. Hem him in from two sides at once. And then—"

There was a knock at the door. "Shall I answer?" Varaile said.

"Who would that be? Well, yes, answer it. —Meanwhile," Prestimion continued, "I'll sail for Stoien city as fast as I can and rendezvous with Akbalik there, and join the troops who'll be setting out for—yes?" he said.

Varaile had gone to the door. An acolyte stood there, holding a message.

"What is it?"

Later word from Akbalik, perhaps? Prestimion broke the seal and scanned it quickly.

"Anything important?" Varaile asked.

"I'm not sure. Your young friend Dekkeret's here. He's made some kind of helter-skelter journey from the Castle to Alaisor and come racing across from Alaisor to the Isle aboard one of the express-mail ships. He's asked special dispensation to come to you up here, and the Lady has granted it. Right now he's on his way up Second Cliff. They expect him here later today."

"Were you expecting him?"

"Not at all. I don't have any idea at all why he's come, Varaile. He says here that he has to meet with me immediately, but he doesn't tell me why. Why is it that I doubt that the news he's traveled halfway around the world at top speed to bring me is going to be anything cheerful?"

Dekkeret's face, so earnest and boyish not so long ago, had hardened now. His whole demeanor was more reserved

and poised. Since Prestimion's first encounter with him at
Normork, Dekkeret had traveled endlessly across the face
of the world; and now, though he looked more than a little
the worse for wear after the furious haste of his latest journey, he radiated an aura of strength and purpose as he entered into Prestimion's presence and offered him the salute
of allegiance.

"I bear greetings from the High Counsellor Septach Melayn and from the Grand Admiral Gialaurys, my lord," was
how he began. "They ask me to tell you that they have
received certain information from Akbalik at Stoien city
concerning Dantirya Sambail, and that they've begun to
make preparations for military action while awaiting your
explicit instructions."

"Good. I'd have expected nothing less."

"You yourself are aware, then, sir, of the Procurator's
location?"

"The news from Akbalik reached me only this morning.
I'm preparing orders to send to the Castle."

"There has been a new development, lordship. The Barjazids have escaped, and are on their way to the Stoienzar
to offer their services to Dantirya Sambail. They have the
mind-controlling device with them."

"What? But they were prisoners in the tunnels! Is that
place such a sieve, that anyone can walk out of it at the
snap of a finger? Anyone but me, it would seem," Prestimion added under his breath, remembering his own bitter
time of captivity there.

"They had been released from the tunnels some time ago,
sir. They were living as free men in the north wing of the
Castle."

"How could that have been possible?"

"Well, sir, apparently it happened like this—"

Prestimion listened in mounting disbelief and dismay as
Dekkeret told him the tale.

That shifty-eyed little man Venghenar Barjazid, in the
days before the civil war, had lived at the Castle in the

retinue of Duke Svor. During his imprisonment in the San-gamor he had somehow made contact, so it seemed, with another former follower of the late duke, who had drawn up fraudulent papers ordering the release of Barjazid and his son from the tunnels and their transfer to modest accom-modations in one of the residential sectors of the Castle.

No one, it seemed, had questioned the appropriateness of such a transfer. The Barjazids had walked out of the tunnels without any difficulty whatever. For a month or more they lived quietly in their new quarters, attracting no attention to themselves. Until, that is, it was discovered one morning that they had managed not only to arrange an escape for themselves—complete with a fine floater to take them wherever they wished—but also to take with them the entire set of mind-control devices and models that the elder Bar-jazid had acquired from the Vroonish wizard, Thalnap Zel-ifor, in the course of escorting the Vroon into exile in Suvrael.

Prestimion passed a hand across his face and muttered dark curses. "And they've gone to join Dantirya Sambail, have they? How does anyone know that? They left a little explanatory note behind in their room, did they?"

"No, sir. Of course not, sir." Dekkeret forced a bleak little grin. "But an inquiry was held following their disappear-ance, and their confederate's identity was uncovered, and his lordship Prince Navigorn placed the man under close interrogation. Very close, my lord. Prince Navigorn has been extremely distressed by this entire incident."

"I can imagine he would be," said Prestimion drily.

"What was learned from the interrogation, my lord, is that the confederate—Morteil Dikaan was his name, sir—"

"Was?"

"Unfortunately he did not survive the interrogation," Dekkeret said.

"Ah."

"The confederate, lordship, had obtained possession of one of the mind-control devices from the storeroom where they had been placed. He brought it to Barjazid in the San-gamor tunnels. And Barjazid used it to make everyone who examined his papers of release accept them as genuine. In the same way he was able to order one of the Castle floaters to be put at his disposal when he was ready to begin his journey south."

"This device of his," said Prestimion in a tone of funereal somberness, "has an absolutely irresistible force, then? It makes someone who wears it capable of compelling anyone in his path to do his bidding?"

"Not exactly, my lord. But it is extremely powerful. I've felt its power myself, sir—in Suvrael, in the place that is known as the Desert of Stolen Dreams. Which was given that name because Barjazid lurked there, entering the minds of wayfarers and altering their mental perceptions so that they were no longer able to tell true from false, illusion from reality: I explained all this to the lady Varaile, my lord. I told her of my own experience with the device's effects while traveling with Barjazid down there, and explained the potential dangers of it."

Varaile said, "Yes, he did, Prestimion. You may recall, I tried to tell you the story, the day you came back from the festival at Muldemar—but you were so busy, of course, with the plans for the trip to the Isle—"

Prestimion winced. It was true. He hadn't even taken the trouble to question Dekkeret himself about what had befallen him in Suvrael. He had brushed the whole thing aside very quickly, filing Dekkeret's tale for future reference and never giving it a moment's thought again.

A machine that controls minds! And Barjazid on his way to turn it over to Dantirya Sambail.

It was another terrible blunder in a reign that was beginning to seem pockmarked with them. A Coronal, he thought, must never allow himself even to sleep, for fear that disaster will envelop the world if he closes his eyes for the merest moment. How, Prestimion wondered, had Confalume succeeded in keeping everything on an even keel for better than forty years? But of course Confalume hadn't had a civil war and its aftermath to deal with, and Dantirya Sambail, may demons blast his soul, had elected to wait until the end of Confalume's reign before beginning to make trouble.

He looked toward Dekkeret. The boy was staring at him with respect verging on adoration. Dekkeret had no clue, it seemed, that the Coronal's mind was boiling with uneasiness and bitter self-accusation.

"Describe for me in detail," Prestimion said, "the sort of things that Barjazid's machine was able to do to your mind."

Dekkeret gave Varaile an uncertain look. She responded with a firm nod.

To Prestimion he said, after a moment's further hesitation, "At first it was just a nightmare. I thought I was being summoned to the Lady, and that was a glorious thing; but as I ran toward her she disappeared and I was left looking down into the crater of a burned-out volcano. It's never possible for one person to feel the real force of someone else's dream, is it, my lord? You must experience it from within. I can describe it to you as a bad nightmare, very bad, and you may think you understand, remembering certain bad dreams of your own. But no one else can ever understand how terrifying another person's dream actually was. Still, I tell you, sir, this was the worst imaginable experience. I felt invaded—drained—violated. Barjazid knew what had happened. He tried to question me, afterward, to get details of my dream from me. He was carrying out experiments on people's minds, you see: testing his equipment, sir."

"That was it, then? He sent you a nasty dream?"

"If only that were all, my lord. But a nasty dream was only the beginning. I dreamed again the next time I slept. There was this woman I met in Tolaghai, someone in the Pontifical service. She came to me in my dream; we were both naked; she was leading me through a lovely garden. I should say that in Tolaghai this woman and I were lovers for a little while. So I followed her gladly enough; but once again everything changed, and the garden became a frightful desert with ghostly figures lurking in it, and I thought I would die there of the heat and the ants that had begun to sting me. So I woke up and found that Barjazid had caused me to walk in my sleep and I was lost in the desert at the worst time of the day, naked, far from camp, without any

water, sunburned and swollen from the heat. A Vroon who
was traveling with us found me and rescued me, or else I
would have died. I am no sleepwalker, sir. Barjazid made it
happen. He gave me the command to get up in my sleep
and walk, and I got up. I walked."

Prestimion, frowning deeply, nibbling at his lower lip,
gestured without a word for Dekkeret to go on. There was
more, he knew. He was certain of it.

Yes. "Then, my lord, the third dream. In the Khyntor
Marches, that time when I was hunting steetmoy with Prince
Akbalik, I committed an atrocious sin. We had guides with
us, March-men, and my guide was struck down by the steetmoy I was hunting, but I was so obsessed with the hunt that
I left her lying where she fell and ran off after the animal I
was chasing. And when I came back to her much later I
discovered that she had been killed and partly eaten by some
scavenger-beast."

"So that was it," Prestimion said.

"That was what, sir?"

"The thing you did. The reason you went to Suvrael.
Akbalik sent word that you had done something in Khyntor
that you felt great shame about, and had gone off to Suvrael
hoping that somehow you would suffer enough there to
make atonement."

Dekkeret's face was bright red. "I would rather not have
spoken of this. But you asked me to tell you what Barjazid's
machine did to my mind. With its help he went into it, my
lord, and found the tale of the steetmoy hunt there, and made
me live through it again; only it was ten times as painful as
the real event had been, because this time I knew all along
what was going to happen, and had no way of preventing it
from happening again anyway. At the climax of the dream
Barjazid was there with me in the snowy forest, questioning
me about my having ignored the guide-woman for the sake
of following after my steetmoy. He wanted to know every
detail of it, what I felt about putting the pleasures of hunting
ahead of a human life, was I ashamed, how was I going to
cope with my guilt. And I said to him, still in the dream,
'Are you my judge?' And he said, 'Of course I am. See my

face?' And pulled his own face apart, removing it the way
you'd remove a mask; and under it there was another face,
a mocking laughing face, and the face was my own, my
lord. The face was my own."

He hunched his shoulders high and looked away. He
seemed appalled even now by the mere recollection.

Varaile said, "You didn't go into these details the first
time you told me the story. The hunt, the guide-woman, the
removal of the mask."

"No, milady. I thought it was all too horrible to speak
of. But it was the Coronal's request that I—that I tell—"

"Yes. It was," Prestimion said. "What happened then?"

"I awoke. In great pain. Saw Barjazid with the machine
still in his hands. Seized him, forced an explanation out of
him, told him that I was taking him into custody and bringing him back to the Castle so that I could make all of this
known to you."

"But I was too busy with other things to listen," said
Prestimion. "And now Barjazid's on the verge of handing
this thing over to Dantirya Sambail."

"I have explained everything to the lord Septach Melayn,
sir. He has given orders for Barjazid and his son to be intercepted if at all possible."

"If at all possible, yes. But he's equipped with a machine
that lets him fool around with realities, isn't he? He'll walk
through the patrol lines the way he walked out of the tunnels, and then out of the Castle itself."

Prestimion rose. "Come with me, both of you. It would
be a good idea for me to discuss this business with my
mother, I think."

The Lady Therissa, sitting at her desk in her little private
study, listened in sober silence as Prestimion sketched the
outlines of Dekkeret's story for her. She was quiet for a
time even after he had finished.

Then she said, "There is real danger here, Prestimion."

"Yes. I see that."

"Has he joined forces with the Procurator yet?"

"That's something I have no way of knowing. But I suspect that he hasn't. Even with that diabolical gadget of his to help him, he'll still have a difficult job getting down through Kajith Kabulon and locating Dantirya Sambail on the Stoien coast."

Varaile said, "I think you're right. He probably isn't there yet. If he had reached Dantirya Sambail, they'd be using the mind-control machine to amplify the madness by now. We'd be hearing about whole cities going crazy, don't you think?"

"I'm sure of it," said Dekkeret, who had been standing to one side, visibly awed at finding himself in the innermost sanctuary of the Lady of the Isle. Even as he spoke, he seemed astonished by his own audacity at opening his mouth unbidden in the presence of two of the three Powers of the Realm, and he made a little gesture with his head and neck as if to pull himself back out of view. But the Lady Therissa smiled and beckoned him to continue, and he said, "I don't know much about the Procurator, though nothing I've heard about him is anything but bad; but I know Barjazid only too well. I think he's capable of using the machine in any way that Dantirya Sambail would want him to."

The Lady said, "Can it really be as powerful as you make it seem, though? We have devices here at the Isle, you know, that can reach very deeply into minds. But nothing that can compel someone to rise up in his sleep and walk out into a lethal desert. Nothing that can take a dream of one kind and transform it into another."

"The one you allowed me to try, mother—the silver circlet that I wore, when we had the dream-speaker wine—is that the most powerful instrument you have here?"

"No," said the Lady Therissa. "There are stronger ones, ones which not only can make contact with minds but also are able to instill sendings in them. I didn't dare allow you to experience their power, not without the months of training that their use requires. But even those things aren't nearly as powerful as the device that this Barjazid evidently uses."

"You've used the equipment of the Isle?" Dekkeret asked him. "Tell me what it was like, my lord!"

"What it was like," Prestimion said, in a musing tone. He cast his mind back to that strange journey, feeling the potent memory of it returning to him. "What it was like. Oh, Dekkeret, that gets us into the same problem you raised when you said that no one can really feel the force of someone else's dream. The only way you could really know that was to wear the circlet yourself."

"But tell me, my lord, anyway. Please."

Prestimion stared far into the distance, as though looking through the walls of Inner Temple, out across the three cliffs of the Isle, off to the sea beyond, glittering golden in the midday light. Very quietly he said, "It was like being a god, Dekkeret. It gave me the power of having mental communion with millions of people at once. It allowed me to be everywhere on Majipoor at the same time. The way the atmosphere is everywhere, the way weather is, the way gravity is."

He narrowed his eyes to slits. The room, his mother, his wife, Dekkeret, all disappeared from his ken. It seemed to him that he heard the sound of a rushing wind. For a dizzying moment he imagined that he had the circlet on his forehead again and was soaring upward and outward, rising higher than the Mount itself, expanding into the vastness of the world by taking on an incomprehensible vastness of his own, touching minds everywhere, thousands of minds, hundreds of thousands, millions, billions, the healthy minds of the world and the poor sad sick disrupted ones also, reaching into them, offering a word here and a caress there, the comfort of the blessed Lady, the healing power of the Isle.

Everyone in the room was looking at him now. He realized that he had drifted off into some strange remote state of consciousness while standing here before them. Another moment passed before he felt that he had fully returned.

Then to Dekkeret he said, "What I learned, wearing that silver circlet, is that when the Lady is at her tasks she ceases to be an ordinary human being and becomes a force of nature—a Power, a true Power, in the way that neither the Coronal nor the Pontifex, mere elected monarchs that we are, could ever be. I haven't said this to you, mother. But the day I wore the circlet I saw very clearly, and now can never forget, how important your function is to the world. And I understood how it must have transformed your life to become the Lady of the Isle."

"But," Dekkeret persevered, "as you traveled around the world using the power of the circlet, did you ever think there might be some way to implant dreams in people's minds? Or to have such power over them that they would automatically have to obey your commands."

"No. I don't think so." Prestimion turned toward the Lady. "Mother?" She shook her head. "It is as I said: the sending of dreams, yes. Commands, no. Not even with our most powerful devices can I do that."

Dekkeret nodded grimly. "Then what Barjazid has, and is about to give to Dantirya Sambail, is the deadliest of weapons, my lord. And if those two are not stopped they will shatter the peace of the world. Which is why I brought my message in person, sir, instead of using the ordinary channels of communication. For no one who has not felt the force of the Barjazid device could possibly understand the threat that it holds. And I am the only one who has done that and lived to tell the tale."

9

FROM HIS OFFICE HIGH above the Stoien waterfront Akbalik watched the royal fleet arrive. Three swift ships, flying the Coronal's banner and the banner of the Lady of the Isle.

"I should go down there and be waiting on the pier when they land," he said. "I will go down there. I have to."

"Your leg, sir—" said Odrian Kestivaunt.

"Damn the leg! The leg's no excuse! The Coronal is coming, and the Lady with him. My place is down there on the pier."

"At least let me change the poultice, sir," said the little Vroon mildly. "There's time enough for that."

It was a reasonable request. Akbalik lowered himself to the stool next to the window and offered his injured calf to the Vroon's ministration. Deftly, tentacles flying so swiftly that Akbalik could scarcely follow their busy motions, Kestivaunt stripped away yesterday's bandage, laying bare the angry red wound. It looked worse than ever: puffy, swollen, the area of its jurisdiction over his leg expanding steadily despite the medication. Kestivaunt bathed it in some cool and faintly astringent pale-blue fluid, gently probed the raw place surrounding the wound with the tip of a tentacle, very carefully spread the lips of the cut and peered within.

Akbalik hissed. "That hurts, fellow."

"I ask your pardon, Prince Akbalik. I need to see—"

"Whether any baby swamp-crabs are hatching in there?"

"I told you, sir, there is very little likelihood that the one that bit you was old enough to—"

"Ow! For the love of the Divine, Kestivaunt! Just give it a new poultice and make an end to this poking around, will you? You're torturing me."

The Vroon apologized again and bent low over his toil. Akbalik could not see, now, what the small creature was doing; but it hurt less than what he had been doing a moment before, at any rate. Applying some mental emanation with those little wriggling tentacles, a Vroonish spell of healing? Perhaps. And a sprinkle of dried herbs, and more of that cooling blue fluid. The clean bandage, next. Better, yes. For the time being, anyway. Momentary surcease from the furious throbbing, the burning pain, the stomach-turning sense that slender tendrils of infection and corruption were gliding along the hidden pathways of his leg, reaching up toward his groin, his gut, ultimately his heart.

"All done," Kestivaunt said. Akbalik rose. Gingerly he put his weight on the troubled leg, grimacing a little, catching his breath. He felt shafts of pain running up the entire left side of his body into his neck and onward to his cheek, his jawbone, his teeth. For the millionth time he saw the great purple swamp-crab, the hideous domed bulgy-eyed thing half as big as a floater, rising up menacingly out of the sandy muck before him. Saw himself adroitly turning away from the monster, smugly pleased with his swift response—stepping back from peril so quickly that he failed entirely to notice the other and much smaller crab, not much bigger across than the palm of his hand, slyly reaching one razor-sharp nipper toward his leg from its shelter in the crotch of a stinkflower bush—

"The cane," he said. "Where's my damned cane? They're practically in port already!"

The Vroon indicated the cane, leaning against the wall by the door in its usual place. Akbalik limped across and took it and went out. As he reached the ground floor he paused, looking out into the bright sunlight, breathing deeply, composing himself. He didn't want to seem like a cripple. The Coronal depended on him. Needed him.

It was no more than fifty yards across a broad cobbled plaza from the doorway of the customs-house where Akbalik maintained his office to the gateway of the piers. Akbalik moved slowly, carefully, holding the head of his cane with a tight grip. Today the distance felt like fifty miles.

Midway to his goal he became aware of the greasy tang of smoke in the air. He looked off to the north, saw the curling black strand climbing into the spotless sky, then the little red tongue higher up, licking out of a smallish building that stood atop a brick pedestal at least sixty feet high. Now he heard the sirens, too. So the crazies were at it again, Akbalik thought—first fire in three or four days, wasn't it? And today of all days, with the Coronal's ship landing at this very moment!

A line of Hjort customs-men stood across the entrance to the wharf, blocking access. Akbalik, not bothering to produce his identification, simply scowled at them and waved them out of his path with a sharp backhanded sweep of his hand. Moving past them without a glance, he went limping out toward Pier 44, the royal pier, draped for the occasion today in green and gold bunting.

Three ships, yes, the big cruiser *Lord Hostirin* and two escorts. The Coronal's honor guard had come down the gangplank and was lining up along the pier. A little gaggle of Mayor Bannikap's people was stationed just beyond them as a welcoming committee, with Bannikap himself visible in the midst of the crowd. "Prestimion!" they were crying.

"Prestimion! Lord Prestimion! Long life to Lord Prestimion!" The usual chant. How tired he must be of it!

And there he was, now, at the rail, with Varaile beside him and the Lady Therissa a short distance to their left, half hidden behind her son. To their rear, rising up out of the shadows, Akbalik saw the lofty figure of Prestimion's two-headed magus Maundigand-Klimd. How ironic, Akbalik thought, that Prestimion, who once had no belief in sorcery at all, never seemed to go anywhere any more without that Su-Suheris magus at his side.

There in the group too—Akbalik was startled to see him—was young Dekkeret, hovering at the Lady Varaile's elbow. That was a surprise. What was Dekkeret doing aboard a ship coming in from the Isle? Shouldn't he still be off in Suvrael, seeking in the discomfort of the desert heat the Divine's pardon for letting that guide-woman die—or else, what was more likely, have gone back to the Castle by this time?

But maybe Suvrael hadn't supplied him with a sufficiently gratifying degree of the atonement, the penance, that he had so desperately seemed to want when Akbalik last saw him in Zimroel, and that strange spiritual hunger of his had led the boy to go from the bleak southern continent to the sanctuary of the gentle Lady for further repairs to his soul. Where Prestimion had encountered him during the course of his own visit to the Lady, and now was bringing him back. Yes, Akbalik thought. That must be it.

He hurried forward, wincing again and again as the stress of hurried movement brought him fresh pain. Shouldering his way into the midst of the scene, he took up a position right in front of the honor guard. This was Bannikap's city, yes, but it was at Akbalik's request that Lord Prestimion was here, and Akbalik wanted to cut through the official folderol as quickly as possible. He had hardly any patience at all left any more, not with that fiery pain gnawing at his left leg all the time.

"Lordship!" he called. "Lordship!"

The Coronal saw him and waved. Akbalik offered him a starburst. And then, as the Lady came into clearer view, he gave her her special sign of respect too. They began their descent to the pier. Mayor Bannikap came forward, his jaws already moving in the preamble to his speech of welcome, but Akbalik cut him off with a stinging glance and went to the Coronal's side first.

Prestimion held out his arms for an embrace. Akbalik, not knowing what to do with his cane, tucked it under his arm and clasped it awkwardly to his side as he returned the Coronal's greeting.

"What's this thing?" Prestimion asked.

Akbalik tried to seem casual about it. "A minor leg injury, my lord. Annoying, but not particularly serious. There are many more important matters than this for us to discuss."

"Yes," Prestimion said. "As soon as I can get the stupid formalities out of the way." He indicated Mayor Bannikap with a quick toss of his head and winked.

Akbalik turned from him and offered his homage to the Lady, and to the Lady Varaile. Dekkeret gave him a shy, uncomfortable grin. He was still keeping to the background.

At a quick glance it seemed to Akbalik that the Lady Varaile was with child. Her manner of dress indicated that. She had that radiant maternal look already as well. That was interesting, the thought of Prestimion as a father so soon after taking on the tasks of the crown. And in these troubled times, too. But he should have expected it. This was a new Prestimion, deepened by responsibility, plainly eager for greater stability in his life, continuity, the ripeness that was maturity.

The Lady Therissa looked magnificent: serene, graceful, steady of soul. All the things that Akbalik himself had been before his ill-fated expedition into the depths of the Stoienzar. He felt better simply from being this near to her.

"Is that smoke I smell?" Prestimion asked.

"A building's on fire up the street a little way. There's been a lot of that lately." Akbalik lowered his voice. "Crazy people carrying bales of straw up to rooftops and setting fire to them. A very popular pastime, suddenly. The mayor will be able to give you more information."

The mayor, a portly red-faced man related in some remote way to Duke Oljebbin and every bit as self-important, was already asserting his place anyway, coming forward to loom over Prestimion's slight figure in a fashion that the Coronal was highly unlikely to enjoy. But protocol was protocol, and this was Bannikap's moment. Akbalik deferred to him. He told Prestimion, who was staring pensively at that black curl of smoke spreading across the sky, that he would attend him later at his suite at the Crystal Pavilion, and made his limping exit.

A wall of continuous windows two hundred feet long gave the Crystal Pavilion its name. It was a relatively young building, put up by Duke Oljebbin during Prankipin's time as Coronal, that stood in a magnificently solitary position in central Stoien atop a colossal pedestal of whitewashed brick. From Lord Prestimion's splendid three-level suite atop the pavilion the view took in the entire city, which unfortunately made it all too easy today to see the pillars of smoke arising from the nine or ten fires that were burning in the downtown area.

"This happens every day, these fires?" Prestimion asked.

Akbalik and the Coronal sat before platters of small cubes of smoked sea-dragon meat. Lady Varaile, weary after the hasty and sometimes turbulent voyage, had retreated to her bedchamber. The Lady Therissa was in a suite four levels down from Prestimion's, resting also. Akbalik had no idea where Dekkeret and the Su-Suheris had gone.

"More or less. It's a little unusual to have this many going at once."

"The madness, is it?"

"The madness, yes. This is the dry season: there's a lot of fuel sitting around. Those pretty vines that flower all summer long turn to immense mounds of straw. As I told you, the crazies gather up bundles of it and go up on rooftops to set it afire. I don't know why. I suppose there are more fires today than usual because they heard the Coronal and the Lady were coming, and that excited them."

"Bannikap tried to tell me that the damage is generally pretty minimal."

"Generally it is. Not always. There's been a big effort, the past two weeks, to demolish and clear away the really seriously ruined buildings, so you won't have to look at them while you're here. Wherever you see a little park about big enough to have held a single building, with freshly planted flowering shrubs, you're looking at a place where they had a bad fire. —May I have more wine, my lord?"

"Yes, of course." Prestimion pushed the flask across. "Tell me what you did to your leg."

"We should discuss Dantirya Sambail, sir."

"We will. What about the leg?"

"I hurt it while I was out hunting for Dantirya Sambail. The Procurator's been moving around very freely within that hell-hole where he's been making camp, pulling up stakes every few days, going up and down through the jungle as it pleases him. He's become very good, lately, at covering his tracks. We're never quite sure where he is on any given day. Using a magus, I suppose, to cast a cloud of unknowingness all around himself. Last month I took a few hundred men and went looking for him, just a reconnaissance mission, to make sure he wasn't going to slip out of our reach altogether. I saw the place where he had been. But he had moved along, a day or two before."

"He's definitely aware that we're on to him?"

"He must be, by now. How could he not? And if we lose him in there for more than a day or two at a time, finding him again will be the old needle in a haystack problem. He's been amazingly tricky about staying beyond our reach. Anyway, about the leg—"

"The leg, yes."

"The scouts said that they thought the Procurator's current location was about two hundred miles inland from the town of Karasat, which is on the southern coast between Maximin and Gunduba, if those names mean anything to you. So I sailed over from Stoien to have a look. You know, my lord, people speak of the Suvrael desert as being the most unpleasant place in the world, with the Valmambra a distant second. But no, no, we've got the prize-winner right here in lower Alhanroel. I've never been to Suvrael, or the Valmambra either, but I tell you, sir, they can't possibly be a patch on the southern Stoienzar for sheer nastiness. It's full of creatures that must have migrated over from Suvrael looking for an even more horrible place to live. I know. I had an encounter with one."

"Something bit you, you mean?"

"A swamp-crab, yes. Not one of the big ones—you should see the size of those monsters, my lord—" Akbalik spread his arms in a broad gesture. "No, it was a little one, a mere baby, lying in wait, clipped me with its nipper, snap, just like that. The worst pain I ever hope to feel. Some kind of acid venom, they say, in the bite. Leg swelled up five times normal size. It's not so bad now, I think."

Prestimion, frowning, leaned forward for a better look. "What are you doing for it?"

"I have a Vroon secretary, name of Kestivaunt, very capable. He's looking after it. Puts medicine on it, does a little Vroonish hocus-pocus also—if the spells don't cure it, the herbal ointment ought to." A fresh spasm of blazing pain traveled up Akbalik's side. He clenched his teeth and turned away, determined not to let Prestimion see how much anguish he was in. A change of subject seemed the best idea. —"My lord, tell me what Dekkeret was doing with you on the Isle, if you will. I would have assumed that he'd have finished up his business in Suvrael—you know, his expiation, his redemption, after that affair in the Khyntor Marches—and returned to the Castle a long time ago."

"He did return," said Prestimion. "Late last summer, it was. Bringing someone with him who he had had a little run-in with in Suvrael. Do you remember a certain Venghenar Barjazid, Akbalik?"

"Knavish-looking little fellow who used to do odd jobs for Duke Svor?"

"The very same. When I sent that troublesome Vroon Thalnap Zelifor into exile in Suvrael, I picked this Barjazid to go with him and make sure he got there. One of the infinite number of mistakes that I've made, Akbalik, since

I took it into my head that I was qualified to be Coronal."

Akbalik listened in growing concern as Prestimion sketched the tale for him: Barjazid doing away with the Vroon and appropriating his mind-controlling devices for his own purposes; the episodes of predatory experimentation on hapless travelers with those devices in Suvrael's Desert of Stolen Dreams; then Dekkeret's own encounter with Barjazid in that desert, his capture of Barjazid, his bringing of Barjazid and his machines to the Castle.

"He lost no time asking for an audience," Prestimion said. "I didn't happen to be at the Castle that day, so he met with Varaile, and very carefully explained the power of these devices, and the danger in them, to her. When I returned she tried to tell me the story, but I confess I paid very little attention. One more black mark on my record, Akbalik. Well, now Barjazid has slipped out of the Castle somehow and made his way down to the Stoienzar to put his machines to work on behalf of Dantirya Sambail. Which is what Dekkeret came running out to the Isle to tell me, and why I've come over to Stoien so quickly myself. If Barjazid and Dantirya Sambail manage to join forces—"

"I'm sure they already have, my lord."

"How do you know that?"

"I said that the Procurator has become very good at eluding our scouts. A magus, I said, who's casting a cloud of unknowingness around him. But what if it's not a magus at all? What if it's this Barjazid? If these devices of his are as powerful as Dekkeret says they are—" Once again Akbalik felt fire in his leg, and hid his shudder of pain from Prestimion. "A lucky thing for us all that the boy did go to Suvrael, eh? And I tried so hard to discourage him. What is your plan, my lord?"

"I've already told you, I think, that Septach Melayn and Gialaurys are leading a force of troops down to the Stoienzar from Castle Mount. They'll go after Dantirya Sambail from the western end of the peninsula. I mean to assemble a second army here in Stoien city that will enter the Stoienzar from the other side. My mother will guide our movements: she thinks she knows a way of employing the arts of the

Isle to search him out. Meanwhile, to keep him from escaping from the area as we go toward him, we blockade the ports everywhere along the peninsula, north and south—"

"May I ask you, my lord, who will command the army out of Stoien city?"

Prestimion seemed surprised at that. "Why, I will."

"I beg you, sir, no."

"No?"

"You must not go into the Stoienzar jungle. You have no idea how awful a place it is. I don't just mean the heat and the humidity, or the insects half as long as your arm that buzz in your face all day long. I mean the dangers, my lord, the terrible perils that lie everywhere around. Do you wonder why there are no settlements there? It is one vast sticky marsh, where your boots sink ankle-deep at every step. Beneath you lurk hidden venomous monsters, the swamp-crabs, whose bite is death, unless you're lucky enough to be bitten by a very small one, as I was. The trees themselves are your enemies: there is one whose seed-pods explode as they ripen, sending long fragments in every direction that strike deep into a man's flesh like flying daggers. There is another tree, the manganoza palm, it is, whose leaves are as sharp as—"

"I know all this, Akbalik. Nevertheless, the task of leading the troops falls to me, and what of it? Do you think I'm afraid of a little discomfort?"

"Many men will die while marching through those swamps. I've seen it happen. I came close to dying there myself. I say that you have no right to risk your life there, my lord."

Anger flared in Prestimion's eyes. "No right? No right? You overreach yourself, Akbalik. Not even Prince Serithorn's nephew should venture to instruct the Coronal in what he ought or ought not to do."

Prestimion's rebuke struck Akbalik with almost physical force. His face went red; he muttered an apology and offered a hasty starburst. To steady himself he took a long draught of the wine. Some different sort of approach was required. After a moment he said in a low voice, "Can your mother really use her arts to help you in this war, my lord?"

"She believes that she can. She may even be able to counteract the mental powers that Barjazid wields."

"And so—forgive me again, Lord Prestimion—you mean to take her with you, do you, into the Stoienzar jungles? The Lady of the Isle is to ride at your side as you make your way through those deadly swamps? Do you really intend to place her in that sort of jeopardy?"

He saw at once that he had scored a point. Prestimion looked stunned. Plainly had not been expecting a thrust from that direction. "I need her close beside me as matters unfold. She will have a clearer view than anyone of the Procurator's movements."

Akbalik said, "The Lady's powers work at any distance, do they not? There's no need to bring her so close. She can stay safe in Stoien while the jungle campaign is mounted. And so can you. You and she can devise strategy together and your wishes can be relayed easily enough to the battle-front." And quickly added, as Prestimion began to reply: "My lord, I plead with you to listen to me. Perhaps Lord Stiamot may have led his army into battle seven thousand years ago, but such risks on the part of a Coronal are un-acceptable today. Remain here in Stoien city and supervise the conflict from a distance with the Lady's help. Let me lead the imperial troops against the Procurator. You are not expendable. I am. And I've already had some experience in dealing with the conditions that the Stoienzar presents. Let me be the one to go."

"You? No. Never, Akbalik."

"But my lord—"

"You think you've been fooling me, with that leg of yours? I can see how you're suffering. You're barely able to walk, let alone go back into that jungle on a new mission. And how can you tell that the infection won't get worse than it is right now before you start to heal? No, Akbalik. You may be right that it isn't wise for me to go in there, but you certainly aren't going to."

There was a steely note in the Coronal's voice that told

Akbalik it was useless to object. He sat in silence, massaging his throbbing leg just above the wound.

Prestimion went on: "I'll attempt to direct operations from here, as you suggest, and we'll see how that works out. But as for you, I relieve you right now from active service. The Lady Varaile is going to leave for the Castle in a few days—she's pregnant, do you know that, Akbalik?—and I'm assigning you the job of escorting her back to the Mount."

"My congratulations, sir. But with all respect, my lord, let Dekkeret take her. I should stay here in Stoien city with you and assist you in the campaign. My understanding of the nature of that jungle—"

"Might be useful, yes. But if you lose that leg, what then? It's idiotic for you to remain in Stoien. This is a provincial backwater. We have the best doctors in the world at the Castle, and they'll repair you in short order. As for Dekkeret, I need him here with me. He's the only one who understands anything about how this Barjazid device actually works."

"I implore you, my lord—"

"I implore you, Akbalik: save your breath. My mind's made up. I thank you for all you've accomplished here in Stoien. Now get yourself to the Castle with my lady Varaile, and have that leg properly taken care of."

Prestimion stood. Akbalik rose also, with an effort he was unable to conceal. His injured leg did not want to support him. The Coronal seized him around the shoulders, steadying him as he struggled to find his balance.

From outside, far below, came the sudden sound of sirens. People were yelling in the streets. Akbalik glanced toward the window. A new pillar of black smoke was rising in the city's southern quarter.

"It gets worse and worse," Prestimion muttered. He turned to go. "Some day, Akbalik, we'll look back at these times and chuckle, won't we? But I wish we could do a little more chuckling right now."

*   *   *

It was late the next afternoon before Akbalik had any
opportunity to speak with Dekkeret. The last time he had
seen the young man was in a simple mountain tavern in
Khyntor, on a night two years before in early spring, as they
sat together over flasks of hot golden wine. That was the
night Dekkeret had announced his intention to go to Suvrael.
"You judge yourself too harshly," Akbalik had said then.
"There's no sin so foul that it merits a jaunt in Suvrael."
And he had urged Dekkeret to make a pilgrimage to the Isle
instead, if he truly felt a need to cleanse his soul of its stain.
"Let the blessed Lady heal your spirit," Akbalik had told
him then. It is foolish to interrupt your career at the Castle,
he said, for the long absence that the trip to Suvrael would
require.

But Dekkeret had gone to Suvrael anyway; and to the
Isle as well, it seemed, if only for the briefest of visits. And
his travels did not appear to have done any harm to his
burgeoning career after all.

"Do you remember what we agreed," Dekkeret said,
"when we were sitting together in that Khyntor tavern? That
you and I would have a happy reunion on the Mount two
years hence, is what we said, when I was back from Suvrael.
We would go to the games in High Morpin together, is what
we promised each other. The two years have come and gone,
Akbalik, but we never managed to get to High Morpin."

"Other matters interfered. I found myself here in Stoien
instead at the time we were supposed to be holding our
reunion. And you——"

"And I went to the Isle of Sleep, but not as a pilgrim."
Dekkeret laughed. "Can you imagine, Akbalik, how strange
my own life seems to me these days? I, who had simply
hoped to be a knight of the Castle, and maybe hold some
modest ministerial post when I was old—I find myself keeping company with the Coronal and his wife, and with the
Lady herself, and drawn into the midst of the most complex
and delicate affairs of state——"

"Yes. Rising fast, you are. You'll be Coronal some day,
Dekkeret, mark my words."

"Me? Don't be foolish, Akbalik! When all this is over,

I'll be just another knight-initiate again. You're the one who might be Coronal! Everyone says so, you know. Confalume might have another ten or twelve years to live, and then Lord Prestimion will become Pontifex, and the next Coronal might well be—"

"Stop this nonsense, Dekkeret. Not another word."

"I'm sorry if I've offended you. I happen to think that you'd be an entirely plausible person to succeed—"

"Stop it! I've never spent a moment thinking about my becoming Coronal and I don't expect to become Coronal and I don't want to become Coronal. It's not going to happen. Just for one thing, I'm the same age as Prestimion exactly. His successor is going to come from your generation, not from mine. But for another—" Akbalik shook his head. "Why are we wasting this much time on anything as idiotic as this? The next Coronal? Let's do what we can to serve this one! —I'm going to be escorting the Lady Varaile back to the Castle in another few days. You'll be staying here, advising Lord Prestimion on ways to deal with Barjazid and his mind-gadget, do you know that? I want you to promise me something, Dekkeret."

"Name it. Anything."

"That if the Coronal takes it into his head to go off into those jungles looking for Dantirya Sambail despite all I've said to him about that, you'll stand up before him and tell him that that's an insane thing to be doing, that he absolutely must not do it, that for sake of his wife and his mother and his unborn child, and for the whole world's sake, for that matter, he has to keep himself far away from the reach of the things that live in that ghastly hothouse of a place. Will you do that, Dekkeret? No matter how angry you make him, no matter what risks to your own career you may run, tell him that. Over and over."

"Of course. I promise."

"Thank you."

For a moment neither one spoke. It had been an awkward conversation through and through, and it seemed now to have hit a wall.

Then Dekkeret said, "May I ask you a personal question, Akbalik?"

"I suppose."

"It worries me to see you limping around like that. Something really bad must have happened to that leg. You're in a lot of pain, aren't you?"

"You sound just like Prestimion. My leg, my leg, my leg! Look, Dekkeret, my leg's going to be all right. It isn't going to drop off, or anything. While I was sloshing around in the Stoienzar I got a nasty nip from a miserable little crab, and it got infected, and, yes, it hurts, so I've been walking with a cane for a few days. But it's healing. Another few days and I'll be fine. All right? Is that enough about my leg? Let's talk about something cheerful, instead. Your little holiday in Suvrael, for example—"

It was still early in the morning and already the bitter scent of smoke marred the sweet fresh air: the first fire of the day, Prestimion thought. This was the day of Varaile's departure for the Castle. A seven-floater caravan was lined up in front of the Crystal Pavilion, a regally grand one for Varaile and Akbalik to ride in, four lesser ones for their security escort, and two for their baggage. The sooner Varaile was back in the safe environment of the Castle, high up above the turmoil that appeared to be engulfing so many of the lowland cities, the better. Prestimion hoped he would be back there himself before the new prince—Taradath, they were going to call him, in honor of the lost uncle that the boy would never know—was born.

"I wish you would come with me, Prestimion," Varaile said, as they emerged from the Pavilion and walked toward the waiting floaters.

"I wish I could. Let me deal with the Procurator, first, and then I will."

"Are you planning to go into those jungles after him?"

"Akbalik insists that I mustn't. And who am I to disobey Akbalik's command? —No, Varaile, I won't be going in there myself. I want my mother beside me as we reach out to crush Dantirya Sambail, and the Stoienzar is no place for her. So I've given in. I tell you, though, it galls me to remain comfortably ensconced here in Stoien while Gialaurys and Septach Melayn and Navigorn are sweating their way through the saw-palm forests looking for—"

She cut him off with a laugh. "Oh, Prestimion, don't be such a boy! Maybe the Coronals we once read about in *The Book of Changes* went into the forests and fought terrible battles against the monsters that used to live in them, but that isn't done any more. Would Lord Confalume have gone thrashing around in a jungle, if he had had a war to fight? Would Lord Prankipin?" She looked at him closely, then. "You won't go, will you?"

"I've just explained to you why I can't."

"Can't doesn't necessarily mean won't. You might decide that you don't really need to have the Lady Therissa at your elbow while the war's going on. In that case, will you leave her in Stoien city and go into the jungle anyway, once Akbalik and I are far away?"

This was making him uncomfortable. He had no more desire to enter that abomination of a jungle than anyone else. And he understood that a Coronal's life should not be placed lightly at stake. This was not the civil war, when he had been only a private citizen seeking to overthrow the usurper: he was the anointed and sacred king, now. But to fight a war by proxy at a distance of two thousand miles, while his friends were risking their lives among the swamp-crabs and saw-grass—?

"If somehow it becomes essential for me to go there, absolutely unavoidable, then I will," Prestimion said finally. "Otherwise, no." He touched his hand lightly to the front of her body. "Believe me, Varaile, I want to be back at the Castle myself, all in one piece, before Taradath is born. I won't take any risks except those that I have no choice about taking." Then, taking her hand in his, he kissed her fingertips and led her toward the floater. "You should be on your way. But where's Akbalik? He ought to be here by now."

"That's him, isn't it, Prestimion? All the way over there?"

She pointed far across the plaza. A man with a cane, yes. Walking very slowly, pausing now and again to rest and take the weight off his left leg. Prestimion stared balefully toward him. This was a troublesome thing, this infected leg of Akbalik's. Vroonish wizardry could go only so far; the man needed to be in the hands of the Castle's best surgeons for this. Akbalik was important to him. Prestimion wondered just how serious this wound of his really was.

"It's going to take him forever to get here," Prestimion said. "Why don't you go into the floater and sit down, Varaile? All this standing around can't be good for you." She smiled and entered the car.

Just then something that had been bobbing in and out of Prestimion's mind for many weeks drifted back into it, something that he had been meaning to ask again and again, without ever quite getting around to it. He peered in after her. "Oh: and one question before you leave, Varaile. —Do you recall, when we were at Inner Temple and I was telling the story of the memory obliteration to my mother and you, I mentioned that the name of the son of Lord Confalume who seized the throne was Korsibar? You seemed very surprised when I said that. Why was that?"

"I had heard the name before. From my father, in his ravings one day. He seemed to think that Confalume was still Coronal, and I told him no, there was a new Coronal now, and he said, 'Oh, yes, Lord Korsibar.' 'No, father,' I said, 'the new Coronal is Lord Prestimion, there isn't any such person as Lord Korsibar.' I thought it was the madness speaking in him. But then, when you told us that the usurper whose name had been wiped from history by your mages was Korsibar—"

"Yes. I see," said Prestimion. He felt a sudden shiver of apprehension. "He knew the name. He remembered Korsibar. Can it be, I wonder, that the obliteration is wearing off, that the true past is breaking through?"

That was all he needed right now, he thought. But perhaps only those in the deepest extremity of madness were experiencing such flashbacks; and no one was likely to take what they said very seriously. "My father in his ravings," as Varaile had just put it. Even so, it was something that he would have to bear in mind. Consult one of his mages about it, he thought: Maundigand-Klimd, or perhaps Heszmon Gorse.

It was a problem for some other time. Akbalik had arrived at last.

He flashed a broad, unconvincing grin. "All ready, are we?" he cried, with a cheeriness that was all too obviously forced.

"Ready and waiting. How's the leg?" Prestimion asked. He thought it seemed more swollen than it had been the night before. Or was that just an illusion?

"The leg? The leg is fine, my lord. Just a tiny little twinge here and there. Another few days—"

"Yes," Prestimion said. "Just a tiny little twinge. I think I observed you getting a couple of those tiny little twinges as you were crossing the plaza. Don't waste any time getting that leg looked at once you're back at the Castle, eh?" He looked away in an attempt to avoid seeing the enormous difficulty with which Akbalik was entering the floater. "Safe journey!" he called. Varaile and Akbalik waved to him. The vehicle's rotors began to hum. The other floaters in the caravan were coming now to life also. Prestimion stood in the plaza looking eastward for a long while after the five vehicles had disappeared from sight.

10

"TELL ME HONESTLY," SEPTACH Melayn said, "did you ever expect to see this part of the world again in your life?"

"Why not?" Gialaurys said. They were entering the Kajith Kabulon rain-forest once more, having made the journey southward through Bailemoona and Ketheron and Arvyanda following the same track they had taken two years before. That time, though, they had been Prestimion's companions on a small exploratory expedition; now they were coming at the head of a great military force. "We serve the Coronal. Prestimion tells us to go here, we go here. He wants us to go there, we go there. If that involves making ten trips to Ketheron the same year, or fifteen to the Valmambra, what should that matter to us?"

Septach Melayn laughed. "A heavy answer to a light question, my friend. I meant only that the world is so big that one never expects to visit the same place twice. Except, of course, going back and forth among the cities of the Mount. But here we are, plodding through the muck of soggy Kajith Kabulon for the second time in three years."

"I repeat my reply," said Gialaurys grumpily. "We are here because it is the pleasure of the Coronal Lord Prestimion that we get ourselves down to the Stoienzar, and the shortest way from Castle Mount to the Stoienzar runs through Kajith Kabulon. I fail to see any point to your question. But this wouldn't be the first time you've opened your mouth just to let some noise come out, is it, Septach Melayn?"

"Do you think," Navigorn said, as much to break the rising tension as for any other reason, "that anyone's ever lived long enough to see the whole world? I don't mean just getting from here to the far side of Zimroel: the Coronals all do that when they make their grand processionals. I mean going everywhere, every province, every city, the eastern coast of Alhanroel to the western coast of Zimroel, and from the land around the North Pole down to the bottom end of Suvrael."

"That would take five hundred years, I think," said Septach Melayn. "Longer, I suspect, than any of us is likely to live. But see: Prestimion has been Coronal just a short while, and already Gialaurys and I have been deep into the east-country of Alhanroel, and then down south as far as Sippulgar, and now we are to have the great pleasure of visiting the beautiful Stoienzar—"

"You are very irritating today, Septach Melayn," Gialaurys said. "I will ride in a different floater, I think."

But he made no move to halt the vehicle and leave it, and they continued onward. The forest canopy grew deeper. This was a green world in here, but for the occasional contrast that the brilliant fungi of the treetrunks provided, mainly scarlet in this part of the forest, occasionally a vivid yellow brighter even than the sulfury yellow of Ketheron. Although it was still only early afternoon, the sun was no longer visible through the tightly interwoven vines that linked the tops of the tall, slender trees flanking the road. The unending downpour's persistent drumbeat sound was making everyone edgy: a light rain, unvarying in its intensity, but continuing hour after hour without a break.

A long line of floaters stretched behind them. Each one was emblazoned with the Labyrinth symbol of the Pontifex, since officially this was not an army, merely a peacekeeping force engaged in a police action, and—officially speaking, at least—it was under the command of the Pontificate. The whole system of enforcing the law was a matter for the Pontificate. There were no armies on Majipoor, just Pontifical troops charged with keeping the peace. The Coronal had no troops of his own beyond those who served as the Castle guard. The army that Korsibar had sent against Prestimion during the civil war had been a greatly expanded and probably unconstitutional version of the Coronal's bodyguard; the army that Prestimion had assembled in his successful campaign against the usurper was a volunteer militia.

A constitutional expert, one whose nose was buried all the time in the Synods and Balances and Decretals, would probably have raised some objections to the legality of this brigade, too. Septach Melayn had requisitioned these troops from Vologaz Sar, the Pontifex's man at the Castle, by presenting him with a decree already signed by himself as High Counsellor and Gialaurys as Grand Admiral, acting in the name of the absent Lord Prestimion, and, for good measure, by Navigorn and Prince Serithorn as well.

"I will have to send this to the Labyrinth for countersigning, of course," Vologaz Sar had said.

"Yes. By all means please do. But we need to leave for the Stoienzar immediately, and we'll be collecting troops from the various Pontifical encampments along the way. So if you'll add your own signature here, giving us authorization to levy troops on a strictly provisional basis pending formal approval by the Pontifex—"

Whereupon Septach Melayn produced a second copy of the decree, identical to the first.

"This is extremely irregular, Septach Melayn!"

"Yes. I rather suppose it is. —You need to sign over here, I think, just above the Pontifical seal, which we have already had engrossed on the document to save you the trouble."

In return for Vologaz Sar's cooperation, Septach Melayn had spared him the necessity of providing Pontifical officers to take part in the action against Dantirya Sambail. It would be simpler, he said, if command responsibilities remained concentrated in the hands of the Coronal's own trusted men. The enormity of the request was too much for the outmaneuvered Vologaz Sar. "Whatever you wish," he muttered, abandoning all resistance, and scrawled his signature on the sheet.

Now it was the fourth day of their passage through rainy Kajith Kabulon. They had turned off the main highway, which would have taken them to the provincial capital and Prince Thaszthasz's wickerwork palace once again, and were making their way sluggishly along a spongy-bedded secondary road that ran somewhat to the west. Everything in this part of the rain-forest grew with crazy tropical excessiveness. Thick tangles of spiky purplish moss festooned the trees so heavily that it was hard to understand why they were not choked by it. Angry blotches of crimson lichen clung to every rock; long ropy strands of a swollen blue fungus coiled along the sides of the road like sleeping serpents. The rain was omnipresent.

"Does it ever stop?" Navigorn asked. He alone, of the three, had not been to Kajith Kabulon before. "By the Lady, this weather can drive a man berserk!"

Septach Melayn gave him a thoughtful glance. The strange convulsive seizures that had plagued Navigorn intermittently almost since the beginning of the madness epidemic still troubled him from time to time, particularly when he was under stress. Would the steady pounding of the rain send him into another one now? That would be awkward, here in the cramped confines of the floater that they shared.

Probably it would have been wiser, Septach Melayn thought, for Navigorn to have remained behind at the Castle, serving once more as regent, instead of subjecting himself to this expedition. But he had insisted. He still felt that his reputation had been badly compromised by the Procurator's escape from the Sangamor tunnels. The very similar escape of Venghenar Barjazid and his son from that same prison, although Navigorn could not in any way be blamed for it, had reawakened those feelings of shame and guilt in him. Dantirya Sambail would be causing no trouble today if Navigorn had been able to keep him safely locked up in the tunnels. And so, evidently by way of achieving a redemption of some sort, he had insisted on coming along. Poor frivolous Serithorn, finally, had been stuck with the job of running the government in their absence, aided in that to some extent by Prestimion's brother Teotas. But the strain of the rain-forest climate was telling on Navigorn. Septach Melayn peered anxiously ahead, hoping for a glimpse of sunlight soon.

He turned to Gialaurys. "What do you say we sing, good admiral? A lively ballad to while away the time!" And launched in lustily on a tune ten thousand years old:

When Lord Vargaiz came to the Shapeshifter hall
And asked for a flask of their wine,
They brought him instead, for the slaking of his thirst
The juice of the glaggaberry vine.

Gialaurys, whose singing voice would have done discredit to the great toad of Kunamolgoi Mountain, folded his arms, glowering, and looked at Septach Melayn as though he had succumbed to the madness himself. Navigorn, though, grinned and joined in immediately:

Now glaggaberry juice, I tell you, friends,
Is a drink to be drunk with care.

But the fearless Lord Vargaiz gulped it all down
In the midst of the Shapeshifter lair

Then the Coronal said, with a sly little smile,
I like the taste of your wine,
It goes down well, but then, I find—

"If you will stop that bellowing for a moment," said Gialaurys, "we can consider which highway we need to take here. For there seems to be a fork in the road. Or does that not matter, if only we sing loudly enough?"

Septach Melayn looked over his shoulder. They had the Vroon guide Galielber Dorn with them, but the small being was huddled up in the back of the vehicle, shivering with some Vroonish malady. The damp climate of Kajith Kabulon seemed not at all to his liking. "Dorn?" Septach Melayn cried. "Which way?"

"Left," came the unhesitating reply, a sickly moan.

"But we need to go toward the west. A left turn will take us the other way"

"If you know the answer, why do you ask the question?" said the Vroon. "Do whatever pleases you. A left turn will bring us to the Stoienzar, however." He groaned and slid down under a pile of blankets.

"We go left, I suppose," said Septach Melayn, shrugging. He shifted the floater's course. It would be just splendid, he thought, if this whole procession of vehicles were to set out down the wrong fork. But one did not argue with a Vroonish guide. And indeed the left-hand branch of the highway, after a few hundred yards, began gradually to loop around on itself, doubling on its own course. Septach Melayn saw now that it was curving to avoid a round muddy-looking lake, heavily congested with drifting vegetation, that blocked further progress in the other direction.

The lake's great mass of floating plants looked sinister, almost predatory: humped tangled masses, leaves like horns of plenty, cup-shaped spore-bodies, snarled ropy stems, everything dark blue against the lighter blue-green of the water. Huge aquatic mammals moved slowly through it, feeding. Septach Melayn had no idea what they were. Their tubular pinkish bodies were almost totally submerged. Only the rounded bulges of their backs and the jutting periscopes of their stalked eyes were in view, and now and then a pair of cavernous snorting nostrils. They were cutting immense swaths through the water-plants, which writhed angrily as the animals gobbled it, but did not otherwise react. At the far side of the lake new growth was already hastening to fill the gaps that the grazing beasts had opened.

"Do you smell something odd?" Navigorn asked.

The windows of the floater were sealed. Even so, a whiff of the lake's fragrance was coming through. The aroma was unmistakable. It was like breathing the fumes of a distillery vat. The lake was in ferment. Evidently one by-product of the respiration of these water-plants was alcohol, and, having no outlet, the lake had turned into a great tub of wine.

Septach Melayn said amiably, "Shall we sample it? Or will it delay our journey too much to stop here, do you think?"

"Would you go among those pink beasts for a sip of wine?" Gialaurys asked. "Yes. Yes, I think you would. Well, here, then: get down on your knees and swill to your heart's content!" He yanked at the rotor control and the floater began to halt.

"Your constant hostility starts to bore me, Admiral Gialaurys," Septach Melayn said.

"Your brand of humor long ago began to bore me, High Counsellor," Gialaurys retorted.

Navigorn started the floater up again. "Gentlemen—please, gentlemen—"

They went on.

The rain was ceasing, now. They were emerging at last from the forest of Kajith Kabulon. It was possible to see the sun again, blazing with tropical force straight ahead of them in what was undoubtedly the west. Golden Sippulgar and the Aruachosian coast lay off to the south with the waters of the Inner Sea beyond. Before them lay the Stoienzar Peninsula and Dantirya Sambail.

*　　*　　*

An end came to the bickering. This was new territory to all of them, and with every passing mile the landscape was turning stranger and more menacing. The roadway had diminished until it was hardly more than an unpaved track, barely wide enough to let the floaters go through. In places it was completely overgrown, and they had to halt and cut a path for themselves with their energy-throwers. And then, after a time, there seemed to be no road at all, and it was necessary to have the floaters bull their way onward by main force, with frequent interruptions while they hacked at vines or even trees that blocked all forward access.

There was no rain here, but this country was more humid, even, than Kajith Kabulon had been. A perpetual steamy fog prevailed everywhere. The ground itself exuded moist vapor, belching steam upward at the merest touch of the sun's rays. Shrouds of furry parasitic plants dangled from every branch of every tree. And the trees themselves were nightmarish things. One, that seemed to create forests all by itself, sent up thousands of slim vertical shoots from a single thick horizontal stem that ran like a black cable along the ground for close to a mile. Another grew with its roots facing upward, rising ten or fifteen feet out of the ground and waving about as though trolling for passing birds. There was a third kind that seemed to have melted and run at the base, for its trunk emerged from a swollen woody mass, a kind of botanical tumor, at least fifty feet across and taller than the tallest man.

These were mere oddities, though, curious and strange, that posed no dangers for the travelers. And there were others that were actually charming in their peculiarities, like the tree whose multitudes of brilliant yellow flowers dangled at the ends of long ropes, like so many lanterns, or the one of somewhat similar structure whose suspended blue-gray seed-pods clanged in the breeze to make a pleasant tinkling sound. A little way onward they came to a huge grove of trees that entered into bloom all at the same moment, at sunrise. It was Septach Melayn, rising early, who saw it happen. "Look at this!" he cried, awakening the others, as giant crimson blossoms began opening everywhere at once around them, creating a symphony of color, a single great chord. All day long they passed through this wondrous forest of flowering trees; but at twilight the petals began to drop with the same singleness of timing as had marked their unfolding, and by dawn they all were fallen and the ground had become a carpet of pink.

But as the expedition proceeded westward such moments of beauty came further and further apart, and what they encountered now seemed increasingly threatening.

First came a few manculains, creeping about sullenly in the underbrush: solitary long-nosed many-legged creatures, sluggish and timid, with narrow red ears. They were covered all over by long yellow spines sharp as stilettos whose black tips, breaking off easily at the lightest touch, or, seemingly, only at a glance, could burrow deep into your flesh as though they had minds and volition of their own.

Then some round hairy insects with double rows of malevolent eyes were seen feeding on a small mikkinong that had injured one of its fragile legs: they reduced it to picked bones in mere moments. And then, in an open place in the forest, the travelers met a hovering swarm of energy-creatures, each one a brilliant white flash no bigger than one's thumb. When they realized that they had been seen, they quickly elongated into horizontal forms two yards long that danced about in the air in unattainable groups a hundred yards away. One unwary officer drew too close to them and they fell on him with a wild buzzing sound of glee, surrounding him in such numbers that he could not be seen at all within that cloud of zigging streaks of light, and when they withdrew from him nothing remained but blackened cinders.

The energy-creatures did not reappear. But the heat and humidity, which had been overwhelming from the moment of the expedition's entry into the peninsula, increased with every mile. They were not far from the coast, now. The breeze here blew straight from Suvrael, so that the southern continent's searing blowtorch heat mingled with the vapors

rising from the warm sea that separated the continents and
turned the air of the Stoienzar's maritime lowlands into a
salty soup.

Bugs of all sorts grew huge and mighty here: meaty
things with bristly legs and clacking jaws, crawling about
everywhere over the moist sandy muck that passed for soil
in this place. The first swamp-crabs came into view, also,
baleful purple-domed crustaceans of tremendous size resting
half-submerged in the marshy ground. Here, too, were
groves of the celebrated animal-plants of Stoienzar, things
that were rooted permanently in place and manufactured
their food by photosynthesis, but which had fleshy arms that
slowly moved about, and rows of shining eyes about the
upper section of their tubular bodies, and slit-like mouths
below. They came in all sizes, and swung about in an unsettling way to stare at the travelers as their floaters passed
by. They would, said Galielber Dorn, seize and devour any
small animal that came within reach of their grasping hands.

"We should torch them all," Gialaurys muttered, shuddering.

But they knew they would need their energy-throwers for
more immediate purposes. This was the land, now, of the
manganoza palms, ungainly slouching trees that grew one
up against the next with so little space between that they
formed a well-nigh impenetrable wall. These trees had clusters of long, arching feather-like leaves, lined along every
edge with astonishingly sharp-edged crystalline cells. The
slightest breeze was enough to make these leaves stir and
flutter about. It took no more than a glancing touch to draw
blood; a harder gust of wind and the trees were capable of
lopping off hands, arms, even heads.

Now the journey became truly appalling. There no longer
was any road at all, and the only way to penetrate the saw-
palm forest was to get out of the floaters and blow a pathway
through it with energy-weapons. But every such blast expended here was one less that could be used against the
forces of Dantirya Sambail.

Eventually, thought Septach Melayn, it would come
down to the necessity of having to advance through this stuff

on foot, prepared for ambush and hand-to-hand combat with the Procurator's men at any moment. And, he reflected, they must know this country well by now, whereas we are strangers in it. In every way the advantage lay with them.

But he kept his misgivings to himself. All that he said aloud was, "This is the perfect place for Dantirya Sambail to have chosen as his camp. His kind of place exactly: everything here is as stubborn and vile and dangerous as he is himself."

11

IN STOIEN CITY IT was still at least an hour before dawn. Prestimion had scarcely slept at all. He stood now at the great curving window of his bedroom atop the Crystal Pavilion, staring intently eastward as though by the force of his gaze alone he could somehow hurry the rising of the sun.

Out there in the east, hidden from him now by the darkness that lay like a shroud across western Alhanroel, the future of Majipoor was being shaped. The history of the reign of the Coronal Lord Prestimion was being written. The entire course of the period that would bear his name was going to be determined in the next few weeks. And somehow he was here in Stoien, thousands of miles from the scene of action, passively allowing others to act in his name. He was a marginal player in his own destiny. How had he contrived to allow that to happen?

There was Dantirya Sambail, huddling like a malign spider at the center of the web he had spun for himself in the ferocious jungles of the Stoienzar Peninsula, preparing to launch whatever campaign of subversion and disruption he had been hatching since his escape from the Sangamor tunnels. And there were Septach Melayn and Gialaurys and Navigorn hacking their way toward him through those jungles from the west at the head of one armed force, while a second band of soldiers was moving eastward across the same peninsula to the same destination—an army that the

Coronal himself should be leading, or, at the worst, Akbalik
or Abrigant, but which was instead commanded by some
Pontifical captain whose name Prestimion could not seem to
remember more than two days running.

It infuriated Prestimion that he had trapped himself here
in Stoien city, unable to take his precious anointed self, or
his mother's, any closer to the zone of peril. Abrigant was
back at Muldemar now, exercising the princely responsibilities that had fallen to him when his elder brother became
Coronal. And Akbalik, on whom Prestimion had come to
rely to the extent that he had begun to think of him as his
own successor, surely was somewhere in central Alhanroel
by this time, heading for the Castle, weary and perhaps mor-
tally ill from the wound he had suffered in the jungle.

Prestimion had tried to pretend that he needed Akbalik
to escort the Lady Varaile back to the Castle to await the
birth of her child, just as Akbalik had attempted to persuade
Prestimion that his wound was not as serious as it was. But
neither of them had been fooled. There were plenty of captains other than Akbalik who could have accompanied Varaile on her journey across Alhanroel. The reason why
Akbalik was traveling with her, instead of playing a key
role in the attack on Dantirya Sambail's camp, was that the
venom of the swamp-crab was seeping deeper within his
body day by day, and the only physicians who could save
him were half a world away on Castle Mount.

If Akbalik dies—

Prestimion shook the thought away. He had enough to
contend with just now without speculating on contingencies
like that. Other beloved friends of his were at risk in the
Stoienzar at this moment, while he himself remained cooped
up here, wild with the frustration of knowing that he must
remain safe behind the lines, where his sacred person would
be shielded from the risks of battle. And Dantirya Sambail,
surely aware that the moment of reckoning was drawing
near, was very likely making ready to burst forth from hiding in all his diabolical fury.

Then, above all, there was the plague of madness steadily
spreading through the world, the pernicious disruption that

threatened to unhinge everyone's sanity before it was done, and for which Prestimion alone, however blameless his motives had been, stood responsible. What kind of world had he created, that terrible day at Thegomar Edge, for the son who would soon be born to Varaile and him? What would be the legacy of the Coronal Lord Prestimion to the world, other than a time of the most horrific chaos? The pitiful struttings of the Procurator of Ni-moya were trivial by comparison. It was easy enough to envisage the defeat and overthrow of Dantirya Sambail at the hands of the armies now converging on his camp. But the madness—the madness—he was at his wit's end for a solution to that!

He heard a knocking at his bedroom door.

Prestimion turned from the window. Someone coming to him at this early hour? What else could it be, but news of some new catastrophe?

"Yes?" he called hoarsely. "What is it?"

From the hallway came the voice of Nilgir Sumanand. "My lord, I beg your pardon for disturbing you, but Prince Dekkeret is here to see you, and he will not wait. It is a very urgent matter, so the prince tells me," said the aide-de-camp, with a certain note of dubiety in his tone. And then another voice, Dekkeret's, saying impatiently, "No, no, not Prince Dekkeret. Just Dekkeret, that's all."

Prestimion frowned. He was rumpled and bleary-faced, stale from the long night's unrest. "Tell him to wait a moment, will you, while I put myself together a little."

"I could let him know, if you wish, that it would be better for him to return later in the day."

Dekkeret seemed to be speaking again out there, explaining something to Nilgir Sumanand in low, emphatically stressed phrases. Prestimion choked back his annoyance. This could go on all morning if he didn't intervene. He strode to the door and pulled it open. Nilgir Sumanand, looking half-asleep, blinked up apologetically at him. Dekkeret stood just behind the older man, looming up like a wall.

"You see, sir," Nilgir Sumanand said, "he rousted me up and very insistently declared—"

"Yes. I quite understand. It's not a problem. You can go, Nilgir Sumanand."

Prestimion beckoned Dekkeret into his suite.

"I very much regret the earliness of the hour, my lord," Dekkeret began. "But in view of the gravity of the situation and the importance of this new development, I felt that it would be wrong to wait until—"

"Never mind all that, Dekkeret, and get to the point. If I hear one more groveling apology I'll explode. Just tell me what all this is about."

"Someone has come to us in the night from the Procurator's camp. I think you'll be very interested in what he's brought us. Very interested indeed, lordship!"

"Ah, will I be, now?" said Prestimion, ashen-voiced. Already he regretted having allowed himself to be burst in upon this way. Dantirya Sambail had sent a message, evidently. An ultimatum, perhaps. Well, whatever it was, it probably could have kept a little longer.

But Dekkeret was throbbing with barely contained excitement; and that, too, made things worse. Suddenly Prestimion felt an almost paralyzing sense of tremendous fatigue. The sleepless night, the strain of the recent weeks, the onslaught of self-doubt and self-accusation that he had lately launched against himself, all were taking their toll. And there was something about Dekkeret's youthful bubbling exuberance, his awkward coltish eagerness to please, that intensified Prestimion's own sense of exhaustion. He was still a relatively young man himself; but right now he felt at least as old as Confalume. It was as if Dekkeret, bounding in here full of energy and vigor and hope, had in just these few moments drained him of whatever vitality he still had left.

It would be cruel and foolish, he knew, to dismiss Dekkeret out of hand. And this ostensible message from the Procurator, though it probably was just some mocking screed, was at least worth hearing about. Wearily Prestimion signaled Dekkeret to proceed.

*   *   *

"When we were at Inner Temple, my lord, you told me that you had donned the silver circlet of your mother the Lady, and had looked out into the mind of the world as she does every night. It was like being a god, you said. The circlet permits the Lady to be everywhere on Majipoor in a single moment, is what you told me. And yet, you said, there are limitations to the godhood of the wearer of the circlet. The Lady can enter the mind of a dreamer and take part in his dream, and interpolate certain thoughts of her own, offer guidance, even a degree of solace. But to shape the dream herself, or to create a dream and implant it in a sleeping mind—no. To give commands to the sleeper that must be obeyed—no. Do I have it correctly, my lord?"

Prestimion nodded. He was maintaining his patience through a supreme effort of self-control.

"And what I told you then, sir, is that the device that Venghenar Barjazid used on me in Suvrael is far more powerful than anything that is available to the Lady, and that if he allies himself with Dantirya Sambail, together they will shake the world to pieces. And as we have recently discovered, lordship, Barjazid has reached the Procurator's camp, and has begun to use his devilish device on Dantirya Sambail's behalf."

Prestimion offered a second curt nod. "You tell me a great many things I already know, Dekkeret. Where are you going with all this? There's been a message, you said, from Dantirya Sambail?"

"Oh, no, lordship, I never said that. What has come is not from Dantirya Sambail but from his camp, and it is not a message but a messenger. May I ask him to come in here, my lord? He's waiting just outside."

More and more mystifying. Prestimion assented with a perfunctory wave of his hand.

Dekkeret went to the door and called someone in from the hall.

A boy, it was, fifteen or perhaps sixteen years old, slender and hard-eyed and self-possessed. There was something oddly familiar about his features—those thin lips, that narrow jaw. He looked like a street-beggar of some sort, deeply tanned, dressed in little more than tattered rags, his cheeks and forehead marked by the scars of newly healing scratches as though he had been scrambling through brambles not very long before. Dangling from his left hand was a bulging burlap sack.

"My lord," said Dekkeret, "this is Dinitak Barjazid. Venghenar Barjazid's son."

Prestimion made a spluttering sound of astonishment. "If this is some sort of joke, Dekkeret—"

"Not at all, lordship."

Prestimion stared at the boy, who was looking back at him with a curious expression that seemed to be compounded equally of awe and defiance. And—yes, by the Divine—he was plainly his father's son! These were the elder Barjazid's features that Prestimion saw before him. All of Venghenar Barjazid's savage determination and fiery drive were mirrored in the taut lines of the boy's face. But that face lacked some key aspects of his father's. It was insufficiently crafty, Prestimion thought; it did not project the disingenuous subtlety of Venghenar Barjazid; there was no glint of treachery in the boy's eyes. Time, no doubt, would put those things there. Or perhaps old Barjazid had created an improved model of himself in this boy, one that knew better how to conceal the darkness within.

"Will you explain?" Prestimion said, after a time. "Or shall we just go on standing here like this?"

But there was no rushing Dekkeret, it seemed. He was evidently determined to do this at his own rhythm. "I know this boy well, my lord. I met him for the first time in Suvrael, on that journey I took through the desert, the time when his father amused himself by playing with my mind. And when I seized the dream-stealing machine from the father and said I would bring it—and him—to Castle Mount to show to the Coronal and the Council, it was this boy who urged old Barjazid to cooperate. 'We should go,' he said. 'It is our great moment of opportunity.'"

"An opportunity to carry their mischief right into the Castle, eh?"

"No, lordship. Not at all. The old man, my lord, is a

rascal. He has nothing but evil on his mind. The boy you see here is something quite different."

"Is he, now?"

"Let him tell you himself," said Dekkeret.

Prestimion felt his eyes beginning to sag shut. What he really wanted more than anything was to have these two go away and permit him to get some sleep. But no: no, he must get to the heart of this mystery. He indicated to young Barjazid that he should speak.

"My lord—" the boy began.

He looked toward Prestimion, then to Dekkeret, then to Prestimion again. It was curious, Prestimion thought, how his face changed as he turned from one to the other. For Prestimion he donned a look of deep respect, almost subservience. But it was a desultory and mechanical expression, a subject's automatic acknowledgment that he was in the presence of the Coronal Lord of Majipoor and nothing more; and Prestimion thought he saw a subtext even of resentment there, a hidden unwillingness to concede full acceptance of the power that the Coronal indeed wielded over him.

When Dinitak Barjazid looked at Dekkeret, though, a glow came into the boy's eyes that spoke of sheer worship. He seemed mesmerized by Dekkeret's personal force, his charisma, his vibrant strength. Perhaps it is because they are closer in age, Prestimion thought. He sees me as a member of some senior generation. But it was a distressing demonstration of the erosion of his own youthful vigor that just these few years at the summit of power had brought about.

"My lord," the young Barjazid was saying, "when my father and I came to the Castle, it was my hope that we could offer the dream-machine to you, that we could enroll ourselves in your service and make ourselves of value. But through some error we were imprisoned instead. This left my father greatly embittered, though I said again and again that it was a mistake."

Yes, Prestimion thought. And I could tell you whose mistake it was, too.

"Then we escaped. It was through the help of an old friend of my father's that we did. But the Procurator of Ni-moya's people were also involved. He has his influence among the Castle guards, you know." Prestimion exchanged a glance with Dekkeret at that, but said nothing. "And so it was to the Procurator, who seemed to be our only ally, to whom we fled," the boy continued. "To his camp in the Stoienzar Peninsula. And there we learned that it is the Procurator's plan to wage war against your lordship and against his majesty the Pontifex, and make himself the master of the world."

That phrase had a fine resonant sound, Prestimion thought: master of the world. He speaks very well, Prestimion told himself. No doubt the boy's been rehearsing this little speech for weeks.

But it was a struggle to pay attention. Another wave of weariness had come over him. He realized that he had begun rocking rhythmically back and forth on his feet in an effort to keep himself awake.

—"My lord?" the boy said. "Are you not well, my lord?"

"Just a little tired, is all," he said. Mustering all his self-control, he brought himself up toward something close to wakefulness again. It was very shrewd of the boy to have noticed, in the midst of his own narrative, that I was flagging, Prestimion thought. He poured a drink of water for himself. "How old did you say you were, boy?"

"Sixteen next month, sir."

"Sixteen next month. Interesting. All right, go on. Dantirya Sambail wants to be master of the world, you were saying."

"I said to my father when we heard that, 'There is no future for us in this place. We will only find trouble here.' And also I said to him, 'We should not be part of this rebellion. The Coronal will destroy this man Dantirya Sambail, and we will be destroyed along with him.' But my father is full of anger and bitterness. It is not that he is an evil man so much as he is an angry one. His soul is full of hatred. I could not tell you why that is. When I said that we should leave the camp of Dantirya Sambail, he struck me."

"Struck you?"

Prestimion could see the fury in the boy's eyes, even now.

"Indeed, my lord. Lashed out at me the way you might lash out at a beast that had nipped at your foot. Told me I was a fool and a child; told me I was incapable of seeing where our true advantage lay; told me—well, no matter what he told me, my lord. It was nothing very pretty. That night I left the Procurator's camp and slipped away through the jungle." Again the boy glanced at Dekkeret, that same worshipful glance. "I had heard, my lord, that Prince Dekkeret was in Stoien city. I decided that I would go to Prince Dekkeret and enroll in his service."

"In his service," Prestimion said. "Not mine, but his, eh? How flattering that must sound to you, Dekkeret. Prince Dekkeret, I should say. Since everyone seems to think you're a prince, I suppose I'll have to make you one when we get back to the Castle, won't I?"

A look of shock appeared on Dekkeret's usually stolid face. "My lord, I have never aspired—"

"No. No. Forgive my sarcasm, Dekkeret." I must be very tired indeed, Prestimion thought, to be saying such things as that. Once more he glanced toward Dinitak Barjazid. "And so. To continue. You made your way through the jungle—"

"Yes, my lord. It is not a pleasant journey, my lord. But it was one that I had to make. —Shall I show it to him now, Prince Dekkeret?" he asked, looking aside.

"Show it, yes."

The boy reached down and scooped up the burlap sack, which had been lying at his feet all this while. He drew from it an intricate circular object fashioned of rods and wires of several different metals delicately woven together, gold and silver and copper and perhaps one or two more, with a series of glittering inlaid stones and crystals, sapphire and serpentine and emerald and what looked like hematite, affixed along its inner surface within an ivory frame. It had something of the look of a royal crown, or perhaps some talismanic instrument of magery, on the order of a rohilla, though much larger. But what it actually was, Prestimion saw, was a mechanism of some sort.

"This," the boy said proudly, holding the thing forth for Prestimion's inspection, "is one of the three working models of the dream-machine. I took it from my father's tent in the jungle and brought it safely here. And I am willing to show you how to use it in your war against the rebels."

The coolly delivered statement struck Prestimion like a bolt from on high.

"May I see it?" he asked, when he had regained a little of his steadiness.

"Of course, my lord."

He placed it in Prestimion's hands. It was a beautiful gleaming thing of complex and elegant design, scarcely heavier than a feather, that seemed almost to be throbbing with the force of the power locked up within it.

Prestimion realized that this was not the first time he had seen something like this. During the civil war, when they were camped in the Marraitis meadowlands west of the Jhelum River on the eve of the great battle that soon would be fought there, he had gone into the tent of the Vroon Thalnap Zelifor and observed him working over an object of somewhat similar design. It was, the Vroon had explained, a device that would enable him when it was perfected to amplify the waves coming from the minds of others, and read their inmost thoughts, and place thoughts of his own into their heads. In time he had indeed perfected it, and eventually it had fallen into the hands of Venghenar Barjazid, and now—now—

Abruptly Prestimion lifted the instrument toward his own forehead.

"My lord, no!" the young Barjazid cried.

"No? Why is that?"

"You must have the training, first. There is tremendous strength in the instrument that you hold. You'll injure yourself, my lord, if you simply put it to your head like that."

"Ah. Perhaps so." He handed the thing back to the boy as though it were about to explode.

Could it be, he wondered, that this youngster had actually

brought him the one weapon that might give him hope of
countering the uprising that confronted him?

To Dekkeret he said, "What do we have here, do you
think? Is this boy to be trusted? Or is it all some new plot
of Dantirya Sambail's to send him here among us?"

"Trust him, my lord," Dekkeret said. "Oh, I beg you,
Lord Prestimion: trust him!"

12

TRAVELERS RETURNING TO CASTLE Mount from Stoien began their eastward journey by going up along the coast to
Treymone, where they could take a boat up the River Trey
as far as it was navigable. Then it was necessary to swing
to the north to avoid the grim desert that surrounded the
ruins of the ancient Metamorph capital of Velalisier. The
route led up into the broad, fertile valley of the River Iyann,
which they would traverse as far as Three Rivers, where the
Iyann took off on its northward journey. There one turned
slightly to the south again, entering the grassy plain known
as the Vale of Gloyn, and crossed west-central Alhanroel to
the midlands mercantile center of Sisivondal, where the
main highway to the Mount could be found. From there it
was a straight path across the heart of the continent to the
foothills of the mighty peak.

Prestimion had provided Varaile and Akbalik with a
floater of the most capacious sort for their homeward journey to the capital. They rode in cushioned comfort while
platoons of tireless Skandar drivers guided the big swift vehicles as they hovered just above the bed of the highway.
An armed escort of Skandar troops occupying half a dozen
armor-shelled military floaters accompanied them, three vehicles preceding theirs and three traveling aft, as safeguards
against any disturbances that the convoy might encounter.
Not that any sane man would dare to lift his hand against
the Coronal's consort, but sanity was beginning to be a com-
modity in short supply in these districts, and Prestimion intended to take no chances. Again and again, as the floaters

halted briefly for supplies in some town or village along the
way, Varaile saw wild, distorted faces peering at her from
the roadside, and heard the harsh cackling cries of the de-
mented. The Skandars, though, kept all these troubled folk
at a safe distance.

They were beyond Gloyn now, moving along through a
series of unfamiliar places with such names as Drone, Hun-
zimar, Gannamunda. So far Varaile had had a fairly easy
time of the journey. She had expected much more discomfort, especially as the passing days brought her ever closer
to the hour when the new Prince Taradath would enter the
world. But aside from the growing heaviness of her body,
the sagging weight of her swelling belly, the occasional
throbbings in her legs, the pregnancy had little effect on her
well-being. Varaile had never given much thought to moth-
erhood—she had not even had any lovers, before Prestimion
had come like a whirlwind into her life and swept her
away—but she was tall and strong and young, and she could
see now that she was going to withstand whatever stresses
were involved in childbirth without serious challenge.

Akbalik, though—it was clear to Varaile that he was
finding the trip east very much of an ordeal.

His infected leg seemed to be getting worse. He said
nothing about it to her, of course, not a word of complaint.
But his forehead glistened with sweat much of the time,
now, and his face was flushed as though he suffered from
a constant fever. Now and again she would catch him biting
his lower lip to hold back pain, or he would turn away from
her and let a stifled groan escape his lips while she pretended
not to notice. It was important to Akbalik, Varaile saw, to
maintain a pose of good health, or at least of steady recovery. But it was easy enough to tell that all that was a mere
facade.

How sick was he, really? Could his life be in danger,
perhaps?

Varaile knew what high regard Prestimion had for Akbalik. He was a bulwark of the throne. It was possible, even,
that Prestimion saw Akbalik as a likely choice for Coronal
in case anything should happen to old Confalume and it

became necessary for Prestimion to move along to the senior throne. "A Coronal has to keep the succession in mind all the time," Prestimion had said to her more than once. "At any moment he can find himself transformed into a Pontifex—and it'll go badly for the world if there's no one ready to take over for him at the Castle."

If Prestimion had already selected the man he would call upon in such an eventuality, he had never said a thing about it to her. Coronals did not like to talk about such matters, apparently—not even with their wives. But she saw already that Septach Melayn, though Prestimion loved him more than any other man in the world, was too whimsical a person to entrust with the throne, and Gialaurys, Prestimion's other dear great friend, was too credulous and slow.

Who, then? Navigorn? A strong man, but troubled greatly by what looked very much like the onset of the madness. There was Dekkeret, of course: full of promise and ability and fervor. But he was ten years too young for a Coronal's high responsibilities. Very likely he would be horrified if Prestimion were to turn to him tomorrow and offer him the starburst crown.

Which left only Akbalik, really. To lose Akbalik to the stupid bite of a vicious little Stoienzar crab, then, would be a terrible blow to all of Prestimion's plans. Especially in a challenging time like this, when troubles seemed to sprout like mushrooms on every side.

We will be in Sisivondal before long, Varaile thought. That was an important city: her father had owned warehouses there, she remembered, and a bank, and a meat packaging company. Surely there would be competent doctors in a city like that. Would it be possible to persuade Akbalik to go to one of them for treatment? It would have to be handled very delicately. "Akbalik was so wonderfully sensible that we all used to go to him for advice about our problems," Prestimion had told her. "But the wound has changed him. He's turned touchy and strange. You have to be very careful not to offend him, now." But certainly she had legitimate reasons of her own now for wanting to stop in Sisivondal for a medical checkup; and would it greatly upset him, she

wondered, if she were to suggest in a mild sort of way that
he might just as well get that leg of his looked at too, while
they were there?

She would try it. She had to.

Sisivondal, though, was still many hundreds of miles
away. It was too soon to bring the subject up.

They sat side by side in silence, watching for hour after
hour as the flat monotonous landscape of west central Alhanroel's dusty drylands flowed past their windows.

"Can you tell me if any battles were fought here in the
civil war?" Varaile asked him, finally, purely for the sake
of having some sort of conversation at all.

Akbalik looked at her strangely. "How would I know,
milady?"

"I thought—well—"

"That I fought in it? I suppose I did, milady. Many of us
did. But no memory of it remains to me. You understand
why that is, do you not?"

Fresh perspiration had broken out on his brow and
cheeks. His deep-set gray eyes, nearly always bloodshot
now, took on a haunted look. Varaile regretted having said
anything at all.

"I know what the mages did at Thegomar Edge, yes,"
she said. "But—listen, Akbalik, if talking about the war is
something painful for you—"

He seemed scarcely to have heard her. "As I understand
it, there were no engagements close by here," he said, looking not at her but at the scene outside, a parched brown
landscape punctuated by occasional sparse clumps of gray-
green trees that grew in strange spiral coils. "There was a
battle northwest of here, at the reservoir on the Iyann. And
something by the Jhelum, off to the south, and one in Arkilon plain, I think Prestimion said. And of course the one
at Thegomar Edge, which is far off to the southeast. But the
war bypassed this region, so I do believe." Akbalik turned
suddenly in his seat to stare at her with wild-eyed intensity.

"You know, do you not, milady, that I fought against Lord Prestimion in the war?

Varaile would not have been more startled if he had revealed himself just then to be a Shapeshifter. "No," she said, with as much control as she could muster. "No, I had no idea! You were on Korsibar's side? But how can that be, Akbalik? Prestimion thinks the world of you, you know!"

"And I of him, milady. But even so, I believe I was on the other side during the rebellion."

"You only believe that you were? You aren't sure?"

Something that could have been a spasm of pain passed across his face. He tried to turn it into a wry smile. "I told you, no memory of the war remains to me, or to any of us, except for Prestimion and Septach Melayn and Gialaurys. But I was at the Castle when the war broke out, that much I know. Even though the manner of Korsibar's coming to the throne would have to have been unusual and irregular, I still would have regarded him, I think, as the true Coronal, simply because he had been anointed and crowned. So if I had been asked to fight on his behalf—and certainly Korsibar would have asked me—I would have done so. Korsibar was at the Castle, and Prestimion was off in the provinces, raising armies from the local people. Most of the Castle princes would necessarily have served as officers in what would have been regarded as the legitimate royal army. I know that Navigorn did. And I, being Prince Serithorn's nephew, would surely not have defied my powerful uncle by going off to join Prestimion."

Varaile's head was swimming. "Serithorn was on Korsibar's side too?"

"You ask me about things I no longer remember, lady. But yes, I think he was, at least some of the time. It was a very complicated period. It was not easy to know who was on which side, much of the time."

He half-rose, suddenly, wincing.

"Akbalik, are you all right?"

"It's nothing, milady. Nothing. The healing process—a little painful, sometimes—" Akbalik managed another unconvincing smile. "Let us finish with the war, shall we?—Do you see, now, why Lord Prestimion wiped it all from our minds? It was the wisest thing. I would rather be his friend unto death than his former enemy; and now I have no recollection of ever having been his enemy, if indeed I ever was. Nor has Navigorn. Septach Melayn has told me that Navigorn was Korsibar's most important general; but all that is forgotten, and Prestimion trusts him implicitly in all things. The war is gone from us. Therefore the war can never be a factor in our dealings with one another. And therefore—"

Another groan came from him now, one that he was altogether unable to conceal. Akbalik's eyes rolled wildly in his head, and sweat seemed to burst from his every pore, coating his face with a bright sheen. He started to rise, spun about, fell back against the cushion of his seat, shivering convulsively.

"Akbalik—Akbalik!"

"Milady," he murmured. But he seemed lost in delirium, suddenly. "The leg—I don't know—it—it—"

She seized a pitcher of water, poured some for him, forced the glass between his lips. He gulped it and nodded faintly for more. Then he closed his eyes. For a moment Varaile thought he had died; but no, no, he still was breathing. A very sick man, though. Very sick. She dipped a cloth in the water and mopped his burning forehead with it.

Then, hastening to the fore cabin, she rapped on the frame of the door to get the driver's attention. The driver, a brown-furred Skandar named Varthan Gutarz, who wore amulets of some Skandar cult around the meaty biceps of three of his four arms, was hunched over the floater's controls, but he looked up quickly.

"Milady?"

"How long before we're in Sisivondal?"

The Skandar glanced at the instruments. "Six hours, maybe, milady."

"Get us there in four. And when you do, head straight for the biggest hospital in town. Prince Akbalik is seriously ill."

*   *   *

Sisivondal appeared to be a thousand miles of outskirts. The flat dry central plain went on and on, practically treeless, now, the emptiness broken only by little clusters of tin-roofed shacks, then more emptiness, then another small group of shacks, perhaps twice as many as before, and then emptiness, emptiness, emptiness, with some scattered warehouses and repair shops after that. And gradually the outskirts coalesced into suburbs, and then into a city, a city of great size.

And great ugliness. Varaile had seen few ugly places in her recent travels about the world, but Sisivondal was somber indeed, a commercial city with no beauty of any sort. Many major roads met here. Much of the merchandise being shipped from Alaisor port to Castle Mount or to the cities of northern Alhanroel had to pass through Sisivondal. It was a starkly functional city, mile after mile of gigantic warehouses fronting broad plain boulevards. Even the plants of Sisivondal were dull and utilitarian: stubby purple-leaved camaganda palms that could stand up easily to the interminable months of Sisivondal's long rainless season, which lasted most of the year, and massive lumma-lummas, which could be mistaken for big gray rocks by the casual eye, and the tough prickly rosettes of garavedas, which took a whole century to produce the tall black spike that bore their flowers.

It looked as though the boulevard that had brought them in from the west would take them straight to the center of town. Varaile saw now that the incoming roads were like the spokes of a great wheel, linked by circular avenues that diminished in sweep as they moved inward. The public buildings would be at the center. There had to be a major hospital among them.

Akbalik was dying. She was certain of that now.

He was only intermittently conscious. Very little of what he said made sense. He had one lucid moment in which he opened his eyes and said to her that the swamp-crab's poison must finally have reached his heart; but the rest of the time he babbled of things that she could not comprehend, jumbled accounts of tournaments and duels, hunting trips, even fist-fights—boyhood memories, perhaps. Sometimes she heard the name of Prestimion, or that of Septach Melayn, or even Korsibar's. That was odd, that he would be speaking of Korsibar. But her father had done the same in the throes of his madness, she reminded herself.

The hospital, at last. To her dismay Varaile found that the chief doctor was a Ghayrog, a terribly alien thing to encounter at such a time. He was dour-faced and aloof, remarkably unimpressed at finding the wife of the Coronal standing before him and urging him to drop everything he might be doing so that he could look after the nephew of Prince Serithorn.

The forked reptilian tongue moved in and out with disconcerting rapidity. The gray-green reptilian eyes displayed little compassion. The calm and measured voice might have been that of a machine. "You come at a very difficult moment, milady. The operating rooms are all in use now. We have been overwhelmed with all manner of unusual problems here, which—"

Varaile cut him off. "I'm sure that that's so. But have you heard of Prince Serithorn of Samivole, doctor? By the divine, have you heard the name of Lord Prestimion? This man is Serithorn's nephew. He is a member of the Coronal's inner circle. He needs immediate treatment."

"The Messenger of the Mysteries is among us today, milady. I will ask him to intercede with the gods of the city on behalf of this man." And the Ghayrog beckoned to a mysterious, sinister figure in the hallway, a man who wore a strange wooden mask, that of a yellow-eyed hound with long pointed ears.

She felt a surge of fury. The gods of the city? By the Divine, what was the creature talking about? "A magus, you mean? No, doctor, not a magus. Medical help is what we came here for."

"The Messenger of the Mysteries—"

"Can bring his message to someone else. You will place Prince Akbalik in your care this moment, doctor, or I tell you, and I swear it by whatever god you may happen to believe in, that I will have Lord Prestimion shut this hospital and transfer every member of its staff to the back end of Suvrael. Is that clear enough?" She snapped her fingers at one of her Skandar escorts. "Mikzin Hrosz, I want you to go through this place and get the name of every doctor in it, and everyone else's name, too, down to the Liimen who swab down the operating tables. And then—"

But the recalcitrant Ghayrog had had enough. He was giving orders of his own, now; and suddenly there was a gurney to place Akbalik on, suddenly there were earnest-faced young interns, Ghayrogs and humans both, gathered around it. They wheeled Akbalik away. The Messenger of the Mysteries marched along beside the gurney as though it was the plan to give him the benefit not only of conventional medical treatment but also of the fantastic religious cult that seemed to have taken hold of this city.

Varaile herself was offered a comfortable room in which to wait. But she did not have to wait long. The Ghayrog doctor returned soon. His mien was as frosty as ever; but when he spoke there was a gentleness in his tone that had not been there before. "What I was trying to tell you, mi-lady, was simply that no useful purpose would be served in interrupting the care of some other seriously ill patient to look after Prince Akbalik, because I could see immediately that the prince's condition was already so critical that—that—"

"That he's dead?" she cried. "Is that what you're trying to tell me?"

But she could read the answer in his face even before he managed to speak the words.

13

NOT EVEN IN THE most unfettered dreams of his boyhood had Dekkeret ever imagined himself in the midst of a scene such as this. A palatial royal suite atop a towering building in Stoien city, halfway across the world from his native city

of Normork on Castle Mount. Standing just to his right: the
Coronal Lord of Majipoor, Prestimion of Muldemar, with a
dark and brooding expression on his face. Behind the Coronal his Su-Suheris sorcerer, Maundigand-Klimd, on whom
he seemed to rely for advice in all things. On his other side,
the sublime Lady of the Isle of Sleep, the Princess Therissa,
with the silver circlet of her office around her brow. Across
the room, the boy Dinitak Barjazid of Suvrael, holding in
his hands the sinister thought-controlling helmet that he had
stolen from his treacherous father in the rebel camp.

The fate of the world was in the hands of these people.
And somehow Dekkeret of Normork found himself in their
midst as everything unfolded. No, not even in a dream
would he have indulged in such a fantasy. Nevertheless,
here he was. Here he was.

"Let me see that thing again, boy," the Princess Therissa
said to Dinitak Barjazid.

He brought the helmet to her. His hands trembled as he
put it in hers. He too, Dekkeret thought, is astonished to find
himself in the thick of events such as these.

She had already examined it extensively, its metallic
wires and its crystal and ivory attachments. And she and the
boy had had a long discussion, utterly incomprehensible to
Dekkeret and evidently to the Coronal as well, of its technical aspects.

The device was beautiful, in its sinister way. It reminded
Dekkeret of some of the implements of sorcery that that
deranged magus had destroyed, just before jumping overboard himself, during the riverboat journey that he and Akbalik had made from Piliplok to Ni-moya.

But this helmet was a scientific instrument, not any kind
of magical apparatus at all. Perhaps that made it all the more
frightening. Dekkeret did not have much faith in the work-
ings of magic, though he was well aware that some mages—
not all—had genuine powers. Most of what the sorcerers
did, he was convinced, was fraud and charlatanry designed
to awe the credulous. Maundigand-Klimd himself had said
as much more than once. But this helmet was something
other than a charlatan's gimcrack. Dekkeret had heard the

Lady and Dinitak Barjazid speaking of the instrument not in terms of the demons one could invoke through it by uttering certain spells, but in terms of its ability to amplify and transmit brain-waves by electrical means. That did not sound like sorcery to him. And he knew that the Barjazid helmet worked. He had felt its terrible power himself.

The Lady put her own circlet aside and held the helmet above her head.

Prestimion said, "Mother, do you think you should?"

She smiled. "I've had more than a little experience with devices of this sort, Prestimion. And Dinitak has explained the basic principles of this one to me:"

She donned it. Touched the controls, made small adjustments.

Dekkeret could hardly bear to watch as she allowed the power of the device to enter her. She was, he thought, the most beautiful woman he had ever seen, ageless, glorious, altogether superb. Her regal grace of bearing, her serene features, her splendid lustrous black hair, her elegantly simple robe with that astonishing purple-red jewel gleaming in its golden hoop on her bosom—oh, truly she was the queen of the world! What if this monstrous machine of the Barjazids were to damage her mind as it lay upon her brow? What if she were to cry out and turn pale before them, and crumple and fall?

She did not cry out. She did not fall. She stood as erect as ever, utterly motionless, transfixed by whatever she was experiencing: transported, it would seem, to some far-off realm.

There was no indication that the helmet was harming her. But a frown appeared on her smooth white forehead as the moments went on, and her lips tightened and turned downward in a grim expression that Dekkeret had never seen on her face before, and when, after what had seemed to him like an eternity, she finally raised the helmet from her brow and handed it back to Dinitak, there was the barest hint of a tremor in her fingers.

"Extraordinary," she said. Her voice sounded deeper than usual, almost hoarse. She pointed to her circlet, lying before her on a table. "It makes this seem like a toy."

"What was it like, mother? Can you describe it?" Prestimion asked.

"You would have to put it on yourself to understand. And you are far from ready for that." Her gaze came to rest on young Barjazid. "I felt your father's presence. I touched his mind with mine." That was all she seemed to want to say about her contact with the elder Barjazid; but Dinitak's face grew stern and dark as though he could understand precisely what she must have felt. Turning again to Prestimion, she added, "I encountered the Procurator's mind too. He is a demon, that man."

"You can actually identify individual minds, your worship?" Dekkeret asked.

"Those two stood out like beacons," the Lady replied. "But yes, yes, I think I could find others, with some practice. I sensed the emanations of Septach Melayn farther to the east—I do think it was he I touched—and perhaps Gialaurys, or it might have been Navigorn. They are moving toward him through the most terrible of jungles."

"What of my wife? And Akbalik?"

The Lady Therissa shook her head. "I made no attempt to rove as far from here as they must be by now." And, to Dinitak: "I found your father so easily because he was wearing the helmet too. When I cast my mind forth to see what I could find, the first thing I felt was the mental broadcast coming from him. The one he has is more powerful than this, isn't it, boy?"

"It is, ma'am, yes. A later model. I didn't dare try to take it: it never leaves his side."

"He's employing it to spread the madness, just as we feared. I saw how easily that can be done. The spell of forgetfulness that you had the mages cast at the end of the war, Prestimion: just as you said, it created places of impairment in many minds, structural weaknesses, easily breached. Not much stress is needed to break through them. And if this man, using his helmet, simply touches such people—"

A sound that seemed almost to be one of pain came from

Prestimion. "Mother, this has to be stopped!"

His anguish was profound. Dekkeret stared at him in horror.

"That may not be so simple," said Maundigand-Klimd somberly. "He is using the helmet to defend himself and his master against attack, is he not, Lady Therissa?"

"Yes. You sensed that, didn't you? He's setting up some kind of shield that made it difficult for me to make contact with him. Even when I did at last penetrate it, I met with great murkiness. And could not tell you, within five hundred miles, where his camp is located."

"Of course you couldn't," Prestimion said. "There's every likelihood that Barjazid's using the helmet to keep Dantirya Sambail's camp concealed from attackers. Akbalik spoke of that. 'A cloud of unknowingness,' he called it. He thought the Procurator might be using a magus to create it for him with some sort of incantation. But then, when I told him Dekkeret's tale of his encounter with Barjazid and his helmet in Suvrael, Akbalik suggested that Dantirya Sambail's constant disappearances were probably Barjazid's work."

"You may be certain of it, my lord," said Dinitak. "It is no difficult thing to use the helmet to cast this cloud of unknowingness, as you term it, over someone's mind. I could do it myself. I could stand right here and you would think I had vanished before your eyes."

Prestimion turned toward the boy. "Do you think," he said, "that one of these helmets could be used to counteract the power of another?"

"That should be possible, my lord. It would not be an easy thing—my father is highly adept with these devices, and he is always a dangerous opponent—but yes, I think it can be done."

"Well, then. The answer to our problem's obvious. We use the helmet we have here for a counterstrike. If all goes well for us, we remove Barjazid and his device from the equation, and the spreading of the madness is ended, and Septach Melayn and Gialaurys will be able to find and attack

Dantirya Sambail. What do you say, mother? Is that something you think you could do?"

The Lady Therissa met her son's gaze levelly. And said in a flat calm tone without any warmth in it at all, "I'm accustomed to using my powers for healing, Prestimion. Not for making war. Not for launching attacks on people—even someone like this man Barjazid. Or Dantirya Sambail."

Her unexpected response obviously jarred Prestimion badly. His eyes flashed amazement and color flared in his cheeks. He regained his poise quickly, though, and said, "Oh, mother, you mustn't think of it as an attack! Or at least try to see it simply as a counterattack. They are the aggressors. What would you be doing, if not defending innocent people against their attacks?"

"Perhaps. Perhaps." But the Lady sounded unconvinced. A certain darkening of her brow revealed the depths of the conflict within her. "You also need to bear in mind, Prestimion, that I barely know how to use this thing. Before we can even think of using it as you suggest, I'd need to gain more skill with it—to master its subtleties, to get a deeper understanding of its power and range. All that will take time. Assuming that I agree to do such a thing at all. And I am by no means sure that I will."

The look of exasperation on Prestimion's face intensified. "Time? We have no time! There are two armies of ours in that horrible jungle at this very moment. How long do you think I can keep them sitting there, mother? And the madness, spreading hour by hour at that man's hands—no. No. We need to strike right away. You have to do it, mother!"

The Lady did not reply. She enfolded herself in her regal grandeur and calmly regarded her son in silence—a silence that was itself an answer, Dekkeret thought. The temperature in the room seemed to approach the freezing point. A quarrel between the Coronal and the Lady of the Isle: what an extraordinary thing that was to find oneself witnessing!

Then the high, clear voice of Dinitak Barjazid broke through the frosty stillness: "I could do it, my lord, if the Lady won't. I could. I know I could."

"You would strike out against your own father?" Dekkeret cried at once, amazed.

The boy looked at him scornfully, as though Dekkeret had said something impossibly naive. "Oh, Prince Dekkeret, why not? If he chooses to make himself the enemy of all the world, surely he's my enemy as well. Why did I bring this helmet here, if not to offer it for use against him? Why did I flee from him at all?" His eyes were shining. His whole face was aflame with youthful zeal. "I am here to serve, Prince Dekkeret. In any way that I can."

Prestimion was staring at him too, Dekkeret realized.

He understood suddenly that young Barjazid had put him in a precarious position. He was the one who had brought the boy to Prestimion, after all. He was the one who had urged the Coronal to have faith in him. From the moment Dekkeret had wrested the dream-stealing helmet out of the elder Barjazid's grasp in Suvrael, Dinitak had taken the position with his father that it would be wise for them to go with Dekkeret to Castle Mount and demonstrate the power of their device to Lord Prestimion.

But suppose what was happening now was—as Prestimion had proposed at the time of Dinitak's startling defection to his side in Stoien city—simply part of some intricately treacherous scheme of Dantirya Sambail's? What if the boy, wearing the helmet that he claimed to have brought here for the sake of putting it at the Coronal's service, were to join forces across these thousands of miles with his father in Stoienzar, who was wearing one of the others? Together they would create an invulnerable force.

It was a rash gamble, Dekkeret thought. They were staking everything on a ragged youngster in whose veins ran the blood of a man for whom betrayal and deceit were as natural as breathing. Could they risk it?

And yet—even so—

"What do you say, Dekkeret?" the Coronal asked. "Shall we accept the boy's offer?"

Dekkeret looked past Prestimion toward the aloof and enigmatic figure of Maundigand-Klimd, who had remained on the periphery of the discussion throughout.

Help me, he begged the Su-Suheris, speaking only with
his eyes. I am beyond my depth here. Help me. Help me.

Did Maundigand-Klimd understand?

Yes. Yes. The four green eyes of the magus were looking
directly into his own. From the left head came the slightest
of nods. Then a second one, from the right. And then again,
unmistakably, both heads nodding at once.

I thank you, Maundigand-Klimd. With all my heart.

In a bold voice Dekkeret said, "I told you when he first
came here that we should trust him, my lord. I still believe
that we should."

"So be it, then," Prestimion said immediately. Plainly he
had already made the same choice. He glanced toward
young Barjazid. "We'll meet again later today," he told the
boy, "to discuss how to go about making our counterstrike."
Then, to the Princess Therissa: "Mother, you are excused
from attending. I won't ask you to take part in this task,
since you find it so disagreeable, though I still have other
work for you." And finally, speaking this time to Dekkeret
and Dinitak and Maundigand-Klimd together: "You may go,
now, all of you. I want to have a few minutes alone with
my mother."

From a cabinet below the window Prestimion took a flask
of the wine of Muldemar, a rare vintage that he had brought
with him to Stoien from the Castle, and poured it liberally
for them. They saluted each other solemnly.

"I ask your pardon, mother," he said, when they had had
a few sips and put their bowls down. "It pained me very
much to put you into such a difficult position in front of the
others."

"I took no offense. You are the Coronal Lord, Prestimion:
you are responsible for the welfare of the world. These men
threaten us all, and you need to take action against them.
I'm willing to do all that I can to help you in that. But you
asked something of me that I'm not capable of giving."

"For which I'm sorry. I should have seen that before I

spoke. For you to employ your training and powers in order to commit an act of aggression—"

"You understand it now," she said, and smiled, and reached across to take his hand. She kissed it lightly, the merest brush of her lips against his skin. "But the attempt must be made, with or without me. Will the boy succeed in besting his father, I wonder? Just from my own brief contact with his mind, I can see how formidable he is. And how evil."

"If at the very least Dinitak can hamper his father somewhat, that will help. An unexpected jab that weakens his guard—a distraction—a diversion—" Prestimion shrugged. "Well, we'll see soon enough." He picked up the Lady's silver circlet, lying where she had left it on the table. The tingling sensation that heralded its power immediately manifested itself to him. "You need to give me further training in this," he said. "And I'll want to learn how to use the Barjazid helmet also. If I'm required to sit here far behind the battle lines, as everyone seems to insist, I want to be able to take whatever part in the struggle I possibly can, even at this distance."

"I can help you with that."

"Will you? The Barjazid device too?"

"Mastering it won't be easy for you. To use it is to ride the lightning. But yes, Prestimion—yes—I'll give you all the assistance I can. Which means I must learn to master the thing myself, I suppose. What wine is this? It's splendid stuff."

He laughed. "You don't recognize it? It comes from our own cellars, mother!"

She drank again, savoring the wine more closely this time, and asked him to fill her bowl once more.

"Gladly," he said. And then, after a little while: "Take up your circlet once again, if you will, mother. Cast your mind far afield for me. There are things I need to know. Tell me how my army fares in the Stoienzar jungles, and find Varaile for me as she travels eastward, and my poor suffering Akbalik."

"Yes. Of course." She donned the slender silver band and

closed her eyes for a moment, and when she opened them again Prestimion saw that she had slipped into the trance-state through which the wearer of the circlet was able to rove freely through the world. She seemed unaware of his presence entirely. He scarcely dared breathe. She was gone a long time; and then that far look, that look of absence, went from her eyes and she was herself again.

But she was silent. "Well?" Prestimion said, when he could wait no longer. "What did you see, mother?"

"It was Septach Melayn I encountered first. What a dear man he is, ever charming, ever elegant and graceful! And so deeply devoted to you."

"How does he fare, then?"

"I found him restless and troubled. He moves on and on through the jungle. But the enemy is nowhere to be found. His scouts come back again and again with reports of the Procurator's camp, but when the full army goes to the place, there is no one there. And apparently never was."

"The cloud of unknowingness," Prestimion said. "With young Barjazid's aid we'll help him overcome that. —And Varaile, and Akbalik?"

"They are far from here by now, are they not, well beyond the midpoint of the continent?"

"I certainly hope so. But crossing such a distance is no great task for you, is it?"

"No," she said, and returned to her trance. This time, when she emerged from it, her jaw was tightly set and her eyes looked alarmingly grim. Again she was maddeningly slow to speak. Evidently it took her some time to collect herself after these voyages.

"Is something the matter?" he burst out finally. "With Varaile? The baby?"

"No," she said. "All is well with your wife and the child she carries. —Your friend Akbalik, though—"

"His condition's grown worse, has it?"

She paused just a moment. "His suffering is over, Prestimion."

The quiet words hit with savage impact. For an instant Prestimion was almost stunned by them. Then, gradually recovering, he said quietly, "I sent him to his death when I let him go into that jungle. Not the first good man whose life was shortened on my account. Not the last, I fear. —I thought he might be Coronal after me, mother. That was how much regard I had for him."

"I know you loved him. I regret bringing you such tidings."

"I asked for them, mother."

She nodded. "There is more trouble, I think, in another quarter. I had only the barest suggestion of it as I cast my mind outward. Let me look again."

A third time she entered trance. Prestimion drained his wine-bowl and waited. This time when she came forth he threw no impatient questions at her.

"Yes," she said. "So I thought. There is a great fleet gathered on the coast of Zimroel, Prestimion. An armada, in truth. Scores of ships, perhaps more than a hundred, waiting at sea off Piliplok for Dantirya Sambail to give them the order to sail."

"So that's it! He's quietly been assembling an invasion force all this time, and now it's on the way! But how strange, mother, that it was able to come together unobserved, unreported—"

"I had the greatest difficulty in detecting it. It moves as though under cover of perpetual night, even in daytime."

"Of course. The cloud of unknowingness again! Which has hidden not just the Procurator from us, but an entire navy!" Prestimion rose. To his great surprise he felt a curious kind of tranquility stealing over him. The news was bad, most of it, but at least he had heard the worst of it now. "So be it," he said. "We know what kind of enemy we face, at any rate. We'd better get down to the job of dealing with him, eh, mother?"

"Darkness is coming on," Navigorn said. "Shall we make camp here, do you think?"

"Why not?" said Septach Melayn. "It's as bad a place as any, isn't it?"

And worse than some, he thought. It was a pity that
young Dekkeret was not along on this expedition: if he still
had the taste for penitence and punishment that had driven
him to undertake his journey to Suvrael, he would find these
jungles ideal for additional self-flagellation purposes. There
could be few regions in the world less hospitable than the
southern Stoienzar.

They had seen an endless procession of hideosities in
their westward journey through the peninsula. Trees that
sprouted and grew and died all in one day—springing out
of the ground at dawn, rising to a height of thirty feet by
noon, unfolding ugly black flowers then that gave off pungent noxious fumes, within another hour producing swollen
ripe fruit of the most intensely lethal sort, and finally per-
ishing of their own miserable poisonous nature by sunset.
Purple crabs as big as houses that came rumbling up out
their hiding-places in the sandy ground right under your
nose, clacking murderous claws sharp as scimitars. Black
snails that spit red acid at your ankles. And the damnable
vile sawpalms everywhere, the foul manganozas, gleefully
waving their savage fronds at you as though daring you to
come near their impenetrable and impassable thickets.

This campsite of Navigorn's, now: a broad, dusty gray
beach of sharp-edged gravel along the banks of a dry gravelly river. That was perfect, thought Septach Melayn. A
river that seemed to be altogether without water, that offered
the eye nothing but a long barren expanse of small broken
stones. There had to be water somewhere beneath its rocky
bed, though, for if one stood and watched for a time one
could see that the pebbles were in steady slow movement,
as though they were being dragged sluggishly along the
river's course by the force of an underground stream flowing
deep down below. To while away the time, he thought, you
could stand beside it and fish for precious stones, trying to
spy the occasional emerald or ruby or whatever, borne along
like a brightly glittering fish through all the dreary slow-
moving debris. But he suspected you could wait here for
fifty thousand years before you found anything worth finding. Or forever, perhaps.

Gialaurys stepped from his floater and came toward them. "Are we going to make our camp in this place?"

"Have you seen any better site?"

"There's no water here."

"But also no manganozas and no swamp-crabs," Navigorn said. "I could do with a night's respite from those. And in the morning we can go straight on toward the Procurator's camp."

Gialaurys laughed harshly and spat.

"No," said Navigorn. "This time we're actually going to find it. I have a feeling that we will."

"Yes," Septach Melayn said. "Of course we will."

He sauntered away from them and found a seat on a saddle-shaped boulder by the river's edge. Scaly many-legged things the size of his hand were rummaging for provender through the topmost level of the gravel, burrowing down to seize smaller creatures lurking below, then coming up to feed at the surface: bugs of some sort, he thought, or crustaceans, or maybe they were the air-breathing fishes of this dry river. Fishes with legs would fit well with a river that had no water. One of them clambered up atop the gravel and peered at him out of half a dozen bright, beady eyes as though it might be contemplating making a run at his ankle to sample his flavor. Everything wanted to bite you in the Stoienzar, even the plants. Septach Melayn shied a rock at the thing, not making any serious attempt to hit it, and it scrabbled out of sight.

For all the buoyancy of his resilient nature, this place was a severe test even for him. As for the others, they must be suffering intensely. The unremittingly hostile nature of the peninsula was so excessive that it was almost funny; but one could find amusement only so long in the challenges of a district where every moment brought some new discomfort or danger. And they were swiftly growing weary of the entire adventure. It was beginning to seem to everyone that they had been chasing after Dantirya Sambail all their lives: first in the east-country, then in Ketheron and Arvyanda and Sippulgar, and now on this interminable trek through the Stoienzar.

How long had they been in here, actually? Weeks? Months? One day flowed unaccountably into the next. It seemed like centuries since they had entered this monstrous place.

Three times, now, scouts had gone forward and returned with reports of having found the Procurator's camp. A lively, bustling place, hundreds of men, tents, floaters and mounts, stockpiles of provisions—but everything vanished like a phantom in the night when they brought the army forward and made ready for an attack. Was what the scouts had found merely an illusion? Or was it the absence of the camp, when they went back for a second look, that was the illusion?

Whatever it was, Septach Melayn was sure, sorcery had to be at work. The abracadabra of the mages operating on their minds, some devilish conjuration. Dantirya Sambail was playing with them. And doubtless getting things ready, all the while, for the long-planned stroke of violence by which he meant to take his revenge on Prestimion for having thwarted his hunger for power in so many ways.

Another of the scaly little creatures of the river was staring at him, perhaps a dozen feet away. It stood half erect, weaving a busy pattern in the air with its multitude of little legs.

"Are you one of the Procurator's spies?" Septach Melayn asked it. "Well, tell him Septach Melayn sends him this gift!"

Once again he tossed a rock, aiming this time to hit. But somehow the little thing succeeded in dodging the missile, deftly moving just a few inches to one side. It continued to peer at him as though defying him to try again.

"Nicely done," he said. "There aren't many who sidestep the thrusts of Septach Melayn!"

He let the small creature be. Sudden drowsiness was coming over him, though it was only the twilight hour. For a moment or two he fought it, fearing that the creatures of the river would swarm up over him as he slept; and then he recognized the telltale signs of a sending from the Lady, and let the spell take possession of him.

The dream-state came over him within instants, there by the shore of the gravelly river. No longer was he in vile Stoienzar, but rather in some green and leafy glade of Lord Havilbove's wonderful park on the slopes of Castle Mount, and the Lady of the Isle was with him, Prestimion's mother, the beautiful Princess Therissa, telling him to fear nothing, to move ahead and strike boldly.

To which he replied, "Fear is not the issue, milady. But how can I strike at something I can't see?"

"We will help you to see," she told him. "We will show you the face of the enemy. And then, Septach Melayn, it will be your time to act."

That was all. The moment passed. The Lady was gone. Septach Melayn opened his eyes, blinked, realized that he had been dreaming.

Before him stood half a dozen of the little scaly things of the river. They had clambered up out of the gravel and were arrayed in a semicircle before him, no more than ten inches from the tips of his boots, standing in that odd semi-erect posture of theirs. He watched them weaving their forelegs about, in much the same way as the first one had. It was almost as though they were entangling him in some spell. Do we have a conclave of tiny sorcerers here? he wondered. Were they planning a concerted assault? Did they mean to rush forward in another moment and sink their little nippers into his flesh?

Apparently not. They were just sitting there, watching him. Fascinated, perhaps, by the sight of a long-legged human being dozing on a boulder. He did not feel himself in any danger. The sight of them, arranged as they were in an earnest little congregation, seemed amusing and nothing more.

So far as he could recall, these were the first inhabitants of the Stoienzar he had encountered who did not seem inherently pernicious.

A good omen, he thought. Perhaps things will be changing for the better, now.

Perhaps.

14

"Now," Prestimion said. "If you're ready, let it begin!"

They were gathered about him, the four of them, in the room that he had made his battle headquarters at the royal suite of Stoien city's Crystal Pavilion: Dinitak, Dekkeret, Maundigand-Klimd, and the Lady of the Isle. It was just before dawn. They had been preparing for this moment with the most single-minded concentration for the past ten days.

Dinitak wore the dream-helmet. He would spearhead the attack. The Lady, using the silver circlet of her power, would monitor all aspects of the struggle as it developed and report on them to Prestimion.

"Yes, my lord, I'm ready," young Barjazid said, giving Prestimion an impudent wink.

The boy closed his eyes. Adjusted something on the rim of the helmet. Hurled his mind upward and outward toward the camp of Dantirya Sambail.

An eternally long moment crawled by. Then Dinitak's left cheek quivered and he drew the side of his mouth back sharply in an ugly grimace; he lifted his left hand and spread its fingers wide, and they began to tremble like leaves fluttering in a hard wind.

"He is focusing the energy of the helmet against his father," Princess Therissa murmured. "Locating him. Making contact."

The boy was trembling. Trembling. Trembling. Trembling.

Dekkeret turned to Maundigand-Klimd. "Are we right to do this?" he asked in a low voice. "I know what the father is like. He'll kill the boy if he can."

"Be calm. The Lady will protect him," the Su-Suheris replied.

"Do you really think she—"

Angrily Prestimion waved them both to silence. To his mother he said, "Are you in contact with Septach Melayn also?"

She answered with a nod.

"Where is he? How far from Dantirya Sambail?"

"Very, very close. But he's unaware that he is. The cloud of unknowingness still screens the Procurator's camp."

From Dinitak Barjazid came now a sharp grunting sound, almost a yelp. He did not appear to be aware that he had uttered it. His eyes were still shut; both his hands were fiercely clenched into tight fists; convulsive tremors now ran up and down both sides of his face, so that his features were twisted and distorted into constantly changing patterns of disarray.

"He has made contact with his father," the Princess Therissa said. "Their minds are touching."

"And? And?"

But the Lady's eyes were closed now, too.

Prestimion waited. It was maddening to be fighting a battle by proxy like this, across a distance of—what?—two thousand miles, was it? He chafed at his own inactivity. Somewhere out there was Dantirya Sambail, with the helmeted Venghenar Barjazid at his side. Somewhere not far to the east of the Procurator's camp were Septach Melayn, Gialaurys, Navigorn, and the army that had followed them through the Stoienzar. A second army, a regiment of Pontifical forces led by an officer named Guyan Daood, was closing in from the other side. Meanwhile the Coronal Lord of Majipoor stood idly by in this luxurious room far from the scene of battle, a mere observer, depending on an untried and virtually unknown boy from Suvrael to open the way for his armies and on his own mother to tell him what was going on.

"The father knows he is under attack," the Lady said, speaking as though in trance. "But he has not yet discovered its source. When he does—ah—ah—"

She pointed a stabbing finger across the room. Prestimion saw Dinitak go jerking backward as though a hot blade had touched his flesh. He staggered, lurched, nearly fell. Dekkeret, moving swiftly toward him, caught him and steadied him. But the boy did not want to be steadied. Brushing Dekkeret aside as though he were a mere buzzing fly, he planted his feet far apart, threw his head and shoulders back, let his arms dangle at his sides. His whole body was trembling. His hands coiled and uncoiled, now forming fists, now spreading wide with the fingers rigid.

A new sound came from Dinitak's lips, stranger than before. It was harsh and low, a bestial throbbing sound, not quite a growl, not quite a whine. It seemed to Prestimion that he had heard a sound like that before, but where? When? Then he remembered: it was the krokkotas, the caged man-killing beast of the midnight market of Bombifale, all jaws and teeth and claws, that had uttered the same hideous droning noise. And later it had come from Dantirya Sambail as well, that day in the Sangamor tunnels, the krokkotas growl again, a frightful cry of throttled rage and hatred and threat.

And now it was coming from Dinitak. "The father speaks through the boy's throat," whispered the Lady. "Crying out his rage at this betrayal."

Prestimion saw Dekkeret's face go pale with fear. He knew at once what the young man must be thinking: that Venghenar Barjazid must surely have the upper hand in this encounter, that his superior skill with the thought device, his wily unscrupulous nature, his savage determination to prevail, would inevitably prove to be too much for Dinitak. They might well see the boy destroyed before their eyes.

But Dinitak had told them over and over that he was confident of success; and in any case they had no choice but to go forward now. This was the path they had chosen; no other was available to them.

And Dinitak Barjazid appeared to be withstanding his father's counterthrusts.

That terrifying growling had ceased. So had much of the trembling. Dinitak stood firmly braced as before, deep in his trance, nostrils flaring, eyes open now but unseeing, his teeth bared and his jaws agape. His whole aspect was a strange one, but strangely calm as well. It was as though he had passed through a zone of terrible storms into some unknown tranquil realm beyond.

Prestimion leaned forward eagerly. "Tell me what's happening, mother!"

"Yes. Yes." She seemed very far away herself. Her words came with great difficulty. "They are—contending for power. Neither one—is able to budge—the other. It is—a stalemate—a stalemate, Prestimion—"

"If only I could help, somehow—"

"No. No need. He is holding his father at bay—preventing him—preventing him from—"

"From what, mother?"

"From sustaining—sustaining—"

Prestimion waited.

"Yes?" he said, when he could wait no longer.

"From sustaining the cloud of unknowingness," said the Princess Therissa. For a moment she returned from her trance and her eyes focused squarely on Prestimion's. "The father is unable to do both things at the same time, to fend off his son's attack and also to keep the cloud of unknowingness in place around the Procurator's camp. And so the cloud is lifting. The way is clear for Septach Melayn."

This part of the jungle seemed just like all the rest, a habitation for monsters. Heat. Humidity. Sandy, moist, marshy soil. Thickets of manganoza palms everywhere. Strange plants, strange birds overhead, strange little animals peering hungrily at them from the underbrush, clouds of sinister little buzzing things in the air, the great unrelenting eye of the sun above them, seemingly filling half the sky. The ocean close at hand on their left and a solid wall of green on their right. The populous northern shore of the peninsula was somewhere off beyond those trees, a pleasant land of thriving harbors, bountiful farms, sumptuous resorts, bayfront villas; but one had no sense here that any of that existed. The north shore might as well have been on some other world.

In this place plants and animals both were indefatigable foes. Nightmare things with teeth and claws lurked everywhere. And again and again it was necessary to leave the safety of the floaters, come forth with energy throwers, blast away at the stubborn tangles of inimical sharp-edged greenery that blocked their path. And for what? For what? The pursuit of an invisible enemy who vanished before their advance with will-o'-the-wisp stealth?

Today, though—today was going to be different. They had the Lady's promise of that.

"Can you feel her with you?" Gialaurys asked. He and Septach Melayn were riding in the lead floater today. Navigorn was just behind them.

"I feel her, yes."

The sendings had been coming to him, waking and sleeping, for the past day and a half. It was an experience such as Septach Melayn had never before had in his life, or even imagined was possible: the constant presence of the Lady in some corner of his mind, speaking softly to him, often without the use of words, simply touching him, steadying him, comforting him, lending him her strength.

She was with him now.

Rise before dawn. Go forward unhesitatingly. You are within striking distance of your enemy.

"What is she saying?" Gialaurys demanded. "Tell me, Septach Melayn! Tell me! I want to know!" He was like some big, eager, overfriendly tame beast, clambering all over him. "Are we really near him? Why can't we see anything? The smoke of their campfires, for instance—"

"Peace, Gialaurys," Septach Melayn replied. One had to be patient with the great burly fellow: he meant well, his heart was good. "The cloud of unknowingness still hangs over everything in front of us."

"But if the Lady says it's going to lift—"

"Peace, Gialaurys. Please."

"I find you very strange today, Septach Melayn."

"I find myself very strange. I am not my own self at all. But let me be: let me hear the messages of the Lady undistracted by your chatter, eh?"

"She speaks to you even now, while you're awake?"

"Please," said Septach Melayn in a tone compounded of irritation and weariness and anger, and this time Gialaurys withdrew sulkily to his side of the cabin and said no more.

It had been just after dawn when they set out, and now, an hour later, the sun was rapidly climbing in the sky. They seemed to be following a vaguely northwest course through the jungle, although always remaining within a few miles of the sea. It was the Lady, speaking through Septach Melayn from her place beside Prestimion at the western tip of the peninsula, who was directing their route.

Some mysterious enterprise, Septach Melayn knew, was unfolding back there in Stoien city under Prestimion's command and with the aid of the Lady. He had no idea what it was, only that they had found some way of striking at Dantirya Sambail from afar, and that very shortly they would lift the shroud of darkness which for weeks had kept him and his forces from striking at the foe they had come into this ghastly jungle to find.

Was it so? Or was this all some sorry hallucination, born in his tired mind out of the long travail of their journey? How could he tell?

What could he do but obey the guiding impulses that arose in his mind, and hope they were real ones? And struggle on and on until this business had reached its conclusion, if such a thing was ever to be granted them.

This was not how he had expected things to be, this life of constant toil and frustration, when Prestimion first had been named as heir to the throne.

How strange it all had been since then, Septach Melayn thought, looking back over the short and troubled years of the reign of the Coronal Lord Prestimion. "Lord Confalume has told me that I am to be the next Coronal," Prestimion had said one day when they all were much younger than they were now, thousands of years younger; and they had rejoiced, he and Gialaurys and little Duke Svor, they had caroused far into the night, and Akbalik had come in eventually to help them finish the last of the wine, and Navigorn, and Mandrykarn, who would die in the war, and Abrigant and perhaps one of Prestimion's other brothers, and even Korsibar—yes, Korsibar had been there, joyously embracing Prestimion with all the rest, for the crazy idea of seizing the

throne for himself had not yet entered his mind. And the
future had looked bright indeed for them that night. But
then—the usurpation, and the civil war, and the memory
obliteration, and this new business with Dantirya Sambail—
why, the whole reign thus far had been nothing but sorrow
and toil. What had it gained any of them that Prestimion
was Coronal Lord, except a life of hardship and pain and
weariness and sorrow for the loss of good friends?

And now—now—this awful unending trek through the
Stoienzar, pursuing a phantom that would not allow itself to
be found—

Septach Melayn shrugged. Like everything else, this was
part of the plan of the Divine. Who someday would summon
them all to return to the Source, as was the destiny of everyone who had ever lived, great and small, and what difference
would it make then that they had had to endure these little
moments of discomfort in this jungle when they would
much rather have been carousing at the Castle?

Therefore, he thought, utter no complaints. Go on and
on, wherever you must. Do your task, whatever it may be.

He stared forward through the windscreen of the floater.

"Gialaurys?" he said suddenly.

"You told me that you wanted no conversation."

"That was before. Look you, Gialaurys! Look there!"
Hastily bringing the floater to a halt, Septach Melayn
pointed toward the north with a frantic jabbing finger.

Gialaurys looked, rubbed his eyes, looked again. "A
clearing? Tents?" he said, amazed.

"A clearing, yes. Tents."

"Is Dantirya Sambail in there somewhere, do you think?"

Septach Melayn nodded. They had stumbled onto the
verge of an actual road, two floater-widths wide, that cut
straight across the rough track that they had been following
westward. It began to their north, amidst the manganoza
thickets, and appeared to run down toward the sea. Through
the opening that it made in the saw-palm grove they could
see the tawny tents of a good-sized encampment in the midst
of the jungle, the sort of hastily improvised bivouac that
their scouts had come upon more than once, but which no

one had ever been able to find again the next day.

And there was the Lady's sweet voice in his mind, letting him know that they had reached their goal and should make ready for attack.

Leaving the floater, he trotted back to the one just behind theirs, Navigorn's, which had halted also. Navigorn was peering out, looking puzzled.

"Do you see it?" Septach Melayn asked.

"Do I see what? Where?"

"Why, the Procurator's camp! Open your eyes, man! It's right over there—"

But as he turned to point it out for Navigorn, Septach Melayn blinked uncomprehendingly, clapped his hand to his mouth, grunted in astonishment.

It was all gone. Or, perhaps, never had been at all. There was no road crossing their path. No clearing; no encampment; nothing but the familiar solid green wall of manganoza palms.

"What are you talking about, Septach Melayn? What do you see?"

"I see nothing at all, Navigorn. That's the problem. I saw it—Gialaurys did too, just a moment ago—and now—now—"

Within his soul Septach Melayn cried out to the Lady for an explanation. At first no answer came. She did not seem to be with him at all.

Then he felt her with him again. But when she came to him, her presence felt distant and unclear, as if she had suffered some great diminution of her strength. It was with the greatest difficulty that he derived any meaning from the uncertain pulse of the wordless contact that ran between them.

Slowly, though, he came to understand.

What he had experienced just before, the sight of the roadway in the jungle and the tent camp beyond it, had been no illusion. The enemy they had sought so long was indeed hidden right behind those nearby trees. And for one brief tantalizing moment it had become possible for his eyes to

penetrate the cloud of unknowingness that had concealed
the Procurator from them for so long.

But the means by which that cloud had been stripped
away had lost its force. The effort had proven too great. The
cloud had descended once more.

They could, of course, attempt an attack against the
nearby position where they now knew Dantirya Sambail to
be hiding. But it would be like fighting a battle blindfolded.
The Procurator and all his men would be invisible to them.
And they themselves would be in plain view as they
launched a charge against a foe they could not see.

It was plain to Prestimion that Dinitak was faltering, now.
His face was strangely pallid despite the darkness of his
Suvrael-tanned skin, his eyes were bleary, his thin cheeks
were sagging with monstrous fatigue. He seemed to be shivering. Now and again he pressed his fingertips against his
temples. His helmet was slightly askew, but he did not seem
to notice.

The operation was hardly two hours old, and already they
were on the verge of losing the key player.

"Will he hold out, mother?" Prestimion asked quietly.

"He's weakening very quickly, I think. He has been able
to disrupt his father's power of illusion but not to overcome
it. And now his strength is beginning to flag."

The Lady, too, was showing signs of the strain. Since
well before sunrise she had maintained contact through her
circlet with Septach Melayn deep in the Stoienzar jungles,
had observed at a careful distance the camp of Dantirya
Sambail, and had linked herself to Dinitak Barjazid also,
while the boy endeavored to use his helmet against his father. The effort of keeping three bridges of perception open
at once had to be draining her strength.

Is our attack on Dantirya Sambail going to fail, Prestimion wondered, before we have even struck our first blow?

He looked toward Dinitak again. No question of it: the
boy was on the edge of collapse. His face was gleaming
with sweat and his eyes seemed not to be in focus. They

were rolling wildly around, so that now and again only the whites were showing. He had started to sway erratically back and forth, rocking eerily on the balls of his feet. A low droning sound came from him.

There was no way that Dinitak could be acting effectively against his father any longer. More likely he was taking a frightful buffeting from Venghenar Barjazid through that helmet. And at any moment—

Yes. Dinitak swung about to the side, froze for a moment in a kind of huddled crouch, quivered wildly from head to toe, and began to topple.

Dekkeret, at Prestimion's side, cried out and moved toward the boy with the same swiftness of reaction that he had shown long ago when that madman with the sickle had erupted from the crowd in Normork. Dinitak, pivoting as he fell, was already crumpling to the ground. With a quick lunge Dekkeret caught him about the shoulders and eased him the rest of the way toward the floor.

Dinitak had knocked the helmet from his forehead in that last convulsive movement before falling: for one dismaying moment the fragile thing seemed almost to be floating across the room. Prestimion, snatching at it almost unthinkingly as it flew past, plucked it from the air with two hooked fingers. He stood staring at it in awe for an instant as it lay in his hands.

Then he realized what must be done in this moment of crisis.

"It is my turn with it now," he said. Without waiting for a reaction from any of the others, he raised the helmet high over his head, looked upward at it for the merest moment, and pulled it down into place.

This was not the first time he had worn it. At Prestimion's stubborn insistence, Dinitak Barjazid had given him three sessions of training with the device over the last two weeks: the most minimal kind of exploration, mere brief tastes of what the helmet was capable of doing. He had learned how to operate the controls in a rudimentary sort of way and he had made short hopping excursions to the outer reaches of Dinitak's own mind and Dekkeret's. But there

had been no opportunity for any real experience at long-
range use.

There would be now.

"Help me, if you can," he said to Dinitak, who lay
sprawled in a heap on the floor, propped up against Dekkeret. "How do I find the Stoienzar?"

"The vertical ascent dial first," the boy said. His voice,
faint and reedy with exhaustion, was next to impossible to
hear. "Go up. Up and out. Then choose your path from
above."

Up and out? Easy enough to say. But what—how—

Well, there was nothing for it but to begin. Prestimion
touched the vertical ascent dial, giving it just the lightest of
twists, and was caught up instantly and carried on high. Like
riding the lightning, yes. Or a climbing rocket. His mind
went soaring upward at infinite velocity through the steel-
blue band that was the atmosphere and out into the black-
ness beyond, heading toward the sun.

Its great blazing golden-green bulk hung before him in
the pure emptiness of space, terrifyingly close, sending
bursts of flame outward in every direction. By its stunning
light Prestimion saw Majipoor far below him, the merest
tiny globe, slowly revolving. The single jagged peak of Castle Mount that came thrusting out from one side of it looked
from here like nothing more than a slender needle; but Prestimion knew that it was the most colossal of needles, pushing high up through the envelope of air that surrounded the
world, extending deep into the dark night-realm outside it.

The planet turned and Castle Mount moved beyond his
view. That shining blue-green expanse below him now was
the Great Sea, whose shores so few explorers had seen. He
saw the coast of Zimroel, then; there was the Isle of Sleep,
and the Rodamaunt Archipelago, and now, as Prestimion
hovered for a timeless time suspended between the stars and
the world, he perceived Alhanroel coming back into view
once more, the side that faced Zimroel, this time. From a
position somewhere over the midpoint of the Inner Sea he
saw it clearly, up ahead. There was the long southward-

tending sweep of its western coast, and there, the slender jutting thumb that was the peninsula.

I am much too high, he told himself. I must descend. Already I have stayed far too long. Years have been going by, centuries, while I soar out here. The battle is over; the world has moved along; the history of my reign has been told.

I have stayed too long; I must descend.

He let himself drift downward. With surprising ease he moved himself toward the coast of Alhanroel.

Steady, now. There is Stoien city. We are in it at this moment, somewhere, even though I am out here as well. And now let us go eastward along the southern shore. Yes. Yes. The peninsula. The jungle.

From a million miles away came a voice that might have been Dinitak Barjazid's, saying, "Search for the point of flame, my lord. That is where you will find them."

The point of flame? What was that supposed to mean?

All was chaos before him. The closer Prestimion came to the surface of the world, the more incomprehensible everything became. But he found the helmet's lateral control and forced himself forward through the thick shroud of haze and murk that confronted him, cutting into it like a living sword, and gradually the confusion gave way to some degree of clarity. The effort was enormous. His brain was ablaze. He was entering the zone of Venghenar Barjazid's defensive screen, now. Great rocking waves of explosive force went shuddering through the firmament all about him, so that he had to fight to keep from tumbling like a spent meteor into the sea, which leaped and foamed like new milk below him.

He regained his balance. Held himself in perfect equipoise. Pushed himself deep into the dark barrier and struggled on toward its farther side.

He could see blazing light beyond.

A point of flame, yes, just as young Barjazid had said, a searing zone of brightness shining through the incomprehensible cloud that still was wrapped about him.

"There they are!" he cried. "Yes! Yes! I see them. But how do I reach—"

Suddenly Prestimion felt support: a friendly hand at his elbow, holding him upright. He sensed that his mother was reaching out to him through her circlet, touching his mind, lending her own strength and wisdom. And she in turn must be drawing on whatever instructions Dinitak Barjazid was able to gasp out to her.

Now was his way clear.

With one of the fine dials on the helmet he centered his mind on that point of flame and the fiery glow thinned and dimmed, and he clearly saw the jungle camp as though he were down there on the ground in the middle of it. The tents, the heaped-up weapons, the bonfires, the floaters and mounts.

Through whose eyes was he seeing all this? he wondered. The answer came immediately. He probed his host's mind and quickly discerned a bright core of malevolence, burning with terrible intensity; and shuddered at the feel of it, for he recognized within instants that he was touching the soul of the Procurator's second-in-command, the odious Mandralisca.

To be within that mind was like swimming in a sea of molten lava. It was impossible for Mandralisca to harm him, he supposed, not without one of these helmets. But any sort of contact with the man at all was a foul experience that ought not to be prolonged.

Prestimion shoved. Mandralisca went reeling away and was gone.

It is Venghenar Barjazid that I want. And then Dantirya Sambail.

"Mother? Help me to find the man with the helmet."

No need. Venghenar Barjazid had already found him, and was fighting back against the intruder in the camp.

The opening defensive move came quickly and stunningly. Prestimion felt a sensation as of a powerful blow on the back of his head, and another at the base of his stomach. He gasped and reeled, tottering under the onslaught. Desperately he fought for breath. But Barjazid was unrelenting.

He had the more powerful helmet. And he was a master of his device and Prestimion was a novice.

Prestimion, his consciousness divided, part of him in a room in Stoien city with his mother and Dekkeret and Dinitak and Maundigand-Klimd, and part of him in a clearing in the jungles of Stoienzar, began to doubt, in the first fury of the struggle, that there was any means at all by which he could fend off this ferocious assault. It looked certain that he must inevitably be destroyed.

But then he pushed, as he had pushed against Mandralisca, and Barjazid seemed to yield to the pressure, and Prestimion pushed again, harder; and this time the force of Barjazid's fury seemed to diminish, either because Prestimion had succeeded in shoving him back or, perhaps, because he had simply drawn aside to gather his strength for a more conclusive blow. Whichever it was, the lull gave Prestimion a much-needed respite.

But he knew it would not last long. He could see the little man as though he were actually standing before him: thin-lipped, sly-eyed, an old necklace of poorly matched sea-dragon bones around his neck and the dream-helmet on his brow. Barjazid looked supremely confident. His eyes were gleaming with malign pleasure. Prestimion had no doubt that he was readying himself to deliver a second and perhaps final thrust.

He braced himself for it.

Are you still with me, mother? I need you now.

Yes. Yes. She was still there. Prestimion felt her unquestionable presence at his side.

And now, abruptly, he became aware of a second potent power joining the effort also, a new bulwark for him in his battle. A strange force came from this ally, nothing at all like the gentle and loving radiance that emanated from the Lady. Through the eyes of the newcomer he seemed to be seeing in some other dimension of perception altogether. After an instant Prestimion recognized the source of that odd alteration of his field of view, that strange doubleness of vision that had come over him just now. It had to be Maundigand-Klimd who had linked himself somehow to the chain of attack. What other explanation could there be, if not the entry of the Su-Suheris magus into the conflict?

Now, Prestimion. Strike!

Yes. He struck. Even as Barjazid was gathering his strength for the blow that would finish the struggle, Prestimion rushed at him with all the might at his command.

Barjazid's skill with these devices was far greater than Prestimion's; but the spirit that had propelled Prestimion to the throne of Majipoor was a stronger one than the dark soul that sizzled and flared within Venghenar Barjazid. And Prestimion had the Lady and Maundigand-Klimd standing at his side, adding their power to his. He lashed out at Barjazid with a tremendous thrust of force and knew at once that he had broken through the other man's defenses with it. Barjazid went reeling backward, thrown off balance by that single great rush of strength coming from his opponent. He swayed and spun about, striving frantically to remain upright.

Again. Again, Prestimion!

Again, yes. And again and again and again.

Barjazid crumbled. Fell. Lay with his face against the marshy soil, making soft moaning sounds.

Nothing now guarded the path to Dantirya Sambail.

15

"CAN YOU SEE IT now?" Septach Melayn cried. "The tents? The floaters? Is that not Dantirya Sambail himself? Come on, before it vanishes a second time!"

He had no real understanding of what had happened, or why, for the Lady no longer rode within his conscious mind. All that was certain was that the Procurator's camp, which only a little while before had been cloaked once again in renewed invisibility, had burst into view before their astounded eyes and lay open and undefended before them. Now the world was churning with a mighty strangeness, the web of destiny crossing and recrossing upon itself, and Septach Melayn knew that this was the moment to bring matters to a conclusion. There might not be another opportunity.

It seemed strange, to have the barriers drop away so easily like this. But Septach Melayn greatly suspected that making such a thing happen had been no simple matter, that some tremendous unseen battle had cleared the way.

"There—yes," Navigorn said, looking baffled. "I see the camp. But how—"

"This is Prestimion's doing," said Septach Melayn. "I feel him at work here. He stands close beside us now. Come, brothers! Quickly!"

He ran forward into the clearing, sword already in his hand. Gialaurys was at his right shoulder, Navigorn to his left, and the troops they had brought with them from the north came rushing up behind them from their floaters to join the fray. This was not to be a carefully structured battle but simply a wild raid, headlong and fierce.

"Find the Procurator!" Gialaurys cried in a voice like a great crack of thunder. "Get him first!"

"And Mandralisca also," Septach Melayn called. "Those two must not escape!"

But where were they? All was in confusion in here. The camp was full of bewildered soldiers milling in such hectic tumult and disarray that there was no telling who was where.

As they advanced into the camp a thin, parched old man who had been sprawled on the ground rose uncertainly to his feet and shambled aimlessly up toward them, his eyes dull and almost blank, his face distorted, one side of his face drawn downward as though he had lately suffered a stroke. Some sort of metallic instrument was on his head—a magical device, perhaps. The man was making thick unintelligible sounds, mere incoherent gabblings. He reached out with trembling hands toward Navigorn, who was the closest to him. Navigorn flung him contemptuously to one side and sent him sprawling out on the ground like a heap of discarded clothing.

"Ah, but don't you know him?" Gialaurys said. "The Barjazid, it is! The damnable maker of all this mischief! Or what's left of him." And he turned to run the man through.

But Septach Melayn, ever quicker, had already despatched him with the quickest flick of his sword.

"That is Mandralisca there, now, I think," said Navigorn, pointing to the far side of the clearing.

And indeed the Procurator's poison-taster could be seen lurking there, creeping along the wall of manganoza palms, searching for some opening through which he could escape. "He is mine," Navigorn said, and ran off toward him.

"The Procurator, there," cried Septach Melayn. "I claim him for my own!"

Yes. Dantirya Sambail stood fifty yards away, smiling at him across the tumultuous uproar of the battlefield that his camp had become. He did not appear to be prepared for combat: all he wore was a simple linen tunic, belted at the waist, and soft leather shoes with peaked tips jutting far out in front. But he had obtained a sturdy saber from somewhere and also a long narrow dagger. He held one weapon in each hand as he looked toward Septach Melayn and beckoned him on toward single combat. The Procurator's strange purple eyes were gazing almost lovingly at him out of that fleshy and florid face.

"Yes," Septach Melayn said. "Let us try our skills, shall we, Dantirya Sambail?"

They moved slowly toward each other, each man's gaze fixed rigidly on his opponent as though there were no one else anywhere around them in the clearing. The Procurator had his stiletto in his right hand, the saber in his left. Which was odd, Septach Melayn thought, for as far as he knew Dantirya Sambail was right-handed, and a massive saber was always his weapon of choice. What was he planning to do? Try to knock Septach Melayn's own sword aside with a swinging side-stroke of the saber, and strike for his undefended heart with the dagger?

No matter. It would not happen. Septach Melayn was certain that this was the moment for him to send that great monster from the world at last.

"On the field at Thegomar Edge you came at Prestimion with two weapons also, did you not, Dantirya Sambail?" Septach Melayn asked him cordially. "And struck at him

with an axe, I think, and then went for him with a saber as
well. But still he bested you, I'm told." They were circling
each other as they spoke, maneuvering for advantage. Septach Melayn was the younger and taller and quicker man,
the Procurator the heavier and stronger one. "He bested you,
yes, and spared your life. But I am not Prestimion, Dantirya
Sambail. When I best you, it will be the end for you. And
none too soon, I'd say."

"You talk much too much, you man of flowers and ringlets. You trifling fop! You overgrown boy!"

"Fop, am I? Well, perhaps it is so. But a boy? A boy,
Dantirya Sambail?"

"A boy is all you are, yes. Come, Septach Melayn, let's
see that famous swordsmanship of yours at last!"

"I offer you a demonstration with all my soul."

Septach Melayn stepped forward, deliberately opening
his guard as an encouragement to the Procurator to reveal
what it was he had in mind to do with those two weapons
of his. But Dantirya Sambail only moved in a crabwise scut-
tle, brandishing dagger and saber as if uncertain himself of
which to use. Septach Melayn flicked a quick elegant thrust
at him, only for the sake of letting the Procurator see the
flash of sunlight against his swiftly moving blade. Dantirya
Sambail smiled and nodded in approval. "Ah, well done,
boy, very well done. But you drew no blood."

"Not when I choose to slice the air, no," said Septach
Melayn. "But try this, though. Boy, you say?"

Now was the time for summoning all his mastery of the
weapon and making a quick end of the combat. He had no
yearning for playing games with Dantirya Sambail. This
man had escaped destruction too many times already. Prestimion somehow had opened the way for this moment and
it was up to Septach Melayn to complete the act; now it
was time to bring Dantirya Sambail quickly to his finish,
Septach Melayn thought, without fighting any drawn-out
elaborate duel, or giving the Procurator a chance to work
some new kind of treachery.

Coming in quickly on the attack, Septach Melayn feinted
idly to the left, chuckling to see how easily Dantirya Sam-

bail mistook that for his real thrust. As the Procurator parried the feint with his saber, Septach Melayn whipped his light sword around the other way and slid its point through the meaty part of the arm that held the dagger. The drawing of first blood brought a sudden flaring of fury and, perhaps, fear, in Dantirya Sambail's remarkable eyes. With an angry howl he struck at Septach Melayn, a downward blow with the saber that would have cut another man in half. Dancing easily aside, Septach Melayn offered the Procurator a pleasant smile and went straight in on the left, arcing his wrist neatly and putting his blade between Dantirya Sambail's ribs, tickling it forward until he was certain he had reached the heart.

There, Septach Melayn thought. It is done. And this tower of evil is gone from our midst.

They stood close together a moment, the Procurator leaning against him, breathing heavily, and then not seeming to breathe at all. A tremor shook the Procurator's body the way a volcano's eruption shakes the ground, and a gush of bright blood spewed from his lips. Then all was still, and Dantirya Sambail was a dead weight against him. Septach Melayn reached out and flicked the saber from Dantirya Sambail's nerveless grasp. It went clattering to the side. With a single light shove he sent the lifeless Procurator after it.

"An overgrown boy, yes," Septach Melayn said. "A trifling fop. No doubt you were right. That is surely what I am. —Goodbye, Dantirya Sambail. You'll not be greatly missed, I think."

But he felt no great sense of triumph, not yet, only a quiet feeling of satisfaction within, of release from a burden. He looked around to see how the others were faring.

Gialaurys was dealing with three or four of the Procurator's men at once. He seemed not to be in need of help. In the midst of the struggle he glanced across, saw Septach Melayn standing beside the fallen form of Dantirya Sambail, and gave him a wildly gleeful grin of congratulation.

But it appeared as though Navigorn had had poorer luck. He was returning now from the manganoza thicket, looking disconsolate. A trail of bloody scratches ran down one side of his face. "Mandralisca got away, damn him! He walked through those miserable palms as though they weren't there and disappeared. —I would have followed but for the trees. You can see they've cut me half to pieces as it is."

In this moment of glory Septach Melayn would accept no disappointment, not even this. He clapped Navigorn heartily on the shoulder. "Well, it's a pity, that. But come, man, don't be so hard on yourself, Navigorn. The fellow's a demon, and chasing demons is no easy game. But he's not likely to get far on his own, is he? May he be devoured by crabs as he wanders around in the jungle!" Septach Melayn pointed then to the bodies strewn all around. "Look! Look you! There lies the Procurator! And the Barjazid over there! The work is done, Navigorn. We've nothing left to do here but a little mopping-up!"

To Prestimion, two thousand miles away, the snapping of the tension came to him like the breaking of some giant cable. He staggered under the impact of it, reeling backward in a sudden access of dizziness.

Instantly Dekkeret was at his side, steadying his arm. "My lord—"

"I don't need any help, thanks," said Prestimion, disengaging himself from Dekkeret's grasp. He must not have sounded very convincing, though, for Dekkeret continued to hover watchfully by his side.

Prestimion thought he knew what had happened just now in the Procurator's camp, but he was not certain. And in any event his voyage with the helmet and the battle with Venghenar Barjazid had brought him by now to the brink of exhaustion. He felt chilled, as though he had been swimming in icy waters, and his head was whirling. He closed his eyes, drew two or three deep breaths, struggled to find his equilibrium.

Then he looked toward the Lady. In the hollow, thin voice of a very tired man he asked her, "Is he really dead, then?"

She nodded solemnly. She looked pale and drawn. Surely she was weary as he was himself. "Gone, and no question of it. It was Septach Melayn who slew him, was it not?" And Maundigand-Klimd, to whom she had addressed the question, nodded, both heads at once, full confirmation.

"Then there will be no second civil war," said Prestimion, and the first warm flickers of joy began to cut through the shroud of fatigue that had engulfed him. "We can give thanks to the Divine for that. But there's still much for us to do before the world is whole again."

Dekkeret said, "My lord, you should put the helmet down, now. Simply the wearing of it must draw energy from you. And after what you have done—"

"But I've just told you that I'm not finished. Stand back, Dekkeret! Stand back!"

And put his hand to the ascent control of the helmet once again before anyone could protest, and sent himself soaring upward a second time.

Was this wise? he wondered.

Yes. Yes. Yes. While he still had strength left in him after the voyage to the Stoienzar, this was something he must do.

He drifted in silence like a great bird of the night above the mighty cities of Majipoor. They sparkled below him in all their glittering majesty, Ni-moya and Stee, Pidruid and Dulorn, Khyntor and Tolaghai and Alaisor and Bailemoona.

And he felt the weight of the madness in them. He sensed above all else the anguish of the myriad sprung and riven souls who had suffered such harm in the moment when he had ripped the tale of the war against Korsibar from the collective memory of the world. His own heart was drawn downward by sorrow as he perceived, far more clearly even than when he had traveled the world with the Lady's circlet on his brow, how much damage he had done.

But what he had done then, he hoped to undo now.

The helmet of the Barjazids had enormously more power than the circlet of the Lady. Where she could reassure and comfort, the wearer of the helmet was able to transform.

And heal, perhaps. Could it be done? He would find out. Now.

He touched a shattered mind with his own. Touched two, three, a thousand, ten thousand. Drew all the tumbled pieces together. Made the rough places smooth.

Yes! Yes!

It was a fearful effort. He could feel his own vital force flowing outward like a river, even as he healed those with whom he came in contact. But it was working. He was certain of it. He went on and on, making a secret and silent grand processional around the world, swooping down here in Sippulgar, here in Sisivondal, here in Treymone, here in his own Muldemar, touching, mending, healing.

The task was immense. He knew he could not hope to achieve it all in this one journey. But he was determined to make a beginning here and now. To bring back this day from that bleak realm in which he had forced them to wander for so long as many as he could of those whom he had condemned to madness.

He moved randomly about the world. The madness was everywhere.

He halted here.

Here.

Here.

Again, again, again, Prestimion descended, touched, repaired. He had no idea, any longer, whether he was moving from north to south or from east to west, whether this was Narabal he was passing over or Velathys or some city of Castle Mount itself. He went on and on, heedless of the expense of spirit that he was undertaking. "I am Prestimion the Coronal Lord, the Divine's own anointed king," he said to them, a hundred times, a thousand, "and I embrace you, I bring you the deepest of love, I offer you the gift of your own self returned. I am Prestimion—I am Prestimion—I am Prestimion—the Coronal Lord—"

But what was this? The contact was breaking. The sky itself seemed to be shaking apart. He was falling—falling—

Plunging toward the sea. Whirling, plummeting, descending headlong into darkness—

"My lord, can you hear me?"

Dekkeret's voice, that was. Prestimion opened his eyes, no easy thing to accomplish in his dazed, numbed state, and saw the burly broad-shouldered form of Dekkeret kneeling beside him as he lay stretched full length on the floor of the room. The helmet of the Barjazids was in the younger man's hands.

"What are you doing with that?" Prestimion demanded.

Dekkeret, reddening, laid the thing beside him, putting it down beyond Prestimion's reach. "Forgive me, my lord. I had to take it from you."

"You—took—it—from—me?"

"You would have died if you wore it any longer. We could see you going from us, right here. Dinitak said, 'Get it off his head,' and I told him it was forbidden to touch a Coronal in that way, that it was sacrilege, but he said to take it off anyway, or Majipoor would need a new Coronal within the hour. So I removed it. I had no choice, my lord. Send me to the tunnels, if you wish. But I could not stand here and watch you die."

"And if I ordered you to give it back to me now, Dekkeret?"

"I would not give it to you, my lord," said Dekkeret calmly.

Prestimion nodded. He forced a faint smile and sat up a little way. "You are a good man, Dekkeret, and a very brave one. But for you nothing that we have achieved this day would have happened. You, and this boy Dinitak—"

"You are not offended, my lord, that I took the helmet from you?"

"It was a bold thing to do. Overbold, one might almost say. But no: no, Dekkeret, I'm not offended. You did the right thing, I suppose. —Help me get up, will you?"

Dekkeret lifted him as though he weighed nothing at all, and set him on his feet, and waited a moment as though fearing he would fall. Prestimion glanced around the room: at his mother, at Dinitak, at Maundigand-Klimd. The Su-Suheris was as inscrutable as ever, a remote figure displaying no emotion. The other two still showed evidence of the fatigue of the battle, but they seemed now to be making a recovery. As was he.

The Lady said, "What were you doing, Prestimion?"

"Healing the madness. Yes, mother, healing it. With the aid of the helmet it can be done, though it's hard work, and won't be finished overnight." He looked down at the helmet, close by Dekkeret's foot, and shook his head. "What appalling power there is in that thing! I find myself tempted to destroy it, and any more like it that may be found in Dantirya Sambail's camp. But what has been invented once can come into the world a second time. Better that we keep it for ourselves, and find some good way to put its great force to use—beginning with the task I commenced just now, of going among the poor mad ones and bringing them back among us."

Turning then to Dekkeret, he said, "Dantirya Sambail has assembled a fleet off Piliplok. Its captains are waiting for an order from their master to sail toward Alhanroel. Let them know, Dekkeret, that the order they await will never come. See to it that they disperse peacefully."

"And if they don't?"

"Then we will disperse them by force," said Prestimion. "But I pray it won't come to that. Tell them, in my name, that there are to be no more Procurators in Zimroel. That title is now extinct. We will divide the powers of the one who held it among other princes who are more loyal to our crown."

And then, to the Lady: "Mother, I thank you for your great help, and I release you now to return to your Isle. Dinitak, you will come with me to the Castle; we'll find work for you there. And you, Dekkeret—Prince Dekkeret, you are thenceforth—and you, Maundigand-Klimd—come, we'll prepare for our return to the Mount. This sorry business has kept us away from home long enough."

16

"AND THIS IS PRINCE Taradath," Varaile said, bringing forth a small fur-wrapped bundle. A wrinkled red face was visible at its upper end.

Prestimion laughed. "This? This, a prince?"

"He will be," said Abrigant, who had come quickly up from Muldemar that morning when news of Prestimion's return to the Castle from the west country had reached him. They were gathered in the great sitting-room of the royal apartments of Lord Thraym's Tower, Prestimion's official residence. "He'll be as tall as our brother Taradath was, and just as quick with his wit. And as good an archer as his father, and Septach Melayn's equal with the sword."

"I will begin his instruction as soon as he can walk," said Septach Melayn gravely, "and by the time he is ten there will be none who can stand against him."

"You are all very optimistic," Prestimion said, peering in astonishment at the small wrinkled visage of his newborn son. Every baby looks like every other one, he thought. But yes, yes, this one is a Coronal's son and the descendant of princes, and we will make something special of him indeed.

He looked toward Abrigant. "Since you see such aptitude in store for him, brother, what skills do you propose to offer him yourself? Will you take him down to Muldemar and teach him the secrets of the winery, do you think?"

"Make a vintner of him, Prestimion? Oh, no: it's metallurgy I'll guide him toward!"

"Metallurgy, eh?"

"I'll put him in charge of the great iron-mines of Skakkenoir, on which the foundations of the prosperity of your reign are to stand. —You do remember, Prestimion, that you promised me that I would be given a second chance to go in search of the metals of Skakkenoir, once this little matter of Dantirya Sambail was dealt with? And I have politely sat on my haunches at Muldemar ever since, waiting for my moment. Which is now at hand, I think, brother."

"Ah," Prestimion said. "Skakkenoir, yes. Well, then, take five hundred men, or a thousand, and go to look for Skakkenoir, Abrigant. And come back from there with ten thousand pounds of iron for us, will you?"

"Ten thousand tons," said Abrigant. "And that will be only the beginning."

Yes, Prestimion thought.

Only the beginning.

He had been Coronal how long now? Three years? Four? That was hard to say, because of Korsibar, and the thing that had been done at Thegomar Edge to make it seem that no civil war had ever happened. He had no clear idea of the date of his own reign's starting-point. In the public chronicles of the realm it would be set at the hour of Prankipin's death and Confalume's ascension to the Pontificate; but Prestimion himself knew that there had been the two years of strife, his wanderings in the provinces and the battles far and wide, before he had truly come to the possession of the throne. And even then, hardly had he been formally crowned but there had been Dantirya Sambail to deal with all over again, and everything else—

Well, there would be a new beginning now, once and for all.

He took the baby from Varaile and held him very gingerly, not at all certain of the best way of doing it, and he and Varaile walked off a little way to stand by themselves, leaving the others—Septach Melayn and Gialaurys and Navigorn and Abrigant and Maundigand-Klimd, those who had been the pillars of his reign thus far—to gather by the table where an array of the wines of Muldemar had been laid out to celebrate the Coronal's return. Out of the corner of his eye Prestimion saw Dekkeret somewhat shyly standing at the edge of the group, Dekkeret who would surely be a figure of great importance in the land in the years ahead, and he smiled as Septach Melayn beckoned him to the table and affectionately put an arm around the young man's shoulders.

To Varaile, Prestimion said, "And your father? He's made an extraordinary recovery, I hear."

"A miracle, Prestimion. But he's not really his old self, you know. Hasn't said a word about all the properties I signed away while he was sick. Hasn't spent so much as a moment meeting with the moneymen who used to take up all his time. He's lost all interest in making money, it would seem. The baby, that's what appears to matter to him the most. Though he said to me yesterday that he hopes he can be some use to you as an economic adviser, now that you're back at the Castle."

That was an odd notion, taking Simbilon Khayf into the Council. But these were new times, and Simbilon Khayf, it seemed, was a new man. Well, we will see, Prestimion thought.

"His help will be very valuable, I'm sure," he said.

"And he's eager to give it. He has the greatest respect for you, Prestimion."

"You must bring him to me in a day or two, Varaile."

Then he turned away and stood for a time by the window, peering into the courtyard below. There was a good view from here of much of the Inner Castle, the heart and nucleus of the entire great structure, the high domain of power. This Castle in which he dwelled was called Lord Prestimion's Castle now, and would be until the end of his reign. The world had been given into his hand to rule; and though he had made an uncertain beginning of things, he was certain now that his mistakes were behind him, that an age of miracles and wonders was about to commence. And for the first time since they had come to him to tell him that the Pontifex Prankipin was dying and he would very likely be selected to take Lord Confalume's place as Coronal, he felt a sensation of something very much like peace stealing over his heart.

He let his mind go roaming outward, beyond the Inner Castle and beyond the uncountable multitude of rooms that surrounded the Castle's core, and on past the Mount at whose summit it stood, and the wondrous multifarious sprawl of the Majipoor lowlands farther on. In a moment's flicker of his mind he undertook a journey that no man could hope to complete in a lifetime, from one end of the world to the other, and returned just as swiftly to the Mount, to the Castle, to this tower that was his home.

"Prestimion?" Varaile said, as if from a great distance away.

He looked around, startled by the intrusion on his reverie. "Yes?"

"You're holding the baby upside down."

"Ah. Ah, so I am." He grinned. "Perhaps you'd better take him back, eh?"

Well, perhaps not all the mistakes were behind him yet.

He handed the baby to Varaile and leaned forward and kissed her lightly on the tip of her nose. And went back across the room to see if Septach Melayn and Gialaurys and the rest had left any of the best wines for him.

AVON EOS PRESENTS
MASTERS OF FANTASY AND ADVENTURE